The Truth About Ruby Cooper

'Liz Nugent never fails to surprise and capture and shock. The writing was sublime as always, and the themes dark and hooky. I bloody loved it' Louise Beech

'Deeply dark and utterly unexpected, only Liz Nugent can create characters like these. Drawing us deep into Ruby Cooper's world, this is a maestro at work. Another sensational read' Sam Blake

'Dark, fearless and compelling – in other words, classic Liz Nugent. Utterly distinctive and unique, this is another unforgettable work from an outstanding and brilliant crime writer' Jane Casey

'Liz Nugent is an unflinching storytelling genius. Unique characters, explosive revelations, tantalizing pacing and heart-stopping twists, not to mention utterly original plots. She is a master of the dark side of human psychology and human nature. I loved it' Edel Coffey

'Liz Nugent is fearless in the places she will go to uncover our basest, darkest impulses. Ruby Cooper is her most morally complex character yet. Utterly compelling' Tammy Cohen

'Only Liz Nugent could have written this book and only Liz Nugent could have conceived of a character like Ruby Cooper. An unflinching, frequently and darkly funny, sometimes disconcerting and always gripping story that will stay with readers long after the final page has been turned' Sinéad Crowley

'God, I loved it! I am such an admirer of Liz Nugent's writing, which is so precise and cool and somehow immediately classic and timeless. *The Truth About Ruby Cooper* is fearless and unforgettable. Just like its protagonist, this book nudges its way into your life until you can think about little else. A story of nightmares, but so beautifully told' Abigail Dean

'Liz Nugent's finest, boldest, and most accomplished novel to date. And that's saying quite a lot. Consistently surprising and richly evoked. Big-hearted and provocative. A triumph, truly – ambiguous, seductive, infuriating, and both sad and full of life. Much like Ruby herself' A. J. Finn

'A brilliant page-turner about family secrets, sibling rivalry, and sex as a weapon. This is another dark, twisted Liz Nugent winner. I loved it!' Robyn Harding

'You will struggle to find darker characters and more wickedly clever tales than those from the mind of Liz Nugent' Susi Holliday

'Utterly compelling and brilliantly imagined . . . all the way to the last dark twist' Anthony Horowitz

'Lydia Fitzsimons, Sally Diamond and now Ruby Cooper – only Liz Nugent can create deeply dark, disturbing tales with flawed female characters that are an absolute pleasure to read. Addictive and awe-inspiring, from the first page to the last' Diane Jeffrey

'Liz Nugent is a genius and this is her best book yet' Lisa Jewell

'An absolute belter of a book. Every time I put it down, I couldn't wait to get back in. *The Truth About Ruby Cooper* is Liz Nugent at her dark and twisty best' Louise Kennedy

'A dark, twisted and grippingly addictive read, that drags you in by the lapels, and won't let go' Neil Lancaster

'How to do this dazzling book justice? An utterly gripping story about how one incident reverberates across time, damaging and destroying lives. No one plumbs the human condition, its moral quandaries, quite so deeply and brilliantly as Liz Nugent. I read it as if in a fever' Shari Lapena

'You know that feeling when you're loving a book so much you have to put it down occasionally, just to savour it a little longer? This was one of those rare reads. It was absolutely gripping. From beginning to end, I felt like I was right there in every house, tangled up with this dysfunctional family, practically shouting at them to make better choices. Another utterly compelling, dark and unsettling piece of work that's going to give me a book hangover for weeks' John Marrs

'I loved this book so much! I was invested in every character so deeply that I couldn't stop reading until I got to the last page! Absolutely a triumph!' Freida McFadden

'Unputdownable, acid-sharp, and emotionally brutal – Liz Nugent at her most compulsive' Dervla McTiernan

'A brilliantly dark and tangled web that every reader will be completely ensnared by. Liz Nugent weaves these sorts of twisted tales better than anyone else. Such a wild twisty ride and yet every moment has the ring of emotional truth' Graham Norton

'An author of extraordinary talent. I don't doubt that Liz Nugent's novels will become literary classics sitting alongside Christie, Highsmith and P. D. James' C. L. Taylor

The Truth About Ruby Cooper

LIZ NUGENT

SANDYCOVE

an imprint of
PENGUIN BOOKS

SANDYCOVE

UK | USA | Canada | Ireland | Australia
India | New Zealand | South Africa

Sandycove is part of the Penguin Random House group of companies
whose addresses can be found at global.penguinrandomhouse.com.

Penguin Random House UK,
One Embassy Gardens, 8 Viaduct Gardens, London SW11 7BW

penguin.co.uk

First published 2026

003

Copyright © Liz Nugent, 2026

The moral right of the author has been asserted

Penguin Random House values and supports copyright.
Copyright fuels creativity, encourages diverse voices, promotes freedom
of expression and supports a vibrant culture. Thank you for purchasing
an authorized edition of this book and for respecting intellectual property
laws by not reproducing, scanning or distributing any part of it by any
means without permission. You are supporting authors and enabling
Penguin Random House to continue to publish books for everyone.
No part of this book may be used or reproduced in any manner for the
purpose of training artificial intelligence technologies or systems. In accordance
with Article 4(3) of the DSM Directive 2019/790, Penguin Random House
expressly reserves this work from the text and data mining exception

Set in 13.2/16 pt Garamond Premier Pro
Typeset by Six Red Marbles UK, Thetford, Norfolk
Printed and bound in Great Britain by Clays Ltd, Elcograf S.p.A.

The authorized representative in the EEA is Penguin Random House Ireland,
Morrison Chambers, 32 Nassau Street, Dublin D02 YH68

A CIP catalogue record for this book is available from the British Library

HARDBACK ISBN: 978–1–844–88679–1
TRADE PAPERBACK ISBN: 978–1–844–88573–2

Penguin Random House is committed to a sustainable future
for our business, our readers and our planet. This book is made from
Forest Stewardship Council® certified paper.

For Richard, again and always

'No guilt is forgotten so long as the conscience still knows of it'

– Stefan Zweig, *Beware of Pity*

For the second time in six weeks, I woke up with the wrong husband.

This time, in a strange house, somewhere in Dublin. Under the sheets, I was naked. How could I have done this again?

I thought about my gentle husband who deserved so much better than I could give. My beautiful daughter who may have inherited that badness at the core of my soul.

My clothes were scattered around the room like that time in Boston, and I tried not to think about that.

I blame my sister.

PART ONE

1
Ruby

If my sister hadn't been beautiful, none of it would have happened.

Erin's hair was blonder than mine. Her eyes were pale blue like Mom's. Mine were ordinary blue. But everything was perfectly in proportion with her. She never had to wear a retainer like me because her teeth were straight and even. Mine were crooked. And my chin was too pointy. I was thin and bony while Erin was curvy in all the right places. My feet were too big for my body. Side on, I looked like a golf club. I didn't smile with my mouth open for the two years I wore that retainer. One time in school, I forgot, and a senior guy said I looked like Steve Buscemi. I was really upset when I found out who he was. Mom said the curves would come and the pointy chin would go as well as the retainer. I couldn't wait.

Everyone talked about how pretty Erin was, and then, when they noticed me, they'd hastily say something like 'and Ruby's freckles are *so* cute'.

I struggled a little at school. I was never bottom of the class. I hovered around the middle. In 1999, I was sixteen and Erin was eighteen, in her senior year. She was top of her class. We were both in Altman High. Dad would sigh before he opened my report card. He never expected it to be good. The comments from teachers said things like 'We hope to see a more mature

Ruby next year' and 'We know that Ruby is capable. If she can memorize the entire script of *Titanic*, I'm sure she'd be able for Robert Frost.' Dad was mad about that one. I got mostly Cs with one or two Bs and an A in drama. Erin was a straight-A student. She was hoping to study English at Harvard. Her boyfriend, Milo, was in his first year at Boston College doing pre-med because he wanted to be a doctor.

Erin wrote stories, but she said I wasn't allowed to read them. Milo said they were excellent, but he thought everything she said or did was awesome. He said she was beautiful and talented and sweet, and that was true.

My dad, Douglas Cooper, was the pastor and founder of the Holy Divine Church of the Fourth Way, and he was also an investment broker. Dad ruled the roost in our house in Fisher Hill, a respectable neighbourhood in Brookline, a suburb of Boston. He led us in prayer before meals, and Sunday was a day of observance when we were supposed to spend our time in contemplation and gratitude for what the Lord had provided. Dad's churches had a congregation of thousands and missions in four states. He was kind, a good dad, but he was out of town a lot, away visiting his other churches, conferring with the ministers he had personally ordained and meeting with investment clients.

I think Mom preferred it that way. When I went to Laquanda or Tasha's houses, I noticed their parents being in agreement. My mom and dad were affectionate with each other in front of us, but they argued a lot, and it had always been that way. Erin and I were used to it. In fact, it worked to our advantage. If Dad said no to something, we could always ask Mom, and fifty per cent of the time we got the right answer. We were a normal family, I guess, franks and beans or clam chowder on alternate Saturdays. Dad was a Red Sox and Patriots fan. Erin, Mom and I weren't interested in sports.

Mom was Irish, I mean properly Irish, born in Ireland. That's where Erin got her name: it means 'Ireland'. Mom's name was Maureen. Dad got to name me, thank God, and he said I was like a precious jewel so I was Ruby. I got a better name than Erin. That was the only perk I got from my parents.

Mom had come over to America for the summer when she was a teenager and was working as a nanny in a house close to where Dad grew up in Worcester, west of Boston. I think it was a love story. He was her knight in shining armour, and he rescued her from having to go back to Ireland. That's the way he told it. Mom would say it wasn't quite like that. They got married young and started a family straight away. Boy, was she homesick, though. By 1999, Erin and I hadn't been back to Ireland in four years, but Mom visited every year and spoke to Grandma once a week on a Saturday at 3 p.m.

I would eavesdrop sometimes. Mom would exclaim at various points, 'No' in disbelief, or 'She didn't' in astonishment, when she clearly did. Grandma's stories were then reported to us, but they concerned cousins we'd met once, or old school friends of Mom's. They involved an unmarried girl getting pregnant, or a fight over a will, or the neighbour's new dog. Mom missed home. The last time Erin and I had visited, it was a rainy and grey summer, but I loved Grandma. She was like the grandma you see in fairy tales. She wore her grey hair in a bun, she was softly chubby and she was always baking. She read bedtime stories and cuddled me, and even though I was probably a bit too old for that by then, I didn't mind it. I think she preferred me to Erin. I don't know how Mom and her brother and my grandparents had lived together in that tiny house. Grandpa had died young a year after his only son was born so I never met him. Dennis was eleven years younger than Mom. Mom and Dad's wedding photos showed him as a young boy. She never spoke about him much. He had emigrated to Australia some years previously and I don't think she kept in contact with him.

Much as I loved Grandma and a trip to Ireland, as we got older we chose to go to Bible Camp, which was way more fun than it sounded. We learned to cook and swim, and we did first aid, knitting circles, book club and singing. Not all the songs were hymns, though we weren't allowed to sing Britney Spears – not in front of the camp leaders anyway.

Erin's boyfriend was wicked smart. Milo had been in Altman High with us until he graduated the previous summer. Everyone wanted to be his girlfriend, but my big sister, Erin, took his attention. Slim and sandy-haired, he looked like a pale version of Bailey from *Party of Five*, and he was fun too. He was from Southie. His clothing was a little shabbier than most students, but apart from that and the accent, you would never know his background. His manners were impeccable, though they didn't come naturally. The first time he came to dinner, when Mom called out 'Dinner's ready' and bid us all to sit at the table, Milo politely began to offer the bread basket around, but Dad coughed and said, 'Let's say grace first, yes? Maureen, will you lead us in prayer?' Milo turned beetroot red. 'Yes, sir, ma'am, I'm sorry, sir.' Dad smiled reassuringly at him. Everyone closed their eyes as Dad intoned the holy words, but I sneaked a peek at Milo, and he was looking at each of us in turn. He caught me looking, jammed his eyes shut tight and then opened them again and winked at me with a grin. It was my turn to blush. He watched carefully how we used our knives and forks. Mom could have been more subtle about that. She narrated the whole table etiquette thing – 'and now we put our napkins on our laps' – and I knew she had learned table manners from Dad's family, because Grandma sometimes ate with her mouth open, or ate peas from her knife, and Mom didn't learn manners from her.

My parents grew to trust Milo, especially Mom, because he was Irish from a few generations back. Despite his good looks and physical presence, he was bookish like Erin. He adored her, and Dad even let him sleep over in the downstairs spare room on weekends or sometimes if they were studying late during the week. He was not allowed to go upstairs where Erin's room was, next to mine. They pretended that they stayed in their respective rooms, but I knew better.

My room was in the middle of the house upstairs and separated Erin's room at the top of the back stairs from Mom and Dad's room at the other end of the house beside the main staircase that led down into the hall. There was a full-length mirror on the wall in my room and I spent a lot of time in front of it, waiting for my teeth to straighten with the retainer and the pointy chin to change as I got older, for the curves that Erin had. Like Snow White's wicked stepmother, I checked the mirror impatiently several times a day, hoping for this miraculous change. One day, I got so frustrated that I banged my fist on the mirror, and it fell off the wall. The nail and the plastic thing that held the nail in place fell out too. There was now a hole in the wall. If it was a bit deeper, it would come out on Erin's side, and I'd be able to see into her room. What did she get up to on her own? Did she have a secret diary? I'd searched her room before. Laquanda showed us her older sister's secret diary and it was full of scandalous thoughts about what she wanted to do with boys and what she wanted boys to do to her. I got some nail scissors and tunnelled through the tiny hole until I could see straight on to the opposite wall of Erin's bedroom. Then I scratched a bit more until the hole was about half an inch wide. The wallpaper in her room was a crazy floral pattern that she'd chosen herself. Mom said it made her dizzy. Erin would never notice a small hole in the wall.

Now I could see Erin's bed and her vanity unit and almost her whole room. I used to spy on her now and then. I watched her removing make-up from perfectly unfreckled skin. I watched her change out of her clothes into her nightgown. I watched her in her most private moments. When I wasn't watching, I put the mirror back against the wall, on top of a shoe box. And I put a large pink Band-Aid over the hole in my pink wallpaper. You wouldn't spot the tape unless you were looking for it. The mirror had only hung six inches off the floor. When Mom noticed and talked about re-hanging it, I told her not to bother, that I liked being able to move the mirror around.

One morning, I woke early and saw a shadow passing under my door, but there was no sound of footsteps. I was immediately alert because I knew that Milo had stayed over the night before. I got out of bed quietly and peeled back the tape on my wall. Milo was in Erin's room. I expected her to shout at him to get out, but they were fooling around, French kissing and more. I was mesmerized and horrified and turned on. It became a regular thing for me, to wake up early and watch them on the nights he stayed over. They never made a sound. The guest room was downstairs behind the kitchen. I don't know how they never got caught.

Sometimes, we would all be working in the study at home, and I would examine him, taking in his fair hair, his square shoulders, his jutting chin, his strong arms. I watched how he was with Erin; how physically comfortable they were together. He would lift her up and throw her over his shoulder while she yelled at him to put her down even though she was clearly enjoying it. They sat together, pinkie fingers intertwined. They were inseparable. Mom insisted he was a good influence on Erin and it's true that she was not slacking in the study department. We all thought how Erin was lucky to have such a supportive boyfriend.

I wasn't one of the cool girls in school. I trained hard to be a cheerleader but never got picked. My friends included Laquanda Rice, Tasha Danziger and Janet De Vere Kennedy (yes, she was one of *those* Kennedys, a third cousin or something). I guess we were cliquey, but we'd been friends since kindergarten. We didn't deliberately exclude anyone from our group. None of us had boyfriends and we wore our virginity as a badge of honour. It didn't stop us talking about sex, though. We all knew the mechanics of how it worked from sex ed classes, but we talked endlessly about how it would feel. Janet said it might be like having Pop Rocks down there, but I thought it had to be better than that. The faces Erin and Milo made didn't look like the ones you made when eating Pop Rocks, from what I could see through the hole in my bedroom wall.

Erin said we were obsessed. But we weren't the ones with boyfriends in our bedrooms. I was ashamed to think my sister was one of the girls who was nearly doing sex. I didn't dare tell anyone. My friends and I talked about saving ourselves for our wedding day. We were going to marry pop stars. We were all to be each other's bridesmaids. We prayed for the souls of the girls who we knew were having sex. We went to Dad's church together. We had taken a pledge there to be virgins until we were twenty-one years old, but we thought we'd be married by then. We had posters of our dream boys on our walls – all the Backstreet Boys, Ricky Martin, Will Smith and Leonardo di Caprio.

At sixteen years of age, I wanted to be an actress. Laquanda said I would have to go to LA for that, but I guess I was more of a homebird than I thought. California seemed far away, and besides, I wanted to be a Broadway star rather than a film actress. Film actors, especially women, were often naked on camera. There was less nudity on stage. Tasha said there was no money in acting and that for every Broadway star there were thousands of bit-part actors. It didn't matter in the end. I never made it on to Broadway. Maybe things would have been different if it hadn't been for Milo Kelly.

It was 10 a.m. on a Wednesday, 15 September 1999, when he called at the house. I had come home from school on my own with a stomach ache and Mom had gone out somewhere with

Erin. The pain wasn't so bad. I told him that Erin wasn't home but that he could come inside and wait. He wondered when they'd be back, but I didn't know. He said he'd wait a while. That wasn't unusual. He spent a lot of time hanging around waiting for Erin. I offered him a coffee, and he accepted. I didn't even like coffee, but it seemed grown up to be sitting with Milo and sipping coffee. This time I sat beside him on the sofa. He was more chatty than usual, asked me about school and my friends. He was teasing me about wanting to be an actress. He reached out to tickle me – 'You want to be in *Dawson's Creek*. You want to kiss Pacey Witter' – and then he grabbed me around the middle and the mood turned dark in a split second. What happened next comes back to me in glimpses, like a series of photographs or glitchy radio static. The sound of my shirt ripping. My panties dropping to the floor. Staring at the vase on the sideboard, hearing my voice yelling, 'No, no, no.'

Dad found me wrapped in a blanket on the sofa when he came home. I wasn't crying yet. He was alarmed to see me like that and asked me what had happened. When I told him, in a robotic monotone, he called the police. He said I was in shock and made me drink a glass of brandy.

I was taken downtown, examined and swabbed and photographed, tested for pregnancy and all sorts of diseases including AIDS. They looked at the bruises on my inner thighs that were caused by Milo's thumbs digging into me, the marks on my wrists caused by his closed right hand, the cut on my head from where I'd banged it off the table trying to get away from him. These sounds and images were scrambled in my mind. I made my statement and answered the graphic questions. The lady police officer and the nurse said I had done excellently, as if I had scored an A on some exam paper.

Dad had called Mom from the police station. Mom and Erin were at home when I got back after midnight, and then all hell broke loose. I often wondered if it could have been dealt with in a different way. If Milo had admitted it, everything would have been simpler.

Over the next week, Erin was hysterical and then that turned to anger. I was sickened that she believed him over me. She had known him for just over a year, and she had known me all my life. But she was adamant I'd made it up and it hurt almost as much as the incident with Milo. She had trusted him completely, but I remember overhearing some friend of Mom's saying, 'Well, what can you expect from a boy from Southie? I certainly wouldn't have let him in my home.' I knew that was wrong. It wasn't Mom's fault for welcoming him into our house, and it wasn't because he was from South Boston, but I was too distraught to defend her. Everyone said I shouldn't feel guilty. But I shouldn't have sat beside him. I shouldn't have laughed when he began to tickle me.

2

Erin

I was seventeen the first time I really noticed Milo. I could see his back and one shoulder, his tanned neck, the side of his head, sandy hair falling into his eyes. The collar of his shirt was frayed, but clean. His hair was long on the top and short at the back. I'd seen him around school, but this was the first time I saw him in our church. He was part of the congregation, and I was two rows behind him. Dad said we should show humility by not taking the front pews. Mom and Ruby and I always hovered around the back. I think folks appreciated that. It made them trust Dad more. He wasn't going to show favour to his own family, but after the service we were expected to stand near him at the exit so that he could introduce us to his flock if required as they left.

Everyone poured out when the service was over, and the boy disappeared into the crowd. Mom had got talking to Marcia Little's mother and, by the time we got outside, he was gone. He was with an older lady. I guessed she was his mom.

The following week they were there again with a girl, older than him but with the same-shaped face as her mom – a sister, I assumed. She had black nail varnish on, and I thought that was kind of inappropriate for church. I rushed out at the end, but the three of them didn't stop. The mother muttered, 'Thank you, Pastor Cooper,' as she passed my dad. I looked at the boy's face then. He must have been older than me because we weren't in any of the same classes. Freckles crossed his nose and cheeks. He was good-looking in an old-fashioned way. His floppy hairstyle was out of date, but I liked that he didn't try to look like everyone else. For the next few weeks, I watched out for him at school. I saw him twice, once leaving the schoolyard and another time leaving Principal Bermingham's office with a grin on his face.

Dad's congregation came from all over Boston. He was not a snob. The marquee sign outside said GOD IS FOR EVERYBODY, and we had all ethnicities, all colours, rich and poor. Dad did his best to preach the word of Jesus in the way of Jesus. When we were planning church picnics or Bible Camp, everyone put unlabelled envelopes containing what they could afford in the donation box. Sometimes there would be envelopes containing a thousand dollars, and some would contain pieces of newspaper cut into the shape of dollar bills. Dad said that people would do that because they wanted to be seen to put an envelope in the box and we mustn't judge them. Ruby and I were allowed to open the envelopes and count the money with calculators by our side. I guessed that the sandy-haired boy was not wealthy. The jacket he wore was a bit too small, and shiny at the elbows. I asked Dad about the family, but he didn't know who I was talking about.

'The boy and his mom have come every Sunday for the last four weeks and sometimes the sister comes too. You should say hello, Dad,' I told him.

'Maureen, have you noticed them?' he said to Mom and she nodded enthusiastically.

The following week, I nudged Dad as they approached at the end of the service. The mom tried to scurry by, but Dad reached for her hand and said, 'You are welcome to the Holy Divine Church. I don't believe we have met?'

She looked up at him, startled, and quickly composed herself. 'Pastor Cooper, it is a pleasure to meet you. I'm Elaine Kelly and this here is my boy, Michael – we call him Milo – and my daughter, Margaret.'

The girl interrupted. 'Margie,' she said.

Dad said, 'We're all friends in this community, call me Douglas or Doug,' and he laughed and introduced all of us then. We shook hands and exchanged greetings, but I failed to make eye contact with Milo. 'What brings you to our church?' Dad asked.

'Well, we were all baptized in the Catholic Church, but I wanted somewhere . . .' She struggled for words.

'Less strait-laced?' said Dad.

'Yes.' Her face brightened, and Milo and Margie looked at the ground.

On this first encounter, I smiled at Milo as they were leaving, and as he moved away, he turned and smiled back. His blue eyes sparkled, and I saw his crooked nose. It made him more attractive to me. His mother pulled him closer to her.

Milo later told me that the priest in their Catholic parish had been moved to another parish for molesting some children. He and Margie had not been targeted but Mrs Kelly was furious that nobody had called the cops. She wanted her children to have a strong Christian faith like she had, but she no longer trusted the Catholic Church to protect children. I was vaguely aware of abuse stories coming out of the Catholic Church in Ireland where Grandma lived. She was upset about it all, but I hadn't heard of anything like that happening in our own city.

The Kellys had tried seven churches before they settled on ours, Mrs Kelly said. They liked Dad, he told Bible stories and then made them relatable to things that happened here and now, locally. He was liberal, much more so than your average preacher. He was not a fire-and-brimstone kind of guy. He was accepting of divorce, interracial marriage, contraception and homosexuality, but he preached chastity for boys and girls up to the age of twenty-one.

In Dad's other role, as an investment broker, he did well. The churches in Massachusetts, Rhode Island, Connecticut and New Hampshire were self-sufficient and supplied him with wealthy investment clients. Dad was a straight shooter. Everybody trusted him. He was away a lot, but always at home at least three Sundays each month for 'church and family, the two things that mean more to me than anything else in the world'. The fourth Sunday, he would be the star attraction at one of his other churches in the other states.

Mom was delighted to meet some Boston Irish; she missed Ireland so much. She was disappointed to hear that Mrs Kelly had never been to Ireland. Mrs Kelly's grandparents had come over in the early 1900s. Mom grasped on to every Irish thing she could. Even though Mrs Kelly was third-generation American, she knew her ancestors were from Donegal and Mom was able to tell her how beautiful her home place was.

Mom was very defensive about Ireland. She was the most elegant woman I ever saw and would say that Ireland had culture and tradition, and people did not live with pigs in the parlour like the old cartoon images. Dad knew this, of course, because he had visited Ireland with Mom to see Grandma. But him mocking the old country annoyed Mom intensely and she always reminded him that on their wedding day he had promised her they could retire to Ireland. He would say that was at least twenty years away and maybe by then you might be able to get a decent cup of coffee in Dublin, but they never stayed mad with each other for long and soon they would be hooting with laughter over some shared joke.

I made sure to talk to Milo every time after that first occasion. Church was now the highlight of my week, rather than hanging out at Filene's or the mall with Ginnie or Saima. They saw him too at church and agreed that he was dreamy. I discovered later that he had won a scholarship to our school, Altman High. You could tell his mom was proud of him, the way she looked at him. His uncle ran Billy's Diner downtown and Milo picked up shifts before and after school and most Saturdays. Sundays, he attended church and occasionally a Red Sox game at Fenway Park.

He was in his senior year. He told me that when he was a kid, his father was sick a lot and then died of heart failure, and he used to fantasize about being a doctor who could cure his father. He was hoping to get into Boston College.

Milo's sister, Margie, did not like that I was friendly with him. One Sunday, she warned me, 'My little brother isn't your type. I can see he's sweet on you, but there's no sense in pulling him into places where he doesn't belong.' I didn't know what she meant. I think she was jealous of her brother. As she sauntered away, hands deep in her pockets, my heart soared. Milo was sweet on me.

In Altman High, I knew that I wasn't the only girl who noticed Milo. Any time his name was mentioned, all the girls commented on how handsome he was. He stood out a little and it was plain as day that he cut his own hair. Some of the school jocks ribbed him about it, but it turned out that Milo had an encyclopaedic knowledge of the Red Sox and every penny he earned at his uncle's diner on evenings and weekends went towards days out at Fenway Park, after he'd given his mom half. Even though he wasn't a great player, the jocks adopted him, almost as their mascot. It could have been patronizing in different circumstances, but they genuinely liked him. He made friends easily and my girlfriends were flirting with him on the daily.

Milo told me that he lived in a triple-decker house. He and his mom and Margie lived on the top floor, and his uncle Billy and uncle Pat lived with their families on the floors below. His dad had been a delivery truck driver but, when he died, he left behind some debts. Margie and his mom worked full-time in a florist at Boston South Station; they all contributed to the household. Southie was up and coming then, and there were cranes all over the place – it was being developed. Milo was relieved that his uncle owned the building.

Dad's church downtown had opened Milo's eyes to new possibilities. He told me that when they first started coming, his mom had expected to be ignored or patronized at best and was delighted when Dad went out of his way to welcome them. Milo loved our church, although he never could take part in Bible Camp or the summer barbecues because he was always working.

I told him he was welcome to come and study at our house any time he wanted. We lived a short walk away from the school on his route to the T Station. I told Mom and Dad I'd made this offer, and they were pleased that I was encouraging him, though I don't think they understood why. Well, maybe Mom did.

The first time Milo came to our house, he said, 'Wow, this place is awesome.' Mom did her best to make him feel comfortable: 'I used to think like that too, but you should have seen the little house that I grew up in. There wasn't room to swing a cat.' Mom was flirting with Milo more than I was. She was embarrassing.

Ruby was shy around him. Ruby was two years younger than me, but she was in a real hurry to grow up. She would stuff her bra with tissues and the posters of the pop idols in her room were covered in lipstick smooches. Dad's church was big on virginity and Ruby and her friends were particularly prudish and immature. Contradictorily, they could not wait until their wedding night.

Ruby was funny and would often sing and dance for us on Saturday night or do impersonations of people on TV. She took her drama classes seriously. We were close, growing up. I often found her in my room trying on my clothes. I didn't mind. She always preferred to get my hand-me-downs to new clothes for herself. That was cute.

The first time that Milo came into the house, Ruby stared at him. It was damn rude. I kicked her under the table. I could sense that Milo was uncomfortable. He said 'Hi', but she didn't say anything. When he became a regular visitor to the house, I think she got more used to him, until a year later when she said he raped her.

3

It was as if the world stopped turning that day in September 1999. My sister lied about what happened. I knew it. She swore Milo had raped her, but he wouldn't. I knew him better than anyone. He was gentle. He was already locked up by the time I got home that night, and it would be many years before I saw him again. I attacked my sister when she came home from the police station late that night, first verbally and then, when she insisted it was true, I attacked her physically, and Mom and Dad had to separate us. Her story didn't even make sense. Milo would never tickle a sixteen-year-old girl, especially Ruby.

Milo was prone sometimes to dark moods. I was aware of it, that there were days when he wouldn't want to talk or hang out, not just with me but with anyone. His best friend in school was a guy called Ben Roche, who advised leaving him alone when he got like that. It only happened three times in the year or so that I knew him. And then he would emerge again, apologetic, unable to explain what had come over him. It was 'a dose of the blues' he said. But that didn't mean he could ever be violent with anyone. He didn't even get in any schoolyard fights when he was a kid, as far as I knew.

Dad decided that I should go and stay with Aunt Rachel a few days later. She was my dad's younger sister, living in Worcester, fifty miles west of Boston. Milo was locked up while the investigation was ongoing. I was not allowed to go and see Milo's mother or sister, or to call them. I only had a rough idea where they lived.

I never went to Milo's house and Dorchester was a big area. Mom told me that they kept calling our house, but she hung up every time. I was angry to be banished from my home like that. I hadn't done anything wrong. My sister had told a vicious lie and soon the police would find out, and Milo would be freed. I decided that when that happened, Milo and I would run away together, to New York, and start over. I couldn't bear being separated from him. Aunt Rachel tried to reason with me: 'Girls don't make up stories like that, Erin, and your sister is a particularly innocent child. She and her friends are proud virgins, aren't they?' I was a virgin too, though I didn't shout about it like Ruby and her friends. If Milo had wanted to have sex badly, I would have given in. I told Aunt Rachel this. She was five years younger than Dad and way cooler. 'But, Erin, rape isn't about sex, it's about control. Now why would your sister lie about something like that? Has she lied before?'

I had to think about that. Ruby was not a habitual liar. She had told childish lies, denying stealing chunks from Mom's birthday cake when the evidence was in the crumbs on her face, but we didn't tell lies in our family. She was an excellent actress and could impersonate every teacher in Altman, but I was never aware of her lying before. This made it more difficult for anyone to believe Milo. It turned out that he had been charged with a misdemeanour by the police two years ago for trespassing in a derelict house. He had never told me about that, but then why would he? I never told him that I had successfully shoplifted a pair of jeans from Old Navy until Mom discovered the labels in the trash can in my room and marched me back to the store to pay for them. It had been a dare among a group of us at the mall. They didn't even fit me. It was a stupid prank. She docked my allowance for ten weeks – four weeks to pay for the jeans and six weeks to make sure I'd learned my lesson. She never told Dad or Ruby, though. Maybe Ruby had done things Mom hadn't told us about?

I was supposed to keep it all a secret, but I had to tell Ginnie and Saima. I did not go back to school that year, and they had been calling the house. I called them from Worcester. Ginnie said that everyone in school already knew and that most people believed Ruby. Saima said she believed me, but she asked me why Ruby would make up such a monstrous lie and I couldn't answer that.

Three weeks later, DNA test results came in. There was no doubt. Milo had raped my sister. Dad drove up to Worcester to tell me. 'You have to accept it, honey. That man is an evil son of a bitch, and he defiled your sister.' I had never heard Dad use such language before. I was shaking with shock. I thought of all the ways his DNA could have got on to my sister. A shared towel perhaps? Dad had to make it clear. 'Erin,' he said sternly, 'the DNA came from semen that was *inside* Ruby, do you understand what I'm telling you?' I understood the words he said to me, but it took a while for them to truly sink in. How could I believe that snow was white if the guy I loved with all my heart had raped my sister? But he had, and I was wrong. Aunt Rachel tried her best to comfort me, but I was angry, first at myself and then at Milo. I was horrified that I had called my sister a liar.

I got a summons to appear as a witness for the defence. Mom and Dad were outraged but I was over eighteen by then and there was nothing they or I could do to stop it. I worried myself sick in the weeks leading up to the trial. I had constant nausea. I did not know what I was going to be asked. Would Milo have told them about how intimate we had been? It turned out that he had. In a full courtroom in front of my parents, Aunt Rachel, their friends, Mrs Kelly, Margie, Milo's friend Ben Roche, Mr Bermingham the school principal, the judge, jury and a whole load of strangers, I had to reveal the private details of my life. I could not look at Milo. I could not look at anyone.

Then it was the prosecutor's turn. He asked me who suggested that Milo sneak into my room against my parents' rules in the middle of the night. I had to admit that it was me. I had been the one who wanted to get closer to him. I think he had expected a different answer. He asked me how hard I had to persuade him, and I told the court that Milo didn't argue at all. I watched my mother leave the courtroom in tears. The prosecutor talked about how this was a sign of Milo's deceptive behaviour, how he had manipulated his way into my bedroom, against the rules of my parents, who had been so good to him. He also asked me about his moodiness. Where did I think he went during those times when he refused to talk to anyone? I didn't understand what he meant. He went to school and to work and home, like normal. He asked if I had proof that he went to work and home during his 'thunderous moods'. Milo's lawyer objected to his words and the judge asked me if his moods were thunderous. I said no. She asked me to describe them. I said that it just seemed like depression to me. The prosecutor resumed his questions, asking again if I knew for sure that Milo went home and to work during these moods. I had no proof. He asked if I knew anything about Milo's previous girlfriends. I did not, except that they were older than him. I don't know what the relevance of these questions was, but Milo's defence let them go unchallenged. There were unsaid implications, though, and they were not good for Milo.

Milo's defending attorney used my information to demonstrate how gentle Milo had been with me and how he had never pressured me into oral or full penetrative sex. I wept through this testimony. I glanced quickly at Milo. He lifted his head from his hands and mouthed the word 'sorry' at me. I hated him by then. I was angry with him for putting me through this.

Months later, right on the day of Milo's sentencing, Mom said we'd have to go to Ireland for Ruby's sake. 'How is Ruby ever going to recover when there are reminders everywhere?' I thought it was an unnecessarily drastic step but Mom was adamant. We had to move to Dublin. Mom and Dad argued about it, and this time the arguments were loud and serious. Doors slammed and voices were raised. We hid in our rooms. Ruby's friends visited, but they never stayed long.

I couldn't talk to her. I don't think she could talk to me either. Milo would never have been in our house if it hadn't been for me.

4
Ruby

The DNA results proved that what I said was true. The investigation and the court case and the verdict took seven months and then there was the sentencing weeks after that. The court case was gruelling and way more traumatic than the incident itself. It was a jury trial. It went on and on and on. Milo had to admit that I'd said no three times. He admitted that he'd told me, 'This never happened, nobody has to know,' but he didn't admit the incident. He didn't try to say it was consensual. He said that I had tried to seduce him. I was quizzed many times by his attorney about what I was wearing. He'd said I was wearing shorts, but I told them I was wearing jeans. And the prosecutor insisted that it didn't matter. I was a sixteen-year-old innocent, and he was a nineteen-year-old working man. But the DNA was the biggest, most undeniable factor.

Neither Erin nor I went to school that academic year. Erin came back from Aunt Rachel's to appear as a witness in the trial. She was a different person. She grabbed me and hugged me and sobbed how sorry she was, but then she went to her room and rarely came out. We stayed home for months, unable to offer comfort to each other. Dad tried to persuade me to come back to church, but I was ashamed. I was no longer pure in the eyes of God.

After the sentencing, Mom's solution was to take us out of

Boston and back to her home in Ireland. 'It's for a few weeks,' said Mom. 'Your grandma will be pleased to see you and Erin.'

I nodded along when the trip was suggested. Mom had been asking Dad for years about moving back to Ireland. Now Dad and Mom fought about it. 'Move *there?*' said Dad, incredulous, then he saw me in the doorway and his voice softened. 'Hey, Ruby, how are you today?' he said, but the smile didn't reach his eyes, and I knew how he wanted me to respond, to run into his arms for comfort so he could kiss the top of my head, like he used to. But I turned away and went back up to my room and shut the door behind me. The trial had been awful.

Erin did not want to go to Ireland. She was broken-hearted and broken.

'You girls need to stick together,' said Mom. Erin looked at me and I saw her shame and anger.

It was agreed that Mom and I would go on our own four days after she suggested it. Erin refused to come. She went to some prayer retreat instead. Nobody talked about what would happen after the summer.

I said goodbye to Laquanda and Tasha and Janet, who promised they'd write. I was glad to be getting away. Milo had his supporters who apparently called me horrible names. My name was graffitied all over walls in South Boston. I had been out of school for eight months and I was desperate to get away. Grandma's little house had always felt safe to me. And I needed to feel safe.

Leaving was horrible. We all cried, Erin and I clinging on to each other, telepathically saying all the things that had gone unsaid. Mom and I had one-way tickets. I didn't know if we were going to come back. Dad's eyes were red-rimmed, and my mother sobbed as they parted at the airport. Once again, I felt guilt for breaking our family in two, but this was only four days after the thirteen-year sentence had been handed down. I had hardly processed what had happened yet.

5
Erin

Milo and I had our first kiss in a deserted gym in high school. We were both nervous, but once we'd kissed, it kind of sealed the deal. Mom and Dad liked him and his mom. Milo was not allowed into my bedroom under any circumstances. We respected their rules for a long time. Being with Milo was exciting and interesting and we laughed a lot. We loved the same books; we watched the same movies over and over. *Good Will Hunting* was our favourite. He was Matt Damon and I was Minnie Driver and we made up the happiest endings for ourselves. Milo couldn't afford to take me out for meals or buy me jewellery, but I didn't need those things.

Milo was not a virgin. He had slept with a few girls. I wasn't entirely surprised by this. I think I was one of the last virgins in my class, but I was struggling with it. My body yearned for him, as if it was a different entity to my mind. I knew that God was testing me, but Milo said he would wait. We didn't go the whole way, though we came close. We had worked out which steps on the back stairs of the house squeaked and I had oiled the handle of my bedroom door. On the occasional nights when Milo stayed over in the spare room downstairs, he could creep up and quietly enter my bedroom at the top of the back stairs without anyone hearing, where we would make out and fool around. We would whisper to each other about what felt good and what didn't, manoeuvring each other's hands and bodies until we were both satisfied. We stifled our moans. Nobody knew. Ruby's bedroom was between mine and my parents' room. She had famously slept through a storm that had taken the roof off the shack directly behind our bedrooms a couple of years earlier. Nothing would wake her.

I think at the time I trusted Milo more than anyone I knew. He told me he'd wait until I was ready, but I was God-fearing in those days. We knew that we were going to get married as soon as I graduated high school. I knew Dad would go crazy, but as they had got married when Mom was twenty-one years old and he was twenty-two, he couldn't say too much. We planned to have three children after he qualified as a doctor. We were stuck about where we were going to live. Milo wanted to support me, but it was going to be a long time until he would be able to do that. Besides, I wanted to go to Harvard. I reckoned that Dad could probably buy us an apartment as a wedding present, but Milo was uncomfortable with that. He had got into Boston College on a scholarship that didn't cover everything. He had student loans too. The principal at Altman had helped him with his applications. Principal Bermingham always took a special interest in Milo. He mentored him and said he could see Milo's potential. So could I.

I used to write short stories for my own amusement. They were usually stories about wacky characters. They were all different. One was about demon children who were born to this loving couple but who grew up to be psychopaths and murdered their parents. Another was about a single mother who refused to feed her children; they were taken from her and put into foster care, but they were traumatized. They refused to eat until they were put back into their mother's care and then they ate her. These stories were often disturbing. I was afraid to show them to anyone but Milo and he suggested I show them to my teacher. I don't know where these ideas came from, but Milo loved them – he said I should send them in to competitions. Even though

I was top of the class in English at school, my English teacher didn't like them. She found them distasteful and encouraged me to write about the real world. I didn't think Dad would have approved, especially if my teacher didn't, and Mom wasn't much of a reader. I loved books and reading, though. Ruby once said that prettiness was wasted on me because I was such a geek. She was funny.

Milo thought I should be a writer, and I thought that was something I could maybe try in my spare time, but I wanted to read books rather than write them. It was a huge surprise to discover that Milo had entered one of my stories into a competition in a literary journal and they had agreed to publish it. Dad demanded to read the story and, to my surprise, he liked it. I don't think Mom understood it, but she was super proud and took me to New York on the train for the day to see *The Lion King* on Broadway. We wouldn't be home until late. That was the day Milo raped Ruby.

I wondered if it had all been a fantasy. Was Milo playing me all this time? Did he like my stories at all? He had told me he'd slept with girls when he was younger, he'd said the girls were older than him, but were they? Did he ever plan to marry me? The shock of what he did to Ruby was overwhelming.

I thought about Milo's dark moods. At the time we were planning our future together, I thought it was depression. In those times, he wouldn't call me or talk to me in school. Once he had shouted, 'Leave me the fuck alone,' and punched a wall while I walked alongside him trying to engage him in conversation. I was shaken by his aggression. I had not told the court about that. I should have. Afterwards he had apologized, and he was back to his sweet old self, but I couldn't forget the sudden rage and hostility. Would he have hit me if I'd tried to hug him? Maybe he was a psychopath. You read about these people all the time:

'He was so mild-mannered, wouldn't hurt a fly.' Milo hadn't planned to rape Ruby, I was sure of it, but if one of those black moods had taken him, who knew what he could do?

I knew that Milo masturbated because sometimes, on those nights when he crept up the back stairs into my room, I helped him jerk off. But there was no way around it: his semen was inside her vagina so he must have come inside her. The whole time he could have said it was consensual, but he insisted that Ruby came on to him, that she wrapped herself around him and that he had stopped her, that she fell and knocked her head. He insisted there was no penetration at all and that he'd had to fight her off. A tiny girl like Ruby? The DNA sealed his fate and broke my heart in two.

Some time after I returned from Worcester, Margie was lurking outside the house one day when I was getting in the car to go to the supermarket. I went to the gate to meet her.

'He didn't do it, you know he didn't.' She was half crazy with rage. 'I warned you something would happen if he started mixing with you rich kids. I never imagined it would be this. Your sister is a liar, and you fucking know it. He's not stupid, Erin, why would he do such a thing and think that he wouldn't be caught?'

Dad heard the commotion and came out and threatened to call the police. He ran her off the property.

Mrs Kelly had come to the house twice, begging to talk to Ruby until Mom and Dad got a restraining order against her. Ruby and I stayed home, thinking our lives were over, and perhaps they were, because nothing was ever the same again.

Sometimes, Ruby could forget and laugh at *The Simpsons* or *Friends* on TV, and we encouraged that. Dad was angry and silent for months. He said his faith was being challenged and prayed about it endlessly.

The story wasn't in the newspapers but some people in the

church knew and everyone in Altman knew. I had only told Saima and I'm sure she didn't tell anyone, but Ruby's friends were less discreet.

And then, four days after Ireland was suggested, Mom and Ruby left. I thought it was temporary. They'd stay for the summer and then they'd come home. Mom begged me to come with them, but I needed a break from Ruby. I knew it wasn't her fault, but I couldn't bear to see her pale face and sad eyes. It was one of the worst days among many terrible ones. Dad thought I should go to a prayer retreat for a while. It was a kind of religious retreat with daily massages as well as group baking, prayer circles, flower arranging, music therapy and painting sessions. I slept a lot and talked a lot in group sessions, about trust and betrayal and family, and I made cupcakes for a party I would never attend, funeral wreaths for my heart; I wrote angry songs that nobody would ever sing, and I painted my soul in shades of grey and green with splashes of rotting yellow. I did not mix with the other guests.

Two weeks later, Dad came to pick me up, a fake cheerful smile on his face, and I noticed his hair was greying at the temples. Milo's actions had taken their toll on everyone.

The house was quiet all the time now, and the tension was gone. I don't know if that was because the trial and sentencing were over or because Ruby was no longer there. I missed Mom badly and called her often. She always wanted me to talk to Ruby, but those conversations were brief and awkward. Dad and I got along okay. I had missed a school year; I was going to have to repeat it. Dad hired a maid to cook and clean for us, but I ironed Dad's shirts in the particular way he liked. He got back to full-time work and his ministries, and Saima persuaded me to spend the summer working as a supervisor with her at a camp for middle school kids in Vermont. I felt bad about leaving Dad alone, but he encouraged me to go. It also gave me an excuse not to go to Dublin to see Mom and Ruby with him. That summer in Vermont was freedom. Nobody knew anything about what had happened. There were no sympathetic looks. I could be normal.

Dad returned from Dublin upset. Mom was pressuring him to move there, but even I knew it was a ridiculous idea. Dad had no friends there, no business contacts, no church community. He broke the news to me that Mom and Ruby were not coming back to Boston. Ruby had refused and Mom couldn't leave her there on her own. I tried to hide my distress from Dad, but it was hard. I was technically an adult, but I still felt like I needed my mom. Mom came back to see me, leaving Ruby with Grandma, but she was still convinced Dad would change his mind and that we would all go to Dublin. I could see their relationship was frayed but there was nothing I could do about it.

Back at school in the fall, things were different. Saima had graduated and gone to Boston University College of Fine Arts. I was doing my final school year. I knew some of the kids in my class, but I didn't feel like mixing with them. Milo had made some real friends during his time in Altman, and they all knew what had happened. The boys shunned me, and I only spent time with the girls in my class who were in Dad's church. Principal Bermingham avoided looking at me when we passed in the corridors. After a few weeks, we heard that he had quit. I realized he must have other things on his mind. Not everything was about me.

In my spare time, I studied. There was nobody to write stories for, so I stopped writing them. I'd applied and got accepted into Harvard. Dad took me out for dinner when I got the letter of acceptance. He said Saima could come too, thank the Lord, because Dad and I had run out of conversation a long time ago.

6

Ruby

Mom and I landed in Grandma's house in Dublin in May 2000. Grandma's house was in a cul de sac. The houses were all squeezed together in one square terrace. Three small bedrooms, a living room and a kitchen and one bathroom for the whole house. The neighbours would say hello and introduce themselves, but I didn't feel like I should be too friendly to anyone. Mom did not grow up rich like Dad did, that's for sure, but I didn't care that much about my surroundings. Grandma always made me feel better.

Mom was happy to be home. She was determined that Dad and Erin would join us soon. She was house hunting. She reconnected with lots of old friends and went out to lunches and dinners and trips to the cinema. She wanted me to meet her friends' children, but I resisted strongly. How could I have anything in common with Irish kids? They seemed rougher than us. When I saw them messing about in the grocery store or in the local park, they cursed a *lot*. Especially the boys. Grandma agreed with me. Dad would have been shocked at the profanity. When Mom went out, Grandma and I would bake together, or she would dig out old photo albums and show me pictures of Mom growing up. My uncle in Australia was handsome when he was a boy. Grandma said he'd been gone so long but that she still missed him. Phone calls to and from

Australia were very expensive and Dennis was not a good letter writer.

Grandma thought Mom should never have come home without Dad, even though she disapproved of him and his church. She kept asking when he was joining us. Grandma was a strict Catholic. The teachings of Dad's church were much more relaxed than her own faith and the observance of it was different. We didn't say grace before dinner like we did at home. There was no Bible Camp, and I missed that, but we went to Mass on Sunday. It was a lot different from going to church back home. Irish people didn't dress up, the music was incredibly dreary and there were few people there of my age. I wasn't expected to contemplate anything or read the Bible on Sundays, and I was allowed to watch TV and play Mom's old records from when she grew up here. There were fewer rules. I liked that.

On the night of the incident, before we went downtown, Dad had poured me a large brandy for the shock. The taste was awful but it warmed me from my toes to the top of my head. I knew I had been through something utterly terrible but, somehow, the brandy took the edge off it. In the days and weeks that followed, I found myself working my way through my parents' liquor cabinet without alerting them, topping up the gin and vodka with water, and the whiskey and brandy with tea. They rarely drank and didn't notice. I continued this little practice when I got to Ireland. I spent most of my allowance on liquor and beer. I was seventeen by then. I could drink legally in Ireland at eighteen, but I was only asked my age once in the liquor store. I lied.

While we were welcome in her home, Grandma made it clear that a wife's role was to be at her husband's side, regardless of his faith. Mom said that maybe Dad could set up a mission in Ireland, just like he had set up his church by himself before.

Mom assured Grandma she could persuade him. Dad had given guest lectures in Ireland a few times. I vaguely remembered going to one five years earlier, when Dad was mad because there was only a handful of attendees. He missed us, Mom said. Grandma sniffed with disapproval. I was sure Mom would persuade Dad.

Grandma never mentioned what Milo did to me, not once. I think it suited us both to sweep it under the carpet. I liked Grandma. She let me be, though I didn't cause her any trouble, not then. I appreciated the fact that she never asked me, and Mom was happy about it too. She knew I never wanted to talk about *that*.

Laquanda and Tasha did write diligently for the first few months; Janet, only twice. I was even allowed to call them on the phone, though Grandma paced up and down the hall muttering about the phone bill when I did. I had permission to call two friends once a week for fifteen minutes. Mom had brokered that deal with Grandma, even though we had enough money to call our friends any time we liked. We were rich compared to other kids in my school in Boston, never mind the kids on this Dublin street. 'Wasteful,' said Grandma. Mom said that we would get cellphones of our own. Grandma didn't trust cellphones. 'If you want to fry your brains, go ahead,' she said.

But even with my new cellphone, my friendships couldn't survive the width of the Atlantic Ocean. There was no more conversation about our wedding days. Laquanda and Tasha kept asking when I was coming home and I'd say 'Soon', thinking that I could never go back. The letters and calls eventually dried up. There were only so many ways to answer 'How are you?' when the answer was 'I don't know'. In the last call I had with Tasha, she said everyone had moved on. Nobody talked about us now. Milo had been sent to Whiteshore Prison. I knew his family were fundraising to appeal. I guess they had believed him too.

Dad visited us in time for the July 4th weekend, five weeks

after we arrived. Erin didn't come at all. The excuse was that she'd got a job supervising at a kids' summer camp in Vermont. I was upset about that. Erin had been good at telephoning regularly, but the conversations were always short. Even before we left home, things had been awkward between us and I'd hoped that when she came to Ireland, to this new environment, that we could all reconnect.

Dad told me I was not to worry about Milo's appeal. It was never going to happen because there was no new evidence. That was a big relief. The thought of ever having to go through a court case again was terrifying. Dad was adamant that he was not ready to retire even though Mom said he didn't need any more money. Mom had set up all these meetings for Dad with religious people he didn't know and didn't wish to know. He referred to them as tadpoles. Mom didn't know any heads of banks or investment brokerages. Dad wanted us to come home. We wanted him to stay in Dublin. I was the most resistant to returning to Boston and grew hysterical at the thought. Mom said she couldn't leave me here on my own.

Dad only stayed eight days. Mom was glassy-eyed and devastated. Before he left, Dad said that he loved me very much but he couldn't start over in Ireland. He told me that I shouldn't blame myself. Mom blamed me, though she said she didn't. 'The important thing is that I love you and that's never going to change,' Dad said. I howled and cried, but that made Mom even more upset, and Dad charged me with looking after Mom. 'You two need to support each other. I'll come over when I can, and when you are properly recovered, you can come back, and we'll be a family again.' I knew for a fact I would never be fully recovered. I was devastated that Dad was choosing his job and his ministry over us. He told me that Erin really missed me. I missed her too. The phone calls were awkward, but I knew that if she were to come to Ireland, we could get back to normal.

When Grandma heard that Dad was going home on his own, she was upset too. And to get away from Grandma's judgement, Mom bought a large apartment for us on Mount Merrion Avenue with a spare room for Erin that went unused ninety-nine per cent of the time. Neither of us believed that this separation was permanent. We thought that Dad would miss us too much.

Mom had several friends in Dublin, some of whom I'd met and some who were strangers to me. I'm sure she told some of them what had happened, but nobody mentioned it to me. They arrived with dinners and cakes and wine. It was good to hear her laughing. She went out to dinner parties and concerts, and I encouraged her. She had sacrificed enough for me.

I started high school, or secondary school as they called it, in September 2000 in a school that was girls only (unusual back home but entirely normal in Ireland). The school was called St Anne's and apparently had a Catholic ethos, not that I saw much of it. It came up in class one day that my father had founded his own church. I think they were confused by that. When asked if it was a Catholic church or a Protestant church, I wasn't sure how to answer. I said it was a Christian church and that we followed the teachings of the New Testament. They didn't ask me anything else and, thankfully, I was left alone again. Our teachers were all female and two of them were nuns. I had two years till graduation.

School was okay. Stricter than Boston, but then home was no longer as strict as Boston. I was scared to make friends. I kept to the corners and tried not to engage. I didn't think I deserved friends. The incident had caused mayhem in the lives of all the people I cared about. I had nothing in common with these girls. Without our church group, there was nothing to bond us. I liked U2, I guess, and The Cranberries, and sometimes I swapped CDs with girls, but I never invited anyone home and I never got invited to their houses either. I was sick with loneliness but terrified to join in.

Erin visited during summer vacation the year after in 2001, but she had changed into a different type of girl. Outwardly, she was still beautiful, and attracted a lot of male attention, but she had no interest in guys. She had been such a cheerful, outgoing big sister, but now she wanted to stay home. Mom had sighed one day when we were both sitting glumly sipping wine on the sofa, 'I guess I have two nuns on my hands.' Erin burst into tears and fled to her room. I was stricken by the thought that I had ruined her future by letting Milo tickle me. That night, I took Erin out to a bar. I'd never seen her drunk. I thought it would be good for her to let her hair down, but she didn't enjoy it at all. After three drinks she wanted to go home and refused to come to a nightclub with me. We only made passing references to what had happened in the fall of '99.

Living in Ireland was weird in the beginning because I didn't always get the cultural references, but it did seem that America was the centre of the universe for Irish people. Mom and I went into Dublin city centre when President Clinton visited that first December. Hillary and Chelsea were there too. I got a glimpse of them through a lowered car window. There were thousands of people there waving American flags. I mean, everyone knew that he'd made a big mistake a few years back with Monica Lewinsky, but Irish people were more than willing to forgive. Dad had tried to protect us from the details when it happened, but Dawn Linskey in Altman told us what a blow job was. Laquanda had said it must be illegal.

After 9/11 in 2001, Irish media went nuts. It was all everyone talked about for ages afterwards. I never knew how connected the two countries were. It seemed like anyone you met in Ireland had only two degrees of separation from someone who lost their life in that terrorist attack. Everyone in school sympathized with me even though I didn't know anyone who died. I felt such a fake, accepting condolences on behalf of New York, a city I didn't even know all that well.

A teacher, Miss Wallace, took me aside one day and asked me if everything was okay at home. She had noted that I didn't mix with my classmates and that I ate my lunch alone. I insisted that I preferred it that way. She sent me home with a letter for Mom suggesting that I seemed to be extremely antisocial. Mom was annoyed at me. 'For God's sake,' she said, 'could you not make an effort to fit in?'

I think Miss Wallace asked Lindsay Dillon to try to befriend me. She didn't seem to have friends either. She was tall with straight hair and still wore an Alice band in her hair. She was not a cool girl. Her school skirt was long, and she wore socks up to her knees, whereas the other girls rolled their skirts up and pushed their socks down, exposing as much bare flesh as they could. Lindsay began to seek me out at lunchtimes and occasionally we swapped our snacks. She didn't ask why we'd moved to Dublin, although the concocted story was that my mom wanted to be close to her ageing mother. We became friends, but not like Laquanda or Tasha. Lindsay was much more serious. We did go for a drink occasionally, but Lindsay always wanted to go home earlier than me. Mom didn't mind what hours I kept. It was unexpected, because back home I'd always thought Mom was the disciplinarian in our house but maybe she had been enforcing Dad's rules.

Lindsay was nice but it was a different kind of friendship to the one I'd had with my American girlfriends. I learned quickly not to say 'girlfriend' when referring to female friends. Girlfriends were girls who were in a relationship with boys. But Lindsay didn't talk about boys or pop music or sex or celebrity gossip. We talked about movies and books, and I occasionally accompanied her to classical concerts. I think, from the taunts and whispers of the other girls, they thought we were lesbians. Lindsay and I went to the theatre together a few times. They didn't have anything equivalent to Broadway in Dublin, but sometimes they would put on American plays with actors doing terrible accents.

In January 2002, I had to fill in a form to say what college I wanted to go to. There was only one course that I was interested in and that was Drama and Theatre Studies in Trinity College. Lindsay wanted to do Law there. We studied like crazy. I had to go do an interview. They asked about a show I had seen, and I had to give my critique on the spot. I talked about musical theatre and the shows I had seen on Broadway. *Riverdance* was the only musical Ireland had ever produced as far as I knew. They asked who were my favourite non-musical playwrights and I was able to talk about Arthur Miller and Tennessee Williams and Lillian Hellman. They were more impressed when I dropped those names. A few weeks later, I got a conditional offer in the mail, depending on my final exam results. I had also signed up for English and Philosophy, but I planned to drop those as soon as I could. I was happy for the first time in many months – I didn't have to force a smile or pretend. When I went to tell Mom, I found her in tears in her bedroom.

Dad was looking for a divorce. He had met somebody new. Kathy.

We had held on to the idea that Dad would eventually come and join us, but apart from a week around Independence Day and Christmas, he had never visited. Mom had gone back to spend time with him every few months, but it wasn't enough to sustain a marriage. I held off telling her about my college success, but she and I got drunk together that night while she told me all about falling in love with my dad. There were details I hadn't heard before. How he had charmed her and pursued her and how she made the difficult decision not to go back to Dublin for

Christmas that first year, leaving Grandma on her own. I guess Mom was totally smitten. Poor Grandma.

Now that a divorce was imminent, and after the shock wore off, I think she was relieved not to have to go back to Boston. Dad had been out of my life for two years, but I was still sad. Even when he'd come here on vacation, I could tell he didn't like it. I got a laptop and an iPod from Dad to alleviate my upset and his guilt. Mom did a course in basic computer skills and got a job through a friend in a boys' school as an administrator. She didn't need to work, but she liked earning her own money, even if it was a pittance compared to what Dad paid in alimony. She was single for the first time in her adult life. I wondered if she would start dating again, but she showed no interest in that, and it wasn't the sort of thing I could talk to her about.

Grandma was the most upset. 'Having a divorced child on top of everything else,' she said. The 'everything else' meant me and the incident. Grandma should have been kinder to Mom. None of this was her fault. It was mine.

7

I started my degree course in Trinity College in September 2002. I moved out of the apartment into one in the city with my schoolfriend Lindsay Dillon. Dad was obliged to pay maintenance, and my allowance was always generous.

That year, in my first week of college, Erin called to tell me that Milo's mother had jumped off the John W. Weeks Bridge into the Charles River and died. I was devastated by this news. Poor Mrs Kelly. I remembered her in church, shivering in a coat that wasn't warm enough for a Boston winter.

'How do you know, Erin?'

'It was on the news,' she said, but I could tell she was lying.

'Are you in touch with Milo's family?' She had never been friendly with his sister, Margie, back in the day, but maybe they had talked to each other.

'No.'

I didn't pursue it. Another life not just destroyed, but over. I couldn't think about that. I pretended not to care. It was easier than talking about it.

I loved Drama and Theatre Studies. We studied all kinds of theatre from puppetry to Japanese Noh. I discovered lots of new (to me) playwrights. I learned about mime and *commedia dell'arte* and the structures of classical plays. I loved acting. The ease with which I was able to slip into another character's head was thrilling to me and noted by my classmates. I was still shy, but if my character called for me to burst into a room and berate a group of strangers, I had no issue with that. I also had a gift for accents. Bizarrely, every accent except the Irish one, despite being surrounded by it. Sometimes we were encouraged to spend entire days living in another character's shoes. I loved that. Even before the end of my first year, I had been offered work in a stage play by a director who had come to see a showcase I was in. It was a reasonable-sized role, but the college didn't approve of students taking professional work during term time. I had to turn it down.

Lindsay had a boyfriend, Stuart, a nerdy, tweedy guy. She had met him on her first day in Trinity. After about two weeks, he stayed the night in our apartment. Lindsay blushed all the way through breakfast next morning. We had never spoken about sex to each other, but I could tell she had done it. Stuart wasn't unattractive, I suppose. Tall and rangy, he wore thick glasses, but when he took them off, his face was pleasant and open. He was polite to me as well.

Irish kids drank alcohol a lot more than Americans did. They didn't have to wait until they were twenty-one. That's not to say there weren't American kids who drank at a young age but my fellow students in Trinity got wasted a lot.

When I got to Ireland, Mom was more relaxed about my drinking. I was seventeen then, but she didn't know the extent of it. I drank in my room and hid the bottles.

In college, it was different. I was drinking with fellow students, and no longer felt I had to hide it. I liked the way it made me feel. It helped me with the shyness. If I had a glass or two of wine before I went out, I was able to walk into the student bar on my own. It was liberating. Soon, I was experimenting with all kinds of liquor and what they called alcopops, drinking as much as my classmates, if not more. I liked being drunk. I was someone else then. Confident, chatty, attractive, wild and promiscuous. Sex was normal. Everyone was doing it. I don't remember much about the first guy. I know he had rooms in Trinity because that's where I woke up. I had turned into the girl that I used to pray for.

In college, I was trusted to study on my own, to go to bed in a timely fashion, to dress appropriately, to attend lectures, to eat sensibly. By the beginning of my third year in September 2004, I did not do any of these things. I spent twice as much time in the student bar as in the library or at classes. I hooked up with a guy once a week. And I didn't care if they had girlfriends. I wasn't looking for a relationship; I was having the time of my life. I had lots of friends, kids from my class and other classes, other courses. My life was chaotic, but it matched my mood. Oblivion was where I wanted to be. Not having to think about Boston, or my broken sister, my absent father or Mrs Kelly. I remember going into a bar in town where UCD and Trinity students hung out, and Gillian MacArthur found my name carved on the back of the toilet door: RUBY COOPER IS A SLUT. There weren't a lot of Ruby Coopers in Ireland so I knew it was about me. Outwardly, I laughed at the person who wrote that, pitied them for how uptight they must be. Privately, I was hurt and lay low for a while, drinking in my room.

Lindsay told me I had to grow up. I didn't think I was causing any more havoc than the other kids in my year, but Lindsay pointed out that we weren't 'kids' any more. She didn't like the smell of weed in our home, or that I brought different boys back all the time, or that I kept her awake playing music, and she definitely didn't like that I drank myself into a blackout twice a week. 'Look at yourself,' she said, 'drinking doesn't suit you' – spoken like a teacher. Why did she have to be like that? I was growing up. As one of my drinking buddies had put it, 'It's a rite of passage to have a few blackouts in your teens', though she probably didn't realize I was older than all of them, because of missing a year of school after the incident and then being held back a year in Ireland in order to do their two-year cycle for Leaving Certificate exams. By then, I was twenty-three.

8

Erin

In the summer of 2001, I went to Dublin for a week. I would be moving on to campus that year at Harvard, and visiting Dublin just seemed like something I needed to get out of the way. I suppose I resented Mom. But then she was thrilled to see me, and Ruby was too, I guess. She tried to convince me to stay in Ireland and go to college there, but Harvard had always been my dream. In her hometown, Mom was comfortable, easier. My parents were in a stalemate. Ruby was mad with Dad for not keeping in touch more. In the beginning he would call every week, but by this time a whole year had passed, and the calls were irregular and infrequent. She felt he didn't care about her. She told me that she thought she embarrassed him because of what had happened. I reassured her that he missed her and talked about her all the time. It was a white lie to make her feel better because the truth was that we rarely spoke her name.

Mom encouraged Ruby and me to go out and spend time together, and we decided to go to the movies one night. It was easier than talking, I suppose, because it was still awkward between us. As soon as we left the apartment, Ruby took me to a bar. Nobody carded us. I had only had alcohol a few times before at parties. I had three beers while Ruby drank five vodka Cokes and got completely wasted. Afterwards, she wanted us to go to a nightclub. I put my foot down. I wanted to go home. This new Ruby was a stranger to me, composed and adult in some ways but completely wilful and childish in others. The next night she wanted to go to another bar, and I said no. She sulked the whole evening while we watched some videos of old films that Mom loved, anything with Patrick Swayze in it. Ruby opened another bottle of wine for this. Grandma came over for dinner one evening. It was great to see her, and I could tell she had a special bond with Ruby. Mom opened a bottle of wine and Ruby drank most of it. Mom didn't comment. It seemed like I was the only one that noticed.

I decided to go to Dublin every second year. A week was as much as I could bear. Mom came to visit me in the intervening years, but Ruby never came back to Boston.

Going to Harvard was liberating. Studying English and History meant a whole lot of reading, much more than I'd anticipated, but I was no longer surrounded by echoes of Milo or Ruby. Living on campus wasn't exactly as comfortable as home, and I learned quickly how to survive using a microwave and TV dinners, but I could go home as often as I wanted. Dad and I still took turns to cook on Sundays after church once a month. Occasionally I would bring my room-mate home too. Carla was Puerto Rican and the first girl in her family's history to go to college. Her older brothers all worked in construction, and she was the baby of the family. Dad liked her. She played our keyboard and thought our house was awesome. That's what Milo had said.

One Sunday, I brought Carla home to find that Dad had a guest of his own, Kathy Brown. I could tell that Dad liked Kathy the first time I saw her. She looked exactly like Mom but younger by a decade, and her blonde hair was less natural than Mom's. If Dad had a type, it seemed, it was a beautiful waif or stray that he could rescue. Kathy was from the Blue Ridge Mountains of Virginia, like in the song. She had grown up dirt poor and worked as a nursing assistant in Mass General. She came to our church because of the sewing circle, she said. I don't remember her being there before Mom left. But she stood out. Her clothing was always a little eccentric, patchwork coats and weirdly shaped hats and an awful lot of lace. There was no overlap between Mom and Kathy, Dad was too honourable for that. But when Dad started seeing Kathy outside the church, I knew where it was heading. Dad told me before he told Mom that they were going to be divorced. I was expecting it. It was May 2002. I called Ruby and she said Mom was shocked. Mom did well financially out of the divorce. Though she liked her job as a school secretary, a one-off settlement meant that she never had to work again and I think that softened the blow. She didn't give up the job – I guess it gave her a purpose. Ruby said she didn't care. It sounded to me like she cared a whole lot, but wasn't going to let it show.

In September 2002, I received an anonymous letter hand-delivered to my dorm.

```
I hope you're happy now. Milo's mom,
Elaine Kelly, jumped into the Charles
River two weeks ago. She took her own
life, but I think you took it, Coopers.
She could never accept your family's
lies. You should tell your sister,
wherever she's hiding, that she killed
Mrs Kelly. She'll probably kill Milo
too, he's not doing too well in prison,
but I guess you don't care about that.
Neither of you spoiled brats care about
anyone except yourselves. Burn in hell,
Coopers.
```

It was Margie or maybe Milo's friend, Ben Roche. It had to be one of them, or maybe someone from Milo's neighbourhood. Who would write such a letter? I was shocked by the news, though. Poor Mrs Kelly. She loved Milo so much and he had destroyed her. He had thrown her pride in him back in her face. Though he hadn't even completed his first year in college and had no guarantee of graduating in medicine, she used to say, 'My Milo, a doctor, can you imagine?' I had been fond of her. She always made such an effort for church, and I was never invited to their home because Milo said she was ashamed of how small it was, but I didn't even know if that was true. I called Ruby in Dublin. I wanted her to feel the hurt I felt. She was drunk when she answered her cellphone. She didn't have much to say about Mrs Kelly, just, 'That's terrible, why would she do that?' I hung up on the call. I knew it wasn't logical to blame my sister, but I did.

Even though I realized she would be angry, I called Margie at home. 'Hi, it's Erin. I'm sorry about your mom,' I said and, before I'd finished the last word, the phone went dead. Poor Margie was on her own. Milo had destroyed his own family.

The year 2002 was also when the Catholic Church scandal rocked Boston. Priests had sexually abused minors and there was a network of cover-ups. I remembered Milo saying that was why his mom came to Dad's church, looking for a new start. She knew all about clerical abuse. It was ironic. If only she could have accepted that she had raised a predator.

9

Ruby

At the end of the academic year in May 2005, Professor White called me into his office and told me how disappointed he was. I had screwed up the year's showcase performance because I was drunk on stage. 'I thought you had potential, Ruby, and you have one year to prove me wrong. Get some help or I'll kick you out. We are not putting up with your chaos next year. Pull your socks up.' I was devastated.

The next thing I knew, Lindsay evicted me.

I landed back at Mom's apartment. That summer, the others in my year travelled and worked to pay their way around Europe, the US and Canada. I decided to try my luck with the smaller independent theatre companies, but I did not see the need to change my behaviour. I was an instinctive actor. I was fine when we were doing improv scenes, but the weed was interfering with my ability to learn my lines. I got a part in one small profit-share show in a room above a pub, but after the two-week run, they were going on tour around Ireland, and I was fired and replaced. Mom was aware now how much I was drinking and nagged me about it. I was staying out late a few times per week and drank at home, until Mom banned it. She found the stash of empty bottles in my room. I started staying out later. I was relieved when fall came again, and I could go back to Trinity.

In September 2005, six years after the incident, there was a gas explosion in Altman High in one of the science labs, killing seven students and a teacher. One of the dead kids was Tasha's cousin and I should have written to her or called but I did not want to be plunged into the past. It made headlines in Ireland.

I was only barely on the rails by this time, but this sudden exposure to footage of Altman being beamed into my bedroom in Dublin shattered me all over again. Alcohol and then drugs were the only cure. Weed alone wasn't really doing it for me any more. It wasn't enough to make me forget, especially when every new person mentioned my accent and I'd have to lie about how I'd come to live in Ireland. Ecstasy made me feel wonderful, speed gave me a buzz, and as my tastes developed I discovered cocaine, which made me feel invincible, but always alcohol first. I don't think I'd ever have had the courage to take the drugs if I hadn't been drunk in the first place. I began to hang out with a dealer who was on the fringes of college life and would sell coke to middle-class girls like me. Darren claimed to be a mature student, but I never figured out exactly what he was studying. I knew he liked me, though. In the beginning, I paid for the drugs with sex, but Darren soon demanded money instead. I stole money from Mom and Grandma and then began to sell the things in our flat to pay for my habit. I had a lost weekend on Mom's engagement ring. She didn't need it any more. Mom threatened me with the cops, but I knew she'd never do that. She did throw me out, though, back to Grandma's house. I had stern phone calls from Dad. He was just a voice on the end of a line with a time delay. He meant nothing to me by then. Grandma, tearful, told me she was ashamed of me. Shame was something with which I was deeply familiar. I didn't bother to tell her we had something in common.

One night, Darren and I were in an upmarket club, snorting speed off the top of the cistern in the gents, when the bouncer caught us and, instead of throwing us out like a normal person, locked us in a room and called the cops, or the guards as the Irish call them. Darren was arrested and I arrived home in a squad car with a warning. Grandma was outraged.

The next day, I was dragged from my bed by Dad. Grandma had bypassed my mom, who she deemed to have no control over me, and Dad had flown in that morning. He repeated the same shit I'd already heard: 'You're wasting your life', 'You'll end up on the streets', 'Drugs will kill you', 'Do you want to go to jail?', 'You're mixing with criminals'. But Dad's words had an extra edge. It wouldn't do to have it known back home that the daughter of the Pastor was on drugs. And then there was what he didn't say. I knew what he was thinking. Here it was again, the past being thrown in my face, like I was to blame.

I yelled at him, 'I'm sorry that my rape inconvenienced you.'

He looked startled. 'I'm sorry, Ruby. I failed you. I should never have let that boy into the house.' His eyes flicked away from me. And there it was, the blame, the guilt and the shame. That was when I should have stopped drinking.

Darren was out on bail. I headed straight to his seedy room above a butcher's shop. I had helped myself to the contents of Dad's wallet on my way out and took the money to the bank to have it changed from dollars to euro. Over three hundred. 'Party time,' I told Darren, but he wasn't in the mood to party, with a sentencing hearing hanging over him. He claimed not to have any coke or pills either. He said he'd jettisoned everything down the toilet. I didn't believe him and began to rummage through the drawers in his bedside table. He pulled me by the hair and yanked me backwards, and I slapped him. Then he punched me in the face. I felt the crack of my nose and blood filled my eyes. In shock, I ran down the stairs and out of the door. An old woman in a car stopped me – 'Are you okay? Do you need to go to hospital? What happened?' I told her I'd fallen and let her take me to the hospital. After three hours they had cleaned up my face, but I still had to wait for an X-ray. That was when I should have stopped drinking.

I left the hospital without having the X-ray and went to the nearest pub and drank some of Dad's money. I ended up in a nightclub where I knew I could score some coke. I had to ingest it rather than snort it because my nose was out of position. That made me mad. I was angry about what had happened and took my anger out on a barmaid who questioned whether I'd had enough and whether I should go see a doctor as the bruising around my eyes was by then violently violet. I called her a nosy useless bitch and demanded a double vodka and Coke. The next thing I knew, I was lifted off my feet, dragged down a flight of stairs and dumped in an alley by two bouncers. That was when I should have stopped drinking.

I don't recall the rest of that night. I woke up on the floor of a derelict house surrounded by tramps who were shuffling around and burning furniture in the middle of the room to keep warm. Dad's money had been stolen, or I had spent it. I wasn't sure which. I walked out into the dawn and realized I was in the north inner city with no recollection of how I had got there or with whom. I walked towards O'Connell Bridge and looked down into the murk of the River Liffey. My parents hated me. I had alienated the only college friends I had. I was probably going to be kicked out. My lovely grandma was ashamed of me. My sister didn't want to know me. It was all *her* fault. I didn't seem to have many options left. Nobody cared about me, not even me. I was worthless. I climbed up on to the river wall and jumped in. Like Milo's mother.

I woke in a hospital bed with Mom and Dad by my side and felt such overwhelming relief to be alive. For a fleeting moment, it was as if the last six years had not happened. Mom and Dad were together, but before they realized I was awake, I could hear fierce whispering, Dad saying, 'How could you let this happen, Maureen?' and Mom hotly responding, 'You have no right to criticize me. I told you she was out of control. You never came when I asked you, but when my mam calls you, you come running –'

I zoned out, feigning unconsciousness, and soon, I was.

Apparently, a passing woman on her way to work had jumped in and rescued me, risking her own life. That was when I should have stopped drinking.

Afterwards, I was confronted by both parents. Mom blamed herself. 'I should have watched you more closely, I should never have let you go and live with Grandma. I'm sorry,' she snivelled into a tissue. I made it clear that the only place I was going to live was Grandma's house. Grandma loved me unconditionally.

Dad suggested a spell in rehab. 'Your mother hasn't been there for you in the way that she should have,' dared say the man who I had seen once or twice per year since I came to this country. I agreed to rehab so that he would think he had done his duty and could fly off back to Boston feeling like the big man who had saved his daughter's life.

I went back to Grandma's. I could see that she was worried. Expecting her to take responsibility for me when I wasn't even taking responsibility for myself was too much to ask. At least she wasn't playing the blame game. 'Tell me what I can do to help you, Ruby. You can't live like this and I'm not going to let you die.'

I was due to go into a seven-week rehab. You were supposed to arrive sober. Mom had some words of advice before I went in: 'Remember, Ruby, you are a rape victim, that's the root of your problem. Tell them what you told the police. They'll be able to help you, I'm sure.' I stared at my mom, but she looked away. They wouldn't be able to help me.

10

I was drunk on arrival at Longhurst, the exclusive treatment centre for addicts in the middle of nowhere, that Sunday evening. I had a water bottle filled with vodka, which was confiscated when I was going through registration. Nobody checked it or sniffed it. They just poured it down the drain in front of me. Mom hugged me and was then told to leave. There was to be no contact at all for the first two weeks with any of my friends or family in the outside world. I realized that I didn't have any friends. I had numbers in my phone of party people but nobody I could call in this situation. They took my phone. They had searched my bags thoroughly, I realized that night. At least I had a room of my own.

Longhurst. There was a chain of these residential rehab clinics around the world. On their website there were testimonials from anonymous famous people.

'Longhurst saved my life' – *twice-nominated Oscar actress*

'Longhurst gave me back the ability to work' – *Nobel Prize winner*

How the hell were we supposed to know if this was true if these people were all anonymous? I smelled bullshit.

As Mom drove off down the leafy driveway, I started to cry. Sheila, a counsellor, moved to comfort me. She said the house was full of addicts of all sorts, gamblers, people with eating disorders, sex addicts, as well as ordinary alcoholics and drug addicts 'like you'. I don't know if she meant this to be comforting, but

I found it terrifying. I wasn't an addict. I could give up any time I wanted to. I just didn't want to. I had only started drinking properly a few years ago, for God's sake. It was my rite of passage.

It was bedtime. There was no lock on my bedroom door. Apart from that, it was like any bland hotel room you'd find in a three-star establishment. Without the TV or bedside clock. Or minibar. But I was on my own. I went hunting through my suitcase. They had found the vodka in the mouthwash and confiscated it (vodka mixed with tea made a convincing Listerine, I had thought to myself), they had found the wraps of coke under the insoles of my shoes, the pills in a baggie in my bottle of conditioner. It was almost as if they'd done this before.

I crawled under the duvet and into the foetal position. I cried silent tears into my pillow. Sheila knocked on my door and, entering, whispered, 'The first night is the worst, I promise.' I said nothing and held my breath until she left. How the hell was I supposed to sleep? I stared at the ceiling. There was a crack in the plaster that took on the shape of a devil creature under the light that streamed in from the car park through the thin curtains. I stared at it until dawn.

I had barely closed my eyes when a stocky guy knocked and entered without asking my permission. He ordered me to get showered and dressed and get down to the breakfast room immediately. He was frightening. 'You must have slept through the bell,' he said in a tone that was nothing less than menacing.

When I got down to the breakfast room, somebody introduced the stocky guy as Jack, one of the addicts. 'Coke and booze,' he said. I think he expected me to name my addiction and then we'd high-five in solidarity, but I didn't have an addiction. His authority was strangely attractive. He told me to help myself to cereal.

The house we were in was old and beautiful. The dining-room table seated eighteen people. The others were a mix of old and young, but mostly surprisingly young and, judging by their accents, international. No one said their last name, though a few people were open about who they were. There was an old Dutch man who was a Pulitzer Prize-winning poet, a young pretty Black girl from Nigeria called Lorraine, she said, the daughter of a diplomat stationed in Washington DC, and an expensively dressed Italian woman in her late twenties perhaps, the wife of some industrialist I'd never heard of. Jack was the only Irish inmate as far as I could tell. The rest were all either famous or wealthy in their home countries, or their family members were. People chose to go to Longhurst in a country where they wouldn't be recognized. How much had this cost Dad?

The clock on the wall said five past four. Not breakfast time. Jack said he had just started his sixth week in here. 'None of the clocks in here tell the right time. It keeps you on your toes. The bell tells you when the next session is.' Time would slow down to a crawl in this place. Without any distractions, I was going to go mad.

Jack insisted on taking me on a tour of the house. There was a library crammed to the rafters with self-help books. The yoga/meditation room looked out on to a frosty November lawn. We met various people along the way who introduced themselves by their first names, but I didn't know if they were addicts or counsellors. I felt sorry for the old Dutch guy. He brought up the average age by about thirty years. Jack was thirtyish. And the hottest. Though there wasn't much competition.

A bell rang and we were led into a large room for meditation. I was told to get rid of my thoughts. I closed my eyes. They had no idea. I was thinking that if I stayed sober for ten days, it would prove that I wasn't an addict. Today was Monday – I could leave by Wednesday of the following week. All I had to do was play along. Then I was thinking that if Jack was leaving by the end of next week, I could probably hook up with him before

I left. Sheila, the counsellor and meditation guide, was whispering some 'calming' words in our ears as she paced around the room. I could hear what she was saying to others: 'mountains', 'sea', 'sky'. When she came to me, she whispered 'beach' and it reminded me of the time when a gang of us were kicked out of a nightclub at 4 a.m. and we walked down to Sandymount Strand. I woke up on the beach the next morning with some stranger's coat thrown over me. I tried to remember when that was and who was in the gang.

Sheila tinkled a small bell. 'Now, did anyone achieve an empty mind for any part of that half-hour?' I shot my hand into the air, then realized that Lorraine and I were the only ones with our hands up. The other twelve in the room looked disappointed in themselves. Jack stared at me.

'Liar,' he said as we left the room. 'There's no point, you know. If you want to get clean, the only way is the truth.'

I flashed him my most angelic smile. 'It wasn't a lie; I already feel cleansed. Maybe some people "get it" faster than others.'

Next, there was a lecture in a room in the basement. The theme that day was shame: 'What makes us ashamed? What does it feel like? Where in your body do you feel it? What have you done in your addiction to be ashamed of?' Some people volunteered information. One had beaten up her child (alcohol). Another had set fire to his sister's home when she wouldn't give him more money (coke). A stick-thin girl had eaten an entire birthday cake during a binge on the morning of her sister's twenty-first birthday party (bulimic?). A Canadian guy had forged his mother's signature to mortgage their beach house to get money to pay off debts (gambler).

My parents had put me in a house with freaks. I hadn't done anything I was ashamed of. Stealing Mom's jewellery wasn't that bad. She hardly wore it and could afford to replace it.

There was a break for lunch then. The food was good, simple, nutritious and healthy. It had been a while since I'd eaten healthily. My relationship with food was not good. I either ate for soakage, or it was hangover food. Mostly greasy, calorific stuff. Maybe I could drop a few pounds in here? We all ate together, though there was tension in the air as we tried not to notice Estelle, the thin girl, remove the tortilla from her wrap and spear a lettuce leaf into her mouth, chewing it endlessly until the bell rang again.

Next was group therapy. I was welcomed by Owen and asked to explain why I was here. I wasn't expecting this. 'I don't want to say in front of a room full of strangers.' I couldn't keep the condescension out of my voice on the word 'strangers'. A guy called Martin smiled at me. Too short, I thought.

'By the end of this meeting we won't be strangers,' he said.

I was starting to get twitchy. Annoyed. And thirsty.

'Do I have to speak?' I said, using my scared small-child voice. I was an aspiring actress, after all.

Owen smiled. 'Perhaps tomorrow?'

I put my head down and tried to listen to Lorraine talk about the havoc she had wreaked on her family through her cocaine addiction. I was desperately trying to contain my shaking body. I couldn't act my way out of that.

Just as Lorraine was telling us about crashing her dad's Mercedes on her fourteenth birthday, like a coke-fuelled Ferris Bueller, Owen stopped her and said, 'Sorry to interrupt, Lorraine, but are you okay, Ruby? Would you be more comfortable on the sofa?'

'No, I'm fine,' I said. 'This sweater was washed with a new detergent and I think I'm allergic to it. I'm tired and I didn't sleep last night. May I go and lie down, please?'

'You may go and change your sweater, but I want you to come straight back. Your constant shifting is distracting in the group.'

Jack glared and mouthed the word 'liar' at me, again. I was on his radar. He'd been watching me.

I stayed put then to annoy Owen and everybody in the group. The shakes were getting worse. After that session, another bell rang. Martin was wrong: they were all still strangers as far as I was concerned. I ran back to my room and got under the duvet fully clothed. How was I going to do this? Stay here for ten days with all these mad people? My head was aching. There was a knock on the door. 'Go away,' I yelled. Sheila walked in uninvited. 'Am I not entitled to some privacy?' I was angry. She sat on the end of the bed and smiled at me. 'Get out,' I screamed at her. She sat there saying nothing, smiling benignly, like a simpleton. Obviously, I was not going to be able to get to sleep while she was sitting on the end of my bed. 'What do you want?' I shouted.

'What you're experiencing are withdrawal symptoms, but that does not exclude you from any part of the programme. Please get up and come to your one-to-one with Dr Hardwicke. She is Longhurst's psychiatrist. You have an hour's appointment and you're already late.'

I burrowed further into the bed. Sheila pulled the duvet off me and stood at the door. 'I'm waiting.' She was calm. The anger consumed me. I wanted to lash out, but she looked braced for that, her feet planted firmly on the ground, her arms by her sides, fists clenched. She spoke calmly, but I knew that if this got physical, she could put me back in the hospital.

11

Erin

By 2004, my life was going smoothly. I was in my final year at Harvard doing my BA in English and History, pinning all my hopes on getting a good degree. I had decided to stay on and continue into the MA programme. I was going to do a two-year MA on women writers of science fiction. They were few and far between, but I adored their stories. Ursula K. Le Guin was my favourite, but I also loved Octavia Butler and Margaret Atwood and, the grandma of them all, Mary Shelley.

I had a boyfriend who I liked. Charlie was from Worcester, where Dad grew up. Dad knew his parents; he approved. Charlie was a nice guy, and I finally gave up my virginity to him, aged twenty-three. I still attended Dad's church, though less frequently. I would turn up once a month to keep him happy. I wanted to have sex with my boyfriend like every other adult. I didn't see why God would have a problem with that. I did not say this to Dad. The sex was pleasurable, sure, but I couldn't help comparing how good Milo had made me feel with just his hands, compared to how I felt with Charlie's whole body.

After five months with Charlie, though, I was bored. Charlie took me out to dinner and bought me endless gifts, jewellery and pretty dresses. I was grateful for his generosity, but I only wore dresses to church. I was a sweater and jeans girl most of the time. He always wanted me to dress up when we went out and would only barely try to hide his disappointment if I didn't appear like a 1950s model with coiffed hair and shiny red lips. 'You're beautiful,' he would say, 'don't you want people to notice?'

He was angry when I broke up with him. He told me I was making a big mistake and that I'd live to regret it. He was hard to shake off, regularly showing up at my door, pleading with me to let him in and declaring his undying love. In the beginning I tried to let him down gently, telling him that I didn't think I was the right person for him. He knew I'd been a virgin when I met him, and he seemed to feel like that entitled him to ownership over me. When he turned creepy, I had to get Dad involved. Dad liked Charlie and couldn't understand why I couldn't stay with him.

'I thought he was husband material. A good family, and the boy has prospects too.'

'Dad, he's my first boyfriend since . . .' I couldn't say it. 'And he's being weird,' I said instead, exasperated. 'Please help me to get rid of him.'

Dad called Charlie's parents and apologetically explained that I was not in the right frame of mind for a partner, and would they mind asking Charlie to leave me alone. I never heard from him again. I bumped into him twice in subsequent years at events around the city and, both times, he ignored me.

I returned to my celibate state. It was much safer.

College life was fun, but hard work. Other students had part-time jobs. I knew I was lucky that Dad had money so I could devote the time to study, and I rewarded him by acing my exams, but this thesis was a whole new challenge. Academic writing was not my strong point, but if I could write about the struggles it took for women to be published, maybe it would work in my favour when I wanted to get a job as an editor. I was already making enquiries with New York publishing houses for editorial assistant roles. I must have sent a hundred emails and resumés. It seemed like every publisher had fifty different imprints. I started with the ones who had published my favourite science fiction writers but quickly realized that almost all science fiction editors were men. Two of them wanted me to send a photo, which was an immediate red flag. My qualifications spoke for themselves.

There were other unwelcome and more sinister challenges. Anonymous letters continued to arrive. They were all typed on an old-fashioned typewriter on plain white paper, sent to my dorm or, in the summer, to my home. Sometimes, the letters would demand to know where Ruby was hiding. Neither of us had a MySpace page like most people our age. She had adopted the stage name of Ruby Bean. I don't know whether that was a deliberate attempt to escape from the girl who had been raped but it was a good move.

```
Where is she? She needs to pay for what
she's done.
```

A couple of months later:

```
You are one nasty bitch. You know
he didn't do it. Why are you
protecting her?
```

I didn't think Ben would be the type to name call. It was Margie, I was sure of it. I didn't tell Dad about the letters, because I knew he would act and I felt that Margie had been through enough. It wasn't her fault that her brother was a rapist, and her mother had taken her own life. I'd been fooled too. I called Margie.

'Margie? It's Erin. You have to stop with these letters –'
'What the hell are you doing calling this house?'

'Margie, he did it, he raped Ruby –'

She hung up on me.

About five months later, another letter arrived. It was just one unrepeatable word. That shook me – the level of hatred and anger made me afraid. What if I was to bump into her? Would she hurt me? I knew there was no point in going to the police. It was hate mail but there was no threat implicit. Until the next one arrived.

```
I'm going to make YOU pay for what she
did, bitch.
```

And then, a few weeks later, I received another one.

```
You're all going to pay until you tell
the truth.
```

I was tempted to go to the cops then. But this was Milo's fault. He was making Margie crazy too.

12

I hadn't heard much from Ruby in months, until one day in October 2005 Dad told me she'd had a nervous breakdown. She had jumped into a river, like Mrs Kelly.

I told Dad about Ruby's drinking, and I saw him get upset again. 'She gets that from your mother's side. Your mom's brother was an alcoholic too.' He decided to go to Dublin because, he said, Mom was clearly not able to manage her daughter.

'Dad,' I said, 'she's an adult, she doesn't have to do what you or Mom say any more.'

Dad wouldn't listen. 'She's still my daughter, Erin. My feelings for my children don't disappear when they reach a magic age.'

I'd had one more letter from Margie.

```
The DNA was planted. Your dad knew the
D.A. They were together in a photo.
```

What did she mean about Dad and the District Attorney and the DNA? Didn't she know that it was impossible to just 'plant' DNA inside of a woman?

Dad flew out that night, leaving me feeling guilty. I couldn't afford the time, but the truth is I didn't want to go. I called Ruby after a few days, and she said the whole jumping in the river was a misunderstanding. She said she'd been practising because part of her course was circus performance. She was not terribly coherent. I suspected she was drunk again. I got mad with her and told her she needed to go to rehab. She was training to be an actress, and could be convincing, but I was not easily fooled these days.

'We're not all as prissy as you, Erin,' she said. 'Some of us like to let our hair down and have some fun.'

'Right? Nearly drowning, was that fun?'

I didn't know whether she was trying to commit suicide or not. I do know that she didn't give a damn about how it affected anyone else in the family. I was still traumatized by the events of 1999. I'm not sure if she was. I didn't go visit. Dad came back worried about Ruby. He had found an expensive private rehab place even though she insisted that she wasn't an alcoholic. Mom admitted that she had spoken to Ruby after some of her jewellery had gone missing. She suspected that Ruby was on drugs as well. She often stayed out all night. She went through her monthly allowance in a week and regularly asked Mom and Grandma for more money.

I didn't want anything to do with her when I heard that. I could hardly reconcile my memory of my cute little sister with this wild stranger. If she got so drunk that she fell into a river and didn't see how serious her problem was, I could not help her. I knew that was mean of me, knowing what I did about the source of her trauma.

Five weeks later, Ruby left rehab after just ten days. She was a lost cause. Where had my innocent sister gone?

13

Ruby

An hour with Dr 'Call me Amber' Hardwicke was way more than an hour. She asked me why I had tried to take my life. She had a referral letter from the hospital in her hands.

'That was a misunderstanding. I was trying to walk along the bridge and fell in.'

She looked at me and then back at her notes. 'At six thirty a.m., by yourself, Ruby?'

'Yes, I'd had a few drinks.'

She sat back and let my words echo around the room.

'Okay,' I said, 'more than a few. I was on a bender.'

'Do you accept that you are an addict?'

'Of course, that's why I'm here,' I lied.

'Good for you, that's the first step. You have no control over your drinking. Isn't that true?'

I was still shaking. God, how long was this day going to be? Dr Amber said my shaking was a sign of withdrawal. She gave me a tablet, Ativan, and told me I would get one per day for a week to quell the worst of the symptoms. I was so grateful, I could have wept. 'I want to get better.'

Throughout the rest of the hour, I agreed with everything she said, and asked her to help me recover.

'You know, Ruby, I've seen hundreds of addicts come through these doors, and I'd say probably twenty per cent went straight back into active addiction and died well before their time, and then forty per cent stayed clean and sober for ten years or more, but it still got them in the end. If I was to guess, I'd put you in their category. I'm not here to argue with you, but if you don't tell the truth in the privacy of these walls, you won't recover, and you will either die or end up on the streets or in prison. And then there's the forty per cent who thrive in sobriety. That's the percentage you should aim for. There is no point in telling me what you think I want to hear.'

Scaremongering. And if twenty per cent of their clients died after attending this place, what was the point?

'You are lucky, you know, that you have people who care for you,' she continued. 'A lot of our clients are alone in the world because they have alienated everyone in their family and friendship circle. They think they have nobody to live for. Who do you have to live for, Ruby?'

I listed my family members and my grandmother, though I'm not sure anyone except Grandma actually cared. Erin had rung when I was in hospital and said I should go into rehab. She hadn't called again. Dad had come over to make sure my indiscretions weren't going to impact his beloved church and he and Mom had agreed to put me into this place to get me out of the way.

'Haven't you forgotten someone?'

'Me?'

She smiled indulgently. 'Don't you think you're worth saving, Ruby?'

I couldn't look directly at her. 'Yes, I do. I thought you were talking about other people.'

The session continued past what I thought was the allotted hour. She wasn't going to stop until I told her something. Eventually, I told her about the incident and how I had been taken from America to Ireland to start over. She livened up then. Now she had something on me, something to work with.

'Let me get this straight, Ruby: you were sixteen, your sister's boyfriend raped you, you endured a trial and were taken to Ireland from Boston, away from your home, your friends, your school, familiar surroundings, and then because of the move your parents divorced? And you are estranged from your sister?' She was almost gleeful. 'You know *none* of that was your fault, right, Ruby? Tonight and every night, when you are brushing your teeth, I want you to look at yourself in the mirror, directly into your eyes. I want you to say "I am free of blame" over and over again.'

'Yeah, sure.'

'Ruby,' she said – she sure did like using my name – 'I can help you. Miracles happen within these walls. You can be one of them.'

She was beaming at me. I had graduated from the forty per cent likely to fall back into addiction to the miraculous top forty per cent, *as if* I was an addict. That was quick.

'Yeah,' I said, thinking, *Sure, if I could turn back time*.

'We have a lot of work to do. But the blame stops now.'

Thank God, the Ativan was already taking the edge off the panic I was feeling. Dr Amber noticed.

'That is the only drug you will get in here, Ruby, you understand? From now on, no more Valium, no codeine, not even cough medicine. It's time to face reality. You have an opportunity now to change your life. I'll see you tomorrow, okay?'

I was already dreading tomorrow. I only told her about the incident to give her something to hang the drinking on. Everyone in here was insistent that I was an alcoholic and that there must be a reason for it. I was just a girl who liked to party. Yeah, sometimes I took it too far. I thought about jumping into the Liffey. It was only three weeks ago. What had I been thinking? Was I trying to end my life? The last few months were cloudy, but the way Amber had put it, 6.30 in the morning on my own, and I didn't even remember. I didn't want to. I remembered being relieved when I woke up in hospital. If it was a suicide attempt, wouldn't I have been disappointed? God, I needed a drink.

The next session was a lecture from a German counsellor on Rebuilding Your Life. The chairs were hard, and I suppose that was on purpose to keep us awake because this guy's voice was soothing. My head kept tilting back as I nodded off and then clanked it on the back of the chair.

There was no time to be alone in this house. I could see clearly what they were trying to do. Isolate us from outside sources, no radio, no TV, no internet. This bubble we lived in was a brainwashing machine, but I was not going to fall for it.

14

I had been sober for nine days but, my God, it was difficult – not because I was an alcoholic but because I didn't get a minute to myself. I yawned my way through group sessions, made as little effort at yoga as possible and laughed in the face of other people's crises. In the evenings, we were allowed to watch some specially curated DVDs of films that featured characters crashing and burning. *The Morning After*, *Affliction* and *Who's Afraid of Virginia Woolf* were the favourites among the group. They were supposed to be inspirational, I guess, but I didn't need to see them any more than once. And certainly not two days in a row.

Amber, the psychiatrist, was drilling down into my relationship with Mom and Dad after the incident. She had a problem with me referring to the rape as the 'incident'. 'Why not name it for what it was?' I couldn't answer that.

'It's hard to get rape convictions, it's nearly always the survivor's word' – Amber never referred to me as a victim – 'against the perpetrator's. You are brave to have brought that case, you know? Most women don't. And let's not forget, you were a *child*.' She missed out on the fact that I didn't get a choice about bringing the case or not. Dad called the cops that day and the rest just happened. I don't remember anyone asking me if I wanted to be dragged through the courts.

It sickened me to have to talk about this every day, but she insisted 'the thing you don't want to talk about is the thing you must talk about'. She asked me about Dad's church, why

I felt 'impure' and unable to go back. Did I still feel impure? When we went on to talk about my current sex life, she became excited all over again. 'You don't feel any emotional connection to these men?' I shook my head. 'And how many men have there been?'

I frowned. 'Roughly? About twenty,' I said, though I knew it was more.

'And you have never sought a relationship with any of these?'

I looked at her. 'Are you judging me for behaving like most men? All *they* want is sex.'

'Let's say there were twenty men' – she knew I was lying – 'how many of them expressed an interest in seeing you again?' She didn't get it.

'I chose my sex partners. I chose not to have relationships. What is wrong with that? As a feminist, aren't I within my rights to have control over my sex life?'

Amber seized on the word 'control' as if we'd made some incredible breakthrough. 'Control!' she shouted. 'There it is. That is what you are seeking in life. Well, you know what you can't have with drugs or alcohol? Control! And I'm betting that few of these encounters happened when you were sober. Where exactly is the control you're so proud of?'

How low could she go? But she was right about one thing. I had never had sober sex.

I was sick of her by this stage. Determined to open every old wound and expose it to the elements. 'Fuck you.'

She ignored that. 'Finally, we're getting somewhere. See you tomorrow, Ruby.' She was smug, pleased with herself. I would have slapped her if I were the violent type.

Speaking of sex partners, Jack was proving elusive. I had figured out that his room was exactly above mine on the second floor. I flaunted myself in front of him as much as I could, but he wasn't taking the bait. Mom had been right all those years ago: although I would never be as beautiful as Erin, my retainer was long gone and my face had filled out, and I finally had the curves I'd yearned for. My feet had stopped growing, allowing the rest of me to catch up. I was still prone to acne, but my nose had been reset in hospital and you would never know it had been broken. Jack had called me a liar many times, but I was sure there was a twinkle in his eye. On one of the evenings between movie time and playing charades (I'm not even joking), I found him in the break room making tea. It was the first time I'd seen him on his own since he'd come to wake me that first morning. I brushed myself up against him as I reached into a cupboard to get a mug. He flinched away from me. 'I know what you're doing, you know.'

'I'm sorry, it's a tight space.'

'Even if it is, you could wait five seconds for me to close the fridge door. I'm not going to fuck you.'

I wasn't expecting this, but I went straight to indignation. 'Excuse me? Jack, if you were the last man on earth, I wouldn't touch you.'

'Sure,' he said, 'read the rule book again.'

The rule book. I had read it cover to cover. It was only slightly more interesting than the hundreds of self-help books. There was to be *no inappropriate touching between clients*. There were even rules about what we should wear. *No shorts for men or women. No low-cut tops for women.* Sexist. (I assume this was for the sake of the sex addicts, although nobody had admitted to sex addiction in our group.) *No new relationships in the first two years of sobriety.* I wasn't looking for a relationship.

'Don't flatter yourself, Grandad, who'd want to fuck an old man like you?'

He came over and stood right in front of me, face to face. I had pushed the right button. He leaned down to kiss me, and

I closed my eyes just in time to feel him back away, laughing. 'The last man on earth, yeah? Get your head straight, Ruby.' I was furious. Who did he think he was? I was leaving tomorrow anyway, right after I told Amber what I thought of her.

The next morning, I didn't talk to anyone. I had never spoken in group, and this was the day that Martin decided to pick on me. 'Ruby, I think it's high time you spoke up. Do you have anything to say about Carmen's dilemma?' I had been thinking about lowering a glass of white wine this evening, wondering where I'd get my hands on some money, sure that Dad would have suspended my account.

'Sorry, I wasn't listening,' I said.

Lorraine and Carmen made exasperated noises.

'Why do we have to put up with Ruby?' Jack said. 'She's not doing any of the recovery work. We're all doing our best here and she's sneering at us every day. She even tried to come on to me in the kitchen last night. I'm out of here at the end of the week and I've learned enough to know that she won't shake my resolve, but it isn't fair, especially to the newer people coming in.' Others mumbled their agreement. My cheeks were burning. I wasn't used to feeling embarrassment, even though I'd probably done lots of embarrassing things when I was drunk. I recalled making a pass at Lindsay's boyfriend one night. That was the night before she evicted me. He must have told her.

'Ruby,' Martin said, 'do you have anything to say?'

'No.' I folded my arms across my chest.

'She's sulking now, like a toddler,' said Jack. I could see he hated me. I wasn't used to this feeling. God, I needed a drink.

'Right,' said Martin, 'I'll have to bring it up with the other counsellors today. Ruby, maybe you should reflect on your attitude, what you bring to this group, whether your behaviour is hindering the recovery of the other people in the room.' He looked serious for a moment but then clapped his hands together and said, 'I think we'll call it a day, folks. Lunch a little early, okay?'

Everyone dispersed. I went back to my room, but Sheila came after me.

'Ruby, it's lunchtime.'

Her tone had lost its soft maternal manner – there was an edge to it I hadn't heard before. She glared at me while I put my shoes on and made my way down to the lunch room. Everyone ignored me, except for Jack – who mouthed the word 'liar' at me – and a new woman who had arrived only two days ago. She offered me some salad.

'Is it this hard to fit in?' she asked.

'Yeah,' I said, 'especially when you're not an addict.'

Lorraine overheard me. 'If you're not an addict, why don't you leave? You've done nothing for others who are trying to recover. I hope they kick you out.'

Hadn't I already decided I was going to leave today anyway? But I wanted it to be on my terms. I had been sober for ten days. I'd *proven* I wasn't an alcoholic.

I was about to load my plate into the dishwasher when Sheila came into the kitchen and asked me to come to the office. I followed her and took a seat in front of her desk.

'Ruby, we've had a staff meeting, and I'm afraid we have decided to ask you to leave. Dr Hardwicke believes you were making progress, but all the other counsellors and supervisors feel that you are a negative influence on the house. Please go to your room and pack your bags. We'll call a taxi to take you anywhere you want to go. We don't believe you have accepted that you are an addict.'

'I haven't had a drink in ten days.' Why was I arguing with her?

'That's because you are not allowed to, in here. Not because of your acceptance. If or when you do accept your addiction, we might consider taking you back, but clearly now is not the right time for you.'

I was going to defend myself, but she spoke in such a definitive way, there was no point. The decision had been made for me.

That's when I should have stopped drinking.

15

Grandma was not pleased to see me when I rocked up at her door that night. She had changed the locks and my key no longer worked. But she let me in and gestured me to sit down.

'I heard you left Longhurst. Your mother is distraught. What is it going to take, Ruby?'

'Grandma, I promise you, I've been sober for ten days. I'm sober now. I don't have to stay in that place not to drink. They said I could leave. Please, I have nowhere else to go. And I'm sorry for all the trouble I caused.'

'Ruby, I can smell the drink from you.' I had stopped in a bar and allowed a guy to buy me a few drinks, maybe three, but definitely not much more than that. 'You are lying about this, like you lie about everything. The drinking. I know what the root of it all is. I know what happened back in Boston was terrible. We should have talked about it as a family –'

I zoned out at that point, but I could feel the anger rising inside me. I had been sober for ten days in there. I had only had a few drinks before I came home to give me the courage to face Grandma and apologize to her. I had proven that I could stay sober. I'd had no coke or pills at all.

'Stop talking about Boston,' I said.

She ignored me. 'I decided when you came here that it was best to pretend it hadn't happened, but I see now that was the wrong thing to do –'

'Please, Grandma, I can't –'

'There are specialists, you know, who deal in cases of rape. There's the Rape Crisis Centre in town. All you have to do is call them. Or your father would pay for any help you need with therapy. I've been reading about it. Don't you know how lucky you are to have those opportunities? You probably have post-traumatic stress disorder. You need help.'

'I got help. I told a psychiatrist in there everything.'

Grandma folded her hands on her lap. 'I'm not a psychiatrist, but would you like to tell me what happened? You know I love you. You know I want the best for you.'

This was the last thing I wanted to talk about. I loved her too. How could I explain what happened?

'You were just a child. What that monster did to you was outrageous. You did nothing wrong.'

'It wasn't like that, Grandma,' I whispered. 'He was a good man.'

'He tricked you into believing he was. You can't still think you were at fault?'

I had a devil that lived inside me, and I needed to get it out.

'I lied. He didn't rape me. I wanted to have sex with him, but he wouldn't. I made it up.'

The words fell out of my mouth. I felt nausea rising from the pit of my stomach. I ran past Grandma, who was sitting stock-still, aghast, and threw up in the bathroom.

16

The Incident

Nobody but Kenny Carter knew that I wasn't a virgin. He had shown me what to do and how to do it at Bible Camp just a few weeks before the incident. I had seen him around church that whole summer. All the senior girls flirted with him, but he never came to our group until the last day. He showed us how to do CPR. I was probably the third least attractive in our group of girls, but on that day, he singled me out every time for special praise and attention. When he demonstrated CPR, he used me as the model of the drowned victim, which meant he had his hands on my non-existent breasts, although there was a layer of clothing between us. There were a few giggles, but he took it so seriously, saying that this was a matter of life and death, that the girls soon hushed up. I got hot and excited, but I don't think anyone noticed. He was the best-looking guy I'd ever seen. His teeth were very white and he had dimples on both cheeks.

Later that day, when camp was over and everyone had gone, I helped him to roll bandages and pack up his kit. He was probably about twenty-five, but he treated me like an equal, told me dirty jokes which I pretended to get. He had an infectious laugh. I liked him a lot. I asked him if he was married or had a girlfriend, and he said no, but then he looked at me, really looked, and I just decided to see what would happen if I kissed him. What happened is that he kissed me back, and all at once his hands went everywhere. Then he stopped suddenly. 'What age are you?' he asked.

I was annoyed at the interruption. 'Don't worry, I'm legal.'

'Shit, I could get in so much trouble for this.'

'I won't tell.' We were in the back of the church, in Dad's large office. No one else was around. Erin had gone to meet Saima. Mom had gone for coffee with Marcia's mother.

'We should use the couch,' I suggested.

'Have you done this before?' he asked.

'No, you're going to have to show me.'

I locked the door and Kenny showed me, with enthusiasm. He pulled my clothes off while kissing me. He showed me how to put a condom over his wiener and then he had me straddle him while I pumped it and felt him grow harder until he guided himself inside me, and he showed me how to bounce up and down on him while he held my ribcage and my ass. It was painful and only slightly pleasurable but totally thrilling. I was a grown-up, doing things that Erin hadn't done.

Afterwards, I asked for his number, and he baulked – 'What do you need my number for?' – and I was embarrassed and tearful. 'I'm thirty-one years old,' he said, 'we can't date, honey.' He was almost twice my age.

'But why?' I asked.

'Are you kidding? I'm friends with your mom. She would kill me.'

I began to cry.

'I'm sorry, baby,' he said, 'but I couldn't resist a virgin.' He pulled up his jeans and picked up the condom. 'And don't worry, I'm not going to tell anyone. So next time, you can pretend it's your first time again, or maybe that's what you're doing now – you were pretty convincing.'

'What? No! I would never . . .' And yet, I just had. I asked him if I could keep the condom.

'You little freak,' he said. He kissed me again and ruffled my hair like adults do to kids, and then he pulled a twenty-dollar bill out of his wallet. 'Buy yourself something nice, honey.'

I took the money and he sauntered out as if nothing had happened. I gathered up my clothes and got dressed. I was so confused after that encounter. The first time was supposed to be special, but I had given it away to a stranger who I would probably never see again, and he'd given me money? What did that make me?

In fact, I did see him just one more time, walking out of the church with Mom a few days later. When I approached them, Mom said, 'Hi, Ruby, you know Kenny, don't you?' and he looked very uncomfortable and made an excuse to hurry away.

'How do you know him, Mom?' I asked.

'He's a paramedic who volunteered to help with Bible Camp,' she said.

'But I've never seen him in church.'

'Really? Well, isn't that nice of him, then, to volunteer like that?'

I didn't say anything.

A few days later, the evening before school term started again, I spilled a jug of lemonade over Dad's briefcase after dinner. It was a simple accident, but Dad was mad because the liquid had got inside the briefcase and ruined some paperwork he needed for the next day. He shouted at me, and I told him he shouldn't have left his briefcase beside the dining table. Erin tried to defend me, saying, 'It was an accident, Dad, she didn't do it on purpose,' and Dad said, 'Erin, you are very sweet defending your sister like this but I have yet to hear an apology from her.'

It was just typical. I made a stupid mistake and Erin managed to make herself look good. I burst into tears and ran upstairs to my room, slamming the door behind me. Later, Mom came up with a bowl of ice cream and said I should come downstairs. I took my time and, when I did go down, I stepped outside and sat under *the kitchen window, reading* Harry Potter and the Prisoner of Azkaban. *I overheard Mom and Dad talking in the kitchen. Dad was mid-sentence when I caught my name and tuned in to the conversation.*

'– and Ruby's head is in the clouds. Erin was so grown up at Ruby's age. How can we have two kids that are so different?'

Mom's voice: 'Don't worry, Ruby will catch up. I think she's just finding adolescence hard.'

'Erin is perfect, though, Maureen, we don't have to nag her to study, or to brush her teeth, or pick up after herself.'

'Ruby is just herself. You can't expect to have two identical children. She's in a hurry to grow up too if you hadn't noticed.'

'Well, I think she should take life a bit more seriously.'

'She's sixteen. Let her enjoy this time, Doug. I know she can be silly at times, but she has endless years of responsibility ahead of her.'

'You know I love her, but she doesn't make it easy.'

Those words rang in my ears for weeks.

Two weeks later, Milo had stayed over the night before but left early for his shift at the diner before going to college. That morning at breakfast, Erin got a letter from the New England Journal of Literature *to say that they had accepted her short story for publication. Erin was astonished because she had never submitted a story to this journal. Milo must have done it on her behalf. Erin tried calling Milo, but he wasn't allowed to take calls at work. When Erin showed Mom and Dad the story and the letter, they were over the moon. Dad was a subscriber. He hadn't ever known anything about Erin's writing. She told him that her teacher didn't like the kind of stories she wrote. He said it was a prestigious magazine and, after he read the piece, he was impressed. Mom read the story and pronounced herself baffled, but she was full of pride.*

Dad called some of his friends to share the good news. He said that Erin should have the day off school. We were all excited.

We would go to New York City on the train and celebrate by going shopping, and Mom said we could try and get tickets for The Lion King *matinee. Dad had church meetings until late. Erin looked happy. I assumed I was going too, but then Dad said I couldn't afford to miss school, whereas Erin was ahead of her class and one day wouldn't make any difference to her prospects. Erin wanted me to come too but Dad was firm. 'I'm sorry, kiddo, not this time. You can go when you give us something to celebrate.' Mom even congratulated Erin on speaking up for her little sister. None of them noticed the tears in my eyes. I wiped them away and pretended to be happy for Erin, but I hated her.*

As I set off for school, Erin said that Milo had left a chemistry book behind, and he might call to the house to pick it up. Mom said there wouldn't be anyone in and he'd just have to do without it.

All through the first period in school, I couldn't concentrate on anything. It wasn't fair. I was the one who loved musical theatre, not Erin. It wasn't my fault that she was smarter and prettier than me and that her boyfriend was so besotted with her that he sent her story to a journal. Tasha asked me what was wrong but I couldn't tell her. It would sound like I was jealous. I thought it was unfair that I had this body and this brain, and Erin's were superior. After the first period was over, I went to Principal Bermingham's office and told him I had menstrual cramps and needed to go home. This was famously the way to get out of school. Everyone knew he was squeamish about any 'girl problems'. His face reddened, and he offered to call my mom, but I said she was away. I would go home to bed. He let me leave. It was on my way home that I devised my plan. I hoped I'd get back in time.

17

Ruby

I wiped my mouth and turned to see Grandma standing in the bathroom doorway, her hands to her throat. 'Tell me that's not true.'

I could have, but now that I had in some way vomited up the truth, I could not swallow it down. All those days of talking, pretending not to hear people's horror stories, letting Amber treat me like a 'survivor', Jack repeatedly calling me a liar. Something had changed while I was there, but I did not feel relief at telling the truth. I felt horror and guilt. I curled up on the bathroom floor and started to cry. 'I'm sorry.' But Grandma had already moved down the hall and I heard her pick up the phone. Who was she calling? I ran out and pulled the phone from her hand. Her face was red.

'You destroyed his life, your sister's life, your parents' lives. Now I know why you drink. You can't live with yourself. Well, I can't live with you either.' She reached for the phone again, but I held it tightly. She clutched at her head then and said, 'You have to tell . . .' but her words became indistinct, and she slid down the wall and sat heavily on the floor as she passed out.

'Oh God, Grandma, please, are you okay? Grandma!'

Her eyes were unfocused, one side of her face slackened. 'Grandma!'

She lost consciousness. I knew enough to know this was a

stroke. I had the phone in my hand and I didn't hesitate. I called the emergency services and begged for an ambulance. I had learned that aspirin could help stroke victims – or was that heart attacks? I couldn't remember. I ran to the medicine cabinet and then tried to get some tablets into her mouth, but it was slack and she couldn't swallow. Was she dead?

My mother met me at the hospital ER. 'What happened? What did you do to her? Were you there in her house? Why did you leave rehab?' I was sobbing hard. They had taken Grandma into triage but made me wait outside. She was given a shot of something in the ambulance, but she hadn't woken up. Mom left me and went to the nurses' station and was allowed through to the treatment cubicles. I prayed silently for Grandma to the God I had abandoned. She was the only person I trusted. Maybe it's why she was the second person to whom I finally told the truth.

'You can't live with yourself,' she'd said, and she was right. Oblivion was preferable to reality, but reality had caught up with me.

That's when I stopped drinking.

18

The Incident

By the time I was home, my plan was complete. I was going to give Milo what he wanted. The very thing that Erin wouldn't give him. Full sexual intercourse. I knew what to do, Kenny had shown me step by step. Milo and I would do it. Then he would break up with Erin and I would be his girlfriend. That would show Erin she couldn't have everything she wanted. Milo and I would keep it secret for a while, maybe a month. And then we would tell everyone. And then, I would break up with him. Erin would be so mad.

I would have to change quickly. I knew the way Milo rang the doorbell. He always did two quick buzzes. He used to say, 'a long buzz is aggressive'. He was gentle like that.

I wore my denim shorts, the ones I was only allowed to wear at the beach. And on top I wore a sleeveless shirt, tied up at the navel, and no bra. I'd used Erin's make-up and did it the way she did, like Britney, lots of mascara and glossy lips.

That morning, I'd watched them through the hole in the wall over the mirror in my room. I felt a kind of pulsing between my legs, a yearning, and now I had an opportunity. My friends would have been shocked, but I wasn't going to tell anybody, yet. Milo liked me, I could tell. When I opened the door, he stepped back for a moment before entering.

'Hi, Milo, Altman is shut because of some boiler problem. Erin's out with Mom. She may be an hour or so. But she said for you to

come in and wait. And here's your book.' I handed him the textbook he had left behind.

'Well, hello to you, Daisy Duke. The whole school is shut down?'
Daisy Duke was a sexy character on an old TV show, The Dukes of Hazzard. *I knew immediately what he was thinking. I didn't answer his question. I was pleased. I made us both coffee and then sat beside him on the couch. I sat very close to him. I could feel the heat from his thigh on my bare leg. We continued to chat about my plans to be a Broadway star and I looked deep into his eyes. He looked uncomfortable. 'Ruby, I don't . . .' he said and attempted to move away. I moved quickly to straddle him. I threw my arms around his neck and kissed his mouth, but his teeth were clamped shut. He grabbed my shirt and pushed me away. I screamed and heard my shirt rip. He stopped, shocked, but I smiled. One breast was exposed, and his eyes lingered there for a second before he turned his head away. I put my arms around his neck again, but he pulled them up and away roughly, holding up my wrists in his fist. 'What the hell are you doing, Ruby? Stop.' I hadn't expected any objection.*

19

Ruby

Grandma had had a serious stroke. We did not know if she would walk or talk again, the damage was so great.

Mom was furious that I was out of rehab. I tried to convince her that I had stayed sober for ten days, but she called Longhurst and they told her that I'd been asked to leave. I was angry that they had broken my confidentiality like that, but Mom, via Dad, had paid the hefty fee. Their contract was with her, not me. I told her I'd go back in; I'd apologize to everyone. This time I meant it. Everyone was right, alcohol was controlling me. I could no longer deny it. I had lied, and it was eating me up inside. I knew that one of the steps in the Twelve Step programme was about apologizing. How could I ever do that?

But right now it was all about Grandma. I told Mom that it had just happened while I'd been there. This was true, I suppose. Maybe she would have had a stroke anyway, or maybe my admission of the truth had caused it. Part of me hoped that Grandma wouldn't recover so that she could never tell anyone what I'd said about Milo Kelly, but the bigger part of me wanted her back. I loved and trusted her even though she had no reason to trust me. If God let Grandma live, I would not drink again. After a hellish forty-eight hours in the Emergency Room, she was finally assigned a room of her own. Mom called her brother home from Australia.

Grandma regained consciousness the next day. She seemed to be alert but could only communicate with her eyes. My uncle Dennis arrived at the end of the week. He was tall and good-looking, and seemed much younger than Mom. He had a wife and children back in Perth. He was happy to see Mom and to meet me for the first time. He was sorry that Grandma was in such a bad way and regretted not coming home sooner.

But later, a family secret was revealed. The reason Dennis had left Ireland in his early twenties was to escape the drinking culture. He was a recovering alcoholic who had got himself into a lot of unspecified trouble when he was young. I asked what he'd done, but it was bad enough that, if it had been disclosed, he'd never have got that visa to live in Australia, and nobody would say what it was. Reading between the lines, I guessed he had harmed somebody drink-driving. Maybe even killed them. He managed to find sobriety eventually in Australia, but shame had prevented him from coming home.

When Grandma saw him, her eyes lit up and tears fell down her cheeks. When she looked at me, I could see only disgust.

Living independently was out of the question for her. Mom found a nursing home not far from where Grandma lived. I was terrified that, somehow, she would reveal my filthy secret. But she couldn't speak, and even using a chalkboard was useless because I think she could no longer read or write. I held newspapers up in front of her, but her eyes slid from side to side, up and down. Her entire right-hand side had collapsed, and her left leg was useless without her right. One of her arms still worked and with that she grasped her rosary beads. I could see her mouth moving in silent prayer. Was she giving thanks for having survived, or praying for release? I couldn't tell.

I went through cold turkey by myself. I called Longhurst, apologized, begged to be readmitted. They reluctantly agreed, though they couldn't take me until after Christmas. One wrong move and I would be sent home. For the next month, I was between the hospital and Grandma's flat, doing any shopping or laundry that she needed. I stayed sober. I stayed away from pubs and clubs. I was by Grandma's side when she moved into the nursing home. Her eyes showed fear, but I held on to her good hand. Her room was large and sunny, and the Filipino women who staffed the home were kind. After a few days, Grandma was more relaxed. Her eyes, when they settled on me, glared, until I told her I was going back to rehab. She made a moaning sound, which I took to mean she approved.

My uncle returned to Australia after tearful goodbyes to his mother and well wishes to me. Dennis said, 'Everything is better, you know, when you're sober. When your head is right, come out and visit us, eh? I can find a job for you.' He ran a mining company. I was grateful but couldn't see myself doing anything like moving to Australia. I wondered if I could go back to college. I was notorious there and for all the wrong reasons. I still had that acting itch, but my future was uncertain.

For those next four weeks, it was a constant struggle not to drink. I felt exhausted, I had a permanent knot in my stomach from fear of the unknown and the emotional work ahead of me. Christmas came and went. I stayed home, watched a lot of TV and read a lot of books. But I did not drink. Nobody congratulated me.

My sister called. I could tell by her tone that she was wary. She knew all about me and my errant ways. But she was comforting too. 'You shouldn't be hard on yourself, you know. You did nothing wrong, you were a child.' Poor Erin, the fool.

I went back to Longhurst in January 2006 with those words ringing in my ears. I *was* a child when it happened but did that excuse perpetuating the lie that had sentenced Milo to thirteen years in prison? I thought it was petty revenge for his rejection. I hadn't been old enough to think of the consequences for everyone. I could have spoken out at any time leading up to the court case, but I held fast to my lies. And more than six years had passed. Now I was twenty-three years old, and I still hadn't told the truth. I had to learn to live with the lie and somehow remain sober.

This time in rehab, I listened to all the lectures, took an active part in the group sessions and the AA meetings, got up early and made my bed, and helped with prep for meals like a model prisoner, perhaps like Milo. Amber still treated me like a rape victim. This time I told her about Kenny Carter. She was horrified. She didn't say it was rape but she said it was an abuse of trust and an abuse of status, and when I told her about the twenty dollars, she asked if she could hug me, and I let her and wept. She said he had taken advantage of my immaturity. And then he'd paid me twenty bucks for my virginity to make me feel like a whore and implied that this was a trick I used to pretend I was a virgin. I'd never really felt clean since then. I'd buried thoughts of him for years. But I had never said no. I had allowed him to teach me. Over the next few sessions, we talked a lot about that encounter. She remarked at one stage that I seemed to be more upset about him than about Milo, and she was right.

I couldn't come clean about Milo, though I worked some things out for myself. I had never had sober sex, except for that one time with Kenny. I don't like to think about any of them but particularly him. Some of the men, from what I remembered, were rough and used me like a rag doll. Had I consented to any of that? Had I allowed myself to be raped? Why had I never yelled no? I had gone back to an old man's house in pursuit of drink one night, and he had removed his belt and whipped my naked body. I never told anybody. In the morning, I thanked him for the vodka and left. This brutality was no more than I deserved.

I was a rape victim, but Milo had never raped anyone; he didn't even try to pressure Erin. I allowed myself to think of him in that prison and what horrors he might be facing on a regular basis, a quiet, good-looking man who, as far as I knew, had never even been in a fight.

I had lost my faith in God, and that was the hardest part for me, trying to visualize this Higher Power to whom I was to hand over all my problems. Amber was quick to point out that this was another control issue. By declaring myself powerless in the face of drugs and alcohol, I had to cede control to something greater than me. 'You don't have to believe in God in the traditional sense. I had a client in here last month who decided that his Higher Power was Elvis. And I have no problem with that.' I could not think what my Higher Power might be.

When I had packed my bags for my second stay in Longhurst, I had, as a matter of course, packed tampons. On my third week in there, I felt a sharp pain in my stomach while brushing my teeth. The tampons caught my eye in the bathroom cabinet. When was my last period? I hadn't had one since the previous time I had been admitted and that was seven weeks ago, plus the three-week waiting period before they accepted me the first time. Prior to that, there was the suicide attempt and before that there was chaos and blackouts.

For one sleepless night, I tried to convince myself that my periods had stopped because of the booze and my erratic appetite. I had been absolutely exhausted for months. The strange feelings in my stomach were alcohol withdrawal. I had veered between starving myself and binge eating. Right now, I knew I was carrying weight, but when I'd stopped drinking, I'd discovered an appetite. Don't they say that women are always hungry and tired in the first trimester? I put my hands on my stomach. It was firmer than it used to be and filled out from hip to hip. There was a significant bump. And I'd been throwing up at random times, with nausea a constant companion. I'd thought it was withdrawal, and then nerves about Grandma. I should have lost weight since I'd stopped drinking ten weeks and six days ago, but my jeans, which were low-waisted, were now a squeeze to get into. By dawn, I knew I was pregnant. Exhausted, miserable, terrified, possibly homeless and pregnant.

20

The Incident

I clamped my knees around Milo's waist. He let my arms go and tried to push me off, but I was annoyed and clung on harder. 'You want me, I know you do. You called me Daisy Duke.' Then he dug his thumbs into my inner thighs and pushed with all his might.

'Stop this, Ruby.'

'No, no, no.' I cried and pushed my hand into his crotch, feeling for a hardness but finding none. He was able to sidle forward in such a way that he jumped up. I fell sideways and landed on my back on the floor, hitting my head on the coffee table on the way down. The coffee cups went flying.

'Holy shit, Ruby, what are you trying to do? Are you okay?'

When I put my hand to my head, I felt a clammy dampness. I was defeated and humiliated and hurt. I slumped on to the floor, saying nothing. He put his hand on my head, and it came away crimson with my blood.

'You're bleeding.' He took the blanket from the back of the couch and put it around my shoulders.

'Cover yourself. What the hell were you trying to do?'

I started to cry. 'Don't you want to?' I sobbed.

'With my girlfriend's baby sister? You got to be fucking kidding me.'

'I'm not a baby,' I said as hot tears full of shame poured down my face. He pulled me up from the floor, put me sitting on the couch

and knelt down to eye level like he was talking to a toddler. He took my hands in his.

'Ruby, I'm going to go now, okay? I suggest you put on a different shirt. I'm not going to tell Erin anything, okay? I don't want to embarrass you. This never happened, right?'

21

Ruby

I had to tell the counsellors in rehab that I needed to see a doctor. I confided my fear of pregnancy to Sheila. Despite my previous behaviour, she acted as if this stay was my first time. She arranged an appointment for me. Dr Mitchell was kind and gentle. She quickly confirmed my pregnancy with a urine test, but then the inevitable question: 'When was your last period?' I didn't know if it was three or four months ago, possibly five.

Before she could ask, I told her, 'I don't know who the father is.'

'Okay,' she said as she washed her hands at the sink and I pulled up my too-tight trousers, 'you still have options. Obviously, as you came here from Longhurst, I assume you have been leading a hectic lifestyle, yes?'

What a great euphemism. 'You could say that.' I nodded.

'And how many weeks have you been sober now?'

'Eleven weeks.'

'Well done,' she said, and that was the first time I ever felt like I had achieved something in life. 'You've lived in Ireland long enough to know that terminations are illegal here?'

'Yes.'

'I'm going to send you for an ultrasound to see exactly how pregnant you are, but I think you could still travel to the UK if you wanted to terminate the pregnancy. Adoption is also an option and then you might want to keep the baby. There are choices.'

I was going to have an abortion. How could I raise a baby on my own and cope with recovery at the same time? And I wanted to finish my degree. As I left, Dr Mitchell gave me a sheaf of leaflets, information on all the options.

'You know, Ruby, whatever you decide will be the right decision. I wish you the best of luck.'

I was going to have an abortion and that was the right decision.

I had the ultrasound that afternoon. This time, a male doctor. He didn't flinch either when I told him I didn't know when my last period was. 'Right, let's find out,' he said as he ran a tube covered in gel across my stomach. I heard the *whomp-whomp* of a heartbeat. It seemed fast to me. Was that normal? 'Would you like to see?' he said. I was confused for a moment until he added, 'The foetus?' Did I? I shook my head. 'This foetus looks about four months old to me,' he said. His use of language was deliberate, I think. If I was going to abort, best not to use the B word.

I thought about the foetus a lot. It had been there when I jumped in the river. It had survived despite me. I didn't have any religious hang-ups about having an abortion. In Dad's church, he never mentioned it. Privately, he always said that a woman's health was her own business, and though he was fixated on virginity, he meant it for girls *and* boys. In fact, he was even stricter with boys because, apparently, they had urges more than girls. I'm not sure if he was right about that.

It would be easy to fly to London and have an abortion, there was no identifiable father to argue with.

Dr Corbett confirmed that I was somewhere between sixteen and eighteen weeks pregnant. I asked some questions, wondering if all my bad behaviour would have inflicted damage on this tiny creature. By some miracle she was 'progressing nicely' despite all the abuse I had inflicted on my body and the baby's. Dr Corbett had confirmed that it was a girl when I told him I wanted to know.

The identity of my baby's father bugged me. I could rule out Darren, because he had given up exchanging coke for sex over a year ago. There were two guys in college, but I had vague memories they'd used condoms. There was a long-haired guy at a party. We had stand-up sex in the cloakroom. I didn't remember his face or his name, and I didn't remember whose party it was or even where the house was. There were two men whose houses I went back to after a long night's drinking. I don't remember if I slept with either of them, or both. There were many times in those final weeks at the height of my addiction when I woke up in a stranger's bed. I had to let go of the task of trying to identify him.

Sheila was the only counsellor in Longhurst who knew I was pregnant, and she respected my confidentiality. She reminded me that there would be extra doctors' bills on the invoice my mother would receive, but that who I told was my own business. I didn't think Mom would look at the invoice closely. She'd send it to Dad. But it was only a matter of time before it became obvious.

With renewed determination, I engaged in rehab, attended the meetings, listened to the other addicts, volunteered to help. I stuck to the story of the incident with Amber. There was nothing I could do about that. Part of the Twelve Step programme was making amends. You must go to everyone who you hurt through your addiction and apologize and thank the people who had tried to help you. Almost everyone had tried to help me.

The thing is, I never hurt Milo because of my addiction. I hurt him because I was an immature child and he rejected me, and when I dug deep, I was trying to take something from Erin. I had tried to come clean too late in the day. Lives were destroyed and changed in ways that could never be reversed. I had to let go of that guilt. In my therapy sessions, I told a different kind of rape story to Amber. Some of it was true. I had tried to seduce Michael (I never called him Milo in my sessions). I had dressed provocatively. I had pulled away and that's what caused the rip in my shirt. I had kissed him first. He protested but then, as I described it, 'the mood changed' and he turned aggressive. This was the new version. I didn't want to present myself any longer as this pure-of-thought virginal girl. I apportioned some blame to myself, but Amber didn't accept that.

'What do you mean when you say the mood changed, Ruby?'

'I don't want to talk about it any further.' And I never did. I couldn't go on talking about something that never happened nearly seven years previously. I'd described it in detail back then, though I find it strange that they believed me. It was because of who I was, whose daughter I was, because of who he was and where he came from, and – most importantly – because of the DNA.

22

The Incident

'Nobody has to know about this.' As Milo was saying this, he picked up one cup and the pieces of the other and put them on the hatch shelf that was between our lounge and the kitchen.

'You're too young, too –' he looked at me, a sobbing mess – *'sweet. Does your head hurt? You want me to get some Tylenol before I go? It's just a graze. You're going to be okay.'*

I was angry now. I said nothing.

He said, 'I love Erin. I would never do anything to hurt her, and especially not –' he gestured towards me with his hand – *'this. I'm sorry, Ruby. I had no idea you were thinking like this. I don't think I ever said or did anything to make you think . . .'* He was backing towards the front door and, without finishing the sentence, he left.

I stayed on the couch for fifteen minutes, hot with rage. Then I went upstairs to Erin's room. It was freezing as usual. She always had the air conditioning turned up high.

I used to watch Erin even when he wasn't there. She slept on her back, with both arms above her head resting on the pillow. She looked like a Disney princess when she slept, her mouth slightly open. And every morning, she woke up perfect. I lay down on her bed.

How dare Milo reject me? Why didn't he want me? I thought about all the ways I could take revenge. I would tell Erin that he had tried to seduce me. But would she believe it?

I buried my face in the pillow. I had seen through the tiny hole in the wall what they'd been doing to each other before Mom and Dad woke up this morning. I looked around the room and spotted the trash can under the dressing table. There were several tissues in it. I knew what he used these for. Erin had jerked him off in the early hours of this morning.

I found a tissue in the trash that was still moist. I knew what I was looking for because I had examined the contents of Kenny Carter's condom out of curiosity. The semen was viscous and sticky. I pulled down my panties and wiped the tissue all around my private parts, pushing it up inside myself, before flushing it and the other tissues from the trash down the toilet in the family bathroom. I washed my face clean of all the make-up.

Then I went downstairs and allowed the tears of anger to come. I took off all my clothes and dropped them on the floor around me, adding a bra to the discarded pile, swapping out the shorts for a pair of high-waisted jeans. I wrapped myself in the blanket and waited for Dad to come home, while I made my plan to destroy Milo Kelly. It was perfect. He had ripped my shirt. He'd said, 'this never happened' and 'nobody has to know'. I had said 'no' three times. And I had the trump card. There were, at the very least, traces of his semen inside me. Erin's perfect smile would be wiped off her face.

23

Ruby

Leaving Longhurst the second time in February 2006 was emotional. I thought I'd made friends for life. They all gathered to say goodbye. Sheila said I had gone from the lost-cause category to the best-hope category. The other recovering addicts had made me a card. They sang as I walked down the avenue to my mom's car, 'Pack up your troubles in your old kit bag...'

I sat in the passenger seat and burst into tears. I hugged Mom tightly. 'I'm sorry,' I said. 'I'm sorry for everything, Mom.' Her stiffened body loosened in my arms.

'I'm sorry too, darling. I should never have...' She was afraid to speak the words. We drove away.

I did not tell her I was pregnant. She had said that as long as I stayed sober, Dad would support me financially. After a few fraught weeks at Mom's, wearing increasingly baggy sweatshirts and disguising my nausea, it was agreed that I could move into Grandma's house by myself. Mom gave me the new keys. I deferred college for a year. They were understanding when I told them I'd been in treatment for addiction. Even Professor White said, 'I'm glad you got the help you needed. We'll see you next September.' After missing a year of school and then a year of college, I was going to be the oldest graduate of all my classmates, but that was the least of my concerns.

I had not arranged to travel to London for the abortion.

I wasn't ready to face up to it yet, but I could feel the baby kicking from time to time. I don't know why I wasn't more proactive about it. A trip to London for the procedure would take less than twenty-four hours. But I was too busy staying sober.

We'd had AA meetings in Longhurst, so I was used to the format, but I was still nervous going to my first one outside. I had a list of meetings I could go to in Dublin. There was one in a community centre nearby on a Tuesday at 9 a.m. I sat in my car until the last minute and then crept in and took a seat at the back. The chairs were arranged in a haphazard circle. There was tea and biscuits on a table at the other end of the room. People were still milling about, until a woman rang a bell and asked everyone to take a seat. I kept my head down and tried not to be seen, pulled a baseball cap low down on my head.

I had heard a lot of dramatic stories in rehab, but in this meeting, they talked about their recovery. There was an old man who had been sober for forty-two years who admitted that, even though he never felt a compulsion to drink again, he wasn't going to take the risk and that's why he came to meetings twice a week, to keep him on the straight and narrow. I couldn't think beyond the end of the meeting, let alone forty years ahead. Others told of relationship difficulties: some were living with spouses in active addiction; others were finding it hard to rebuild trust in their relationships. One woman had relapsed after twenty-three years of sobriety. She couldn't think of a single reason why. She had woken up on Tuesday of last week and opened the bottle of champagne that had been bought for her sister's bachelorette party. A young guy told her it didn't matter what the reason was. She had come back to the meeting, and she would receive all the support she needed.

Towards the end, the woman with the bell asked me directly if I was new. I introduced myself in the traditional way. Saying it in a room full of strangers, and meaning it, was liberating. It was like stepping out from a shadow. I clarified that I wasn't a tourist and lived nearby. I admitted to cocaine addiction too. I admitted this was my first meeting since rehab. Everyone applauded, but I was uncomfortable with that. 'Maybe you can clap when I've been here a year,' I said quietly.

'No, this is the meeting that is worthy of applause,' the woman said. 'You have shown courage today. We don't know you, but I can assure you that everyone in this room wants sobriety for you as much as they want it for themselves. It's not impossible to stay sober on your own, but it's much easier to get there with us.'

We ended with the serenity prayer, and then everyone said, 'Keep coming back.' Some of it was a bit corny to me, but it all meant something.

I did feel better after the meeting. It was full of all kinds of people. A boy, who looked like a teenager, came over and said, 'Don't think about a year, think about today. Try to stay sober today.' It wasn't like Longhurst, where everyone was wealthy, but as I'd listened, the stories were similar. Losing jobs, partners, being estranged from parents and children, destroying property. I was lucky, I still had Mom and Grandma. Judging by their clothes and accents and the level of grooming, addicts came in all shapes and sizes. Another woman came over and told me about a Narcotics Anonymous meeting that she went to. She said she'd be there on Sunday if I wanted to go.

As I got up to leave, a man stopped me on the way out. 'Jack.' I recognized him from my first visit to Longhurst. His demeanour was no different here. The hostility he had carried in his body was still there.

'Are you for real this time?' he said, still suspicious of me.

'I'm here, I'm trying.'

'Good for you,' he said. I'm not sure he believed me.

24

The Incident

I didn't think it through. If I had even waited until the next day, my temper would have abated. I would have seen how foolish my plan was, that destroying Milo would also destroy me, and many others. And I know he would have kept his word and not told Erin or anyone.

I gave the police all the evidence they needed. I didn't think ahead to a court case. I never thought that Milo would go to prison.

Once the lies were told, I had to keep track of them. I didn't know what to do. It had all gone too far. Dad withdrew Erin's short story from the New England Journal. *Milo never found out it had been accepted.*

Months later, I gave my testimony behind a screen so that I wouldn't have to face the court, or the jury, or Milo. But it was all very exciting. Before we went to trial, I rehearsed my answers with the prosecutor. I enjoyed the attention and put in my best performance, acting nervous and terrified. I thought it would be all over in a few days. Instead, it went on for weeks. His defence attorney tried to trip me up and at times I got confused. He kept asking about the denim shorts. He also asked about how my clothes had come off, in what order. I contradicted myself but then said I was shocked, confused, and I didn't remember. And that part was true. It was hard to remember things that didn't happen. He suggested I must have removed them myself. I denied it. I answered the same questions, asked in a hundred different ways. I was afraid of making a mistake but, before the final week of the trial, I knew that I was believed. Dad paid attention to me all the time and told me repeatedly that he loved me and that none of this was my fault. I guess I was easier to love now.

One strange thing was that, according to Dad, Principal Bermingham didn't remember me asking permission to go home. He was adamant that I'd lied. But his lie worked in my favour. In court, I said I went home with a pain in my stomach. If he had remembered that I'd said I had menstrual cramps, then my lie would have been revealed by the forensic examiner who would have told the court that I wasn't bleeding. But he also said I could not be trusted. I don't know why he said that. My homeroom teacher verified that I had told her I wasn't feeling well after first period that morning.

I told my mother the truth.

We were home alone. It had been a few weeks since the trial had ended and the next day Milo was to be sentenced. Dad was out and Erin was staying in Saima's house. I think in those days she couldn't bear to be around me. Mom had to be able to fix this. I sobbed my way through my story. I told her everything: how I'd wanted Milo to love me instead of Erin, how I'd come on to him, how I'd planted the evidence inside my body using the tissue. I told her how I had lied to the police, how the blood on his jacket was from where I'd banged my head, and how he had said we would keep it a secret to protect Erin and me. The bruises on my inner thighs, which matched his thumbs, were from when he tried to push me away, and he had gripped my wrists to keep me off him.

I didn't need to tell Mom that I was Doug Cooper's daughter, the Pastor of the Holy Divine Church, a sworn virgin who went to Bible Camp, who had felt sick that morning and came home alone to an empty house. All the odds were stacked against Milo.

'You need to stop it, Mom. You need to help him,' I begged her.

My mother slapped me across the face so hard I fell to the floor. In shock, I looked at her furious face.

'Mother of God, you little bitch. How could you do that to him? To your sister?' she screamed at me. She paced up and down the room, wringing her hands. 'How did you even know what to do?'

I told her about Kenny Carter. She looked like she was going to be sick. I didn't tell her about the twenty dollars. She sat and put her head on the table and covered it with her arms, breathing heavily, and stayed like that until I said, 'Mom, what am I going to do?'

She whispered, 'It's too late now, don't you see? You have had eight months to tell the truth, while Milo has begged for freedom. Nobody believed him when he said you had tried to seduce him. He couldn't explain the DNA, could he? You scheming bitch.' I had never seen Mom lose it this way before. Any trace of an American accent she'd picked up was gone, pure blasphemy and Irish rage pouring out of her. 'Why did you do it?'

'Erin gets everything she wants, all the time.'

'You said he raped you. How did you become so calculating? Taking the tissues out of the trash? You disgust me. What in the name of Jesus do you expect me to do?' She handed me the phone and took our attorney's card out of her bag. 'Milo's life is already ruined. He can never escape your accusation. I don't know if Erin can ever recover. Go ahead, ruin your own life, ruin mine and your father's. Call Donny Bouras and tell him the truth.'

I couldn't take the phone from her hand. 'What will Dad say?'

'What the hell do you think he'll say? His church will collapse. His investment clients will run for the hills. Nobody will ever want to be associated with this family again. We're going to lose everything. Everything.' I could feel her spittle on my face.

'I can't do it,' I said.

Mom sat with her head in her hands and for ten minutes neither of us spoke. I could feel the heat on my face from where she'd struck me. Eventually, she got up and went to the freezer and came back with a Ziploc bag of ice wrapped in a towel. She pressed it to my face.

'If this gets out, do you understand that every convicted rapist will claim that their victims lied and schemed like you did? You will be the poster girl for rapists everywhere. "She lied. She planted the DNA." If you tell the truth, you'll be doing real rapists the biggest favour.'

'Mom, I'm sorry.'

'Jesus Christ, I don't know how you would even think to use his... sperm like that.'

'I saw what Kenny Carter's looked like –'

'Do not mention his name again.'

'What will I do?'

'It's Milo or us. You can never tell anyone the truth, do you hear me? Nobody ever. Especially not Erin. You stick to your story, okay? I have to take you away from here.'

'What?'

'After the sentencing, we'll need to get away. You must live with this for the rest of your life. Live your life as if you are a rape victim. You've been damn convincing so far. You have sent an innocent boy to jail for God knows how many years. Poor Milo. I don't know if he'll survive.' Her eyes filled with tears. 'Now, I'm going to say the same thing to you as Milo did. We never had this conversation. You have to believe your lies. If Dad or Erin ask what happened to your face, I opened the kitchen door on you by accident, okay?'

PART TWO

25

Ruby

I tried several different meetings before I found one I was comfortable with. Although there was both Narcotics Anonymous and Alcoholics Anonymous, I knew that I had never taken cocaine while sober, so I stuck to AA. I even recognized a few faces from my debaucherous days. Those encounters were awkward at first until we both realized that we were embarrassed for the same reasons. I recognized one of the lecturers in Trinity; a woman who I'd partied with the previous summer; an old teacher from school and one of Mom's friend's husbands. But we all respected the anonymity rules.

My 'home' meeting was about twenty minutes' walk from my house, but I didn't always go to the same one. I was surprised to discover there were AA meetings everywhere, thousands of people trying to stay sober one day at a time. It seemed like the biggest private club in the world. It had taken me a while to find a meeting that was evenly split between genders and who were around my own age, in their late teens, twenties and thirties. Even among that age group, there were people who had started drinking when they were ten years old, people who had suffered or caused devastating consequences for themselves and others. People like me.

I chose my words carefully when I shared or when I chaired a meeting after my first ninety days. I talked about finding sobriety, my lowest point, my need to keep the party going at any cost to suspend reality. My self-destructive behaviour that stemmed from a 'childhood trauma'. I kept as close to the truth as I could.

All this time, my belly was growing. Sometimes I imagined I could feel her heartbeat through my skin. I remembered Dr Amber asking me in Longhurst on my first visit who the people were that I wanted to get sober for and I could only think of Grandma, but now there was another person, another reason to get sober and stay sober. Two reasons – my child and her mother. I was aware of the calendar. I knew that by now it was too late to terminate the pregnancy. I guess I was going to have a baby, and the more I felt her moving around, the more I realized that I needed her.

Finally, Mom noticed. I think she realized earlier than she said, but neither of us wanted to confront it. And then, when I was seven months pregnant in April 2006, she could no longer ignore it. 'You seem to have put on a lot of weight around your belly, Ruby.' I said nothing. 'Is there anything you want to tell me?'

'I think you've already guessed,' I said. Her face took on a lot of expressions in the next ten seconds, from dismay to exasperation to hope. It settled on acceptance.

'Well, a new baby is never a bad thing, is it?'

'I think it will be good for me, Mom, honestly.'

'May I ask who the father is?'

'He's not in the picture. I'm doing this on my own.'

'You mean he's not even going to help out financially?'

'I mean I don't know who he is.'

'What do you mean?' She was horrified but said she was relieved that I hadn't had an abortion.

'I nearly did, but then I heard the heartbeat, and I thought about Grandma. I don't think she's going to live long, and she deserves to see one great-grandchild.'

Mom was sombre for a moment but then said, 'You won't be on your own, honey, you've got me,' and we hugged. I was overwhelmed with relief, because I knew the horror stories about how young unmarried Irish women and girls were sent to 'homes' run by nuns and forced into unpaid labour, their babies stolen from them and sold to infertile couples.

Mom came with me to break the news to Grandma. It was the five-month anniversary of my sobriety, and I was now very visibly pregnant, no longer able to hide my belly behind colossal handbags and loose-fitting sweaters. Grandma's face twisted with dismay, but I was calm and explained how out of control my life had been, and that I was going to do right by my child. By the time I finished, her eyes were glassy with tears, and she reached out with her one good hand. I took it in mine and she squeezed it tight. She tapped her wedding ring insistently, and for a few minutes I thought she was urging me to get married until I realized she wanted me to wear it. I took it off her finger as gently as I could and put it on to mine, and she smiled her half-smile and closed her eyes.

Mom broke the news to Dad and told him the father was unknown. Dad was aghast but once he had calmed down he said the child would be a blessing. I was very lucky to have the support of both parents under the circumstances.

Erin wanted to see me. I wondered if Mom had pushed her or if Erin was coming voluntarily. She was shocked by the news of my pregnancy. I hadn't seen her in over a year. Though we had talked on the phone a few times, we had not spoken since I got sober. I owed her an apology that I was never going to be able to make. I was nervous about seeing her.

Mom was delighted. She hosted a big welcome dinner for her. I made cannoli, which were still hard to come by in Ireland. I left out the Marsala wine. Cannoli were one of my cravings and I'd got the recipe down to a fine art. Grandma was able to come out for the day from her care home. When we went to collect her, she was up and dressed and her hair was freshly washed. I applied some lip balm to her dry lips and sprayed her with her favourite perfume. The side of her face that could move lit up. She put her good hand on my belly and the baby kicked right then, like she was saying hello to Grandma. Grandma was happy. She held my hand, rubbing her old wedding ring that I was now wearing.

It was a surprise for Grandma that Erin was going to be at Mom's. Erin didn't talk much. I felt that she was uncomfortable being the centre of attention. She tried to be cheerful, but I knew her well enough to know it was a pretence. We got through the dinner with small talk, making up names for the baby, joking about the fact that at least we wouldn't have to consult the father's side of the family. Grandma did not find that funny. She slammed her good hand on the table. It was easy to forget that she was fully alert – there was nothing wrong with her hearing. After dinner, when we propped her up on the sofa, she made noises and glances that I knew meant she wanted Erin and me to come sit by her. She reached for both our hands and put them in her lap, and I suddenly realized what she wanted. She wanted me to tell Erin what I had told her, that Milo never raped me. I jumped up and went to the table, beginning to clear things away, and ignored the noise Grandma made when she was calling my name.

'Ruby?' Erin said. 'I think Grandma wants you to say something.'

I held up my glass of sparkling water. 'I'll make a toast to all the strong, fabulous women in our family here today.' Mom gave me a funny look, and Grandma's mouth remained downturned.

That night back in my house, when Erin and I were alone, I asked Erin if she was dating anyone. The long-held tears spilled from her eyes. 'How come you're okay?' she asked me.

'Okay? I'm a twenty-three-year-old alcoholic single pregnant drama student thousands of miles from home with few friends. What makes you think I'm okay?'

'But you seem . . . happy? Like, you're over it.'

I didn't have to ask her what she meant by *it*. Erin and I had not spoken of Milo in years now. 'I try not to think about it. I'm not going to let the actions of one man on one day ruin my life.'

'He ruined mine too.'

'Oh, Erin.' I felt bad for her. 'You should try to forget about him. Put yourself out there. It's been over six years.'

'I dated one guy, Charlie, but he tried to control me. I trusted Milo with my life, and I feel guilty.'

It never occurred to me that Erin would feel guilt. 'He loved you.' I blurted the words.

'No, he didn't,' she answered, her voice quaking with anger. 'A man doesn't rape the sister of a girl he loves. But that's how easily we can be fooled. How can I possibly trust another man?'

'They're not all like that,' I said quietly.

'Right? The father of your baby is a fine, upstanding guy, is he?'

'Erin, my life has been a train wreck for the last few years. The only thing that is keeping me upright is Alcoholics Anonymous. But I know there are good men out there.'

I thought of Milo, who had never put a foot wrong, who had adored Erin and had only ever tried to protect me from myself. She'd had a good man who was spending yet another summer in prison because of my lies. The nausea I felt wasn't only because of my baby. I had tried over the years not to imagine what Milo's life might be like, but on this night, sitting with the love of his life, it was unavoidable. Erin was acing her exams as usual. She was looking for an internship with a publishing house in New York, hoping to be an editor. She had the smarts to do it. And she was still stunningly beautiful. It shocked me to see her lack of confidence.

I had a sleepless night, not helped by my baby kicking the hell out of me and having to get up to pee every hour. I could hear Erin crying in her room as I passed. What was I feeling? Was this guilt tinged with glee? My sobriety was being tested. I had no booze in the house and all the pubs were closed, but there were nightclubs. I could slip out without her knowing. But who would serve a heavily pregnant woman on her own? I dug deep. I recited the mantras in my head: 'Easy does it', 'One day at a time', 'This too shall pass'. None of them helped me in this situation. But then the baby kicked again. Hard. And that is what stopped me leaving my sister in distress in the middle of the night to go looking for drink. Instead, I went to comfort Erin.

'None of it was your fault, Erin. Nobody blames you. Look,' I smiled, holding my belly, 'baby agrees.' My little girl kicked again to confirm.

Erin looked at me. 'You don't blame me?'

'I never blamed you. Not for one second. I'm sorry, Erin.'

I did blame her, but not for the reasons she thought.

'You have nothing to be sorry for,' she said.

She had no idea. Nobody realized what a good performer I was.

26

My obstetrician was pleased with how my pregnancy was progressing. Mom had already offered childcare so that I could go back to college and finish my degree in September. I think she had a chip on her shoulder about not having a college education and was determined that I would finish mine. And despite her fears, being an unmarried mother in the 2000s was not as shameful as it was in her day. Ireland certainly wasn't as restrictive as it had been when she grew up. Contraception had been illegal back then and so had divorce and homosexuality. Abortion was still illegal, but you could go to England and get one there. I couldn't understand how Mom had grown up in such a backwards society. Imagine being married to someone who was violent and having no control over how many children you had. I wouldn't have stayed in *that* Ireland. No wonder she got out as soon as she could.

Staying sober was still a challenge. The day after I saw Erin off, I finally plucked up the courage to ask Nasrin Sutton to be my sponsor. She had been sober three years, and she was eight years older than me. She was a haematologist. I admired her style of sobriety. Like a lot of people, I struggled with the Twelve Steps of AA. Even the serenity prayer bothered me a little – why couldn't we change the things we couldn't accept instead of '*accept the things I cannot change*'? Nasrin laughed. 'Yeah, well I see your point there – I'm saving up for a nose job; I'm not accepting living with this conk.' She wasn't a churchgoer, but she had a strong belief in the Higher Power – though she warned me against using it as a crutch. I had to be responsible for myself and my own actions. She was warm and friendly, and although sometimes when I called she was busy, she always called me back. Indeed, like Uncle Dennis had said, everything was better without alcohol, certainly clearer, though my lies cast a long shadow. Honesty wasn't possible in my case. I knew by now that even if I did come clean about what had happened back in 1999, more lives would be destroyed, mine most of all.

Jack appeared occasionally at different meetings. Gradually, he could see I was sincere about staying sober. When it came time for him to share at a meeting we both attended, he talked obliquely about being taken advantage of as a child actor. Afterwards, I approached him.

'You're an actor?'

'How long have you been in Ireland?'

'Six years.'

'Yeah, I'd been written out by then, but I was in a long-running TV drama series shot in London when I was a youngster. I'm Jack Brady.'

The name meant nothing to me except that it was the same name as Tom Brady, the most famous quarterback in the world. Jack had never heard of him. 'Quarterbacks only exist in America, so he's hardly world famous.' He was putting me in my place.

'And are you still acting?'

'No. That lifestyle doesn't exactly lend itself to sobriety.'

'You know I'm a drama student, right?'

'Well, I know you're a drama queen.' He saw the hurt in my face. 'Sorry, I mean you *were* a drama queen, back in Longhurst, before you got kicked out.'

'You're the one who got me kicked out.'

'I think I did you a favour.'

'I think you probably did.'

The conversation was becoming a little intense. He took a step back. 'When are you due?'

'Just a few weeks to go.'

'Is Daddy sober?'

It took me a few seconds to decide how to respond.

'None of your business.'

'Good answer.'

'Yeah, well, I needed somebody to get sober for.'

His brow furrowed. 'Well, that's a shitty reason to have a kid.'

I was startled. The conversation had started okay, then turned a bit awkward, and now it was horrible.

'You asshole. That's not *why* I got pregnant.'

'Sure,' he said, then turned on his heel and left.

Was I using my child to stay sober? No. By now I really wanted someone to love.

27

Erin

It was a while since I'd visited Ireland. Instead of going to visit Saima on Long Island for the weekend, I went to visit Mom and Ruby. The guilt got to me. Dad had told me the father of Ruby's baby was unknown.

Sober pregnant Ruby was different. We talked about Milo for the first time in years. Ruby had never blamed me, and I wept with relief. She urged me to get back out there and live my life. I was grateful that my sister had seen the light, and that we were able to reconnect. She sounded like an adult for the first time. She still planned an acting career. Mom was going to be doing a lot of childcare, but she was a young grandma at forty-nine, and I think she relished the role. I went back to Boston feeling like a burden had lifted off my shoulders.

Ruby's baby was born on 1 June 2006. It was going to be a whole new life for her. I wondered if she realized what she was getting herself into. Mom always came over to Boston twice a year to see me, but Ruby never came. I told Ruby I hoped she would come with Mom and the baby next time. She made no promises.

In the new year of 2007, I realized how lonely I was. Boyfriends had come and gone, but I didn't trust any of them for long enough to build a lasting relationship. College had kept me busy, and now I had moved to New York City and was interning at Schoolroom, an educational imprint of a bigger publisher, Watling and Harris. It wasn't anything close to the type of job I wanted but it was a start. My job was demanding and demeaning and included everything from photocopying and printing documents to collecting the senior editor's dry-cleaning. With Dad's help, I rented a tiny apartment in Brooklyn.

I had not wanted a relationship because I didn't think I deserved one. But Ruby had told me there were trustworthy guys out there, and I guess if she could say it, it must be true. Most of my friends had coupled up and were married with kids or had kids on the way. I'd kissed a few frogs but none of them had turned out to be princes.

I noodled around on the dating websites to see who was out there. My work girlfriends Larissa and Dawn and I tried speed dating and Match.com with some hilarious and some troubling results. I met one man who was upfront by the third date about the fact that he needed to get married and have a baby on the way within the next six months to inherit a quarter of a million dollars. He said he'd give me ten per cent but that we had to stay married for five years before we officially divorced as per the terms of the will. We could put the baby up for adoption as soon as he got the money. He could not understand why I didn't swoon into his arms. He upped his offer to twenty per cent. I deleted his number and blocked his calls.

I had a few months emailing and texting losers and time-wasters, a lot of whom wanted to show me photos of their dicks – as if any woman would be persuaded into a date by a photo of a penis. My friends and I laughed at these, stupid, ugly and offensive at the same time. I will never understand why men do this.

I thought I had found the perfect guy after a few dates with a charming self-described Christian man, particularly well-groomed and a terrific kisser, who never wanted me to go back to his place or he to mine. On the fourth date, I asked him bluntly if he was gay. His shoulders drooped and he begged me to keep his secret. I played along for six months because he was fun and I met his family on one occasion who declared me 'adorable', but after the 'dinner with the folks' I had to tell him that I could no longer keep up the lie. I stayed friends with Cisco and his real partner, Chad. I regularly had them to lunch with Aunt Rachel, when she came to the city.

Then there was the mild-mannered divorcee. He was interesting when you got him talking but cripplingly shy; it took an hour on each date to get him to loosen up. We liked the same music and went to see Prince and Usher. He was an awesome dancer. He was surprisingly skilled in the bedroom department too. I liked him. And then, after three months, he vanished. My calls, texts and emails were not returned. He dropped me like a sack of lobsters. In fact, I never saw him again. I still wonder what happened to him.

One morning, in the office, there was a letter waiting for me, postmarked Boston. I recognized the typewritten envelope. I wasn't hard to find. My name was on the publisher's website.

```
You think running away to New York is
the solution? I'll always find you. I
don't know whose DNA they found but it
certainly wasn't Milo's. You know that.
```

Margie would get tired of this eventually.

28

Ruby

In the last month of pregnancy, I had moved back into Mom's apartment. It seemed like I would yoyo between Mom's and Grandma's forever. The last trimester had been tough-going. Back in March I had decided to build an extension on Grandma's house, and Olivia, who had been doing set design in my year in college, offered to project manage it for me. When Dad learned I was pregnant, he'd suggested I would need more room and offered to pay for it.

In the beginning, the builders wouldn't take Olivia or me seriously, and spoke down to us, but they hadn't reckoned with the rage of a pregnant woman who needed completion by the time the baby was four months old. I was going to stay with Mom until then. I got stuck in with painting and decorating to earn their respect. And Olivia made them aware of who was boss. The back of the house was going to be one large kitchen-diner with folding doors, which would open out to the deck, and we'd also have a new guest bathroom and shower upstairs as well as an en suite bathroom off my bedroom, which doubled in size. The combi boiler would live in the attic. The bedroom that had been my uncle's was going to be the nursery, and Mom's childhood bedroom housed my exercise bike and boxes of books. I hadn't decided what it should be yet.

I went into labour at an AA meeting on 1 June 2006.

The only person I knew well at that meeting was Jack. I sat as far away from him as possible. I felt the first contraction like a rolling wave down my belly but it wasn't too bad and I assumed it was a Braxton Hicks cramp, which I'd been warned about. My obstetrician said most people got them and, unless they were coming twenty minutes apart, I was not to go to the maternity hospital. I was prepared, though, I had been carrying my hospital bag in the trunk of my car for a few weeks. I took a deep breath, and the lady beside me asked if I was okay. I didn't want to disrupt the meeting and assured her I was fine. The next contraction came twenty minutes later. This was a little sharper, and I gasped and held my belly. I saw Jack roll his eyes. Was I in labour? I didn't want to interrupt the woman who was sharing about how she had been able to turn her life around.

When the next contraction came ten minutes later, and the pressure whooshed down the valley of my groin, I knew that my baby was knocking at my pelvic door. I stood up and apologized, and tried to leave the room discreetly as my waters broke. I was mortified; my pregnancy jeans were soaked through. The whole meeting was abandoned quickly and people were talking about ambulances, but I didn't want a fuss. 'Do you know anyone here?' asked the woman I'd been sitting next to.

'No, but I'll be fine. I'll drive myself – it's not far to Holles Street.'

Jack appeared beside me. 'Give me your keys, Ruby, I'll drive. You'll never be able to park.' I was surprised. But there was a look of genuine concern on his face, and right at this moment wasn't the time to quibble about whether he was insured to drive my car.

Outside, I heaved myself into the passenger seat and noted that he'd put his jacket down on the seat so it didn't get wet. I was about to thank him when another wave gripped me and this one was vicious. Everyone from the meeting was crowded around. 'Close the door,' he shouted as I reeled back from the pain. As soon as it was shut, we shot out of the car park and on to the road. 'Christ,' he said, 'I'm not used to driving an automatic. Fucking Americans.'

There wasn't much conversation between us on the way. He told me to call the hospital and to call the father. I didn't feel I owed him an explanation and, in between huffing and puffing and screaming in pain, I called the hospital, told them I was five minutes away and that the contractions were three minutes apart. Then I called Mom and asked her to meet me there. She was with Grandma, and said she'd be there as soon as she could. Jack overheard all this and glanced across at me before he ran another red light. He dropped me off at the hospital entrance and came around and helped me out of the car. I walked in by myself. The orderly at the door on a smoke break took one look at me and said, 'That baby's not waiting around.' He wasn't wrong.

Eight minutes later, the midwife asked me for 'one last big push', and Lucy was born, punching the air and mewling as soon as her tiny body slipped through the birth canal. It had been eight minutes of acute agony, but once I saw her, I no longer felt anything but love. She was perfect. I didn't want to let her go when the nurses tried to take her away to check her vitals and clean her up, while the midwife stayed with me as I still had to push out the placenta. They eased her out of my arms, and they had never felt emptier. Mom wasn't there, Erin wasn't there. I felt entirely alone as all the medics focused on my baby. I could see her over the other side of the delivery suite. The placenta pushed its way out of me and then a flurry of people came around me to clean me up and make sure I was okay.

A nurse came in and said, 'Daddy's here. He had trouble parking the car. Shall we let him in?' I was confused. Had Dad flown in coincidentally on the same day I'd given birth? I wanted to see him. I nodded enthusiastically. But it was Jack who arrived at my side.

'I lied,' he whispered. 'I told them I was the dad. I didn't want you to be on your own.'

Just then, the nurse returned and put the baby back into my arms.

'Wow,' said Jack. 'She's beautiful and so tiny.' Her little scrunched-up face miaowed like a tiger cub. Jack was leaning over, and she reached up and grabbed his finger. 'My God,' he whispered, and I looked at him. His eyes were shining and his whole face softened. And then I looked at my daughter again. She would melt the most hardened of hearts.

29

Erin

I was still friends with Cisco, who had recently broken up with Chad. We were both single, though I was more single than Cisco. He had regular dates and hook-ups. I asked him if he knew any decent straight guys and he set me up on a date with his cousin Fabian, who had broken up with his fiancée six months previously. 'Not a rebounder, thank you very much,' I said, but Cisco insisted that Fabian was over Natasha and ready to dip his toe into the dating pool again.

Fabian was an unusual-looking man, with a low forehead and madly bushy eyebrows, but the widest smile and perfect teeth. He was a tiny bit on the short side, but I didn't mind that. He had longish dark hair and a great sense of humour. He was a high school English teacher and rented a tiny studio in Greenwich Village. He also had a second job, teaching deaf kids how to swim. Dad was heavily hinting that I should settle down and start a family. I wasn't too sure. I liked my independence, and I was now an assistant editor, which was more satisfying than interning. I earned peanuts but I finally got to work on some copy. I hoped to move to their fiction imprint, but it seemed like so did every other assistant in New York.

Much as I enjoyed my independence, I wanted someone to share meals and watch TV with. I had gone to the movies on my own a lot. Apart from Milo, my longest relationship thus far had been four months, and I didn't have high expectations, but I fell for Fabian hard. He fulfilled all my desires, including the more intimate ones. I liked everything about him, and I learned to trust again. I told him all about Milo and what he had done to Ruby, our family being split down the middle, and Ruby's subsequent alcoholism. He was horrified and angry on my behalf, and even though I no longer cried about it, he encouraged me to go back to a therapist. 'You've been carrying around that guilt for years, guilt for bringing him to your home, for not believing your sister, for not being able to talk to her. You should see someone.' And so I did.

I didn't think it would help. However, I was able to rationalize everything, break down every part of the fallout, and realized that there was nothing I could have done. She didn't say it directly, but my therapist clearly disapproved of my mother choosing one daughter over the other. I tried to explain that it wasn't like that, but when I thought about it, Mom could have tried harder to get me to Dublin and she needn't have done the whole move so suddenly. We were all still in shock. Dad had his church community and his business. Mom was right to take Ruby away to distract her from everything that had happened, but I needed the distraction too. I hadn't wanted to go at the time, but she could have insisted. We could have gone to Dublin for the summer and then moved to another city where Dad had a church. I wondered why that had never been an option.

30

Ruby

I called the baby Lucy after her great-grandmother. She was such a perfect child, latched on to my breast easily, slept on schedule, rarely cried, gave us a real smile when she was about six weeks old. I felt like I was being rewarded for . . . what? I didn't know.

Mom was helpful. She was only too delighted to have a baby to coo over. When we took Lucy to see her namesake for the first time, we managed to wedge her into the crook of Grandma's good arm and the two of them stared deeply into each other's eyes. It was beautiful to watch, and there were four generations of us in the room that day.

Lucy changed my life in a way I hadn't imagined. It took quite an adjustment. In those early weeks, she was like an extra limb and a lot of work, but I didn't begrudge a second of it. When she woke several times a night, I fought the exhaustion and relished looking at her beautiful face, which changed from day to day as the wrinkly newborn look smoothed out into peachy cheeks topped by a tuft of white-blonde hair. Mom thought she looked like me. We never speculated about who the father was, but I'd seen photos of me as a baby and Lucy was much more beautiful.

Despite all the exhaustion, I made it to my AA meetings two or three times a week. Jack had texted me to ask how the baby was doing, and I asked Mom to buy Jack a new jacket to replace the one I'd destroyed on the way to the hospital. We arranged to have coffee after the next AA meeting. I had Lucy strapped to me during the meeting, sitting near the exit, ready to bolt if she started to cry.

In the café, I thanked Jack for taking me to the hospital (and for later rescuing my car and leaving it at Mom's apartment). I could tell he was smitten by my daughter, and I felt proud, but then he asked, 'I suppose the father isn't on the scene?'

I immediately grew defensive. 'I don't think that's any of your business.'

'I'm not judging you,' he said.

'I've decided to raise her on my own – well, with Mom's help.' I was frosty.

'That's great. It's cool that you have her support.' He was contrite.

'Yes, I'm lucky, I guess. What about your family?' When he had shared in meetings, he had never mentioned parents or children or siblings, and now I wondered why not. Families were usually part of every recovery story.

His face darkened. 'I have parents, but I don't know if they're dead or alive, and I don't care. I had a sister but . . . but she died.' His face was strained with emotion, and he kept it at bay by shaking a rattle at Lucy, who burbled obligingly at him.

'I'm sorry to hear that. It must be tough.'

'It is.'

Jack's backstory was grim to say the least. His father had been physically abusive with him and his mother had squandered the money he had earned as a child actor. At one point his mother had chaperoned him when he was cast in a fairly big role, filming in LA, when he was ten years old. She abandoned him on arrival, and he stayed in his trailer on his own on location in the desert, or in hotel rooms, preyed upon by a persistent producer, until

Jack attacked him with a broken bottle. It was all hushed up, but production stopped and Jack was sent home. His mother had no idea why, but Jack was greeted at home by an angry father who broke his arm and three ribs for losing the part. Jack was determined from a young age to be free of both parents and became the sole guardian of his little sister when he was just eighteen, but she was killed in a car accident four years afterwards.

We had a lot of shared interests. He ran a private acting school in the south inner city. He had given up acting a few years ago when his booze and coke addiction made him too unreliable to cast. His agent, Svetlana, was his mother figure. She had paid for Jack to go into Longhurst. He was paying her back slowly over the course of years, but he was also talent-spotting for her among his acting students.

Over the next few months, Jack became a good friend. I eventually moved back into my newly renovated home two months later than planned.

In AA meetings we talked a lot about forgiveness. Forgiving others and forgiving ourselves. That was Jack's stumbling block. And mine. He could not forgive his parents for their violence and neglect. He blamed himself for his sister's death. The day she died he had been too hungover to collect her from school. She should never have been in the neighbour's car. I knew that guilt and the inability to forgive oneself. I could never explain why out loud, but I understood him more than he realized.

In September, I went back to college with renewed intentions. I expressed milk every morning, and sometimes if that didn't work, Mom would bring Lucy into college so that I could feed her. The first week was the hardest. I missed Lucy and nearly gave up altogether. Some of my fellow students loved the scandal of having an alcoholic mother in their midst, but most were kind. Lindsay Dillon let me know that she was glad I had cleaned up my act. There were others too. My college friends Jane and Sinéad were exceptionally helpful. They took it upon themselves to make sure I was eating properly and to call me on weekends. I wasn't friendless in college. Some people thought it was cool to hang out with someone like me. But my AA family had become much more important. They were my first port of call when I felt overwhelmed, and I often did.

There was a social worker in Trinity who helped me navigate all the necessary supports I would need, and Mom stepped up in a way she never had before. I think she was delighted to be useful. Mom insisted she was well able to take care of a newborn. She still had a part-time job as a school administrator that she loved and I guess the school loved her too. They were flexible. She worked four half-days per week and was allowed to arrange her hours around my college classes. When Lucy was six months old, she would join a daycare nursery in college.

Tentatively, I began to make real friends in college. I sought out Lindsay and apologized to her and Stuart. Stuart had moved into Lindsay's apartment. They accepted my apology and wished me well with parenthood. I had a reputation to live down at college. At first, the old drinking crowd thought I wasn't drinking because of the baby and, while that was partly true, I was quick to tell them I was in recovery now. Thankfully, they drifted away.

Jack relapsed only once in that first year, when his mother died. He heard about it from a distant cousin. He didn't turn up at any meetings for a few days and, when I asked around, nobody had seen him. When that turned into two weeks, I texted him. He didn't reply. I was worried. I didn't know who his sponsor was – in fact, I wasn't even sure if he had a sponsor. People often took their time finding the right person.

I didn't know whether I should call his colleagues at the

acting school or his agent, Svetlana, but after three weeks he turned up at a meeting, red-eyed and dishevelled. He admitted to his relapse and asked for support from the group. It was hard for somebody like Jack to humble himself like that, but he knew he had thrown away a whole year of sobriety. It was only after that meeting that I began to see him in a different light. He broke down in the meeting and told the story about his mother in LA. Now she was dead, and he still couldn't forgive her. He was vulnerable that day.

I took him back to my house, made him a proper meal and let Lucy crawl all over him. There was no question of anything romantic happening between us, but that was his first time in my house. I explained it had been my grandma's and showed off my new extension. He asked me who had paid for my stay at Longhurst. I told him about Dad, the pastor and investment broker.

'You have never had to worry about money, then?'

I hadn't realized how privileged I was. Obviously, I knew that I was wealthier than most people in my class in school and college, and in AA rooms, but when Jack began to explain the sacrifices he had made to put food on the table for his little sister, Barb, I could understand how oblivion might often have been the better option and how that downward spiral was inevitable. He had no safety net. He was not equipped or mature enough to look after himself at that time, let alone a little girl seven years younger than him. The example his parents had given him of how to look after a child was terrible, but he tried his best. He refused to pull her out of school for acting jobs that came up. He felt terribly uneducated because of the amount of school he had missed. But without acting income from Barb, and his own sporadic earnings and then his addiction, they fell into poverty. I had never known poverty. I thought for the first time about how blessed I was. I'd never had to struggle financially for anything.

The Bank of Dad had paid for my rehab and the house extension. And I still received a generous monthly allowance.

Jack was quick to get back on the wagon. He found out that his father was in some grim nursing home on the edge of an industrial estate. He was torn about whether he should go and see him or not. I offered to go with him if he wanted but he said no. He tortured himself for months, but he did go in the end. Later, he told me his dad was a shrivelled-up husk of a man in a bed. He had no idea who Jack was but smiled at him when he came in. Language was beyond him, but he grinned happily when Jack said hello. He reached out and put his hand in Jack's. There was going to be no apology, no acknowledgement of the damage and chaos he had wreaked on two young lives, but Jack said it was hugely emotional for him. He was able to tell his father he forgave him and emerged into the sunlight feeling at peace for the first time. He never visited again and heard he had died a few weeks later.

It was strange how interacting with Lucy was a kind of therapy for Jack. He brought me many books on childcare and development from the library, but it seemed he had always read them first. He often said he wanted to be a dad, but he was afraid of getting it wrong because he had such poor examples for parents.

31

I graduated with an honours degree in Drama and Theatre Studies, which was a miracle considering I'd had a baby and a spell in rehab while my college mates all took up opportunities to travel and take film and theatre roles. Professor White told me that other mothers made it work, that being a mother had taught me the discipline and responsibility that I had not been able to learn from him. 'Life lessons come in all sorts of ways, but you have come through and deserve congratulations,' he said. I beamed with pride, but I was prouder of my child-rearing and my recovery.

By the time Lucy was a year old, I had successfully weaned her off breast milk to give myself a little freedom, and she graduated to whole milk without too much resistance. I know I was later than most mothers to do that, but I had an extra reason. Any alcohol I drank would go straight into Lucy's system and, if I was breastfeeding, I couldn't drink. But one year was enough. Mom booked two weeks' holiday with her friends straight away. I was a little alarmed. I knew I needed to go it alone as a mother, but I hadn't thought I'd be totally on my own. It was tough. Lucy was a delight, but she was hard work. I hadn't had a full night's sleep since she was born. She cried and cried and cried the first night I placed her in her own room. It was well past time. I cried too but I waited it out until she cried herself to sleep. During the day, she cried a lot. She was restless and squirmy in my arms. She was alert, looking around, probably wondering where Mom was. Me too.

Sinéad and Jane came to the house bearing a home-made casserole and bags full of shopping, including nappies and baby wipes, fresh fruit and ready meals, and a bottle of sparkling lemonade. Their thoughtfulness took me by surprise. I guess crying down the phone to Sinéad the night before because I had literally spilt milk was received like an SOS. They ran a bath for me and changed the sheets in my bed and the baby's crib. They amused and fed Lucy for about two hours while I bathed and napped. When I got up, we toasted my graduation with lemonade, and I felt lucky and blessed. Sinéad was going to London the following month to try to get an acting agent there, while Jane had won her first role in a touring show around Ireland.

I admit that part of me felt left out. I should have been embarking on a career by now but there was no way I was going to put Lucy into full-time daycare yet. I had a few people I could call on as babysitters – my lovely neighbour Helen, and another teenager from the house opposite had offered too – but I thought it would be easier if I stopped going to AA meetings so often. Yes, they helped me stay sober but the emphasis on forgiveness and honesty and making amends were things I could not reckon with. I made up my mind. I was going to have to give up AA. I was sure I could stay sober without it, but I couldn't continue to live a lie with my AA family. I would have to do without them.

I kept myself busy. I started going to auditions, which was tough when you had a child and no agent. All my female college friends went for the same roles, but those with agents were more likely to hear about auditions than those of us without. I would generally hear about these shows through my former classmates. My accent didn't help. It was frustrating that I could do every accent except an Irish one – in fact, in my drinking days, I often pretended to be French or Russian for whole days while on a binge. No agent would take me on because I had become an infamous drunken liability during my college years. It was a label that was hard to shake off. On a few occasions, I'd have lunch with Jane or Sinéad and then bump into them the next day at an audition. The friendships started to become strained. There were few enough roles being cast for theatre work and having to directly compete with friends was tough.

Eventually, I got a supporting part in a stage show and, thankfully, as a result of that, I was introduced at the after-party on opening night to an agent who was also in recovery. We found ourselves leaving for the cloakroom at the same time and struck up conversation. Daphne was honest and upfront. I warmed to her immediately. She was rebuilding her agency after losing a lot of her clients because of her addiction. We were a perfect match. After that, the stage parts got bigger, though they were still few and far between. Still, I was slowly losing my bad reputation. Daphne tried to convince me to audition for TV and film roles, but I never wanted to be on TV. 'You know you are reducing your potential earnings by ninety per cent,' she said. I didn't care. I was still in hiding. I didn't want to take the chance of turning up on a TV screen in Boston.

I stopped going to AA meetings altogether. Nasrin said that she couldn't continue to sponsor me if I wasn't going to do the programme. I told her that I couldn't get past the forgiveness part. I'd told Nasrin about the incident. Not the real one – I'd told her I couldn't forgive my rapist. She urged me to pray for him. She didn't know that I thought of him every night. I asked if we could remain friends and she said yes, as long as I was sober. I tried to stop myself thinking about it and Lucy certainly kept me on my toes. I could stay sober for her. I attended my last meeting in January 2008.

Jack called and pleaded with me to come back. He was adamant that I would never recover on my own. I pointed out that I wasn't the person who had relapsed after a year of AA.

He hung up and I immediately called him back to apologize. There were lots of ways to stay sober, I told him. Thousands of people were sober without going to meetings. He wanted to see me, so we met in a café in Inchicore. I think he was relieved to see me looking well. He admitted that he thought I'd already relapsed. Lucy sat in his lap and gurgled happily. She was always pleased to see him.

32

Erin

Fabian was a great listener. The relationship wasn't moving fast enough for me, though. I wasn't sure he was the marrying kind. I waited for him to suggest moving in together, but despite dropping hints, he either didn't get them or got them but ignored them. In 2007, on the six-month anniversary of our first date, I invited him to move into my small apartment. It was only marginally bigger than his, but by New York standards it was okay. I had more storage space and a tiny outdoor terrace on the roof. I had stayed over in Fabian's a few times, but his bed was narrow, and he didn't have a lot of stuff. He was hesitant. How would it work financially? I told him that what he paid in rent would cover utilities and he'd still have money left over for saving. I was made vulnerable by his hesitance. When I said saving, I had meant for the wedding we were going to have. I might as well have proposed. After a week of talking it over back and forth, he agreed. Nobody was more excited about this than Aunt Rachel. She adored him. She came to New York regularly and took us to lunch in upmarket restaurants. We never knew the celebrities she pointed out. They were painters or musicians of her own era. Sometimes I pretended to recognize them just to make her feel good.

Dad liked Fabian too. We went to dinner together when Dad came to visit, and although he didn't quite approve of us living together without a wedding ring, I had to remind him I was twenty-six years old, and Fabian made me happy. He accepted I was an adult and treated Fabian like a son. He and Dad liked to get into theological discussions.

I didn't dare raise the subject of children, but one day out of the blue three months later, Fabian started talking about names for kids. A friend of his had named his son Bart, as in Simpson, not as in short for Bartholomew, and Fabian asked me what I would call 'our children'. He was talking casually as he stirred more parmesan into the risotto, but I knew him well enough by now to know that he never made eye contact when he was making big decisions. I played along, throwing out comical names to make him laugh. A few days later, he went missing for several hours in the evening. I couldn't get him on his phone. He came home after ten, claiming he'd been at a PTA meeting that he'd told me about. I knew it was a lie, but I let it go. Perhaps he was planning a surprise proposal.

But that was just the beginning of the lies, sudden absences, trips away with the guys. It took me a while to realize because I desperately wanted everything to be okay. I'd convinced myself I was in love, but after another two months I knew that he was emotionally withdrawing from me. I confronted him. The worst part was that he was relieved to be caught. He would have happily lied to my face for God knows how long. He was seeing his ex-fiancée, and he was still in love with her.

I admit I lost it. I threw his stuff out into the hall and changed the locks. Cisco was embarrassed. He said he'd planned his wedding outfit. I told him bitterly that he could wear it to Fabian's wedding to Natasha. Aunt Rachel called Fabian up and unleashed holy hell upon him. I didn't try to stop her.

There was something wrong with me. I attracted bad men, and I could no longer trust myself. Once his stuff had been cleared out, I was relieved to find that I did not miss him.

I missed the companionship, I missed the affection, but I did not miss Fabian. My heart was surprisingly intact. Maybe I hadn't fallen in love after all. Maybe I wasn't capable of it. Milo's fault.

Once again, I buried myself in work. I had been promoted to editor, but I had to do all the assistant administration work as well. I was still at the Schoolroom imprint and there was no sign of me moving to the fiction side of the publishing house. It was frustrating but I was forced to accept it, having no other alternative. The publisher acted like one big family when it suited them, but I felt like an unwanted step-grandchild. I decided to look around to see how other publishing houses worked.

I got a phone call from Margie Kelly a few weeks later. I couldn't believe her audacity. I hung up when I realized who she was but somehow she got my cellphone number and she kept calling over and over again. Eventually, I took the call. She begged to meet me. She said she had some information I needed to know, but I said no. I told her never to call me again. In the aftermath of Fabian, I was still at a low ebb. I was vulnerable and spent two sleepless nights wondering if Milo was going to be released early. Was he going to try to reconnect with me? Was he out already? I called her back and agreed to meet in NYC. She said she'd take the bus.

Margie was two years older than Milo, but in the intervening years, she hadn't changed that much. Her dark hair was lightened, and she was wearing no make-up at all. She chain-smoked as we walked through Central Park, lighting one cigarette from another. We eventually sat down at an outdoor café.

'You know he didn't do it, right?' was her opening salvo. 'Somehow, they got a fake DNA result and framed him.' Milo had served almost eight years by now.

'Margie, first of all, that is impossible and I'm leaving if this is how the conversation is going to go.'

She wouldn't stop. 'Did your sister have a pair of denim shorts? Cos that's what she was wearing when my brother knocked on your door that day.'

As she continued to talk, I shouted over her. 'Margie, DNA does not lie. You can convince yourself as much as you want but it doesn't change facts.'

'Your pop, though, he's got money. He could pay to get the right results.'

I grabbed her arm. 'You have to stop sending those letters, okay? Stop it. You're not going to persuade anyone. They're pathetic.'

'What? What are you talking about?'

'Don't bother trying to pretend, Margie. I know it's you.'

'No idea what you're talking about. But your dad and the DA's office. They're connected. They faked the DNA evidence.'

'My father would never do that. You know that he liked Milo? We all loved Milo. I was going to marry him. Did he tell you that? Right up until the day that he raped my kid sister.'

'But –'

'Stop, Margie, this is pointless. Your brother is responsible for so much pain. Ruby has –' and then I stopped myself speaking further.

'Where is she? How come she's not turning up on Google?'

'Are you trying to find her? Why? Leave her alone. She's had a tough time.'

'So has Milo, as I'm sure you can imagine.'

'I don't think about him any more,' I lied.

'He's sick.'

'So?'

'You don't care?'

I said nothing.

'It's serious. He could die in there.'

'Milo has cancer?'

'Yeah.'

I inhaled deeply as a lump formed in my throat. 'I'm sorry to hear that.'

'You could go see him.'

'I can't, I'm sorry.'

'He wants you to go see him.'

'No.'

I got up from the table and walked towards the exit. Margie shouted after me. 'First your sister has him incarcerated and kills my ma, and now you're going to let him die in there? He still loves you. But you're fucking monsters, both of you. And the DNA is wrong. I don't care what you say.'

I broke down in the office and had to hide in the printer room for half an hour before I could pull myself together to go back to my desk.

The next day, Grandma died in Dublin. I managed to get cover at work. I went to Boston, and Dad and I flew to Dublin together from there. Mom needed us. And I had not met my niece, Lucy, yet. I had stubbornly refused to go to Dublin, but she was eighteen months old now and I was forced to accept that Ruby wasn't ever coming home. Kathy wanted to come to Ireland too, but Dad told her it wouldn't be appropriate. We left her sulking with her knitting needles.

On the six-hour-long flight to Dublin, I asked Dad about the trial, how the DNA was gathered, and how it was matched to Milo. The mere mention of it made him wince. I had not been present for it, except to be a witness at the end, one of the worst days of my life. Dad opened a miniature bottle of bourbon. 'I'm not sure, but in court the forensics woman who had tested the semen found inside your sister said the DNA matched with Milo's. It was a 99.2 per cent match.' He took a long sip of his drink. 'I don't know whether they match it to a hair sample or a swab or his blood. Some of the evidence, I couldn't stay to listen to it. It was distressing, and I felt bad too, you know. I let him stay over in our house. It's part of my faith to trust everyone, but it let me down when it came to that man. Your aunt Rachel stayed for the whole thing. She said that if it wasn't for the DNA, he could have got away with it. I feel bad for calling the cops and for the fact that Ruby had to go through the whole court case, but at least he won't do it again. I think it may have re-traumatized her and led to her alcoholism, but there was no other way to stop him legally.'

I asked him casually how well he knew the Boston District Attorney.

'Met him a couple times at the Mayor's Gala and at some fundraisers. I didn't take to him much. Seems like a slippery kind of guy. A sniffer.' That was the term Dad used for a cocaine user. By the way he was talking, I knew he would not and could not have interfered in any way in the trial. I already knew via Google how DNA was sampled and tested and matched. I only asked Dad to see if there was any way he could have meddled in the process to make sure Milo was found guilty, but Dad was nothing but honest, and if he ever bent the rules, it was to benefit somebody. Now I knew there was no room for doubt. Margie was wrong. I felt bad for her, but she was another victim of Milo. She just didn't know it.

I told Dad about Fabian. He was furious with him for his betrayal. 'That man has no right to call himself a Christian.' That got me thinking about my own Christianity. Was it the right thing to do to turn my back on Milo when he was sick? Maybe I should advocate for him? I asked Dad. At first, he was horrified, but then he suggested that we pray together. We did so with clasped hands, in our aeroplane seats, as the bar trolley passed us by. After about ten minutes, Dad loosened his grasp.

'Let Ruby decide,' he said.

'What?' I gasped.

'Tell her the truth and ask her if it's okay to visit. If you do it behind her back, she might be hurt again, and we don't want to risk her sobriety.'

I felt a stab of guilt. Maybe Ruby would say no.

33

Ruby

'I don't get it,' said Jack.

'Get what?'

'Why you're an alcoholic?'

'There doesn't have to be a reason.'

'There's nearly always a reason but you had every opportunity, every privilege.'

'My parents divorced,' I said.

'Yes, you told me that – fairly amicably, you said.'

'Did I say that? Maybe it wasn't that amicable.'

He sat up straighter, lifting Lucy over his shoulder so that she was facing away from us, as if to give us privacy.

'Did you witness some domestic violence? Or were you on the receiving end?'

I halted, not sure what I should say. 'No, nothing to do with that. The divorce wasn't bad. But I moved here to Dublin with Mom while my sister stayed in Boston, long before they divorced.'

He turned his head to one side, cradling Lucy's head in his hand. 'But why?'

'Genetics, I guess. My mom's brother is a recovering alcoholic too.'

'Yeah, but everyone has a story. Did your parents love your sister more than you?'

This was way too close to the bone.

'There was an incident,' I said and paused. I did not want to tell Jack this lie. He was becoming important to me. He waited, saying nothing. 'I was sexually assaulted by my sister's boyfriend, is that enough for you?' I stood up and took Lucy back from him, strapping her into the stroller beside our bed. She started to wail.

'I . . . I'm sorry. I had no right to pry. Ruby, I'm sorry.'

'You wouldn't let it go, like a dog with a bone. There was no need to be so intrusive.'

'I'm sorry.'

I had my jacket on and my baby kitbag over my shoulder. I left Jack to pay the bill and walked out. Tears filled my eyes. Why did I lie to Jack? I walked away and took the long route home, hoping that he wouldn't follow me. My phone buzzed in my pocket. I knew it was him. I wasn't going to answer it. When I eventually got home, there were two missed calls from Jack and five from Mom.

I called Mom to learn that Grandma had died a matter of hours earlier. Fresh tears blurred my vision. I asked my neighbour Helen to look after Lucy while I drove to the hospital to be with Mom. Poor Grandma had had a sudden stroke after lunch in the care home. It was severe, Mom said, she couldn't have survived. Now she was being taken to the hospital morgue. Mom was inconsolable but I was strangely okay. It didn't occur to me to have a drink. I was too busy. I had to step up and call Uncle Dennis in Australia. I called Erin in New York and Dad in Boston. He was, I think, genuinely sad to hear the news.

'I'll come,' he said, 'your mother will need support at a time like this, and you too.' He coughed. 'Besides, I'd like to meet my granddaughter.'

I was pleased. He had been begging me to come to

Boston – 'Kathy wants to meet you, and I'd love to see your baby' – but I made excuses every time, and it was never convenient for him to come to Dublin either. I had a mental block about Boston. I didn't want to bump into anyone from my past.

For a few days, despite the sadness of the circumstances, it felt like my whole family was pulling together for the first time since before the incident. Mom was desperately upset. I was too but I was being the adult, talking to the undertaker and to Grandma's parish priest, selecting music, choosing clothes for Grandma to wear in the coffin. I deferred my grief until later. There was a lot to be done, and Mom was too upset to do much. It would be a full nine days before we could hold the funeral. My uncle was managing the mining company he worked for in the middle of nowhere, a five-hour drive from Perth, and had trouble getting someone in to replace him while he came home for his mother's funeral. I organized for Dad and my uncle, when they arrived, to stay in a hotel nearby and Erin stayed with Mom first and then a few nights with me.

Lucy did not cover herself in glory the first time she met Dad over at Mom's place. She had an ear infection and was red-faced, screaming, writhing and generally inconsolable, but Dad made all the right noises about how cute she was. We went for a walk with Lucy in the stroller and she eventually cried herself to sleep.

'I wonder if I made a terrible mistake, putting you through a court case at such a young age, and then letting you and your mother go like that . . .'

'What do you mean?'

'I should have tried harder to keep the family together. And the court case, having to relive the . . . the happenings of that day. But that boy had to be punished. You understand that, right?'

Could I tell Dad the truth? I didn't have to tell him that Mom knew. I let the silence grow until he said, 'There might have been other ways of dealing with Milo Kelly.' He spat the name.

'Like what?' I whispered.

'I wanted to kill him at the time, but my faith wouldn't let me. I called the police, but I never asked you what you wanted and I'm sorry about that. I think the whole experience of the trial, when you were so young, I think that might be the root of your, you know . . . problems.'

'You mean my alcoholism and cocaine addiction?'

He winced. 'Yes. What would you have wanted to happen?'

'Nothing.'

'I mean, what would you have wanted us to do about the . . . assault?' He found it as hard to say as I did.

'I didn't want anything to happen.'

He shook his head, confused. 'You would have liked him to get away with it?'

'Maybe.'

He stopped in his tracks and turned to face me. I couldn't meet his eyes. For the rest of his stay, Dad was perfectly polite and civil, throwing money at me 'for Lucy'. We never discussed it, or anything even vaguely personal, again. He couldn't have suspected, and the DNA evidence was undeniable. I don't know what he thought, but I hadn't eased his guilt. I'd made him feel worse.

Erin was more beautiful than ever. She had cut her long blonde hair and grown out the bangs, and it suited her. After the first few nights in Mom's place, she came to my house. 'I guess you'll own this house now, right?' she said.

'Really? I haven't thought about it.' It hadn't occurred to me.

'I don't mind; Dad has a fund for both of us. You might have to buy out Uncle Dennis, but I'm sure Dad will help with that.'

'Do you ever think about how rich we are?' I asked Erin.

'Sure, we got everything we wanted,' she replied in a flat tone.

'Erin, are you okay? You seem a little off.'

'Please, don't you start. Saima is constantly checking up on me.'

Saima had been Erin's best friend in school. 'You and Saima are still friendly? That's good. Did she move to New York?'

'No, but I see her every time I go home for a weekend. She's married with two kids. Are you not still in contact with anyone from Boston?'

I shook my head. 'All my friends are Irish. Tell me about Saima.'

'I don't think she's happy. She was desperate to have a sexual relationship. She married Binto so she could have one.'

'You don't still believe in that virginity oath, do you?'

'No. Besides, I'm well over twenty-one. I've been dating on and off for years, but I've given up now.'

'Oh no, why?'

'Fabian. He cheated, a few months after he moved in with me. I threw him out last week. You can't trust any of them.' Her voice wobbled.

We stared at each other before I turned away to put the kettle on. 'I'm sorry, Erin, I had no idea. That sucks.' I hadn't known she had a boyfriend.

'Would you like some tea or coffee?' I asked. 'I've got a proper Italian coffee pot. We have Dunkin's in Ireland now, you know? Better than Starbucks, right? But we have that too. We're in a boom, apparently.'

Happy to change the subject, Erin marvelled at the number of cranes she had spotted on the Dublin skyline when flying into the city. 'You certainly are. There are buildings going up everywhere. There was a whole feature about it in *The New York Times*.' We laughed at how Mom had always insisted that Ireland was not a third-world country despite what Dad said, and now it seemed very much to be a first-world country. Hotels and housing developments and factories were being launched every other day.

I wanted to hear about her life in New York City. She said it was tough and expensive. She had only seen Broadway shows a few times. I tentatively asked for news from Boston. Erin said she went home once a month. She'd met my friend Laquanda in Faneuil Hall with her boyfriend, who was a six-foot-seven basketball player. He was playing in reserve for the Boston Celtics. I was happy to hear that. I asked about our old neighbour Mr Delancy and his cactus collection, but he had died a year previously. She said home didn't feel much like home since Dad had married Kathy.

'What's she like?'

'Looks like Mom, but ten years younger. Dad tries to keep up with her. I doubt that he ever intended to move to Ireland, not even for retirement. Mom should have known that. But haven't you noticed how tired he looks?'

I had noticed, but assumed he was fighting jet-lag.

'He can't keep up with her,' Erin said. 'She wants to go bowling every Friday.'

'Wow, even we hated bowling.'

We laughed and the relief of the laughter made us both a little hysterical. And then our laughter fizzled away to nothing.

More sombre now, she said, 'We had a blessed childhood, didn't we?'

'I guess so.'

I didn't say what I was thinking, that she was smart and beautiful. I was the ugly duckling. I'd never felt blessed.

'Milo wants me to visit him in Whiteshore.' The sentence was lobbed into the conversation like a hand grenade.

'What?'

'I know, I was shocked.'

'But how did he ask you?'

'Margie tracked me down at work. She's angry.'

I couldn't help the redness flushing my cheeks. My heart was pounding. I couldn't speak.

'She said he's innocent and that you lied. He wants me to visit him in prison. She said he would never . . . have done that.'

I found my voice. 'Well, he did,' I lied.

'I know that. I believe you. His friends and family have given up on the appeal. They wanted the DNA tested in a different independent lab, but they were turned down. There is no new evidence.'

'What else did Margie say?'

'A lot. She repeated everything he said in court. She said he never tickled you and that you sat on his lap and tried to kiss him. She asked if you had a pair of denim shorts and, if you did, how would Milo even know about them?'

'I don't know,' I shouted.

I was flung back into the witness box behind the screen in March 2000, nearly eight years ago. Now my sister was Milo's public defender. I started to cry, deep heaving sobs. Lucy, in tune with me, woke up crying. Her wails grew louder as mine subsided. Erin hugged me and I felt worse.

'I'm sorry, Ruby, I should never have told you. You know I believe you. You probably wore those shorts in the garden that summer and he saw you wearing them. He's a pervert. Margie is mad. Especially after Mrs Kelly . . . Margie won't give up, but what the hell would she know? She didn't realize what her brother was capable of and can't accept it.'

The irony of her statement made me blush to the roots. I turned away to fill Lucy's beaker with fruit juice. When I turned back, Lucy was sitting comfortably on Erin's lap, grizzling.

'Why now?' I asked.

'What do you mean?'

'He's been in prison for eight years. Why is she coming to you now?'

'He's sick. Cancer. She's afraid he'll die in prison.'

'Oh.'

'I was thinking I might go. But only if it's okay with you?' Her eyes brimmed with tears.

'Yes, go.' Why was she crying?

Because of the delayed arrival of Mom's brother, Erin had to go back to Boston before Grandma's funeral, and Dad went with her. Erin got very little holiday or bereavement leave, and Dad had itchy feet. Kathy was calling him constantly. Dad had business to attend to and church on Sunday. Mom was grateful to him for coming. I said goodbye to Dad and Erin at the airport drop-off. Dad said I should come home for a visit soon, and Erin said I could stay with her in New York. I didn't commit. I had made my life in Ireland, lost touch with my friends. The Ruby I had left behind in Boston was not me. At least, I hoped not.

Uncle Dennis, when he eventually came, distracted Mom. It turned out that Mom and her brother had different experiences of Grandma. Dennis obviously wasn't a planned baby, arriving eleven years after Mom. The way he told it, he didn't get much warmth from his mother. Mom admitted that she had resented his intrusion into her life and especially when their dad died a year later of a sudden heart attack while on his way to the bus depot where he worked as a driver. The way Mom told it, Dennis took up all of Grandma's time and, as he got older, Mom was put in charge of him as Grandma tried to reclaim her life. That was why Mom took a job as a nanny in the US, in Worcester. She was doing the job anyway; she might as well get paid for it and earn a little independence and money. Mom and Dennis resented each other, and Grandma resented Dennis for driving Mom away. My saintly image of Grandma dissipated as I learned more about her rejection of her son. No wonder he was an alcoholic. Every family was messed up in some way, generations of us. But it wasn't genetic in my case. I was the one who broke my family.

The funeral went off without a hitch. The priest read a eulogy to a loving mother who capably brought up two children on her own after their father's death. I caught Dennis and Mom exchanging looks. The church was half full. My friends Jane and Sinéad came as well as Nasrin and Jack. I was glad to see Jack. I accepted his apologies this time. I had lied to him and then acted offended. I was the dishonest one.

Of my friends, only Jack came to the burial and to the small reception I had organized in a hotel. I knew he was checking up on me. I passed him the glass of sparkling water I was drinking. 'Taste it,' I said, 'no gin.'

'Any vodka?'

'No,' I said firmly. He was the one who had relapsed. But I guess by then we both knew there was the foundation of a friendship. I'd have checked on him too, if I'd known about his mother dying, but he hadn't told anyone.

A week later, Jack offered me some teaching work in his Academy. I was delighted. Lucy was eighteen months old and I needed to spend more time with adults. He asked me to devise a programme for first years. He warned me they were the trickiest. But he thought they might relate to me better because I wasn't that much older than them.

By now over her ear infection, Lucy showed off her new head-over-heels skills to Jack. He cheered, clapped his hands, and she copied him.

Mom and Dennis established a relationship over those days and promised to keep in touch with each other. Grandma was in the ground and I was heartbroken, but also relieved in a way. Now only Mom knew the truth. And Milo.

34

A few weeks after Grandma's funeral, out of the blue one day, Mom said, 'I wonder what would happen now if you confessed.'

We were in my local playground, watching Lucy playing on the slide, clambering up the ladder, sliding down, clapping her hands and laughing, before running back to take her turn and climb the ladder again. We'd been up all night because she had a temperature. She showed no sign of it now, but I was exhausted and completely unprepared for this bombshell of a statement.

'What do you mean?' I said, though I knew.

'Maybe they wouldn't give a young mother a prison sentence, or maybe it would be a very short one.' She stumbled over her words. She had been thinking about this. 'We could go back. I'd be there if you were sentenced, to take care of Lucy. I'm sure they wouldn't treat you so harshly. You were only sixteen years old.'

'Mom, no –'

'Do you ever think of Milo?'

'Yes, of course –'

She cut me off. 'Eight years. What would happen if you told the truth, Ruby?'

'Why are you saying this now?'

She shifted on the bench so that she was facing me.

'Mam's gone. I don't want to go back to Boston, but if I had to, I could. I'd confess my part too. Perhaps they'd only imprison me. I shouldn't have panicked. I should have told your father. He would have done the right thing, even if it destroyed everything he'd built. I don't think it's too late to do the right thing, Ruby.'

I beckoned Lucy to come and join us. I needed to use her to show Mom what she was suggesting I sacrifice. She climbed easily on to my lap. 'You're not thinking straight. Dad would never forgive us; Milo would sue us. You said at the time, Dad would lose everything, and what if we were both jailed, what then, Mom?'

She started to cry. She'd been crying a lot since Grandma died. 'We did a terrible thing, you and I,' she said.

'Mom, it wasn't your fault. You did whatever you could to protect me. It was a mother's instinct. I have a mother's instinct too and it's telling me to stay here with my daughter. There is no guarantee that either of us would get off with a light sentence.'

Lucy reached towards Mom and stroked the tears from her face. 'Granny sad?' she said.

'Yes, and it's Mamma's fault.' I wrapped her up in my coat and she was quiet. 'Mom, I'm so sorry. Please don't think about this any more. You're not to blame. And, you know, there's another way to look at this. They say that ninety per cent of rapists get away with it, either because the rapes are never reported in the first place or because they cannot be proven in court. It's most often a case of her word against his. If one innocent man goes to prison, doesn't that redress the balance a tiny bit? One or two wrongs don't make a right, but maybe a thousand wrongs do?'

'No. No, they don't. I can't force you to do the right thing and I can't do the right thing without you.'

'Mom, I'm sorry, but I can't take the risk of losing my daughter.'

'You never mentioned Erin, what it did to her.'

Erin hadn't crossed my mind. Now, I thought she might kill me if she found out. That's what I told Mom. That the truth would cause further damage to our family, our careers, the people who cared about us, the people we loved.

'It can't stay a secret forever,' she said as I drove her home. It was the most chilling thing she had ever said to me.

We stayed away from each other for the next few weeks, and then gradually we started talking again. We needed each other and Lucy needed both of us. There was a tacit agreement that we would not discuss it again.

35

I had always known that I was a bad person, ever since Kenny Carter paid me for my virginity, but now the thoughts that oozed around my mind became uglier than ever. If Milo had cancer, then he might die, and it would be over. Then there would be nobody but Mom left who knew the truth.

If Erin saw him, what could he realistically do? Repeat the same story he'd told in court? The DNA overruled everything he could possibly say. I think she was going out of curiosity. She didn't even know what kind of cancer he had. Poor Milo. Life had dealt him a particularly rough hand. And even though I had played a large part, perhaps he was always destined to die young. It's not like he caught cancer in prison. It was the luck of the draw. But then I remembered how kind he was, how sweet even after my misguided seduction attempt. His first instinct was to reassure me that I wouldn't have to worry. Little did he know then that my actions in the aftermath meant he would have to worry for the rest of his probably short life. I told Erin it was okay for her to go see him but that I didn't want to hear anything about it, and she was not to tell him or Margie anything about me. I was curious but I reckoned I was better off not knowing. She totally believed me. I didn't have to worry about Milo trying to persuade her that I was the liar.

Lucy was thriving, hitting all her developmental markers early. She had walked at ten months, and by the age of two she had an extensive vocabulary. I was working part-time at Jack's Academy, doing admin or teaching an improv class. I enjoyed it and refused the money when he tried to pay me. I couldn't help noting the look of relief on his face when I told him I didn't need the money.

Jack ran his private drama school on a shoestring, but I was aware that students were dropping out, or parents weren't paying their bills. He was having difficulty paying the rent on that building, and he had scrapped the plan to install air conditioning to keep it comfortable in the summer. He didn't have the money. The financial crash had arrived almost overnight. Nearly all acting work dried up. Voice-overs for radio ads were probably the most lucrative work you could get but fewer ads were being made.

Jack had had to let one teacher go already. It wasn't as if he had a huge staff. He never volunteered this information, but every time we talked around the summer of 2008, his brow was increasingly furrowed, and I worked at him until eventually he spilled the beans.

'I'm going to have to try and find a cheaper place,' he said. I was surprised. The Academy was in a mixed area, derelict buildings on one side of the street and a Georgian terrace on the other. Tacked on to the end of the terrace was the former cinema that Jack had turned into a drama school.

'It will be hard to find somewhere else with a stage and a rehearsal room.'

'I'm talking about my house,' he said. 'I'm in a mess. I haven't paid my rent for a while. I can't put the letting agency off forever.'

'I didn't realize things were that bad. Didn't you inherit anything from your parents?'

He looked at me. 'Like what?'

I had always assumed that Jack had a family home somewhere or at least a savings account. 'What about relatives?'

'My dad has a brother that I haven't seen since my sister's funeral.'

On the radio and in the newspapers, there was talk of imminent financial collapse, but I hadn't bothered listening too closely. I wasn't worried about my own finances. Strictly speaking, Mom and her brother owned Grandma's house that I was living in rent free, and Dad had never discontinued my allowance when I left college. He increased it after Lucy was born and had already mentioned the necessity of me having a permanent home.

As the weeks went on, the recession hit Ireland in waves. Every day there was news of another factory closing, young people emigrating and long lines at social welfare offices. Jack was talking of trying his luck as an actor in the UK. He went over a few times but his agent, Svetlana, did not have the contacts there that he needed. The big ad agencies in Dublin were resorting to animation or images instead of using actors because they were cutting costs as well. There were fewer films and TV dramas being commissioned or green lit.

In July of that year, I invited Jack for lunch. 'I got a notice to quit from my landlord and I'm thinking of emigrating,' he said, bouncing Lucy on his knee while she built a castle of Lego on the table in front of her.

'No.' I was vehement. Jack was probably my closest friend.

'No, Jack, that's naughty,' said Lucy, who could now throw full sentences together. We laughed and she looked up, surprised and pleased to have caught our attention.

'Move in here.' I didn't think about it before I said it, but although this was a small house compared to what I'd had in Boston, it still had three bedrooms.

'Move in here,' parroted Lucy absent-mindedly.

'As a housemate,' I said hurriedly. 'The box room is full of old junk that should be thrown out or moved up into the attic. You could live here.'

'I can't do that.'

'Why not? Think about it before you say no. My grandparents raised two children in this house, and that was before the extension.'

He looked me in the eye in a way that made me feel uncomfortable. 'Aren't we better off as friends?' he asked.

I was confused for a second and then I said, 'I'm not offering you a relationship.' I decided to bypass his embarrassment. 'If you can put up with living with me and a highly verbal toddler who now answers back, you'd be more than welcome.'

He coughed to clear his throat. 'I don't know, what if we don't get on? No offence, but you're a tricky character.'

'Jack, we only lived together once, for ten days, in rehab. I'm a different person now. We'll get on fine.'

Lucy piped up. Even though she hadn't appeared to be listening, she seemed to know exactly what was going on. 'You come live here,' she said to Jack, looking up at him with her shiny deep brown eyes.

He looked at her sternly. 'Will you put your Lego away before bedtime every night?' She nodded her head emphatically. 'Well, okay, I'll think about it.' He scooped her up and held her upside down, and her laughter took the embarrassment out of the moment.

Afterwards, I replayed the conversation in my head. I was disappointed that Jack still saw me as the nymphomaniac I used to be. He had taken the invitation as a come-on when all I'd been doing was trying to suggest a practical solution to his problems. I thought he knew me better by now.

Three weeks later, his landlord threatened to change the locks and left Jack with no choice. He literally had nowhere else to go. He had surprisingly few belongings: a suitcase and a few large boxes.

'Are you sure about this?' he said on that first day in August 2008.

'Yes. We're sure, aren't we, Lulu?' She nodded her head enthusiastically but, strangely, Lucy took longer to get used to the change than either of us. She would hide when he came into a room, bury her face in my skirts when he sat at our table. I think it was his baking skills that won her over in the end. Every Saturday, he would bake fresh gingerbread men, and she would squeal in delight. And then she would bake with him, and he would give her the jobs of sifting the flour and licking the spoon.

Having Jack around was a good thing. A positive male role model for Lucy and companionship for me. Jack wanted to make himself useful and he was handy. He fixed the boiler and the broken ring on the gas stove. And in the evenings, we watched his DVD collection with pots of tea or mugs of hot chocolate. I hadn't seen *The West Wing*, *The Wire* or *The Sopranos*, and Jack relished rewatching and getting me hooked. It became by far the best addiction I'd ever had. Jack still talked about recovery and, although it was annoying in the beginning because I thought he was trying to bring me back into the fellowship, I soon realized that it was his way to stay sober. If he talked the talk, he could walk the walk. It was probably good for me to hear it.

36

Erin

The smell was the first thing I noticed when I entered the Whiteshore Prison complex. Stale sweat, urine and decay. Normally you get used to a smell quickly, but this was cloying. I felt like I could taste it and it revolted me. The arrangement to visit had not been straightforward. I had to write to the prison to request to be added to Milo's visitors' list and then there was a two-week wait until I was approved.

The amount of bureaucracy and red tape to get into the visiting area took over an hour, but Margie had warned me about this.

There were rules about how to sit in the plastic chairs provided; some touching was allowed, though I had no intention of touching Milo or allowing him to touch me. My heart was pounding and I found myself feeling excited at the thought of seeing him. At the same time, my stomach was flipping and I was terrified of facing him. I had to be very cool. Like ice. I spotted him immediately. We were both nine years older than we had been the last time I'd seen him. Milo's sandy hair was streaked with silver at the sides, he was leaner in his sweatpants and shirt than I remembered, but the sparkling blue eyes were the same. He didn't look particularly sick. He stood up as I approached. A guard yelled at him to sit down. I sat in the chair opposite his, a white painted line on the floor the only thing dividing us. I could not tear my eyes away from his face, which seemed to express many emotions all at once – hope, desire, fear, confusion – and then he grinned. That familiar grin.

'I . . . I didn't think you'd come.'

I'd forgotten how deep his voice was. Many years previously, I had thrown out every memory of him, the love letters, the photos, the silly drawings, the small trinkets of affection. But here he was, older, and though this place had taken its toll on him, he was still handsome. I was momentarily stunned as we locked eyes.

'I heard you were sick,' I said.

A flash of angst crossed his face and the grin disappeared. 'I didn't do it, Eri, you know I didn't.'

He was the only person who ever called me Eri. I'd forgotten. I shoved the sweet memories aside. 'You're sick?'

'What?'

'Where is your cancer?'

'Can we not say hello first?'

'Hello. Where is your cancer?'

'I would never force myself on anybody.'

'I came because Margie said you had cancer.'

'Think about it. Why would I attack her? Your family were good to me. Why would I risk losing you, and them, and losing everything else I was working towards?'

I had to look away and ignore his words.

'Do you have cancer or not?'

'If I had raped her, wouldn't it have been easier for me to say it was consensual? I'm not saying your family did anything wrong but that could not have been my DNA. I did not have sex of any kind with your sister, she was just a kid. They made a mistake or the DA lied –'

I dragged myself up from the chair. This was pointless. A guard looked questioningly in my direction. Milo reached for my hand and pulled it, and the memory of his touch, the heat from his hand, now calloused and red, made me collapse back into the chair. I had to gather myself. I must not cry. I couldn't let him win. I looked at the guard, a nod to assure him that everything was okay. Then I snatched my hand back.

'You did rape her. DNA cannot be faked. It is impossible. You will never convince me otherwise. Now, do you have cancer or not?'

He dropped his head, and I realized then that it was a ruse. Margie and Milo had concocted this cancer story to make me visit him.

'More lies, Milo? Really?'

'It was Margie's idea. I'm not allowed to write to you. I needed to see you. You're still my girl, Erin.'

'Stop talking like that. I am not your girl. I don't know why you thought you could force me to come, use emotional blackmail like that. You know I only came because Ruby said I could –'

'You came because you still care.'

Did I? In the moment, I was utterly confused. Even though I wanted to leave, I found my feet wouldn't carry me away.

'Every single day, I've thought about you,' he said. 'In the beginning, I tried to hate you for not believing me, but –'

'Stop. I can't stay if you talk like that. You lied to get me here, or Margie did, and you went along with it. You're smarter than that, Milo. Why would you think that lying now would make me believe that you didn't lie then?'

'Please, I wanted to see you, to see if there was any chance –'

'Of what?'

'Of you believing me.'

'There isn't. You are a monster. You destroyed my family. My parents divorced. Ruby is an alcoholic –'

I faltered. I'd sworn to her that I would not reveal anything about her to him. The tears came.

'I'm sorry, that's tough, but none of it is my fault. My ma took her own life.'

'I'm sorry about that.'

'There's something wrong with your sister. You didn't lose anyone except me. Please stay a little longer. We don't have to talk about any of that, but please, don't go.'

I wiped the tears from my face with the back of my hand and, again, I saw the concern in Milo's face. I sat back in the chair. 'Your mother. She was a real lady.' He smiled a wan smile. I had to stop myself from reaching out and putting my hand on his cheek.

'Thanks for those care parcels. I really appreciate them.'

'What? I don't know what you're talking about.'

'Sure you do. Every month? I get these parcels with candy and socks and toothbrushes, stuff like that?'

I wasn't sure if this was another manipulation. 'I never sent you one thing, Milo.'

He looked puzzled and then disbelieving.

'If you say so.'

'I do.'

He changed tack. 'How are you, Eri? Are you still writing those amazing stories? You know how I loved them.'

I remembered that Milo never knew that the story he had submitted on my behalf had been accepted, and then withdrawn. I wasn't going to tell him. I shook my head.

'Why not? They were wicked smart stories. Why are you publishing other people's stories?' Margie clearly kept tabs on me for Milo. 'Where are you living? Do you have room-mates?'

'I live with my boyfriend, Fabian. We're getting married next year,' I lied.

His brows lowered. 'You love him, this Fabian?'

'With all my heart.' My eyes skipped away.

There was a short pause and then he said, 'Nah, you don't love him. It would be a big mistake to marry him.'

I couldn't say anything to that. Milo always knew when I was being evasive.

'Why now, Milo? Why did you contact me now?'

'It's been over eight years. I got my first parole hearing coming up next month. My guy says that if I confess to it, I could get out of here. But I'm not going to admit it because I didn't do it.'

'Well, then you're a fool,' I said, 'and please tell Margie to stop with the hate mail, she's wasting her time. I don't read them any more.'

'I don't know what you're talking about. Margie would never do something like that.'

'Yeah, well I never thought you'd do something like rape my sister, yet here we are.'

I saw anger then. 'I did not do that. I loved you.'

'Shut up.' It was all too much. I couldn't bear to stay any longer.

I got up to leave and he said, 'Don't go, Eri, please don't go. We can sit here and say nothing. You're still the most beautiful girl I've ever seen. Please, Erin.' I continued to walk away. 'Write your stories, don't waste that talent, write your stories, Eri.' I never looked back while I waited for the guard and heard him shouting as I went through the door, 'I never did nothing with your sister, nothing. I'll swear that on a stack of bibles until the day I die.'

I left and had to go back through all the gates and doors, and sign all the forms on the way out. It was a half-hour before I got back into the privacy of my car where I could cry like a child. I was done with Milo Kelly, the lying bastard. I hadn't thought that he was stupid too. Denying his crime would never go down well with the parole board.

37

Ruby

The Academy was hanging on by a thread and Jack was only just balancing the books. Then, finally, he got a lucky break. In February 2009, Svetlana, his agent, persuaded him to go for an acting job in a fantasy series shooting in Belfast, *The Round Table*. Jack got a strong supporting role, and it was a four-month shoot with a solid possibility of a second series and beyond – 'If I don't get killed off,' he said. The money was good. They were bringing in some A-listers from the US and every Irish actor worth their salt who looked like they could handle a sword, grow a beard or slay a dragon was hired. I couldn't uproot Lucy and didn't even ask Daphne about a role for me – she knew I would only do theatre. In any case, I hadn't acted in a year or so.

There were three months between audition and shooting, and Jack was working hard at the beard and working out in the gym. He was on the point of closing the Academy, but I persuaded him not to. He'd only be away for four months and if the show's producers' reputation was as good as its budget and it became a hit, his name might attract more students. It was a long time since he'd been a presence on TV. When I first met him, people in AA rooms used to say, 'Isn't that Jack Brady?' or passers-by would nudge each other as he walked down the street, but it was ages since that had happened. He had faded from the public consciousness. I could keep the Academy ticking over for him while he was gone. Lucy was in a kindergarten, and I knew the business well enough by now to handle it. It would take some juggling, but I could do it.

There was no question of him not taking the job. He couldn't afford not to, but he had worries about being away in a new environment, being around booze and inevitably cocaine, but he talked to his AA friends, and I wasn't worried about him at all. I knew he could do this sober. It was too important, and he knew it too. He had a plan for every eventuality: he was going to be honest with them all about his recovery, and there was a gym between the film studio and his apartment accommodation that he could escape to when the cast and crew headed for the bar. He also took a ton of books with him and had made contact with AA members in Belfast.

Jack was gone for the whole summer and I missed him. He would call from time to time and tell me about the bust-ups on set, the unexpected egos of bit-part actors. Lucy would constantly ask when he was coming home, but she chattered away to him on the phone too and whatever he said made her giggle. And then the calls petered out and I reckoned he was too busy, and besides, it wasn't as if we were a couple in a relationship. I never even thought about him that way until I got a five-word text from him.

Hey Rubes, I've met someone.

I felt my heart lurch. Well, maybe not my heart, but there was a sudden pain in my stomach as if someone had punched me. He must have seen that I'd read the message, but my feelings were too complicated to allow me to respond. I decided to reply like a male friend would.

Is she hot? What's her name?

Her name was Isobel Lucas, and I didn't have to google her. She was English, the leading lady in *The Round Table*, and had been Oscar nominated when she was a child. She'd been a Bond girl ten years ago. Maybe not A-list now but definitely B. I googled her anyway. She was thirty-four, divorced but rumoured to be dating one of the lesser known Baldwins. I dug further and found a Facebook fan page that showed her posing at beautiful locations, wearing couture clothing. On YouTube, I was able to see scenes from her films and TV series. She was way out of Jack's league.

I called Jack and quizzed him. He was besotted, and he didn't seem to understand that she existed in a different realm to us, though I kept those thoughts to myself. He told me they'd met first on the set but later he had spotted her at an AA meeting, and they felt a spark. I hadn't even known that I loved Jack before this gilded pixie arrived on the scene, but now I knew. I wanted Jack badly.

I also felt a spark of something that I hadn't felt for ten years. It was the way I'd felt that day when Erin had gone to New York with Mom. She had what I wanted. Now Isobel did.

Jack and Isobel had a weekend off and he wanted to bring her to Dublin, to stay in the Merrion Hotel. I guessed he was ashamed to bring her to our humble home. I played along, with *Delighted for you, dying to meet her.* I reminded myself that I was a trained actress. I was disappointed that he was going to spend much of the money he should have been putting towards the Academy on a five-star hotel for the weekend, but I went ahead and even made the booking for him. He wanted me to meet her. He wanted my approval. Why?

I insisted that he bring her out to the house. Jack didn't object at all, and I realized that it was I who felt the shame of living in a mid-terrace former council house. He didn't want to stay here with his new girlfriend in a single bed, with me and a toddler floating around. Why wouldn't he want to impress her with a fancy hotel? He had been contributing a lot more to the house since he'd taken this role. Lump sums were deposited in my bank account even though I had never asked for them. But he wanted to pay his way.

When she arrived, without entourage or limo or make-up, I was taken aback. Her dark hair was loosely scraped back into a ponytail. Without the flashbulbs, it was far less glossy. She looked nothing like the shiny person on Google or IMDb. She was wearing a pair of boot-cut jeans and an authentic Aran sweater beloved of tourists, but also practical for an Irish summer. She was no less beautiful, perhaps more so. I had piled on the make-up and had a blow-dry that morning in a salon. Lucy went straight for Jack, putting her hands up, demanding to be lifted. Jack let go of Isobel's hand.

'Isobel, meet Lucy and her mum, Ruby.'

She put out her hand and said, 'All right,' in a Cockney accent. I'd watched her in *Gosford Park* the night before and the crystal tones of her accent in that were nowhere to be heard. 'Your house is great,' she said, and I could tell she was being kind, but I also felt that she did not come from money and probably grew up in a house not too dissimilar to this.

'Hi, you're welcome,' I said and stood back from the door to let them pass into the open-plan kitchen. She was slim and at least six inches taller than me. Lucy reached out her sticky hands to grab one of Isobel's loose strings of hair.

'Lulu, no.' I was firm, but too late.

Jack said, 'Lucy, we don't hurt other people, do we?' and he said it in a stern voice that Lucy wasn't used to. I don't care that he was trying to impress Isobel, this wasn't the Jack I knew. Lucy's lip trembled and I lifted her from him while she sobbed.

'It's okay, Lulu. We know you didn't mean to hurt Isobel.'

'The poor little thing, I'm sure she didn't mean no harm,' said Isobel, making herself comfortable on one of the island stools.

I smiled sweetly. 'It's fine, isn't it, Lucy?' I said, and I nuzzled her neck until she giggled. Jack was uneasy. By trying to protect his girlfriend from my marauding three-year-old, he had given the impression that he could be overly strict with children. He desperately tried to remedy the situation by getting down on all fours and snuffling around my child like a dog. It was not a good look.

I offered Isobel some peppermint tea and Jack said he'd have a regular tea. We made small talk for an hour. She had grown up in a tower block in Brixton. From an early age, she sang and danced, first at her primary school and then later at stage school, as her mom cleaned houses to save the money to pay for her talented little girl while her dad worked as a Tube driver. She loved musicals and we bonded over that for a while, and then she left with Jack.

Later, Jack called me. It was about 9 p.m. 'I need to stay the night. Can I come home?'

'Of course. Have you had an argument with Isobel? We thought she was lovely.'

'I can't . . . I need to be home, okay?' There was desperation in his voice.

When he arrived, he told me that as soon as they got back to the hotel, while he went to buy a pair of shoes, Isobel had gone straight to the bar. He'd found her flat-out drunk on the bed when he got back. Jack tried to talk to her, but she wasn't making sense. She had said she'd been four years sober but now he wasn't sure if that was true. He couldn't stay with her.

A few hours earlier, I had added a miniature bottle of vodka to Isobel's pot of peppermint tea and warned her that the kick she might taste was lemongrass. I knew how easy it was to go back to drinking, because I had, several times. I was crafty about it. Waited until Jack was out for the day and Lucy was in kindergarten before I started. I would drink myself into a stupor and fall asleep, and then, on waking, I'd shower and change, eat a pack of Polo mints and an orange.

The first time it happened was an accident. I had called to Deirdre's house to collect Lucy from a play date, and Deirdre had invited me in to join a group of parents swilling wine. I accepted a soda, and someone offered me some salmon paste on toast. I tried it and it certainly tasted great. And on the way home, an hour later, I desperately wanted a drink. I stopped at an off-licence and bought a half-bottle of vodka. The rest of the day went to hell. I can't remember where Jack was, but he wasn't around that night. I know Lucy kept trying to wake me up, saying she was hungry. I let her have a box of dry cornflakes. When I woke on my bed about 10 p.m. I was horrified and had no clue what had driven me to drink, until Deirdre called me the next day to see if I was okay. After I left, Deirdre's sister, who had made the salmon paste, had boasted that the secret ingredient was vodka. Deirdre knew I was in recovery. I was furious but too ashamed to admit what had happened afterwards.

I had other episodes that were planned. Sometimes, life felt hard, and I knew I needed a little alcoholic release. I didn't consider these to be relapses, as they only lasted a day, and I could almost schedule them around Lucy and Jack's comings and goings. As far as Jack was concerned, I sometimes suffered from severe migraines, and if it was the weekend he'd be only too glad to take Lucy out for the day. They didn't affect my work or my relationships, though they sapped my energy, like a bad migraine might. It was a different kind of drinking than before, planned and controlled, but I still felt horrible afterwards.

Isobel would never suspect the tea. Jack had told her it was a sober house. We knew about each other's sobriety. Jack had talked me up as if I was some kind of guardian angel who'd been able to put a roof over his head.

When he came out to the house that night, he was distraught.

I feigned upset too, on his behalf. 'What was she thinking?' I said. 'She knows you're in recovery. Maybe she's one of those Hollywood types. You can't tell whether they're acting or not.' My own performance was worthy of an Oscar.

Poor Isobel went on a bender that weekend. Jack had to drive her back to Belfast on the Sunday night. She ranted and raved and blamed him for leaving her on her own in the hotel. She had a bottle of gin in her bag, and Jack had to throw it out of the car window on the motorway. He called the Second Assistant Director when he got back to Belfast. I don't exactly know the sequence of events, but Isobel Lucas was written out of the show. She was 'taking the rest of the year off' said the gossip columns 'because of a recurring throat infection'. Everyone, certainly everyone in the business, knew that was code for 'problematic'.

I will accept the blame for her slip, but not her relapse, although that might have been caused by Jack breaking up with her and then losing her job. Maybe it was all my fault, but she wasn't right for Jack. Later, he told me that she had a mansion in Essex, drove a Range Rover and kept ponies. They didn't have anything in common. Besides, she was an obstacle and she was in my way.

38

Jack came back at the end of the summer with a new contract for the next season. He had money to invest in the Academy and, he said, he should think about getting a place of his own. I turned to Lucy and said, 'Jack doesn't want to live with us any more.' She cried loud and long, and he had to rock her to sleep.

'I don't want you to go either,' I said tentatively.

'I'm grateful to you, Rubes, but I feel like a teenager in a single bed, and I'm in your way. You're young and beautiful and should be on the dating scene by now.' He had never said I was beautiful before. Nobody had. I was taken aback. I reached out and stroked his beard. I could see his surprise and then a smile that lit up his face.

'Jack, would you like to go on a date with me?'

'Are you serious?'

'Wicked serious.'

'But I thought you weren't interested . . . when I moved in, you said –'

I hushed him with a kiss on the mouth.

'I'm interested,' I said.

He put a waking Lucy gently on the floor and wrapped his arms around me.

'I've loved you from the day you gave birth,' he said. 'You were incredibly brave, determined to do it all on your own. You have guts, Ruby, but I thought as soon as you were properly sober that you would never settle for someone like me. I mean, socially, we're poles apart.'

I recalled sometime in the long-distant past eavesdropping on a similar conversation between Milo and Erin in the kitchen in Boston, but I banished the thought from my mind. Memories like this took root sometimes. Those were the days when I might have a slip and drink again.

'No,' I said, 'you were made for me. Besides, you didn't think Isobel Lucas was out of your league.'

He blushed. 'I was trying to distract myself from you. You have no idea how hard it has been to keep my distance –'

'Oh my God, how much time have we wasted?'

Lucy was sitting at the kitchen table. 'Ages,' she said like a little old wise woman who was resigned to our mutual blindness.

To give and receive love from a partner was a new experience for me. I'd always found Jack attractive, but a relationship was a whole new level. I finally understood what love was. Sex in a committed relationship was a new thing for me too, and I realized now that one-night-stand sex was the worst type of sex a girl could have. There was never any effort by those men to please me. With Jack, the first few times were almost frenzied because we had been holding back our hunger for each other, but gradually we got to know each other's bodies and what we liked and didn't. One time, Jack said that he never wanted to touch me the way I had been touched during the incident. I froze, which turned out to be the correct response, and he apologized and held me, and we never mentioned it again in the bedroom.

Six months later, we were married. We kept it small, a registry office affair. We didn't even tell my parents. Jack's family consisted of one uncle with whom he had no contact, but Svetlana came to be his best woman, and his sponsor, Graham, came along. Jane and Sinéad were there as witnesses and some of our friends who were actors and teachers from the Academy came too. We went for dinner after the ceremony to the Trocadero, in true theatrical style. We made Lucy central to the ceremony. It was Lucy that bound us together. My little angel child.

Afterwards, I called Mom and then Dad and then Erin. Mom and Dad were doubly disappointed. They had both met Jack and liked him well enough, but I hadn't told them we were dating. They also would have liked a church wedding. They would have to get over themselves. Erin wished us luck, but it was the mildest of congratulations.

We took a short honeymoon in Florida, a week in Walt Disney World, Orlando. It was as magical for us as it was for Lucy, walking hand in hand, the three of us, stopping for kisses and ice cream. We availed ourselves of the hotel's Kids' Klub babysitting service and had romantic dinners in outdoor restaurants by ourselves.

Jack wanted to adopt Lucy. It turned out to be more complicated than I thought. I had to produce a death certificate for Lucy's birth father. This was not going to be possible. Jack had casually asked a few questions over the years about the identity of Lucy's dad, and I had shut down the conversation, but a few months before the wedding I was able to admit to Jack that Lucy had been conceived at the height of my addiction and I did not know who her father was. He understood – he had also had a few encounters with women he could not recall. We told Lucy that she could call Jack 'Daddy' if she wanted. We tried to explain that he wasn't her real daddy. She was too young to understand everything, but 'Jack' was quickly replaced by 'Daddy'.

I gladly took Jack's surname, Brady. If I were Ruby Brady, I no longer had to hide like Ruby Cooper. I had avoided social media and photographs and I had adopted Ruby Bean for my stage name, a little homage to my hometown, even though no self-respecting Bostonian would call it Beantown. Ruby Cooper wouldn't be tagged in any photo, but I lurked online. I had accounts under fake names which I used to watch friends, ex-friends and enemies.

Poor Isobel Lucas, she occasionally popped up in made-for-TV movies, years after our encounter. If only I'd known that Jack already loved me. Another life ruined, at least temporarily. She went back into rehab according to TMZ and later married a producer and moved to LA. She'd also made a new career for herself as a screenwriter. She was happy. It all worked out in the end – I probably did her a favour.

39

Erin

Another year went by while I tried to forget about Milo, but the things he said could not be forgotten. Why would he have attacked Ruby in our home? Why not a girl in his own neighbourhood, why *my* sister? And how did he ever think he'd get away with it? He had told Ruby not to speak of it, but he must have known that she would be traumatized, she would have to tell us. Why hadn't he claimed it was consensual? I heard from Dad that at the trial Milo said he never even unzipped his pants. It was such a strange defence against such overwhelming evidence. The prosecutor's job was very easy.

The anonymous letters continued about once every two months. I didn't bother reading them and eventually they stopped. But then, strange things started to happen which made me wish I'd opened them. I was called into the boardroom at work and questioned about sending lewd photographs of myself to a male author who was edited by my boss, using my personal email address. I had no idea what they were talking about. The email address wasn't a match for my personal one but they demanded access to my work email. This horrified me. I had used my work email address for lots of things: buying lingerie online, bitching about my immediate boss to a colleague, searching various publishing houses for employment opportunities. They couldn't prove I'd sent anything to the writer, but my own emails were damning enough. They didn't take action – I guess because they couldn't verify I'd sent the photos, which were clearly Photoshopped. I was embarrassed, though.

A few weeks later, I was called in again. A colleague had anonymously reported me for having sex in the office with an unauthorized visitor after hours. I was outraged by this and demanded to know who the colleague was. They couldn't tell me, but word spread like wildfire and people from different departments were casually passing my desk on the daily. Nothing could be proven, and I guessed that the 'colleague' didn't exist.

The reputational damage was bad, and I worried about what was going to happen next. Margie had got bored sending letters to me and started to email my company instead.

Later, the texts started. She must have had a burner phone.

> I know where you live and I know where your dad lives, and where he preaches.

A week after I received that text, Dad called me from the hospital, distressed. There had been an arson attack on his church in Boston during a service. I left the office immediately and went to his bedside at Mass General. Kathy told me everything. Gasoline had been poured around the rear of the church, nearest the altar. Nobody saw a thing. Because the church was relatively modern, it had side doors as well as the traditional front door and was evacuated quickly and efficiently. Dad kept the congregation calm. But once the church was evacuated, he ran back into the maw of flames to save the tabernacle containing the chalice. Kathy screamed as she saw him dive into the fire. The fire station was only a few blocks away and fortunately the firemen rescued him, but he had severe burns on both hands that caused him lifelong pain. The fire was extinguished before it got into the main nave. Unfortunately, Dad didn't have security cameras around the church. Even after everything that had happened with Ruby, he trusted everyone and didn't think he had any enemies. I didn't think so either. But Margie had warned me.

I called her in a rage. 'Leave my dad alone. He didn't do anything.'

'Is that Erin? Fuck you.' She ended the call.

She didn't deny it.

I went to the church. The damage was bad, though the congregation were already talking about fundraising and rebuilding. Dad was sitting up in his hospital bed with his hands swathed in bandages like a boxer. I hadn't seen my dad cry since Milo's trial. I realized that the church was as important to him as his children. I called the cops on Margie and told them everything for the first time. A detective was assigned to the case, Irene Hernandez. Margie was smart enough to have an alibi: she'd been out of town when the fire started, and the cops searched her studio apartment and couldn't find any burner phone. She did not appear to own an old typewriter. They had also seized her laptop and found no sinister emails.

She called me in a screaming rage after Hernandez paid her a visit. 'Arson? What next? You won't rest until you've destroyed all of us. I'm warning you. Leave me alone. I did not send any letter to you or your office. If I never see or hear from you again, it will be too soon, you hear me? Leave me alone.'

She was angry, but she'd got the message. There was a text after that:

I didn't intend anyone to get hurt. I'm sorry. I went too far.

40

Ruby

My messy situations were now a thing of the past. I didn't drink again. I was happy and fulfilled in my marriage and determined to put the past behind me. I wrote down the rape story and simplified it. I rehearsed telling it. I almost convinced myself it was true.

I knew that if Milo had died of cancer I would have heard. I never asked Erin, but she would have told me, or Dad would have. I was nervous about what would happen in a few years' time when he'd be released. But I couldn't think about that.

Jack was getting more acting work. We agreed that I'd take over the Academy, while he would still be the figurehead. After the lease ran out, we rented another, more modern building which used to be a dance studio. It was perfect for our requirements and cheaper than the previous place. We lowered our prices and gradually started building up the profile again, particularly when some former students started to get work in film and TV in America. We renamed it the Jack Brady Academy.

The Round Table shot for only four months every year. As Jack's role was becoming more prominent, he got offered more work on other shows, some of it abroad. I would take Lucy with me most of the time and we'd visit him in Budapest or London or Prague or wherever the work took him. He didn't like to be away from home for too long.

Jack should have been fulfilled too but he wanted us to have a baby of our own. He had always talked about being a dad. I didn't want a second child, but I couldn't say that to him. I knew that second children could suffer from extreme jealousy and Lucy was perfect. Any other child I might have would be envious of her. Also, what if Jack loved his own child more than Lucy? I distracted Jack by saying now wasn't the right time. We needed to give Lucy time to adjust to our new relationship. Jack didn't think she needed time – he had been in her life since the day she was born – but he let it go for about six months until he said it was time to try again. I didn't object this time, but I was secretly on the pill. I was extremely careful about hiding it in places he would never look.

I would pretend to be devastated every month when my period arrived and he would comfort me, or if he was away, he'd send me flowers. He worked out when I'd be ovulating and would come home for a night or two from wherever he was, or I'd go and meet him.

Another six months later, he tentatively suggested a fertility specialist. He was away shooting, and it was one of those late-night calls. I agreed – it was better to get ahead of these things, in case there was anything wrong, I said.

As it happened, I had diminished ovarian reserve, meaning I wasn't producing as many eggs as the average woman. I was relieved by this news, but then the fertility doctor suggested IVF. It was going to be expensive and the doctor could not guarantee success.

By now we had joint accounts, business in the drama school was up and Jack's earnings were good. Jack had asked Dad not to give me an allowance any more. Dad's wedding present to me had been to buy Uncle Dennis's share of my house and Mom gave up her share to me also. So now the house was in Jack's and my name, and we were mortgage free.

I had never been wildly extravagant and had never worried about money in my life but now we depended on Jack's acting income plus the drama school to keep us afloat. We could afford several rounds of IVF but I didn't want another child. Jack insisted the time was right. He'd been contracted for a third season of *The Round Table* and had more film offers he was considering. The Academy had turned a healthy profit for the first time since the recession. But no matter what reasons I came up with – it would take a toll on me both emotionally and physically, the invasive nature of the procedure reminded me of the rape – Jack wanted this more than anything. Somehow, I had to prove to him how 'scared' I was of going down this road.

It was a Friday morning in September 2011, and Jack was working on a drama series, but they were shooting in Dublin. He'd been picked up at 5.30 a.m. by the production car and driven out to Ardmore Studios. I didn't know what time he'd be back. The schedule often changed depending on weather, light or unexpected hold-ups. I went out to get hammered. But this time I had an excuse, and I *wanted* Jack to find out. I didn't call the Academy to say I wouldn't be in. I dropped Lucy to school that morning and then I went to the supermarket and bought a bottle of wine the moment it was legal to sell it at 10.30 a.m. I drank the bottle as soon as I got home and then decided to drive into town around lunchtime. I left my phone at home. I crashed the car into the pillar at the front gate, so I left it there and walked down to the local pub instead. After striking up a conversation with a gang of women on a bachelorette party, I bought them two rounds of Jägermeister shots. Then one or two of them got a bit hostile and told me to back off, that I hadn't been invited to join their party. I got angry and slapped one of them across the head. I was then thrown out of the pub by the barman, who was watching. 'I knew you were trouble the minute you walked in,' he told me.

I was furious at this injustice. I hailed a cab to take me into the city centre and went to a pub I hadn't been in since college. The Stag's Head catered to a mixed crowd, but I sat on my own at the bar, drinking vodka and Coke, chatting to anyone who sat on the stool beside me. I must have been pretty dull because they all drifted away after a few minutes. Eventually, a young guy, rough around the edges, sat next to me.

'Looking for company?' he said, and I nodded. 'Looking for some Class As?' he added.

It was six years since I'd done any drugs at all but I figured in for a penny, in for a pound.

'How much?'

'Hundred and twenty quid for a gram.'

I fumbled in my wallet and took out three crisp fifty-euro notes. He slid a little cellophane pouch on to my lap under the bar.

'I don't have any change,' he said.

I was drunk but I still had some wits about me. 'Ask the barman,' I said.

He sauntered away, supposedly in search of the barman, but then disappeared with my thirty-euro change. Maybe my final wits were deserting me after all. I remember going down the stairs to the ladies, clutching the walls, but it was impossibly dark in the cubicle. I knew from AA meetings that bars had started doing this deliberately to stop cocaine use on the premises. There was no surface on which to chop out a line. The cistern was high up on the wall. I dabbed my finger into the pouch and rubbed it into my gums. I felt nothing, no buzz at all. Had I just paid €150 for some ground-up paracetamol or worse? I stumbled back up to the bar, thirsty for more vodka. I surveyed the various guys coming and going, and eventually one older man came over and offered me a drink. I think I told him I was an airline pilot who had arrived in Dublin that morning. I don't remember eating anything the whole day. I do remember it being dark when I fell out of the pub and the guy asked where my hotel was. I didn't know what he was talking about. He led me up a laneway nearby where he slammed me up against the wall and began to tear at my skirt. I screamed and he ran. I cried then. This whole day had been a horrible mistake. I managed to get a cab and remember my address. The taxi driver woke me up when I got home. I tried to fit my keys in the lock, but Jack swung the door open and I fell into the hall. Mom came out of the kitchen. Then I blacked out.

Three days later, Jack agreed that we would not have any IVF treatment. He apologized for pressuring me. I apologized for my relapse. He begged me to come back to AA with him, and I agreed. Nasrin, my sponsor, was happy to take me on again.

41

Erin

By 2011, I was tired of New York. I was a senior editor, but since those rumours had spread about me, despite the complete lack of evidence, I wasn't trusted or promoted. I was completely unfulfilled in my job and stifled in New York. I was also homesick for Boston, and worried about Dad. I talked to him about it. His solution, as it was to everything, was to pray about it, and he said I mustn't worry about him. The church had been rebuilt, but he had lost two fingers on his right hand and one on the left. Kathy said he was in more pain than he was admitting to me. 'At least I still have opposable thumbs, honey,' he told me.

A week later, God must have answered Dad's prayers because he came up with a real answer: 'Come home and start your own publishing company here in Boston. I'll help to set you up, financially.' I knew enough agents and had good relationships with them. Most of them also represented fiction writers. I called up my old room-mate, Carla Rivera, from my Harvard days. She was also struggling in New York, trying to pay rent in the Bronx as a marketing assistant for one of the big advertising companies. I put together a proposal for her. She was a Boston girl too, and she was fed up. I knew I could do the editing, but I needed somebody to do publicity, and she had all the contacts from her time in advertising. She knew features editors and some book editors, but she also had contacts for all the major TV shows who might want to interview a writer. Before I handed in my notice to Schoolroom, I had some lunches on their expense account. I figured it was the least they owed me. I knew that New York was the centre of the publishing world, but it didn't have to be.

I registered with the latest edition of *Writer's Market* and placed targeted ads in writers' groups on the internet. I knew I would eventually need a broad spectrum of books, so I appealed for submissions in fantasy, dystopian, speculative, horror, crime, romance, children's and science fiction categories. I went for the most commercial genres and the ones in which I had a particular interest. I needed Dad's money to pay advances and cover the exorbitant rent on an office in Cambridge. The one thing I had learned from my time in New York publishing was that appearances mattered, and Cambridge was a good address. My first publication had to be a great one, and Carla and I trawled through submissions day and night for weeks. I trusted her taste and she trusted mine.

It was a few months before I received a submission I liked enough to publish. Carla was worried we would run out of money and so was I. But I had to be choosy. The author was a medical student in Harvard, and the book was a romance set mostly in the subway of New York city as a young white man and Black woman locked eyes across a subway platform in the early hours of the morning. They then passed each other on subway trains, always missing each other, taking out ads in Craigslist to try to find each other. It was a credible story, charming and sweet, and I felt it would be relatable. I asked the writer, Esha Khan, to fix some timeline issues and character consistency matters, then offered her a $5,000 advance, which thankfully she accepted. I knew that I couldn't have been her first choice, and she was unagented. Marketing was going to be key and Carla swung into action. She was great at the digital end of marketing and understood the power of Twitter and Facebook.

In March 2012, with seed money from Dad and every penny I had been able to save, Carla and I opened the Cooper Rivera Publishing House. I worried that I'd made a mistake. I had no money to pay for a copy-editor or a proofreader, I did all the work myself. Esha was eager to be published. She quickly made all the necessary changes and then I sent the book out in manuscript form to some trusted reader friends. I was relieved that they loved it as much as I did. I paid a designer to create a cover that would have broad appeal, and I let her and Esha talk together to come up with something they both liked. I used the last of my money to pay for the first print run of 5,000 copies. The whole enterprise had cost me all I had. I was worried sick that the book would flop.

The first review from the *Boston Globe* hurt me so much that I can't imagine how Esha felt. We wept together and I tried to reassure her and myself that it was just one review.

> It is hard to care about these characters and their small lives. It might be more interesting if they had aspirational careers. I doubt that any reader is going to care about a maid and a school caretaker.

The critic could not have been more wrong and, to our delight, I had to order a second print run of 10,000 within two weeks and then 20,000 the following week. *Sweet Subway* went viral across social media, and it became THE book that everyone was talking about. Esha was invited on to *Good Morning America* and was interviewed by *The New York Times*.

Suddenly the top agents were sending me manuscripts. My next two acquisitions were children's books, one about a girl pirate and the other a coming-of-age story about a neurodivergent teen. Both books took off and I was finally established. At the beginning of our second year, I hired an assistant, Ruth, and a copy-editor, Suzie, and found a bigger office. I also needed to see a therapist because even though my professional life couldn't have been better, my love life was non-existent. I didn't trust men. That was when the texts started again.

I could destroy your business. You should have stayed away.

Why was Margie starting this game again? Milo would be released within months. What could she possibly have to gain?

PART THREE

42

Erin

Monday, 15 April 2013, is a day that no Bostonian will ever forget. It was Patriots' Day, and it started unusually because a lot of the city was closed off for the annual Boston City Marathon. We were an all-female company, and I let the moms have the day off because schools were out and Carla and Suzie both had family members running the marathon.

I was editing a memoir I had acquired quite by chance by a young woman born a conjoined twin who had lost her sister in the operation that was supposed to separate them at the age of twelve. It was a complicated story of love and loss and sacrifice. The physical struggles they faced together as children and the emotional scars left behind were profound. I hadn't published a memoir before, but Carla had alerted me that this could be big. The writer was forty-five years old and had one prosthetic leg, and she had endured sixty-five surgeries in her lifetime, and yet the story was full of hope and gratitude for her life.

We had a TV in the office lobby, usually tuned to CNN but silenced. I was working through the manuscript at my desk when I heard Ruth saying, 'My God,' and at the same time my phone began to buzz. I picked up and it was Dad.

'Where are you, honey? Are you in the office?' I could hear the concern in his voice.

'Yeah, I'm fine, what's up?'

At the same moment Ruth burst into my office, exclaiming, 'There's been explosions at the marathon. I think they're bombs!'

Dad heard what she'd said. 'That's what I was calling about. Don't leave the office, you hear me?'

I thought of Carla and Suzie, who were lining the route. I walked into the next room. Ruth had turned up the volume. 'Okay, Dad, I'm just watching now.' There were chaotic scenes on the TV as plumes of smoke were seen emanating from two sites near the finish line on Boylston Street. People were running away but there were lots of others lying injured on the ground. The image of one man, a bystander with half his leg blown off, is seared into my brain.

I assured Dad that I was okay. Ruth and I abandoned our work and sat grimly transfixed by the news and the images of horror unfolding in our city, but something else caught my eye too. After a while the same footage was being played over and over. It was shaky, from someone's camera phone I guessed. A blast from the right-hand side of the street, people falling all round and then screaming and shouting.

As the commentators talked over the images, I identified Milo running towards a man on the ground who appeared to have been hit by shrapnel, blood pouring from his right thigh. Milo lifted him up and put his arm around the man's shoulder, then half carried the man out of shot. Another man followed him, pointing away from the blast site. I hadn't known Milo had been released. Surely my family should have been informed. Did Dad know?

But the Boston bombing was a bigger story than Milo, and I spent hours on the phone that day. The cell towers in the area were overloaded, and we could only text. Carla and Suzie were fine but Carla's cousin, who had been standing as an onlooker near the second bomb site further up the street, had bad foot injuries. Surgeons fought to save his lower limb. For days, twenty blocks of Watertown not far from where I lived were on lockdown as it became clear that this was a terrorist attack, and the perpetrators were two brothers with a Chechen background who had been radicalized online. If they hadn't been caught, they intended to target Times Square next.

It was a terrible time in the history of Boston. Three young people died, including an eight-year-old boy, twelve people lost limbs and two hundred and eighty-one were injured.

But Milo was out of prison and, watching the images over and over, I realized that the man who had followed him out on to the street was his old school friend Ben Roche. At least Margie's messages would stop now.

43

In 2015, my therapist suggested something I had never considered. She said that I was letting Milo control my life. I couldn't trust anyone because of him. If I allowed him to dictate my life, I was going to be on my own. I knew she was right. I didn't want to be alone forever – I thought I might die of loneliness. But I couldn't face online dating. How could I trust some random man?

Vince was a friend of Saima's brother-in-law. I met him at a dinner party in her house. Saima and her husband had obviously had an argument before we arrived. Binto was snapping at her, ordering her about, complaining that she'd forgotten the oyster crackers when she was laying the table, while he sat on his ass doing nothing. There were two other couples there, and one older guy. I gave Saima sympathetic looks and Vince, the older guy, seated opposite, caught me and glanced at me while turning his head slightly to the side. I think we were all in silent agreement that Binto was a putz. Later, when Binto went to have a cigar outside with one of his work buddies, while 'the little wife' went to the kitchen to get dessert, Vince leaned over and said, 'I mean, what kind of name is Binto anyway? His real name is Reginald.' I bust out laughing. When we were all saying goodnight on the porch, Vince offered me a ride home, but I had my car. 'Damn,' he said, 'can I at least get your number? Or am I too old for you? I'm too old, right? Just tell me straight out, I promise I'll take it like a man.'

I told him I'd be shocked if he took it like a woman and gave him my number.

On our first date in Legal Sea Foods, I learned that Vincent Delgado's wife, Anjelica, had died in a car crash four years earlier. He was fifty years old and had two boys aged nineteen and twenty. I was thirty-four. Vince was a mechanical engineer and had his own company installing and maintaining air-conditioning units in factories, offices and all kinds of commercial buildings.

His sons were smart boys, living and studying in Berkeley, California. Despite the distance, they were close to their dad and called and visited every vacation. He flew out to San Francisco once a month to spend the weekend with them.

We bonded quickly. He and his boys were ice hockey fans, and we went to see the Bruins play whenever we could, with or without the boys. They were taken aback by my age, I guess. Carmine and Nick did everything together. I thought they were sweet. They never said anything disrespectful to me and I made it clear that I was devoted to their dad and would never try to replace their mom. They were Italian-American Catholics and, though they didn't attend church, they were good people in the way that mattered.

My dad was the one who was upset – he was only nine years older than Vince and couldn't accept that I could fall in love with a man with such an age gap. I was forced to point out the ten-year age gap between Kathy and him, and that stopped him in his tracks. Poor Dad was ageing rapidly as he tried to keep up with Kathy, who loved to travel, particularly to ski resorts in Colorado and Utah. Dad broke a wrist the first time but bravely went the next few years until he broke a hip. This was before the fire that ruined his hands. Without the full use of them, he had slowed down a lot. I talked to Kathy, explained to her that maybe Dad should think about taking early retirement, at least from the investment business. Kathy wasn't the brightest, but she accepted this, I thought, until the following year when they went to Miami, and she took him skydiving. I was horrified, but Dad was totally exhilarated by the experience. He'd been harnessed to an experienced skydiver, and insisted that I should try it. I decided to butt out then, and told myself it was none of my business.

I also had to tell Dad that my relationship with Vince was none of his business. But, feeling bruised by my previous experiences, I hired a private investigator within the first two months. Vince had one DUI when he was seventeen, but apart from that, he was clean as a whistle.

Mom met him when she visited the following year, 2016. She wasn't bothered by the age gap but worried that one of his sons might fall in love with me. Vince and I laughed about that. Both boys were in stable relationships with Californian girls. They had no interest in me. Carmine told me he was glad that his dad had a new relationship, because he'd been broken-hearted by the death of Anjelica, and now that he had me, they didn't have to worry about him as much.

Anjelica was ever-present in our relationship. She had been outgoing and gregarious. Vince's friends often mentioned her when I was around and then would look apologetically at me. In Vince's house, her photo stood on the piano. She looked nothing like me, a striking brunette with a megawatt smile, heavy eye make-up and crimson lipstick. He talked about her sometimes, recalling what she used to order when we were at his favourite restaurant, how she hated the garbage collectors because one of them had wolf whistled at her through the window when she was breast-feeding Nick. She had been outraged and called the cops and the waste-management company. He said she never wore jeans as she considered them too masculine. He was not being critical. Vince rarely commented on what I was wearing – I don't think he noticed.

He proposed a year into our relationship. I had sensed it was on the cards and that maybe Vince thought that five years was a respectable amount of time to leave between burying one wife and marrying another. Apparently, his sons had already given their approval. I said yes. I told myself that this was love. There didn't have to be sparks and whistles, just a man I could trust.

Vince needed to know if I wanted children, and how many. I could see his relief when I told him I didn't want to have any. I said that my career was too important to me. Vince had raised two awesome young men, and now admitted he never wanted to change another diaper in his life. He had been a hands-on dad, and Anjelica had been a wonderful mother. He didn't need to say that it would be impossible for him not to compare us.

I didn't mind having this ghost hovering over our relationship, because I had one too, though I never told Vince about Milo. Since the Boston Marathon in 2013, he had appeared in my waking thoughts and middle-of-the-night dreams even more regularly. Why had he been determined to serve a full sentence rather than admit the truth? It bugged me that he was trying to be some martyr-like figure, all the time Margie was sending me letters and making sleazy insinuations about what I was doing in New York, not to mention trying to have my dad's church burned down. I hated that he had turned into such a manipulator, but as desperate as he had seemed in prison, the wound in my heart had reopened in some undefined way.

I'd expected to hear from him and was scared that he would turn up one day. I kept my distance from Fenway Park where I knew he might be likely to go see a Red Sox game. I'd put out some feelers through my friends. They said he was back working in Billy's Diner. I discovered that he too was keeping tabs on me when a letter from him landed in my office in 2016.

Dear Erin,

I know that you won't welcome this letter, but I've been out for three years, and I need you to know that you're still the most beautiful girl I ever saw and the only one I ever wanted. I hope that guy you married knows how lucky he is. I won't bother you again. Margie says my broken heart will mend one day. I'm not sure I believe her, but I got to make a life for myself though I don't know how I'm going to do that without you. You will be a great wife and an awesome mother, but you can't use the names we picked for our kids, okay? Though I don't imagine you will.

    I appreciated those monthly parcels when I was inside. I got to tell you, they were a godsend and sometimes they saved me from trouble. Thank you very much.

    I don't know what to say about Ruby. When you came to the prison that time and told me she was an alcoholic, I wasn't too surprised and I'm not sorry for her, but if she has to live with a lie her whole life, even now when she's a grown-ass woman, there are consequences to that. I'm not taking responsibility for it. My mom drowned herself because of Ruby's lies and maybe that's why I can't see myself forgiving her any time soon, or ever. I served my whole sentence because I wouldn't tell a lie. I thought you knew me better, and that's what hurts the most.

    By the way, Margie did not send you any emails or letters and I can hardly believe you would think she'd set fire to a church, but then I think of what you believe about me and I'm just not sure any more.

I read all about you in the Globe. They said you were publishing books. I've read them all, even the kids' ones, and you sure know what readers want, but I meant what I said about your stories, Eri. They were better than anything you've published. Please don't waste your talent.

M x

A day later, I got a text from the burner phone I had logged as Margie. There were photos of naked women in crude poses with my head superimposed on them. They looked real. I was totally freaked out. The text read:

> I've uploaded these on to some Boston escort sites. Expect some calls.

The calls came and within two days I had to change my number, which was hugely inconvenient for business. The calls and photos I received were disgusting and depraved. I had to report this to Hernandez. She was as helpful as she could be. They were able to find my doctored image on three escort sites. I had to obtain a court order to get them taken down and it had to be done fast, as my reputation was on the line, though anyone who knew me knew that I was not shaped like any of these women, with their enormous butts and plus-sized breasts. Hernandez talked to Margie, seized her laptop again and came up empty. No evidence. I got another screaming voicemail from Margie on her regular number, begging me to leave her alone. I handled all of this on my own. I did not respond to Margie; I did not tell Dad or Vince.

When was this going to stop?

44

Vince and I celebrated our marriage in June 2016 in the TD Garden, home to the Boston Bruins ice hockey team. Mom and Dad raised their eyebrows at that, but they still came along and enjoyed the day. The venue meant a lot to Vince, and I had developed an interest in the game too, even though, traditionally, the Coopers were a baseball family. Well, Dad was a baseball fan. Sport was always a big thing in Boston. You would have families who were into ice hockey, baseball (the Red Sox), basketball (the Celtics) or football (the New England Patriots, featuring national treasure Tom Brady), or you could get a family who were into all four. Dad had been unable to persuade his wife or daughters to take much interest in his game, but he and Milo could talk about the Red Sox for hours, back before 'the incident', as Ruby always called it.

Ruby did not come to the wedding, but I knew she wouldn't. This time the excuse was that she was running the acting school for the husband I'd never met while he took a job on some series that was shooting in Norway. Ruby had made excuses not to come home every year since she touched down in Ireland. I knew she went on vacations to Italy, France and Spain, and had honeymooned in Orlando, but she avoided Boston. I guessed that some part of her was still afraid, but I was disappointed she wouldn't make the effort for me. It was years since I'd seen her. We had become estranged without ever having an argument.

My wedding was the first time Mom met Kathy too and that

was always going to be awkward. Mom was surprised: 'My God, Erin, she looks cheap – her hair is nearly bleached off her head.' And, yes, Kathy had made herself some kind of Little Bo Peep-style dress with layers of lace in different pastel shades for the wedding, while Mom was demurely dressed in an olive-green linen sheath dress. Both of Dad's wives were beautiful, but Mom had style. I felt sorry for Kathy. She was intimidated by Mom, but Mom stayed in a hotel, and they were civil to each other at the ceremony and reception.

The ceremony took place in Dad's church. That was our compromise. Vince agreed to a non-Catholic ceremony if I agreed to an ice hockey venue for the reception. We were good at compromising. I still attended Dad's church and had a lot of friends there from childhood. It was a big wedding with all our friends and colleagues, though this made the age difference more apparent as a lot of Vince's friends were of a similar vintage to my parents. And some of my younger authors flirted with Vince's boys.

I did not take my husband's surname. It was never an issue. I was not prepared to be Mrs Delgado when I had worked hard to become Erin Cooper, Publisher. I think Dad was more disappointed than Vince.

I wore a simple but eye-wateringly expensive Vera Wang sleeveless ivory dress with a train, and Saima, my bridesmaid, looked stunning in powder-blue satin against her dark skin. Vince's single, married and divorced male friends flocked around my mother as if she was Scarlett O'Hara at a cotillion ball, and she relished the attention, but did not succumb to any offers, as far as I know. I had an awesome day, surrounded by people who loved me. When I reflect now, I realize that despite my vows and my efforts, I did not love Vince at all, though he was dear to me, and I was happy to be his wife. It was cruel of me. I should have let him go and find somebody more deserving of his love than me, but I was lonely, and I thought that Vince could protect me.

45

Since Ruby had failed to invite me to her wedding, and then made excuses not to come to mine, we grew even further apart. She had married her housemate, Jack, in 2010. None of us were invited to the wedding, not even Mom. I'd met Jack once at Grandma's funeral but only briefly. I knew he was an actor and a so-far sober alcoholic. I thought it was a terrible idea. Mom had been upset not to be invited to the wedding, but she reckoned Jack was okay. He was nine years older than Ruby. Maybe Ruby and I were both looking for the same thing, marrying older men. Jack also ran a drama school and gave Ruby work there. He had been with her when she went into labour with Lucy but apparently was not the father. I guess they knew each other well.

Our phone calls grew more and more sporadic. I would hear what she was up to through Mom, and she had a few theatre acting jobs here and there for which she got good reviews. Then, in later years, I saw Jack on TV. He was more handsome and rugged than I remembered. And even though he was just ten years younger than Vince, he looked a different generation. My husband wore pressed shirts and suits to work. He had a small paunch which he managed to keep small through a very strict diet. Vince's casual clothing was an open-necked shirt and a sweater over some chinos. Jack wore designer jeans and T-shirts or hoodies with leather jackets. He clearly spent time in the gym. I don't know why I was comparing my husband to Ruby's. I was not exactly the svelte young thing I had been either. I'd let myself go a little. A few extra pounds and some grey hair that I didn't bother to hide.

Jack appeared in several films and we went to see him in the movie theatre. I read interviews with him, where he often mentioned Ruby as his inspiration. He always referred to Lucy as his daughter too. Who knows what the truth was? Vince and his sons were star-struck that my sister was married to a movie star. But she never invited us to meet him. I wished her well but had to accept that she didn't want me in her life any more. Eventually, I gave up the pretence and stopped the birthday and Christmas cards that were never reciprocated.

Somehow, Margie got hold of my new cellphone number and the texts started again.

> He could have been a doctor by now if it wasn't for your bitch sister.

The tone of these communications was always erratic, from disgusting comments to professional sabotage, from threats of church arson to apology, back to sexual harassment and then hostile regret. Margie was clearly unhinged. I had a constant fear of what the next one would say or threaten, and yet sometimes months went by when there were none. I was forever on my guard. It was exhausting.

46

We were nearly eighteen months married before Vince found out about Milo. We had settled into married life easily and Vince and I bought a new house in Beacon Hill, a fresh start. I hadn't wanted to live in Anjelica's shadow. He still talked about her, but less frequently. I had insisted, after the first year of our relationship, that we take vacations to places that Vince had not been with her. We went to the West Coast a lot to see Vince's boys. Carmine got a job in Cupertino, something to do with tech and Microsoft. I never understood exactly what the job was, but he was well paid and got great benefits. Nick, on the other hand, was struggling. The boys had grown apart since their college years. Nick's girlfriend had dumped him, and he did not take it well. She told Carmine that she was worried about him, that he had started talking about conspiracy theories. He believed in chemtrails, the theory that trails in the sky left by aeroplanes were leaking poison into the atmosphere and brainwashing the population. He stayed in his rental studio most of the time and had sealed the windows shut. Despite his fear of inhaling chemicals, he chain-smoked in that room until his landlord threw him out after an inspection revealed he was a hoarder and was living in total squalor. The neighbours had complained. Vince paid for him to come back to Boston.

When he returned, he was upset that we had sold the family home, though we'd told him at the time, and he had visited with us before in the new house. He acted like it was all new information, something that had been orchestrated behind his back to erase his mother's memory. He also wanted to know why I hadn't had babies yet. Childbirth was a woman's purpose, he said. He didn't like the fact that I worked and said that I should be more like his mom and stay home raising children. He would get angry and sometimes aggressive about these issues. He had latched on to the theory that the moon landings were faked and that humans could not have built the pyramids. He believed that Tupac was still alive and running a motel somewhere in Brazil.

Vince and I tried to get him a psych assessment, but we couldn't forcibly make him go. Then he accused me of having abortions behind his father's back. Vince banned him from the house. Nick was unemployed and Vince paid rent for him in a one-room studio downtown, but the realtor kicked him out when he set fire to the building. Luckily, the fire was contained and nobody got hurt, but it cost us thousands for the refurb. Carmine and his girlfriend, Shelley, flew in from California to try and talk some sense into him. But even his brother couldn't get through to him. We asked what had happened in Berkeley. Carmine was sure it wasn't a drug issue, but said that Nick spent a lot of time on the internet, trawling through conspiracy websites. Some had more credibility than others, but many were outlandish and stupid. Princess Diana wasn't dead and had orchestrated the 9/11 attacks on behalf of the Saudi government. Straight white men were under attack and were being replaced by aliens masquerading as immigrants. I couldn't entirely blame the internet. Nick had developed significant mental health issues.

He started living on the streets by choice, believing that everyone around him was out to get him, and even that his brother was a clone. This was all hard on Vince and Carmine, and though I played it down, I was beginning to fear him, as a lot of his anger seemed to be targeted at women and at me in particular. When we did manage to meet him somewhere for a meal, I felt uncomfortable. A lot of times he would be completely uncommunicative and would stare at me with open hostility, or he would cower in fear until I left the restaurant. I would get my food to go and wait in the car. Vince would emerge as soon as he could, upset and distressed.

In November 2017, we hadn't heard from Nick in six months. Vince was worried. He would visit the places where homeless people hung out, and sometimes I'd go with him. One night, we were down at Haley House, a soup kitchen run by volunteers, when I saw Milo unloading crates of food from a small truck. He was carrying a little more weight than he had in prison. He was wearing a beanie and a Red Sox jacket and had his back to me, but I knew him, like that first day in church. I was so surprised to see him that I froze, rooted to the spot. I guess I should have expected to bump into him sometime. He did a double-take when he saw me and then that huge grin appeared. 'Erin, Eri. How are you?' I started to tremble with shock or nerves, I don't know. I couldn't speak. He walked towards me until he was an arm's length away. 'I was wondering when I'd see you again.'

Vince appeared at my side. 'Hi,' he said, thrusting his arm forward to shake Milo's hand. 'Who's this, honey?' I still couldn't speak.

'Milo Kelly, I'm an old friend of Erin's.'

As he said it, I could see that he was bracing himself for some reaction. But the name meant nothing to Vince, and he had other things on his mind. 'Well, Milo, it's a real pleasure to meet you. I'm Erin's husband, Vince Delgado, and I'm looking for my son Niccolo, or Nick. We're worried about him.' He was handing Milo a picture of Nick with our contact details. 'Do you reckon you've seen him around?'

Milo tore his eyes from mine and studied the photo. 'I deliver food to places like this around the city from my uncle's diner where I work downtown.' The information was for me, but he peered more closely at the photo. 'I'm not sure I've seen your boy, sir, but I'll hang on to this and look out for him, all right?'

'Thank you, my friend, we'd be very grateful, wouldn't we, sweetheart?'

'Yes. Thank you.' I kept any emotion out of my voice. My response was robotic. Vince put his arm around me and led me across the street to our car.

'He seems like a good guy. How do you know Milo?'

In the car on the way home, I told him.

Vince was horrified by what Milo had done to Ruby and by extension to our family. He understood now why Ruby had never come back to Boston. He sympathized with teenage me, but I assured him I was over it. Milo had served his time in prison. Ruby was in Ireland. I begged him to let the past be the past.

47

In September 2018, Dad died. He was only sixty-two years old. He was way too young. He got pancreatic cancer, and it was four months between diagnosis and death. He had felt a twinge in his back, but didn't think it was bad enough to see a doctor. Kathy was distraught. I had to call Mom and Ruby. Mom was upset. She and Dad had become better friends than they ever were as spouses. Since our wedding, Mom had always visited Dad and Kathy when she came to Boston to see me. And despite her initial impressions of Kathy, they found common ground. They even once went to a Dolly Parton concert together.

Ruby may have been upset, but when I called her for the first time in years, I got the exact response I expected. She did not want to come over for the funeral.

'I can't go back there, Erin. I can't ever go back there.'

I was annoyed with her. 'This isn't about you, Ruby, it's about paying your respects to your father. He was a good dad to both of us, I can't believe you don't want to say goodbye. He deserves that much. Mom told me you were in New York a few weeks ago. I could have come to see you.'

'You don't understand, Erin, Boston triggers –'

'For God's sake, that was almost twenty years ago. Are you going to hold it against an entire city forever? You're being ridiculous.'

'He'll be there, at the funeral, I know he will.'

I didn't have to ask who she meant. The thought had also

crossed my mind. Dad had been good to Milo before the rape, and Milo could easily show up.

The funeral was big, with screens broadcasting outside on the lawn in front of the church. Aunt Rachel was devastated. We all were. Since the damage to his hands because of the arson attack on the church, he had struggled. Devotees came from all of Dad's other churches. He had begun to wind down the investment business to concentrate more on what he saw as his mission. The funeral was devastating and uplifting at the same time. People queued up to say nice things about him, kindnesses he had done for them with no expectation of anything in return. Dad was always a 'pay it forward' kind of guy. I was proud of him, and I missed him. If Milo did turn up to the funeral, and I suspect he did, I did not see him. I received a condolence card at the office.

> Your dad was one of the good guys. I don't blame him for believing his own daughter over me, and I'm sorry for your loss.

I put it straight in the trash can.

Kathy inherited the house and enough money to keep her comfortable. Mom, Ruby and I inherited $50k each. The rest was bequeathed to the church and to charities all over Massachusetts. I know that Ruby wasn't happy about it. She had expected to inherit millions, but Mom and Dad had bought her a home and I had got the money to start a business plus a lot of financial help when I was in New York. Ruby had moved a year or two earlier to a much bigger detached house, and Jack was a movie star – I was sure they could afford it. Dad had mentioned to me that he intended to bequeath most of his money to charities. I guess he didn't say it to Ruby because they were rarely in touch. To any normal person, $50k was a good inheritance, but Ruby was shocked. Too bad. Mom knew about it. I guess she never told Ruby either.

Dad had appointed a successor for his church shortly before his death. When he realized his condition was terminal, he was quick to get his affairs in order. Typical Dad. I was mad with God for taking him so young, but in my last conversation with Dad, he told me that God knew what he was doing and that he had served his purpose in this realm and was looking forward to the next one. I felt unsettled after his death for a long time. He had been my rock my whole life. Mom and Ruby were gone. Aunt Rachel was still in Worcester, and we were close, but she could never take the place of Dad.

Vince still held out hope that Nick could be rescued from his demons. He had turned up a year after he went missing, toothless and gaunt. He had been in San Francisco, living in a tented city. He said it was the only place he felt safe from the aliens. He stayed with us for one night, but nobody slept. He roamed around the house all night, constantly checking that windows and doors were locked. When Vince tried to talk to him the next day about seeing a doctor, he disappeared again. It was a pattern that would repeat itself for years.

I could not let the past go. I kept an eye on Milo via the internet. I could see that he was still working in his uncle's diner. He had an Instagram account, but didn't post with any regularity. Once or twice a year, I would dress in as much of a disguise as I could muster, a hat and sunglasses, and go downtown and sit in a bar opposite the diner to watch. Sometimes I wouldn't see him at all. Twice, I saw him standing in the doorway in conversation with some friend or customer. Once, I saw him get into a beat-up Corvette in the alley beside the diner. A couple of times I saw him in the company of a woman, a redhead, short and pretty. I hated him but I couldn't stay away. Once, I saw him outside the diner with our old school principal,

Mr Bermingham, from Altman High. Bermingham seemed to be agitated and Milo looked annoyed. But these sightings of Milo fuelled my anger. I would go home to my husband and lie about where I'd been. How would he understand when I couldn't understand myself?

48

Ruby

I was genuinely sad when Dad died. He was a good man. He had always done the right thing, as far as he knew. Despite our estrangement, I could see that he tried to do his best under the circumstances. I had been too harsh on him. He had so often begged me to come home for a visit. I should have gone to the funeral, but I was terrified. Mom went over and, now that Dad was out of the picture, I was afraid she might say something. He had the most to lose materially, if the truth were ever to come out. But now he was gone, she could sink us both if she wanted to.

Before Mom left, I begged her to keep our secret. She said it hadn't crossed her mind; she was too grief-stricken. She accused me of being cold and calculating, and maybe I was, but I was doing it for my daughter.

The biggest shock came about when Dad's will went through probate. I had always assumed that I would inherit at least two million dollars. Two years previously, we had moved into a beautiful old red-brick detached home in Ranelagh, closer to the city. Ranelagh was quiet but had full access to all the nice restaurants and public transport and was close to the private school I wanted for Lucy.

Jack had been against the move. He hadn't seen the need for a three-million-euro four-bedroom house when we had one child, and he didn't want to be saddled with a huge mortgage in his early forties. *The Round Table* had come to an end after seven series. He was still getting good film and TV roles in limited series, but they were becoming further apart. It was a year since he'd done a prestige role, and his income was never guaranteed.

In those years, it was very difficult to get a mortgage. I told Jack to flirt with the mortgage adviser. He didn't think I was serious, but he didn't realize how much I wanted this house. When I grew up in Boston, we had a big house with a huge lawn front and back, and a double garage. The garden of this new house was beautiful, the kitchen was state of the art, with a separate utility room, and it had a large dining room. 'We'll never use it,' Jack had said. The mortgage adviser was an avid fan of *The Round Table* and was star-struck. I suspect she worked very hard to get us mortgage approval.

When we moved in, I had dinner parties once a month for the first six months to prove Jack wrong about the dining room. But he turned out to be right. We weren't dinner-party people – sober alcoholics rarely are. It was too formal for lunch. The circular table in the kitchen seated eight at a squeeze, and that's where we ended up entertaining lunch parties on a smaller scale. After a year, the only person who went into the dining room was the cleaner to polish the twelve-seater dining table and the candelabra.

I had never worried about taking on a huge mortgage because of Dad, and then I got the shock of my life after he died and I discovered he had only left me $50k in his will. I called Erin and she was snippy with me on the phone: 'What did you expect? He and Mom already bought you a house. You didn't visit him. You never met Kathy. You didn't even come to his funeral.'

I realized with a sinking feeling that paying this mortgage would be a challenge. The Academy was breaking even, but Jack's roles were not as big as they used to be. He was now represented by CAA in Los Angeles, but he was getting less work than he used to. He was not ageing as well as some of his peers. He never wanted to be away from home for long, but I pushed him to take the roles that meant he might be away for five months or more. 'You wanted this big house, and now, to pay for it, I can't be in it. I miss Lucy,' he said down the line from Tunisia.

'Just Lucy?' I was hurt.

'Aw, you know what I mean, Rubes. I miss you too, of course I do, but she's growing up and I'm not there to see it.'

Lucy had turned twelve the summer before Dad died. She had only met him a handful of times, but now she started asking questions about dads, my dad and her birth dad. She had picked up everything she needed to know about the facts of life long before we sat her down, aged nine. At twelve, she was aware of the difference between vanilla sex and kinky sex. I'd had no idea at that age about any sex, except that it was how you made babies. Jack was home at that time. She asked why, if Granny and Grandad loved each other, had they divorced? Was it because they didn't want to have sex any more? Jack laughed until I reminded him privately of the 'real' reason why my parents had divorced.

'I'm sorry,' he said, 'I forgot.'

I never forgot. It was like having a constant zit. I could see the lie in the mirror every day.

A week later, Lucy asked about her real dad. 'I think it's time to tell me the truth, Mum, who is he?' We were alone in the house.

'Don't you love Jack?' I asked her.

'Yes, I do, but it's my right to know. On my birth certificate, it's blank where it should say his name.'

'Oh, Lulu, it's complicated. You know I'm an alcoholic, right? Around the time I got pregnant, I had sex with a lot of people. I couldn't be sure which one was your dad.'

'Like a gang bang?' she asked.

49

In 2020, Jack's work dried as the Corona Virus spread around the world. We were all home a lot more. We should have been a happy family as a result, but despite the large deposit we had paid upfront thanks to Jack's earnings and his fan in the mortgage department, the repayments, on top of Lucy's school fees, were crippling. Jack suggested we should downsize to a smaller house, but how would that look to Lucy's classmates and their parents, and how would it look for Jack's career? 'The appearance of success breeds success,' I read somewhere. I vetoed the move.

Lucy said we should move, and that 'it wasn't fair to put all the pressure on Dad'. I was incensed. I ran the Jack Brady Academy and rarely had time to take the stage roles I was offered before the pandemic. Now we were forced to temporarily close the school and while the government stepped in to subsidize our earnings, they weren't paying our mortgage.

A distance was growing between Lucy and me. I encouraged her towards acting. It was the family business after all, and she had done all the child acting courses the Academy had to offer, but she claimed now she hadn't enjoyed them and refused to do any more. Jack quietly said to me that a film or TV set was no place for a child, and I knew he was thinking of his own childhood and his sister, Barbra. 'We shouldn't push her, she's not interested,' he said, but I couldn't accept that. Her parents were actors.

One evening when Lucy and I were on our own, I said, 'You know you could be a big star, like your dad, if you just tried a bit harder?'

'Or I could be a scientist or a zookeeper or a billionaire like my real dad? I guess we'll never know, because you slept around so much.'

I was shocked by her words. 'Lucy!'

'Well, it's true, isn't it? Dad was an addict too. He didn't have a random child, did he?'

'You are not a random child. I could have had an abortion. I wanted you.'

'Why?' Her question reminded me of the time long before Jack and I were together, when he said that getting sober was a shitty reason to have a baby. 'I had screwed up my own life. I had an opportunity to make a great one for you.'

'How many men did you sleep with?'

'Stop this, Lucy. I am not answering that question. It's unworthy of you.'

'What does that even mean, Mum? Didn't it ever occur to you that I might want to know?'

'I think your dad would be upset by this.'

Lucy snapped back. 'No, he wouldn't. He says he never discussed it with you and that if I wanted to know, I should ask you, and now I'm asking you and you're not giving me any answers.'

'That's because I never knew,' I shouted at her. She glared at me. I could see her judgement. 'It's easy to be promiscuous when you're drunk all the time.' I teared up, but instead of giving me an apology, I heard her walk away, stomp up the stairs and slam her bedroom door.

It hurt me that she and Jack had talked about this without me. Jack knew my situation when she was born, and when he married me. I did not like this growing alliance between them, with Jack telling her she shouldn't be an actress and encouraging her to ask for details of her birth father, details he knew I didn't have. When I confronted him, he said I shouldn't be so defensive, and that Lucy was displaying normal teenager behaviour.

It continued as she got older. In the most minor of arguments, she would take Jack's side against mine. I reckoned her birth father must have been a very bright guy because she was smarter than Jack and me both. She used her 'mystery father' as a weapon against me many times in years to come. She was doing riding lessons and wanted a pony, and when Jack and I both said no, she said it was a shame she didn't know who her birth father was because she was sure he would have said yes.

50

Erin

Around Thanksgiving time in 2020, Milo turned up at my office, masked like everyone else, but I knew those sparkling blue eyes. I was startled; I hustled him out immediately. He begged me for five minutes of my time. He was jumping from foot to foot, clearly excited by something. It was a cold day and there was snow on the ground. We took a socially distanced walk around the block. Milo looked better than the last time I'd seen him outside the diner. His hair was freshly cut and his clothes were neat.

His voice was gentle. 'Look, Erin, I don't mean to upset you, but I've figured it out. I know how your sister got the DNA inside her.'

I stopped dead. 'I am not listening to this.'

'You have to, Eri, it doesn't make any difference to anyone. I served my time. Please?'

I walked faster but he could easily keep up with me. 'Look, just hear me out. That's all I ask. Please.' He was begging. 'You know back in the day when I came to your bedroom, and you jerked me off –'

'Stop, please stop, Milo.' But he wouldn't.

'I cleaned myself up with tissues afterwards, right? And then I put those tissues in the trash can under your desk, right?'

I was horrified and tried to jaywalk across the street to get away from him, but traffic was flying past me.

'I reckon that Ruby was watching us through the keyhole. She picked one of those tissues out of the trash. That's how she knew where to get the DNA and that's how it got inside her. She put it there.'

I was momentarily stunned. How the hell could he even think up something like that?

I whipped around to face him. 'Milo, my bedroom door did not have a keyhole. It didn't even have a lock. There was no key. Now please leave, and if you ever come to my office or approach me again, I am calling the police.'

'She saw us, I'm telling you.'

I turned to go in the opposite direction.

'Hey, did you find Nick yet?'

I hated that he knew anything about my family and my husband. I was furious. Why would he do this? It was over.

The following weekend, however, I found an excuse to visit Kathy in our old home. I reassured myself that, in fact, there was no keyhole. The door was exactly as I remembered. I lay on the floor in the hall to see if there was a gap under the door. All I could see was the carpet immediately inside the room. Why would Milo persist in this lie? It bothered me.

A few days later, a text arrived from Margie's burner number.

> What a dirty little bitch you and your sister are. A pair of dirty little bitches.

I cried.

51

In 2022, I was forty-one and Vince was fifty-seven. We played tennis in the summer, and he coached minor ice hockey in the winter. It was another year during which we had not heard from Nick. Carmine was settled in Marin County, north of San Francisco, with his wife and two beautiful girls, Abigail and Rosie. Once a month, Carmine went down to the shelters and soup kitchens in the Bay Area looking for Nick and invariably found him in one place or another. He would provide him with clothing and hygiene products and try to bring him to a diner to make sure he had a good meal. He reported that sometimes Nick was compliant and sometimes he was outright hostile, accusing Carmine of working for 'the aliens' or of being a clone. He'd had an untreated wound on the side of his head the last time Carmine saw him in August. He wouldn't reveal how he got it, and when Carmine went to Walgreens to get some disinfectant, Nick was gone when he came back. Carmine could not find him anywhere. Vince flew out there and together he and Carmine trawled the streets and the crack dens and derelict houses of the Mission district. Vince was robbed twice while on these searches, and I worried that he would be shot or stabbed. These places were dangerous, full of people desperate or high enough to pull a trigger or a knife, but Vince didn't care. He would have done anything for Nick.

I wasn't a parent, but I understood the depth of love a man could have for his child. It was evident in the way Vince's face lit up when he saw Carmine or when Carmine called to say that Nick was safe. But now there was no trace of him and Vince came back from California despondent.

We were both working a lot, and I couldn't help thinking what it would be like when Vince retired, and he'd be home all the time. After six years of marriage, I had never been able to tell him that I loved him. He told me often, early in our marriage, but I never reciprocated. When he asked me one day if I loved him, I told him that I didn't grow up with declarations of love, and it felt silly and childish to me. The first part wasn't true. Mom and Dad showered us with love and affection when we were kids.

My friends my own age still met up in bars and nightclubs, went to drive-in movies, enjoyed rollerblading and got wasted at their children's birthday parties, but I realized that I was living Vince's life. We did a lot of Netflix and no chill. We tried out every new restaurant as soon as it opened. We were ready with our opinions on the latest book-to-TV adaptation and the latest fine-dining experiences when we had other couples over to dinner. Long, dull evenings, where the men would discuss their golf handicap and the wives would discuss anti-ageing creams, menopause, and of course, books. We all avoided discussing politics, it was becoming too contentious. I didn't resent those women, but I floundered. There was something missing from my life. Business was great – I had one author in the *USA Today* chart and one who had been shortlisted for a National Book Award – but I was unfulfilled. Maybe I did want a baby after all, but our sex life had diminished so much that it would probably be a miracle for me to conceive, now aged forty-two. I stayed on the pill.

Around this time, Vince got an email saying that somebody had found Nick, that he was safe and well in Boston and wanted to meet Vince. I questioned who had sent the email and he showed me: mk123@qmail.com. I knew immediately that was Milo. I had been waiting. I knew that he would try his hardest to find Nick from the moment Vince handed him the flyer five years earlier.

When I explained it to Vince, we wondered if it was some kind of ruse to get back into my life. Vince emailed him and asked him if he was Milo Kelly, and told him that he knew what he had done to my sister. Milo responded that he had never done anything to my sister and that he had spent thirteen years in prison for nothing, but if Vince wanted to meet his son, Milo was happy to arrange it. Vince called him up. Apparently, Milo had befriended Nick slowly over the course of six months. He described it like getting an abused dog to trust a human again. He had asked a psychiatrist friend of his to meet Nick where he lived in a semi-derelict house in Fenway and, together, they had persuaded him that he might feel less fear if he took some anti-psychotic medication. I recognized the name of the psychiatrist, Ben Roche. He was one of Milo's friends when he was in college. They had been together at the Boston Marathon on the day of the bombing. Ben had called my sister a liar. He'd been in court the day I gave evidence. But, apparently, he and Milo had put Nick back together. I did not want to have a reason to be grateful to Milo Kelly after everything he had done to our family.

Vince went to meet him on his own. And, later that evening, he brought Nick home. The years had taken their toll on him. The last time I had seen him, he was emaciated, but now his face was puffed up and swollen, probably a side effect of the drugs, he said. His words came slowly. He cried when he entered the house and said he missed his mom. Vince caught him in a bear hug, and I felt like an intruder. I asked Vince if I should leave, but he wanted me to stay. Nick said I should stay too. He apologized for all the hurt he had caused. He was hazy about how he had met Milo. His memories of the last few years were like shrapnel, a fight here, an arrest there. He had a rap sheet and had served time in correctional facilities, which had made him even more afraid and paranoid. But nobody had ever offered him genuine help until Milo. He was lucid and coherent despite the slurred words and the swollen appearance. I made up the spare room for him.

Nick never said how long he was going to stay, and we didn't ask. He'd realized that he had a mental illness and was accepting of the treatment he was getting from Dr Ben, who had been treating him free of charge. He felt calm for the first time he could remember. It seemed like it should be a happy ending, but all I could think of was how Milo had spent months with Nick in this city until Nick was well enough to come home, and I had no doubt in my mind that he was still trying to prove to me that he was a good guy. How could Vince not be grateful to Milo? He had offered him money earlier that evening, but Milo had refused to accept it. How noble of him.

52

This was Milo's way back into my life. Inevitably, he and Dr Ben were the only ones who Nick trusted completely. Vince was caught between a rock and a hard place. He asked me not to tell Nick what Milo had done, saying 'he has probably saved Nick's life'. Vince even wondered aloud if Ruby's rape had been some kind of flirtation that had got out of hand. We barely spoke for days. Nick went out to meet up with Milo a couple of times a week, and when he asked if he could invite Milo to our house for dinner, Vince said yes. I was livid and wanted to tell Nick exactly how trustworthy his best friend was, but Vince begged me not to.

'Whether you like it or not, that man has turned his life around, and if he did the crime, he has served his time.'

'If?' I said, incredulous.

'I didn't mean that.'

'You don't believe he did it. His DNA was inside my sister, for the love of God.'

'It doesn't matter whether I believe he did it or not. You're talking about something that happened nearly twenty-four years ago. Don't you think people can change?'

'You've been talking to him, haven't you?'

Vince couldn't look me in the eye. 'He has taken exceptional care of my son for nearly a year. He stood by him when everybody else failed him, including me. Milo earned his trust, got him psychiatric treatment and into a position where he seems mentally stable for the first time in years. You don't have to be here when he comes.'

'Sure, you'd like that, wouldn't you? So he can tell you that the DNA was planted, that my sister is a liar, that he's an innocent man. No way. I'm going to be here.'

Vince pleaded with me not to make a scene, not to confront Milo about anything in case it upset Nick. I did not want to be there, but I knew now how manipulative Milo could be. He'd do anything to get into my good books, but he could not unrape Ruby. I was going to be there.

Nick felt absolute loyalty to Milo. He told me that Milo had once been in prison too and that, when he got out, he went to work in his uncle's diner. He would drop off surplus food from the diner at soup kitchens and homeless shelters every week. Then he trained as a counsellor for a homeless charity and helped with recovering addicts and ex-cons. He still worked shifts in the diner. I asked Nick what Milo had been in prison for. He said it was some kind of assault case but he knew that Milo was innocent.

'How do you know?'

'Because he's the gentlest guy I've ever met.'

No wonder Nick had mental health problems – he would believe anything.

In early June 2023, Milo came to dinner. I had put it off as long as I could, using the London Book Fair as an excuse and then being too busy with editing, but I couldn't put it off forever. When Nick walked into the room with him, Milo looked at me with a warm smile, which I did not return. Normally, Vince did the cooking, but on this occasion, I did. I could spend less time in Milo's company. When it was time to serve, I sat in the seat opposite Nick to avoid facing Milo or sitting beside him. The three men were discussing the Bruins. Milo was telling some story about hopping a fence with a cousin to get in to see a game at the TD Garden when he was twelve years old, but they were caught and given a lifetime ban, and that's why he wasn't ever an ice hockey fan. Vince and Nick laughed and told him they were sure that particular security guard was long gone by now. Vince offered to take Milo to a game with them the following weekend.

'I don't go where I'm not welcome,' said Milo, grinning.

'Really?' I said, ice in my voice.

The grin disappeared. 'Yeah,' he said, 'like, that security guy could have made up a story that I stole something and called the police. I don't mess with the law. I haven't found those legal people to be honest or truthful.'

Vince beside me put his hand on my wrist. I took several deep breaths while Nick and Vince went back to discussing the Bruins. I met Milo's eyes briefly but there was no anger or defiance in them, he was unreadable.

For the rest of the evening, I said little, and spent more time than necessary in the kitchen. When it was time for Milo to leave, I avoided shaking his hand. He tried to take my hand, but I shoved them both in my pockets. He said goodbye and thanked me. I nodded towards him and kept my mouth shut.

53

The following year, on a December evening, I was the last one in the office, reading through the latest submissions. Vince called to say it was dinnertime. This often happened, particularly in the winter when it got dark so early. I would get lost in a fictional world and not notice the time slipping by. I locked up the office and headed homeward, a five-minute walk through the snow. There was no moon. It was darker than usual. I had my head down, buried in my thick fleece collar. It was bitterly cold. As I passed an alleyway, suddenly I felt a sharp blade at my throat as a hood was shoved over my head from behind.

'Don't make a sound. If you scream, I'll cut you.'

I was too frightened to absorb the words and too shocked to make a sound. The next thing I knew, I was dragged backwards into the alley and shoved into the back of a van. My attacker took my bag off my shoulder, searched my pockets and found my cellphone, muttering, 'Shut up . . . shut up . . .' all the time, though I was too terrified to utter a word. I felt my arms being wrenched back from my shoulders and something hard and tight – cable ties, I guessed – securing my wrists. Then he pushed me down to the floor on my front.

'Stay down, bitch,' he warned.

I didn't hear anyone else. He seemed to be on his own. There was something vaguely familiar about the voice, but I couldn't place it. I could hear the doors closing and feel the van shift as he sat into the driver's seat.

'What do you want with me?' I said, crying now as the shock wore off and the seriousness of my situation became obvious.

'I told you to shut up, bitch.'

I was almost immobile, but I was able to kick the side of the door with my feet. He roared at me, 'Stop that, stop!' And I did.

For the next fifteen minutes he drove in silence. I tried to remember the route, a right turn and then a left, another left and it felt like we were on the freeway, but then I realized we had stopped at a pedestrian crossing because I heard the beeper for blind people. I was completely disorientated. I couldn't tell where we were. Then the van swerved and stopped. He turned the engine off and got out. I screamed, as loud as I could, but then I heard him pull the back door of the van open, and he must have hit me because I lost consciousness.

I came to. I was in a cold room, probably a basement. I felt pain all over. I must have been pushed down the steps. A sack was over my head and tied around my neck. I could just about breathe through it. I was terrified. I had to fight hard to control my panic. I could hear him shouting on the phone in a room above me.

'But I got her for *you* . . . Don't you think she should be punished? . . . She must pay for what she did . . .'

I realized then that this was the person who was behind all the messages, the letters, texts and emails. He was deranged.

'I only roughed her up a bit, no broken bones . . . What?' Then he was arguing with whoever was on the phone, because he screamed, 'Fuck you!'

I shouted, 'Let me go!' and then a door slammed, and I could hear only muffled sounds as if he was pacing up and down in the room above me, occasionally shouting indistinct words.

The next sound I heard was music to my ears: police sirens, a lot of them. And then there were screeches of tyres and a loudspeaker.

'Come out with your hands in the air.'

I felt like I was in an episode of *NYPD Blue*. Thunderous steps surrounded the building I was in and then there was a splintering sound – a door was being broken in. And then the sweetest sound of all, 'Ma'am, are you okay?' and gentle hands lifted me to a sitting position and removed the hood.

I looked around me. I was surrounded by four police officers, with another one standing at the top of the basement stairs.

'Are you Erin Cooper?'

I nodded but I felt faint. I knew there was a gash on my head. When they snipped the cable ties, I pushed my hair out of my eyes and, looking at my hands, saw they were covered in blood.

'May I have some water, please?' I couldn't stand up straight when I tried, my right ankle would not hold me, and I was embarrassed to discover I had peed myself. Then paramedics came with a stretcher and carefully lifted me on to it and out of that dank basement.

When I got upstairs and outside, I was surprised to find that I was in a very ordinary suburban house. The garage door was open, and cops were all over the van and in the hallway and up and down the stairs. Then I passed out.

Later, I woke up in the hospital, feeling queasy and thirsty. Vince was right beside me. 'My God, are you all right, honey? Erin?'

'It was Milo,' I said, 'one of Milo's friends.'

Vince took his hands in mine. 'Erin, it was Milo who called the cops. The guy who kidnapped you is Leo Bermingham.'

I was confused.

'Principal Bermingham?'

Whatever sedation they had given me was strong. I couldn't process what I was being told.

I woke early the next morning. I had a fractured ankle, which had been operated on, and some cracked ribs, as well as a laceration to my face. He had hit me with a wrench. My skull was intact, but they had to keep me under observation for twenty-four hours because the cut around my eye socket, which had been stitched up, was long and deep. It was black and purple. I was lucky to keep my left eye, they said. I would be only mildly disfigured, a nurse told me, which is not what anybody wants to hear, but I was grateful to be alive.

Vince never left my side. I didn't want to talk much. The girls from the office all wanted to see me, but I didn't want to see anyone.

Detective Sergeant Hernandez paid me a visit later that day. She confirmed that Leo Bermingham had the old typewriter. They had found the burner phone that I'd thought was Margie's, Photoshopped images of me on his home computer, as well as the emails to Watling and Harris. He had already spent several spells in a psychiatric institution and those times coincided with the periods when I got no messages. Hernandez said Leo Bermingham had become fixated on me, because he couldn't get to Ruby. He blamed us for 'framing Milo Kelly'. Milo had been his pet project. He claimed to have been 'a father to that boy'. He had been forced to quit his job the year I left school because of unspecified 'erratic behaviour' but I guessed it must have had something to do with Ruby or me. He had even admitted to the attempt to burn down Dad's church. It was a blessing that Dad wasn't alive to see this. Hernandez and I had let him believe that it was some teenage vandals. Bermingham had been a regular visitor to Milo in prison for the first year or two until Milo took him off his visitors' list. On his release, Milo had tried to get a restraining order against him coming to the diner, but as a convicted rapist, he didn't have much success.

Bermingham fully believed in Milo's innocence and had

decided I was the evil one who had ruined Milo's life. I'd never told anyone about the campaign of hatred against me except for Detective Sergeant Irene Hernandez and my oldest friend, Saima. Bermingham got a four-year sentence.

Hernandez assured me that neither Milo nor Margie was complicit in Bermingham's harassment of me or my abduction. She reminded me that she and I owed an apology to Margie. I tried, but Margie didn't want to see or hear from me. Hernandez gave her a letter of apology from me and told me she tore it up right in front of her. She talked about suing me for harassment and she could have, but I never heard anything.

Vince was angry that I'd never told him about the campaign that had been going on for years. But I could not deal with another angry man. I didn't want anyone to touch me, not even Vince. I stayed in the spare room. From that point on, I drove to the office and back. I constantly looked over my shoulder and startled easily. I was unable to get past the fear I felt in that basement. Even though I probably spent less than two hours there, I had truly believed they were the last hours of my life. I was put on an anti-anxiety medication, a low dose during the day and a higher dose at night so that I could sleep.

Of all people, Nick was the one I related to most. He'd had years of paranoia. He understood fear. He shared books with me, by Gabor Maté and Eckhart Tolle, and taught me to treat my anxious self like another person, to welcome her in with compassion and to meditate in the moment. He taught me some breathing exercises that helped too.

My physical wounds healed. I had my hair cut into bangs again to cover my forehead, and the scar around my eye socket faded. Vince told me it was invisible, but I could see and feel it. I was Frankenstein's monster.

Milo did his best to convince me he had nothing to do with Bermingham's actions and never knew about the messages or the fire or any of it. I wasn't sure I believed him. I did not want him back in my house. Vince understood and kept him away. I let Carla take the reins at Cooper Rivera for a while as I tried to recover from the trauma. I began to write stories again. I could find an escape only in the alternate worlds I created.

PART FOUR

54

Lucy

Growing up with two recovering addicts was not easy. Mum was prone to moods and depression, though she'd never admit it. Dad was not my real dad, but I don't think I could have loved him more if he was. He was always ready to talk about anything I was curious about. But nearly all their friends were sober alcos too. There was never booze in our house and I thought that was normal until I went for a sleepover at my pal Melanie's house when I was about thirteen. Her parents had some of their friends around, and they all got drunk; they were singing and hugging each other at the end of the night. Mel said this often happened and used it to her advantage. She knew that when they were 'merry' was the best time to ask for an Xbox, or a new iPhone, or for cold hard cash. Cash was the best, because their friends would contribute too. That night, Mel and I made a hundred euro each from her parents and their friends, and they were fun. One lady kept running her fingers through my hair and saying, 'A natural blonde, don't ever dye your hair, it's beautiful,' and a man did some magic tricks and pulled a twenty-euro note from behind my ear.

When I came home and told Mum and Dad about it, they seemed embarrassed, and Dad said, 'Don't you think we're fun?' and they were, but not in the same way that the drunk people were. Mum bought a book about magic tricks and tried a few out on me but I could tell her heart wasn't in it. Dad bought me a new iPhone out of the blue about two weeks later.

They sat me down and explained what addiction meant and how recovery was a lifelong commitment. I kind of knew all this stuff already. There were framed affirmations all over the house. But then they told me the story of what their lives were like before they gave up drugs and alcohol. They gave me a sanitized version of events until I was old enough to handle the truth when I was about fifteen.

They were both alcoholics and cocaine addicts. When Mum was bad, she was *bad*, she couldn't stop. She stole money from Granny and almost died after a suicide attempt when she was just a little bit older than I am now. She said she was deeply affected by having to leave Boston after Granny and Grandad broke up and being separated from her sister. That sounded bad to me, but Dad's story was a whole lot worse.

Dad was a child actor in a TV show called *What's Up* for seven years, but he was also in a lot of feature films as a kid. His mother was a pushy 'stage mum', and his schooling suffered because he missed so much. He was on stage or screen from the age of seven to twenty-five. His father was an alcoholic, and violent with it. If Dad failed at an audition, his father would beat him. His younger sister was a kid actor too and she got the same treatment. One time, when he was fifteen, Dad was hospitalized after his father threw him down the stairs. His mother lied to the doctors about how he tripped and fell, but the doctors noticed other bruises and marks on his body and started asking inconvenient questions. The police were called, and Dad spent a week in a foster home with an ultra-religious family who told him that if he prayed hard enough, he would never be beaten again. Dad had already tried that, and it didn't work. He soon landed back at home with his parents because he felt he needed to be there to protect his sister.

The rows between Dad and his father became more violent as Dad got older and began to fight back. He put his own dad in the hospital one time, but his father called the police this time and social services got involved again. It was all entirely dysfunctional. As soon as he was eighteen, he asked his mother for access to all the money he had earned, but his parents had spent it or squirrelled it away somehow. They'd had fancy foreign holidays and lived a lavish lifestyle but had never had the sense to buy a house. Both had given up work as soon as their children started earning a substantial living. Dad moved out of the house and took his little sister, Barbra, with him. His parents didn't put up much of a fight. He changed agent, hired a lawyer and went no contact with his parents. His new agent gave them a place to stay, and various friends in show business helped them out. He never got the money he had worked for from the age of seven, and the pressure of raising his young teen sister was a lot for such a young man.

She died in a car accident on an icy day when he was twenty-two. She was being driven home from school by a neighbour. It was one of those things where nobody was to blame. The road conditions were lethal. Everyone in the car died, including the neighbour and her daughter.

Poor Dad, it was incredibly sad. Sometimes when I was growing up, I thought that he was overprotective of me, but I know he was thinking of Barb. There were photos of her all over the house, a beautiful, clear-skinned girl who never made it past fifteen years of age. I admit I was jealous of her for a time, but when I told Dad how I felt, he was understanding. Photos of me began to replace the photos of her. Dad has always been cool.

Mum has not. She had a few relapses when I was small, but I don't remember them. She had far less reason to go off the rails, but she was always moody, prone to snarkiness. With Mum, I knew that she felt obliged to love me, but I never thought that she liked me much.

55

I was a good student. My teachers said I was a quick learner and, despite Dad's objection, I was allowed to skip fifth class in junior school when I was ten. I think Mum was proud of me in those days. In the summer holidays, I would read the schoolbooks for the coming year out of interest, and I'd joined a CoderDojo club when I was nine because school wasn't stimulating enough, and coding was useful for everything. I didn't want to do transition year either and consequently I did my Leaving Certificate at sixteen and went to college.

I had no intention of following my parents into show business. When I was younger, I had considered it because Mum thought it was a good idea. Dad was against it. I took all the classes in the Academy, but never felt like I was the person I was pretending to be. It certainly didn't come naturally. I know that Mum was disappointed in me. Also there were times when we had lots of money and times when we were broke, but it meant never being able to plan anything. When I was eleven, we moved from a mid-terrace house on a former council estate in Inchicore to a detached house in Ranelagh. Mum and Dad fought about that too. She thought she was going to get some big inheritance from Grandad when he died but she got far less than she expected. In the following years, meeting the mortgage payments was like constantly walking a tightrope. Dad had to be away a lot for work after that. Feature films mostly. I suppose you could say my dad was famous, but as far as I was concerned, he was just my dad.

When it came to career options, I was turned off by anything artsy. I wanted independence and I knew that if I was ever going to move out of Mum and Dad's, I'd have to earn a shitload of my own money. The future seemed to be in FinTech, or Financial Technology as I had to explain to my parents, who looked at each other, bewildered. I was good at maths and science, which also bewildered them. Perhaps I'd inherited those skills from my birth father, whoever he was.

Simon Perry was on the interview panel when I went for the interview for my internship at ComStat Holdings. I was extremely well qualified, having done computer science specializing in cyber security, I was confident and I knew I'd done a good interview. When I started, I was assigned to work with a team that reported to Susan Cunningham, but after a week there was a change. I never knew the reason, but I was reassigned to work for the team that was led by Simon Perry. I was pleased because Simon was more senior. He was a good boss, quick to assign credit when it was due, and when we got things wrong, he explained everything clearly. He didn't look for who to blame, he was all about problem-solving.

We were in an open-plan office and my desk was closest to his. The first thing I noticed about him was how good he smelled. He would sometimes come to my desk and lean over to show me something on my monitor. He smelled clean, of soap or aftershave. He wore a suit well, and he often mentioned going to the gym before going home. I couldn't help noticing what good shape he was in when he would stand up and stretch at the end of the day. Sometimes, his shirt might have come loose, and I'd see a bare tanned patch of his toned stomach. One day we were in the break room together at lunchtime and he was talking about some new café bar that had opened and he said to me, 'Want to check it out for lunch next week?' There was only me in the room, and I wasn't sure if it was a date or not, like, he was about fifteen years older than me, but I said yes, because it seemed rude to say no to your boss.

I'm not a fool: I had googled Simon, and he was married with a baby and an attractive raven-haired wife. I was not interested in having an affair. The next day, leaning over my desk again, he asked me what I thought of a gold bracelet he was going to buy for his wife. It was over €2k. Okay, I thought, it definitely wasn't a date, and over lunch in the shiny new café bar, he talked about his political journalist wife and showed me photos of their holidays in the Seychelles. He was wearing board shorts in the photos which he swiped through. I talked about being the youngest graduate at my college. We drank Cokes and sparkling water, and I came back to my desk a little late, but relieved that there was no question of him seeing me in any romantic way.

But after that, I began to think of him differently. I imagined myself on that beach with him in the Seychelles. I was slimmer than his wife. And a lot younger.

A few weeks later, he found another new restaurant that had just opened, though this one was further away. He asked me if I wanted to go and again I said yes, feeling a little ripple of excitement this time.

When the day came and I saw the others on my team dressed up, I had a slight feeling of disappointment that I was not the chosen one after all. We were all going. This time we did not go back to work after lunch and there were bottles of wine on the table. I never drank that much, but Simon was constantly filling our glasses. He was becoming more and more attractive to me, but he didn't pay me any special attention. Daniel, who'd started in the office at the same time as me, made some comment to me about Simon, that it was obvious I liked him. He'd caught me gazing at Simon while I was supposed to be listening to Steph's tale of hiking in Tibet. Daniel said he wished Simon was playing for his team. Daniel was funny and sweet, and I guess this was his way of telling me he was gay, though he didn't have to. My gaydar was finely tuned, except when it came to myself. I'd had a month-long fling with a Canadian girl in college. I was crazy about her and told Mum and Dad I was a lesbian. They were, as expected, annoyingly laid-back and unshocked. 'Good for you,' said Dad, and then Mum said, 'Nasrin's daughter is gay too. You might get along?' and my eyes rolled so far back in my head that I could see my ass.

Daniel was my work pal, and we were seven weeks into the placement. We'd been told that only five out of fifteen of us would be chosen for full-time jobs. I already knew that I was one of the five. I'd won contracts and had created a database to streamline each approach to a new client, based on seven core criteria. It had been adopted across the entire company, and I'd received a hefty bonus. I was popular with the others in our team too – they wanted to learn from me.

But I was not the centre of Simon's attention on this afternoon that progressed into a drunken evening. At the end of the night, I was feeling out of control. I went to the bathroom and downed a few of the complimentary bottles of water. As I emerged, Simon exited from the gents. He took my arm and twirled me around like a ballroom dance move.

'You're something else, you know that?' he said and, with his arm cradling me, dipped me back, so that my head almost touched the floor. Then he lifted me upright, kissed me a smacker on the lips and moved past me back into the restaurant. It had all happened so fast, I couldn't believe it was real.

As the others began to drift off, I lingered, eyeing Simon, who was now completely ignoring me, showing the boys something on his phone. Daniel said goodbye.

'Remember, he's married and he's got a reputation,' he said as he was leaving.

I wanted to know more about the reputation, but I was watching Simon. 'See you Monday,' I said.

At the end there was Simon, Greg, the accounts manager, Ian, one of the other interns, and me. We were talking about the worst summer jobs we had ever done. I was careful to put my hand across my glass as more wine was poured. 'Spoilsport,' said Simon and then continued his story of working the bar at a golf club in Martha's Vineyard as the Bernie Madoff scandal became public knowledge, and people got up and abandoned their tables during lunch service. We all hung on his every word, and then Simon suggested to the men that they go on to a casino.

I was not invited. I went home alone, feeling humiliated and foolish.

The mixed signals continued for weeks. I couldn't understand it. Simon would often join me for lunch, but I noted he went for lunch with another intern, Gina, too. Daniel was my only confidant. 'Be careful,' he said. 'Don't you think it's weird what he's doing?'

I tried to act innocent. 'What?'

'Come on. He's trying to play you off against each other.'

'That's ridiculous, I like Gina.'

'I'm sure she'd say the same about you, but why don't you go for lunch with her if you're such good pals, instead of waiting to see which of you he's going to choose? Greg told me there was a girl here last year who had the hots for Simon, and one day she called in, handed in her notice and wouldn't give any reason. Everyone thinks he rejected her. He enjoys the flirtation, but he's married. He has a kid.'

'So? That could mean anything. Anyway, I'm hardly going to give up a job like a lovesick puppy. I don't even have the hots for him.'

'Sure you don't.' Daniel did not believe me.

56

At work, I continued to excel, often staying late, or at least being seen to stay late to get Simon's attention. Sometimes I *would* get it. A report due at the end of the week would be on his desk on Wednesday morning. He would come over to my desk and perch on the end of it. 'Well, well, star girl, ahead of schedule as usual. When do you sleep?' I'd laugh and then he might or might not invite me to the newest, shiniest lunch venue. We would discuss work mostly, but sometimes it would get a bit more personal.

'I cannot understand why a beauty like you hasn't been swept off her feet by some knight in shining armour,' he said to me one lunchtime.

I wanted to point out how archaic his attitude was, the idea that women needed a knight, but it was all light-hearted. I wanted to find out more about what he got up to away from work. 'What do you do to unwind after a week at the office?' I asked.

'I do my best to stay out of the house. The chores are endless. We have a gardener and a cleaner, but Adanna insists I repaint the nursery for the new arrival.'

'She's pregnant?' I tried to keep the disappointment out of my voice.

'Not my idea, I can assure you. I thought she was on the pill, but you women are tricky little creatures, aren't you?'

Poor Simon, his first child was only a year old. It was hardly fair of his wife to plunge him back into more sleepless nights so soon.

'I have an apartment nearby,' he continued. 'I used to rent it out but now I stay there at least two nights a week to get some sleep. Adanna is furious about that, but you understand how full-on this job is – I need to be on the ball.'

I sympathized and agreed that Adanna should have consulted him before getting pregnant again.

'You'd never do that, would you, Lulu? Trap a man?'

I laughed. When Mum called me Lulu, I hated it, but the way he said it made me feel kittenish.

A week later, there was a group outing from work to a Billie Eilish gig in the 3Arena on Saturday night. I didn't find out until I heard Gina talking about it on Friday.

'Oh,' I said, in the break room, pretending I knew all about it, 'are we picking up the tickets there or does someone have them?'

She hadn't seen me and faltered, 'I don't know –' but somebody else said, 'Simon must have them, he booked them.'

'Cool,' I said, swinging my hair back and moving on. I was hurt. Almost the whole team was going.

At clocking-off time that Friday, Simon passed my desk. 'How's my favourite little worker bee? Looking forward to the gig tomorrow?'

My heart leapt. I decided to play dumb. 'What gig?' I asked.

He nodded towards the noticeboard behind me. 'I put up a poster on Monday. Didn't you see it?' There was no poster. 'And I asked Gina to send an email round.'

Gina. Of course. 'I wasn't cc'd on the email. And I don't see any poster.' I was a little petulant.

He walked over to the noticeboard and came back. 'I don't know what happened to the poster, but you don't think we'd have a team outing without our best worker, do you?'

I beamed at him.

When I told Daniel that night via WhatsApp what Gina

had done, he told me that he'd got an email invite directly from Simon. When he checked, my name was not in the addressee list.

'I don't think it was anything to do with Gina, hun,' he said. I was sure she'd had a hand in it somehow, but at least now I had been personally invited.

The next night, a lot of people were planning to meet up before the gig but I'd decided to wear a knockout skintight gold dress that I'd bought on Shein on a whim some months earlier. I was determined to make an entrance.

And make an entrance I did. They were all hanging out in one of the VIP bars and mostly a little drunk when I got there. The guys wolf whistled and the girls stared. Simon shouted, 'Here she is,' as if they had all been waiting for me. 'Fancy a Negroni, Lulu?' he asked.

'Oh God, no, too much alcohol in that for me. I'll have a dry white wine, please.'

Gina turned to me. 'You look absolutely stunning, Lucy.' I wasn't sure what to say. And then she introduced me to the guy beside her. 'Have you met my boyfriend, Romero? Simon had a spare ticket and said I could bring him.'

I was surprised. 'Nice to meet you,' I said, and indeed, Romero was the most handsome man in the room. I immediately felt warm towards Gina. I had misjudged her. We chatted for a while before going into the auditorium. I swapped places with Gina and Romero to sit beside Simon. I tried to be subtle.

The concert was great. I knew Billie Eilish's music well because my dad liked her too and played her stuff on Spotify regularly when he was cooking. Mum preferred old-fashioned stuff like Christina Aguilera, who was probably as old as she was. I stood and danced for most of the gig, like everyone else. Simon stayed seated but I could feel his eyes on me. Daniel was in the row below me. I twirled him from above and he blew kisses at some friends on the other side of the arena. Simon didn't dance with me. But he didn't dance with anyone else either.

At the end of the night, we all dispersed quickly. There were few taxis outside. There was news of some riot or protest on the other side of the city. People called their friends or their parents to come pick them up. Simon grabbed me around the waist. 'Want to come to my apartment and call a taxi from there?' I did not need to be asked twice. We snuck off into the night and ten minutes later I was in his apartment. It was opulent and very male. The sofas were pale grey velvet, the artwork was slick, black-and-white photography of bullfighting, wild horses on a mountainside, a raging Atlantic Ocean. The lighting was recessed. I would bet that no child had ever been in that apartment. There were no signs of his wife either, apart from a chic jacket hanging on a peg in the hall. This was Simon's domain. 'Will you have a glass of wine?' he said, already popping the cork.

'Sure, but I should call a taxi,' I said. It was all a bit too real now. Simon was married. I was in his apartment. Adanna, his pregnant wife, was probably home alone. He was much older than me. I needed to put the brakes on.

'I've already called one on the app,' he said. Had he? 'Come here,' he said. 'I want to show you something.'

I followed him down the corridor into another room, the bedroom. I stopped at the door. 'Simon . . .'

'Don't be daft,' he said and pulled back the curtains to reveal a deck with a telescope under an awning. 'Want to see the moon?' He slid back the glass door, and we were outside in the cool night air. He positioned himself behind me while he adjusted the eye piece. I could feel the heat from his body. I had never felt such pure lust. I turned to face him, looked into his eyes and kissed him on the lips.

He immediately stepped back. 'Lucy, I think maybe you've

had too much to drink.' His phone beeped in his pocket. 'And that will be your taxi. You'd better go.'

I didn't say anything as he bundled me out of the door and walked me to the lift. 'Sleep it off. You'll feel better in the morning.'

I cried in the taxi all the way home. How had I misjudged this whole situation? He thought I was a good worker. Yes, he liked me, but not romantically. I was way too young for him. I was mortified by the way I had danced around him earlier. He had implied that I was drunk, but I wasn't. I'd only had two drinks at the gig and one that he'd poured for me. If anything, he was the drunk one – or was he? I couldn't tell how much he'd had to drink.

I woke up in the horrors on Saturday morning and stayed in my room for the whole weekend, dreading what would happen on Monday morning. Mum offered me food from time to time, but I couldn't face her or anyone. I told her I had a cold and only ventured to the kitchen after she'd gone to bed or when she went out. Would Simon tell anyone? Had anyone from the office seen us slipping away together? What kind of reputation did I have now? Would he move me from his team? I couldn't bear to wait until Monday. I had to nip this in the bud. I sent an email. I would pretend I had been drunk. I needed to write in a formal style – he needed to know I was taking this seriously. Other emails between us had started with the word *Yo!* Not this one.

Dear Simon

I'm sorry about what happened on Friday night. I think I was drunk, and I totally got the wrong impression when you invited me to your apartment to call for a taxi. I am extremely embarrassed and don't know how I'm going to face you in the morning. Kissing you was wrong.

I apologize wholeheartedly for insulting you, for even thinking that you were the kind of man to cheat on Adanna and jeopardize your relationship with your family. I am so stupid. I'm sure you must think I am pathetic and immature.

Please, please do not let this affect our working relationship. I have enjoyed working for you and with the team and I would hate for that to change. I know that work nights out are mentioned in the HR handbook as an extension of the workplace, and you could probably have me suspended or dismissed for sexual harassment or whatever.

I'm begging you not to do that and I'm also hoping that you won't tell anyone or escalate this mortifying situation any further.

I am so, so, so sorry. Please forgive me.

Kind regards,

Lucy

57

I didn't sleep a wink the night I sent the email. I knew Simon would probably check his emails on his phone, and I waited and waited for a response. Then I panicked when I thought, what if he showed Adanna? I even tried to retrieve the email, but I couldn't, I knew he'd read it. Eventually, at dawn, I fell asleep and woke up sluggish. I was running late for work. My eyes were puffy from crying and my skin was blotchy. I got to my desk at ten minutes past nine and kept my head down. Simon didn't usually get in until closer to half past. The Monday morning chatter around me seemed normal. Daniel came over to my desk. I tried to pretend I hadn't seen him, but he pulled up a chair beside me.

'Jesus, what's happened to your eyes?' It was obviously worse than I thought.

'I think I'm allergic to this new shampoo.'

'Well, you never replied to my texts over the weekend. Is everything okay?'

I hadn't replied to any texts and had kept my distance from my parents. 'Yeah, sure, I was busy with my cousin. Sorry, I should have replied.'

'Friday night was fun, wasn't it? You caused a stir.'

I paused. 'What?'

'Gina had a stand-up row with her boyfriend, Romero? He couldn't stop looking at you all night. She threw a glass of beer in his face at the end of the gig. Didn't you know? How did you miss that? I couldn't find you – that's why I was texting you.'

The relief I felt was overwhelming, though I hadn't seen Simon yet. At least it appeared that nobody had seen us leaving together. And everyone was talking about Gina, not me.

Just then, Simon breezed in. 'Morning,' he called and got a lot of responses.

'Thanks for the gig, Simon.'

'Great night out on Friday, cheers!'

Some of them started singing the chorus of 'Birds of a Feather' and broke into laughter. I kept my head down again but he passed close to my desk. 'Lulu, will you pop into the meeting room in about five minutes? I need to put you on the Burton project.'

My heart walloped in my chest. I'd never heard of the Burton project. Anything could happen. I could be fired, suspended, or at least moved to a different department on a different floor, with a strike against my name.

As soon as I stepped into the room, I burst into tears. Simon was sitting at the head of the long table. 'Hey, shush,' he said, and his voice was gentle. 'Come, sit here.' He indicated the chair beside him. I sat obediently, pointing my knees away from him.

'I'm sorry. I didn't know what I was doing. I'm such a fool.'

He pushed a box of tissues towards me. This was the room people were brought to when they were fired from the company. There was always a box of tissues.

'I don't want you to be upset, Lulu,' he said. 'But I don't think I gave you any reason to think –'

'No, no, you didn't, I was drunk and, like, stupid, oh God.' Fresh tears poured down my cheeks.

'I think you should go home,' said Simon.

This was it. The end of my career before it had begun.

He continued. 'You're clearly in no condition to work today, but there's no need to be anxious about it. It was a silly mistake, and we can chalk it down to too much alcohol and overexcitement. Go home, watch some mindless daytime TV and relax, maybe get yourself a massage, and please stop crying. There's no need. I deleted that email the minute I read it, and I suggest you do the same. I'll see you in the morning and we shall continue as if nothing has happened, okay?'

My heart lifted with every sentence. No dismissal, no suspension, no HR involvement at all.

I couldn't believe it. I stopped myself from hugging him obviously but thanked him profusely and promised him it would never happen again. I closed the door behind me, overwhelmed with relief. I told Daniel I was going to see a doctor about my eye infection and left the office. I couldn't believe I had gotten off so lightly.

On Tuesday, everything was as normal in the office, though I avoided eye contact with Simon, even though he included me in all the meetings and, as usual, praised my work.

Then it came to Thursday of the following week, and Daniel asked me to come to Angelo's, a new gay bar, with him on Friday. He was a bit of a lost soul in Dublin. His friends and family were in Mullingar. He was living in a soulless apartment block fifteen miles from the city centre, sharing with strangers. I sensed he was lonely. I agreed but, as we were discussing it, Simon appeared and invited himself along. Although I was nervous, I replied, 'Of course.'

But Daniel was peeved. 'It's a *gay* bar, Simon.'

Simon laughed. 'I'm sure they won't throw me out. I'm popular with the gays, you know.' There was a bit of an edge to his voice and Daniel knew his place.

'Fine,' he said. 'The karaoke starts at eight – we'll need to be there by seven to get a seat.'

'Karaoke?' said Simon. 'How wonderfully retro. Do I have to be in drag?'

We laughed, and I felt another wave of relief. Simon wasn't afraid to socialize with me again, and this time I was going to be keeping my hands to myself.

The next day, I dressed carefully. My skirt was short, but it was summer. I wore a high-necked blouse that revealed nothing and a jacket over that.

At the end of the working day, Simon suggested we go to Bar Four before Angelo's. Daniel said, 'Okay, but only for a short while.'

We all walked down to the bar together. I was quiet, not wanting to be seen as too gregarious or needy. When we got there, I asked for a glass of wine, but Simon insisted we should have gin and tonics. He went to the bar while Daniel and I found a table. 'Are you okay?' he quizzed me. 'You hardly said anything on the way over.'

'Sure, I'm tired.' And I was tired. The previous two weeks had taken their toll on me, and I hadn't slept well, thinking of all the things that could have happened.

Simon came back with the drinks. I hadn't drunk spirits before. Maybe growing up in a house with two alcoholics made me wary, but on a night out I'd have three glasses of wine max. The gin relaxed me, though. Simon was good company, telling funny stories about his tiny daughter whose first word was not 'mama' or 'dada', but 'tractor'. Adanna was spending the weekend back at her parents' farm in Cork with little Sadie. Simon ordered another round of drinks. Daniel didn't want one. He wanted to get going to Angelo's.

'Will you go ahead and save us a seat? We've only just started these. We'll follow you down,' said Simon.

Daniel gave me a look, but Simon caught it. 'Don't worry, I won't let her try to ravish me again,' he said, laughing.

I blushed to my roots and Daniel looked confused. 'I'll see you down there, okay?'

'Sure,' I said.

Once Daniel was gone, Simon turned serious. 'You know, I've been thinking about it and I may have led you astray after all, that day in the restaurant when I met you coming out of the bathroom. Remember, I twirled you around and kissed you on the cheek?'

I remembered, though I clearly recollected he had kissed me on the mouth.

'I'm sorry, Lulu. I did it to a few of the girls that night. I remember worrying afterwards that some of them might think I was a lecherous old perve.'

I didn't think anyone thought of him like that. But I appreciated the fact that he was owning up to this. I felt better. I hadn't imagined things. Simon was just one of those flirty guys. He didn't mean anything by it. We got into talking about relationships then. I told him about my first boyfriend in school. I also told him that, strictly speaking, I was queer – that I'd had a girlfriend in college but I was into guys now. I wanted him to know that I wasn't as buttoned up as it might appear because I was such a work nerd. He then had me rate the guys in the office on a scale of 1 to 10. It was cruel but funny.

I think we mutually decided that we weren't going to join Daniel. I texted him to say that I was too tired and that I was going home. It was a lie, and I should have gone to Angelo's, but it was nice to have a proper conversation with Simon, knowing that it wasn't going to lead anywhere. I could relax and be myself. He told me about his childhood, a weak mother and a father who left them both when he was fifteen. We had more drinks and then he announced he was starving and suggested we go to L'Étoile Bleue for dinner.

I remember arriving at the restaurant; I remember trying to refuse more alcohol, but Simon insisted on a bottle of expensive wine. 'You're going to love it,' he said, but after four G&Ts on an empty stomach, I wouldn't have known the difference between champagne and cider. He filled my glass but not his own. 'I'll have some in a minute,' he said, and he ordered food. I had fishcakes to start and duck confit for my main course. My glass never seemed to be empty. I remember saying 'No more wine' and he mimicked me in a baby voice, and we laughed hysterically. Everything was funny.

After that, I remember little. Moments came back to me.

Simon leaning over me outside somewhere. I must have been on the ground. Did I fall?

Simon struggling to get the key in the door of his apartment.

I must have fallen asleep in the chair because I remember being woken up and Simon giving me a glass of wine. Did I drink any of that?

The next thing I remember was waking up naked, and in terrible pain, not just from being hungover. I didn't dare to count the welts and bruises all over my body. There was a terrible ache between my legs. A discarded used condom was on the floor beside me, and an empty wine bottle. Simon was fast asleep on the bed.

As quietly as I could, I gathered my clothes and my bag, and left. I hailed a taxi on the street and went home.

58

Ruby

In early August, Lucy came home early one Saturday morning in a state of hysteria. Crying uncontrollably, breathing erratically.

She had always been fiercely independent. She had desperately wanted to move out of home, but the internship in her company was only covering her day-to-day expenses. The housing crisis meant that she could be living with us for another ten years. At least we had plenty of room. When she was in college, she regularly had friends stay over, sometimes for weeks at a time, essentially because they couldn't find anywhere to live. Jack loved having a house full of people. I was okay with it for a while, but on days when I couldn't find a mug because they were in seven different rooms around the house, it became a hassle. I dared not say anything, though. Jack would take Lucy's side. She communicated with us via WhatsApp. Woe betide us if we called her. She had made it clear that she no longer needed me and that I was not welcome to come into her bedroom without an invitation. She usually cooked her own food and ate in the garden room. She joined us for Sunday lunch every week as if she was visiting. That suited me, though Jack missed her a lot. And yet, here she was, choking with tears and clinging to Jack in a way that she hadn't done since she was a toddler.

Jack tried to calm her. I was alarmed. 'What's happened? What's wrong? Has somebody died? Did somebody hurt you?'

I said. She shook her head and took several deep breaths before the story emerged in bits and pieces.

She told us that on Thursday, her manager, Simon, had asked her and a male colleague, Daniel, out for a drink after work on Friday. Lucy was nineteen years old. Simon was in his mid-thirties and close to the top in this Irish branch of a multinational company, ComStat Holdings. She had often mentioned Simon, how he praised her work, how kind he was, how he did charity work in Eritrea every year.

When Daniel left to go to a gay bar, she said yes when Simon asked her out to dinner. They had more wine with dinner. Lucy, as far as we knew, did not drink much. We weren't sure because we never had alcohol at home. She said he was good fun and that he told stories about his wife and kids. She didn't think he was seducing her. She could hardly remember anything after the main course was served but woke up naked on the floor of his bedroom in his apartment nearby the office this morning, not his family home. She didn't remember getting there.

'He raped me.'

'What?' I clamped my hands over my ears. My heart felt like it had been weighted with lead. Jack swept her up into his arms. Was this my fault? Was this karma?

Jack wanted to call the police. I pulled the phone out of his hand. 'You can't,' I said, 'once the police are involved, we lose control of the whole situation.'

'What are you talking about? That bastard raped our child, just like –'

'Jack!' We had never told Lucy about the incident. I had barely talked about it in fifteen years, and the version I did tell, I almost believed to be true. But I knew. I hadn't been raped. I had framed Milo Kelly. I had planted DNA evidence. I didn't want to have to tell all the lies to my own child.

'Please, Jack, let me,' I said. 'I know what the police will ask.'

Lucy looked from Jack to me, the tears spilling down her face, bewildered.

'Darling, was this what you were wearing?' The blouse was high-necked and sleeveless, the jacket was tight, the skirt was short, the sandals were high and her legs were long and bare.

'Jesus, Ruby, I can't believe you of all people are asking this question.' Jack was annoyed.

'Just shut up, Jack, I'm protecting her.'

'Mum, why does it matter what I was wearing?'

I made her take off the jacket. Lucy had a beautiful shape, curvy in all the right places, like Erin had been at that age. Men would notice her. But there were bruises on her wrists, her upper arms and one shoulder. Her knees were bruised. I felt faint. I had to keep it together.

'Is that what you normally wear to the office?' I asked. Jack groaned and sighed heavily at me.

'No, but I knew I was going out after work.'

'Tell me about that again. Who arranged it?'

A blush passed her face. 'Daniel asked me on Thursday if I wanted to go for a drink with him last night.'

I hadn't met Daniel before, but I'd heard all about him.

'I thought you said Simon had asked you and Daniel on Thursday?'

'Well, he heard Daniel and me talking about it, and then he invited himself along.'

'When you said in the beginning that Simon invited you and Daniel for an afterwork drink on Friday, that wasn't true. Do you see what I mean, Lucy? If we get the police involved, they will grill you like this – you must be sure of everything.'

'Mum, don't you believe me?'

If she was lying, then she wasn't raped, and it wasn't my fault. I prayed that she was lying.

'Of course I do. How much did you drink? In the pub? Before dinner?'

'We had two or three with Daniel –'

'Was it two or three, Lucy? These things matter.'

Jack slammed his fist on the table. 'For God's sake, Ruby, all that matters is whether she consented.'

I ignored him. 'In the pub, was it two or three drinks?'

She looked up at me and I could almost see the cogs in her brain turning. She opted for the truth. 'It might have been four.' I looked at Jack. He closed his eyes, appalled by the irrelevance of the question. Or was he appalled by her lie? I couldn't tell.

'And Daniel was there all the time, for these four drinks? Was it beer, wine, spirits? What did you drink?'

'Gin and tonics. Simon said they were proper summer drinks.' She hadn't answered the first part of the question.

'And Daniel?'

I could see the blush rising to her cheek. 'He left after two.'

'You arrange to go out with Daniel on Friday, and you dressed like that for your gay friend, and then he left after two drinks?'

Jack interrupted. 'Did you consent to sex with Simon?'

'No.' She shouted the word and burst into tears.

'That's all we need to know,' said Jack in a weirdly triumphant way.

'He spiked my drink, he must have.'

'Lucy, I believe you were raped, I do, but there cannot be any doubt.' I lied about believing her. If it was true, that would be my punishment, and I could not accept that.

'I don't want to go to the guards anyway,' she said.

'Why not?' said Jack, taken aback.

'Because they'll never believe me. It will be my word against his. They always get away with it.'

I relaxed a little. I didn't want her to go through that either.

'Lucy, I don't want to upset you, but I must ask this. Did you ever sleep with Simon before, consensually?'

'No.'

'Okay. Were you ever in that apartment before?'

She whispered. 'Yes.'

Jack released her hands and stood up. 'When were you there before? Why? How many of you?' he asked.

'Two weeks ago, we'd been out at the Billie Eilish concert, a gang of us, and we couldn't get a taxi, on the street or on our apps. Simon said I could come back to his place and wait there.'

I jumped in. 'Just you, not the others who were also trying to get taxis?'

'Just me. But, Mum, I swear to you. We had a glass of wine, and I left when the taxi came.'

'Did anything happen between you? Did you kiss, Lucy? That time, when you were alone with him in his apartment?'

A fresh outburst of tears confirmed my suspicions.

'Oh God,' said Jack.

'I was drunk. I didn't know what I was doing. I apologized to him afterwards. And the taxi came that night. It was one stupid kiss.'

My voice hardened. 'Why did you apologize for kissing him? You initiated it?'

'Yes, but I thought he liked me.' Fresh sobbing.

Jack had been silent and was holding on to the kitchen counter with his back to us.

I said, 'You had four gin and tonics and then shared at least one bottle of wine with dinner. Is it possible that he didn't put something in your drink? Isn't it possible that you blacked out?'

'I don't know. I'm not used to so much drink.'

'You weren't roofied, then?' I said.

'Jesus Christ, Ruby, would you go easy on her?' Jack was exasperated with me.

She shouted, 'You don't believe me. Why don't you believe me? He raped me last night. I did not consent to sex. Whether he drugged me or I blacked out, what's the difference? I wasn't conscious.'

'I believe you,' said Jack.

'I believe you,' I said, but I didn't, I couldn't. 'If you kissed him, you were letting him know that you liked him,' I went on. 'Help me understand. Did you want to sleep with him?'

'Maybe. I thought that one day in the future he might leave his wife, and we could be together, but I wanted it to happen slowly. I know it was stupid, I know it probably would never have happened. It was a silly crush.' She was too young to be out in the world. Now I understood why Jack had objected to her skipping a year in school and had really wanted her to take a gap year before she went to college. She was academically brilliant but hopelessly naive.

'But I woke up this morning on the floor of his bedroom, not even near the bed, and I'm covered in bruises and bite marks. I don't remember anything. He was in bed snoring away like nothing happened. There was a used condom on the floor too. And a wine bottle. I think he may have used the wine bottle to . . . I ran out the door and came home.'

'Darling,' said Jack and went to hug her again. 'We'll go to the police if you want, Lucy. Any way you want to handle this, we will support you.' He looked to me for reassurance. I shook my head at him. Lucy wasn't looking at me.

She wanted to take a shower. She knew that taking a shower would mean the erasure of evidence, but she opted not to go to the guards. Jack said, 'You know this means there's a rapist out there who can target other people? Don't you want to stop him? Where does he live? I'm going to go and beat the living shit out of him.'

I turned on Jack. 'Why should it be Lucy's responsibility to stop him?'

Jack was annoyed. 'I can't say anything right. You can at least let me go and sort him out?'

'No, Dad, please don't. He's younger than you. Stronger. He could hurt you.'

'Just give me the address.' Jack was shouting now.

'We all need to calm down,' I said.

'But, Ruby –' Jack started.

'Shut up, Jack,' I cut across him.

Lucy burst into tears again. Jack backed down then. 'I'm sorry, pet. The only thing we are doing today is looking after our girl. Lucy, love, do you mind if your mum takes photos of the bruises and the bite marks?'

I didn't like where this was going. 'Why?'

He ignored me and directed himself to Lucy. 'Do you want to keep working there? For ComStat Holdings?'

'Not if he's there.'

'Fine. I will go and meet him. It's Simon . . . Preston, isn't it? I won't lay a finger on him, but he has to be warned.'

'Simon Perry. Dad, what are you going to do?'

As he asked her these questions I went up to her bedroom, and I fetched towels from the airing cupboard. I needed to get away from both of them, but I could still hear them.

'I'm going to gather evidence. What restaurant were you in?'

'L'Étoile Bleue.'

An upmarket place where the tables were in booths separated by silk hand-painted screens. Jack and I had been there. We had joked that it would be the ideal place to go if you were having an affair.

'I'm going to see if they have CCTV inside or outside. He must have carried you out. Someone will have noticed.'

'Why would they hand over CCTV to you?' Lucy asked.

'Because I will tell them that they will be part of a rape story in the newspapers if they don't hand it over. Don't worry, I'll only say it to make them cooperate. Where is the apartment?'

'In the Docklands, the Zevon Building, number 902. It's a penthouse apartment. He stays there sometimes during the week. His family home is in Wicklow somewhere.'

Of course it was. Lucy wouldn't have fallen for the mailroom guy.

'I will pay him a visit in the office on Monday and show him the photos, screenshots, whatever I can get.'

'Dad, he's going to lie to you.'

'I will *know* if he's lying.' He smiled at her.

I played along. Taking photos of my daughter's bruised body was truly traumatic. There were teeth marks on her breasts, almost as if he had tried to bite her nipple off, bruising across her stomach, teeth marks on her buttocks where he had drawn blood. Her knees were scraped as well, though that might have happened when she fell. She did not remember how she got these marks.

God knows what kind of porn was out there, all available at a click. Twelve-year-olds were watching it on their phones. Sexual activity had certainly changed since my youth. Had their encounter been consensual? Maybe violent sex was a turn-on for some girls, but my Lucy? Then I hated myself for thinking that.

Part of me was thinking 'that bastard' about Simon Perry. And part of me was thinking of how ambitious Lucy was, how driven, how badly she had taken loss or rejection in the past.

When she was five or six at a Sports Day in elementary school, she smacked the girl who beat her in a race, her face red with fury.

When her first boyfriend broke up with her at fifteen, she stole his bicycle. We didn't know a thing about it until spring arrived and Jack went to the shed for the lawnmower and found the bike, immediately recognizable as Tommy's. I thought it was funny at the time. I guess I was relieved that she hadn't done anything worse. In fact, I thought she had handled that rejection well, though we made her return the bike.

And then, when she was older, her team had come second to two girls from another school in the Young Scientist of the Year competition. I was called into the school a week later. Lucy had found the kids on the winning team on Snapchat and Instagram and had left nasty comments about them cheating, suggesting they had won by blowing one of the male judges. God knows how it hadn't become a bigger story, but she had done it using an anonymous account. Both schools got involved and it took very little to uncover her identity. I was ashamed of her. We took her phone and turned off the Wi-Fi router in her room for a month.

Our beautiful Lucy, such a brilliant, smart and funny child from the beginning, and yet she could be devious. And she could be as dishonest as I was.

Had Simon rejected her after consensual violent sex? Had he told her he was never leaving his wife? Was that why she was upset? Had she been obsessed by him? She had certainly mentioned him often enough.

Yes, Lucy was book-smart, but she was younger than her peers, and she wasn't as emotionally mature as them. Maybe she had gone along with what Simon wanted and then regretted it.

I remembered being back in Boston in the cop station making my statement. I lost count of how many times I had to tell my story to different people and then again behind a screen in court. I loved the attention but they tripped me up a few times. I gave two different versions of how I got the cut on my head. The mechanics of how Milo got my jeans off were questioned. He had said I was wearing shorts. I said jeans in my witness statement. I was asked why I thought he called me Daisy Duke if I was wearing ordinary jeans. She famously wore denim shorts. I was asked why I'd invited him into the house when I knew that

Erin wouldn't be back until very late. Lots of little lies that I had to make up on the spot and then remember for the next time.

Lucy's story was full of contradictions, and we were her parents. I *wanted* her to be lying. I needed a drink badly.

Lucy stayed in her bedroom. I left Jack to take care of her and said I was slipping out to get some groceries. Instead, I went drinking. That was the night I ended up in the Merrion Hotel, out-of-control drunk for the first time in fourteen years, in bed with Karl from Austin, Texas.

59

When I arrived home the morning after Lucy appeared, I told Jack I'd been triggered by Lucy's experience, that I'd needed to get away. I'd stayed the night in the Merrion Hotel by myself, I told him. I had been smart enough to shower and sober up with gallons of coffee and breath mints before I came home that morning.

Jack had been worried sick, and Lucy was distraught because she thought I'd relapsed because of her. I went to her bedside and lied that I believed her. We assured her that she certainly wasn't going to have to go back to ComStat Holdings while Simon was there. We would call in sick for her.

I stayed home that day, disguising my hangover as distress, although I *was* distressed. Was my daughter like her mother?

Lucy stayed in bed with the door closed, her tears audible from the corridor outside. Jack ordered takeaway, but Lucy wouldn't come out of her room to eat it. He was angry, furious. He wanted to kill Simon Perry. I tried to talk him down. If Lucy had been a victim of violence, she wouldn't want to see any aggression in her home.

'If?' he said, looking at me strangely.

'Please,' I said, 'let it be.'

'You have to tell her,' he said.

'Tell her what?'

'About your own rape.'

'Absolutely not. We are never telling her that.'

'But she –'
'Never, Jack.'

That evening, Jack began his investigations and duly reported back. There were no cameras outside L'Étoile Bleue, but the manager was more than willing to help Jack when he heard that the restaurant might make headlines for all the wrong reasons. He knew Simon, he was a regular customer, although usually with big groups. According to the manager, Simon and Lucy both seemed a little drunk on arrival. Lucy was alert all the way through the meal. They had ordered dessert and eaten it. This didn't tally with Lucy's assertion that she remembered nothing after the main course. They had ordered a bottle of wine in the beginning and then were given complimentary shots of Sambuca with their bill. He remembered Lucy had drunk both shots. Simon paid the bill. When they got up to leave, Lucy had stumbled out of the booth and Simon had helped her up. She was unsteady on her feet, but still chatty. They had been offered a taxi, but Simon said he lived nearby and indeed the Zevon Building ('the most dazzling example of luxury living' as it was touted at the time of its launch a few years ago) was within walking distance. Simon wasn't exactly carrying her, but he had his arm around her. There was nothing to suggest any bad behaviour on either part. They had laughed a lot, the manager said.

Jack told me these details reluctantly.

'Oh God, she lied,' I said.

He looked at me strangely. 'She was drunk but that doesn't mean anything. It means she doesn't remember that part of it. When we were drunk or high back in the day, we both heard about crazy shit we did after the fact. She liked him, she was planning his divorce before she'd even kissed him. But she has no reason to lie about the rape. I think she wanted to sleep with him. But if it was consensual and nothing untoward happened, why would she come home yesterday morning in pieces and bruised all over?'

I wanted to agree with him, though I had doubts. 'Maybe she fudged the truth to avoid our judgement of her lifestyle. She's the daughter of two recovering addicts. We've all made bad decisions when we were young and drunk. You and I should know.'

He put his arms around me, and I rested my head on his shoulder. Dearest Jack.

'Well, what about Simon? We can't let him get away with it,' he said.

'I'll go see him,' I said.

'No chance. I will deal with Mr Perry,' said Jack. 'You're not going anywhere near him.' Jack wanted to protect me from a rapist.

60

The next day, a Monday, Lucy stayed in her bedroom again all day. I brought her trays of food which were barely touched. It was eerie how her actions mirrored mine in the days after the incident. Jack came back late from work. I had stayed home for Lucy.

'How is she?' he asked.

'The same.'

'I went to see Simon Perry today after leaving the Academy. I think he will be leaving ComStat and not coming back.'

'What did you do? You confronted him? Did he admit it?' I was flustered.

'It's okay. I dealt with him, like I said.'

'What happened?'

'I made a five o'clock appointment with him. He knew my face from TV, but he didn't know I was Lucy's dad. She mustn't have told him.' Was there slight disappointment in Jack's voice? 'I told him I wanted to invest with my shelf company, Orifin.'

'Your what?'

'I'm an actor, remember? And I needed him to take the meeting.'

'In his office?'

'A big meeting room overlooking the Arena. I had to ensure he got the message. He had a young guy bring us coffee while I played the part and then, when I heard all the doors closing and people outside saying goodbye for the night, I showed him the photos of Lucy's bruises. I told him who I was and that I knew exactly what he'd done. He said she was asking for it. I suggested that we call his wife to get confirmation that he liked rough sex.' Jack's hands were clenched into fists as he spoke.

'Simon Perry was completely chilled out, the fucker. He threw some paper at me. "You need to read this. Lucy is obsessed with me." He presented me with an email from Lucy to him, dated about two weeks ago. It was an apology for kissing him and in it she begged him not to fire her. She had put it all in writing.'

I was right. I felt nauseous.

Jack was keeping his voice even, but I could tell he was rattled. 'Simon said that Lucy never objected. He accused me of trying to destroy his marriage over a one-night fling.'

Jack had shown him more of the photos. 'I asked him how Lucy could have consented when she was unconscious. He said she wasn't unconscious and that she had consented. I could tell he was lying. He thought I'd back off after I saw the email.'

'Are you sure you don't believe him?' I asked Jack.

He looked at me incredulously. 'Of course not. I lied to Simon that Lucy has made a full statement to our solicitor. I admitted that Lucy had had a crush on him but she never consented to being violently assaulted, because she was unconscious. I suggested he resign immediately or we would go to his wife and then to the guards. He stood up as if he was going to show me the door, so I kneed him in the balls to drive the message home. He could barely get off the floor. I said to him, "I thought you liked it rough."'

As he was telling me this, Jack couldn't keep the smirk off his face. 'On rare occasions, it's justified. I did it for Lucy.'

'Absolutely,' I said.

61

Lucy

After I left Simon's apartment, I never saw him again. I couldn't get past the fact that it was somehow my own fault. I'd made it crystal clear that I found him attractive. I didn't remember saying no. I didn't remember saying anything. I showered three times per day. Dad took me to our GP after a week, but I wouldn't let him come into the office with me. When I sat in the chair facing her, and she asked me what was wrong, I started to cry and I could not stop. Dr Joyce asked me to take some deep breaths, but I had a full-blown panic attack right in front of her. I thought I was going to die. She helped me on to the reclining bed and checked my vitals and then gave me a glass of water and a yellow tablet, which I later discovered was Valium.

Finally, I could speak. She coaxed the words out of me bit by bit and pieced together what had happened on Friday night. She asked if I wanted to go to the rape crisis centre or the police. I told her no. I agreed to a physical examination. I told her I thought he'd used a bottle to penetrate me and she agreed that he probably did. There was some tearing and lacerations, but they had already begun to heal. She said she was very sorry to hear what had happened to me and wrote down the number for Women's Aid. She also gave me the number for a trauma counsellor and asked if I lived alone. I was feeling a little better by then and told her I lived at home with my parents and my dad was in the waiting room and that my parents knew. She told me to keep talking to them at the very least. She gave me a prescription for Xanax, to take when I felt panicked or overwhelmed, and she signed me off work for a month. She could not have been kinder.

I spent most of the month in bed. Mum stayed home while Jack looked after the Academy. I didn't want to be on my own and Mum was better than no one. I went back to eating meals with my parents, though I couldn't summon up much of an appetite. I blamed myself. I remembered dancing at the Billie Eilish concert, doing my best to catch Simon's attention. I threw up a lot in the first week and thought I could be pregnant, but Dad got me three different pregnancy tests and they were all negative. I had a phone consultation with Dr Joyce. She assured me that it was a trauma response, and it would ease off as I physically recovered. The mental scars would take longer to heal. I felt like my body wasn't my own, as if it was some filthy and worthless appendage that I was doomed to carry around. Women's Aid, when I eventually called them at 5 a.m. one morning when I could not sleep, were very helpful. They assured me that what I was feeling about my body was a normal reaction to a sexual assault. They offered counselling and sent me a list of therapists.

On the work WhatsApp group, the word was that Simon had been mugged and was in hospital. They were organizing a collection, and then, a week later, he resigned with immediate effect. Everyone was shocked. I stayed out of those conversations. Daniel never texted me after that Friday night. I knew he was pissed off that we hadn't turned up at Angelo's and that I'd never called him over the weekend, but I was in no condition to talk, apologize or make small talk. I wished with my whole heart that I had gone to Angelo's with him.

Mum and Dad were being weird. After the morning I came home and told them what happened, Mum did not want to talk about it and that night she disappeared. She had Dad and me worrying all night. She came back the next morning with some lame excuse but we knew she'd been drinking. We both ignored it. Dad tried his best to keep things normal and kept talking to me.

Eventually, I told him the full story of my infatuation with Simon, and the whole thing I had imagined with Gina. Dad looked furious. 'Lucy, don't you see? He was grooming you all along,' and it wasn't until he said it that I realized how true it was. Simon had been giving deliberately mixed signals the whole time. Excluding me from the concert invite and making me blame Gina. The lunches with her and then with me. There was a door on to his balcony in the living room. In fact, the telescope on the balcony was positioned closer to the living-room door. There was no need for him to bring me through his bedroom, except seduction, and when he acted shocked after I'd kissed him, it was all part of his plan. I'd been sick with worry, and I'd apologized to him in writing. How stupid I had been. He was setting me up, and he had the email to prove my complicity. But Dad scared him off and apparently put him in the hospital. I wondered about that other girl who had disappeared from the office. Daniel thought she'd had a crush on Simon, and he'd rejected her. Maybe he'd done the same thing to her. It stoked my anger.

A month after I was raped, I went back to work. Walking into the office felt like walking on a tightrope. I got to my desk and sat down. I had to remember to breathe in for four and out for eight until I stopped trembling. Several people welcomed me back and asked about my gallbladder operation. That was the story I used to explain my absence. I opened my emails. There was nothing from Simon. There was an email to say that Susan Cunningham would be leading the team going forward. I immediately felt better. The atmosphere was normal. At the end of the week,

I subtly asked around about the girl who had left suddenly and got her name, Miranda Hayes. Her number and email address were still in the employee database. I didn't know what I was going to do yet, like, you don't ring someone up and ask if they've been raped. I had her number, though.

I started with a text.

> Hi Miranda, I've been working for ComStat Holdings for 3 mths. Everyone says u were great when u were here. Did u work for Simon Perry? Heard u left before end of ur placement. Was that cos u got a better offer? Wd love to discuss if u have time?
>
> Lucy Brady

I avoided Daniel even though I knew he was expecting an apology from me. I was too ashamed. Despite Dad and my therapist trying to force me to see it wasn't my fault, if I had been a loyal friend to Daniel, it wouldn't have happened. He blanked me in the break room, and I didn't socialize with work colleagues again. I didn't care what they thought of me. I had a lot of absences over the next few months. There were days when I couldn't get out of bed. I knew I was jeopardizing my career, but I couldn't help it.

62

Ruby

I was back at work at the Academy by the end of August. Jack was in rehearsals for a new Mark O'Rowe play. But Monday afternoons were Lucy's therapy sessions and Jack insisted that I should collect her as she was likely to be at her most fragile then. So Lucy and I both left work early on Mondays. I made a big effort with her. Jack said we needed to wrap her in cotton wool.

I sat waiting in the car during her session, scrolling through Instagram. I lurked there mostly. My profile photo was a flower arrangement. I never commented or offered opinions, but it was interesting to see what other people were saying, and from time to time I had to see what *he* was saying, Milo Kelly, the man whose life I ruined twenty-six years ago. He used this name on Instagram, which was clever under the circumstances, and I never saw any negative comments on his posts. Maybe he deleted them quickly or maybe everyone had forgotten. He hadn't died of cancer. He was not a doctor, as he had hoped. When you googled his full name, Michael Joseph Kelly, and Boston rape, it came up in court records from 2000. Michaels usually became Mikes. There were no court records for Milo Kelly.

As far as I could tell, he'd been on Instagram since 2017. I knew that he'd been released early in 2013, after serving his thirteen-year term. Mostly there were photos of him among his colleagues in Billy's Diner in downtown Boston. He wore the white uniform of a chef. Maybe he'd replaced his uncle. There were photos of fish he'd caught at Boston Harbor. It looked like he'd gone back to his South Boston origins. South Boston was different now compared to how it was back in the day. The whole area had been redeveloped. I wondered how he could afford to live there. Or maybe he didn't? He looked old, though, so much older than I would have expected for a forty-five-year-old man. His curly sandy hair was shorn and white. His wrinkles were deep. He'd had it tough. It didn't seem like he had a wife or significant woman in his life. I knew he'd never be able to find me since I went by my married name, Ruby Brady, or for theatre work, my stage name, Ruby Bean.

The urge to drink was back, and I had a feeling that morning I wasn't going to resist it. I'd even parked in front of the off-licence beside the therapist's office. I'd had a slip on the night that Lucy came home with her story of woe, which led to me waking up with Karl from Austin. I lied my way out of that one and Jack believed me because he wanted to. The shame consumed me, and I couldn't tell anyone what had happened. I'd avoided my sponsor since.

I watched Lucy emerge from the counsellor's office where I'd been parked up for fifteen minutes. Her shoulders were slumped.

'Hello, darling! How are you?'

She didn't reply. We travelled in total silence. I remembered that. It was how I had been when I was faking trauma. I knew her game.

I resisted going into the off-licence. Perhaps I could get through this day. I went through all the tools in my AA arsenal: 'A day at a time. Play the tape forward.' The last time could have been a slip but, if I drank today, it would be a relapse. Nearly fifteen years of sobriety down the drain.

When we got back, Lucy went straight up to her room, while

I prepared dinner. Jack came home and I immediately lied and told him that I was going to the theatre with Sinéad and Jane that evening. That was that, decision made. The lie was told. I *was* going to drink. He asked me how Lucy had been after seeing her therapist.

'No different,' I said.

'I know we've spoken about this, but –'

'No.'

'Don't you think it would help her, Rubes?'

'Jack, please.'

I shut down the conversation. We had been through this many times. I thought I had convinced him that Lucy needed me to be strong. She couldn't see me as a victim too, I'd said.

During dinner with our silent daughter, the only thing I could think of was how soon I could get a drink. Jack asked about the show I was going to see, but I'd done my homework. I could name the actors, some of whom were friends. I knew the playwright as well.

'I thought you didn't like him?' said Jack.

'I don't but I'm going to support Julie, you know she hasn't been on stage in eight years. Apparently, she's a nervous wreck.'

Lucy said, 'That's because she can't act.'

It was such a relief to us that she had spoken that we laughed and agreed with her. She seemed somewhat more relaxed today than she had since her incident. Her plate was empty. When Jack got up to fetch more vegetables, she rose from her seat and hugged him, and he wrapped himself around her. Whenever I'd tried to hold her, she'd flinched from my touch. I needed to get out.

'I'll take the bus into town,' I said, clearing the plates away, in a rush now.

'Hey, I'm not finished.' Jack was looking at me curiously. 'And you never take the bus.'

'Yes, but parking is such a pain around there.' I wasn't going to drive drunk. I would be home late. I already had the Polo mints and orange in my bag. I'd sleep in the spare room, say Jack was snoring.

'Okay, but take a taxi home? I don't like you being in the city at night.'

'Yes, I'll be fine. Don't wait up, though, we might go to the Troc afterwards.'

'Sure.'

Lucy was staring at me. 'Mum, I don't want you to go out.'

I couldn't answer her. Jack looked at me and then turned to her. 'Your mum needs some time out, honey.'

'From me?'

I dug my nails into my palms under the table and tried to keep my voice even. 'No, not from you. I need a night out with some friends, darling. I know it must seem impossible to you, but life must go on.' I needed to get away from her badly.

'Will you be talking about me?' Her big brown eyes filled with tears.

'Do you want me to?'

'No.'

'Good, because we have happier things to talk about, like Jane's upcoming party.' I grinned.

Jack glared at me. Lucy pushed her chair back and stormed up to her bedroom.

'Maybe you shouldn't go out –' Jack began.

'We have to live our lives.' Even if it did happen, it had been well over a month ago now.

'I thought that you, of all people, would understand. But your behaviour has been so . . . erratic,' he said.

'Don't you get it? I am triggered by all of this. That's why I needed to get away the night Lulu came home after the assault. A hotel room on my own with the phone turned off. You should be grateful that I'm not drinking.' This was the lie that got me off the hook the morning after.

'Do Sinéad and Jane know?'

'About me? Or Lucy? No, it's none of their business.'

'I know we said we'd keep it private, for Lucy's sake, but it might help you to talk to them about your own experience?'

I closed my eyes as if by doing so I could plug my ears too.

'Shut up, Jack. I'm over it. I did the rehab and the therapy. It's not something that you casually bring up during the interval of a show, is it? "Did I tell you I was raped when I was sixteen?"'

63

I started my evening in the Morrison. I didn't know anybody who hung out there. I pretended to be a tourist. I convinced myself that black was white. It's probably what made me a good actor and drama teacher. Hotels were anonymous. The bars where people my age socialized were few and far between and there was more chance of meeting someone I knew in those places. All my friends and probably most of my acquaintances knew that I was a recovering alcoholic.

The hotel lounge was empty but then it was a Monday night. I sat at the bar and ordered three glasses of wine, one after the other, and I drank quickly. Within an hour, my defences were down. I wanted to be someone else. I was chatting amiably to the bartender. She didn't ask me any questions, we talked about her. She was off to Boston for the summer. She asked if I had any pearls of wisdom to impart. I told her that she should try to catch a Red Sox game at Fenway Park. A few people had come in by this time, young couples who failed to notice me. That happened with increasing frequency. The joys of being in my forties, I guess. A man of about my own age came in. I checked my cleavage and discreetly hoisted it upward. He bypassed me completely, went to a corner table and opened a laptop, having ordered a sparkling water. I looked over a few times, but he didn't look my way. I craved sex like I had when I was in college. I remembered my first time with Kenny Carter. I felt the twenty bucks burning my palm. I got another drink to wash away the memory.

Later, suited men entered, an older man with a young guy. They sat near me on bar stools. The older one was upset and was being comforted by the young man. Lawyers, I guessed. We weren't too far from the courts. Eventually, the younger of the two left, and I caught the eye of the other in the mirror behind the bar. I smiled at him.

'Did you lose your case?'

'Sorry?'

'Lawyer?'

'God, no, much worse. Auctioneer. Estate Agent.' He laughed bitterly.

'A realtor.'

'American?' he said.

'Bingo. How did you guess?' He was not a theatre-goer, then. He showed no sign of recognizing me.

He moved down the bar and, as he did so, he knocked his pint glass across the bar. A spray of dark liquid splashed on to my dress before I could get out of the way. The bartender swung into action, cleaned up the mess on the bar and handed me some clean napkins while the man rambled his apology.

'Shit. Sorry. I guess I'm having a bad day and it's getting worse. I'm sorry. Your beautiful dress.' I was busily sponging off the worst of the stain with tissue. Luckily, it was around the knee-length hem. The man was still jabbering away. 'I blew the sale of a multi-million-euro office building to a Chinese investor. My car wouldn't start and then the taxi ran out of petrol. You couldn't make it up. Turns out that Chinese people are sticklers for punctuality. I was only twenty minutes late. He left before I got there. And then my day gets that bit worse when I throw Guinness on to the dress of a beautiful tourist.'

'It's okay.' I was flattered. I'd had the usual Botox and fillers, but only Jack called me beautiful. I felt sorry for him.

He smiled at me forlornly with even white teeth and for a moment I was reminded of Erin's bright grin.

My sister Erin had married some much older guy nine years previously. Vince was sixty years old and Erin was forty-four now. She invited me to the wedding, but that would have meant going to Boston. Mom had hassled me about going: 'She wants you to be her bridesmaid.' I told her I couldn't go because I had to look after Jack's drama school. The timing was wrong, I told her.

'Let Jack find someone else. You don't owe him anything. Besides, the timing will never be right for you to go to Boston,' she said, narrowing her eyes at me. She was right and she knew exactly why.

When she returned, she showed me a lot of photos. Vince had two adult sons and was a widower. Erin should have married one of the sons, they were cute. We didn't speak much after that. I couldn't remember the last time I'd heard from Erin. Maybe it was the time she told me I was entitled for expecting Dad to leave me proper money in his will. That was 2018. Seven years ago.

'Please let me pay for the dry-cleaning?'

I shook the thought of Erin out of my head and turned my attention to this poor man and his bad day. Maybe I could turn it into his lucky day. He hadn't even tried to hide his wedding ring yet. Mine was in my handbag.

He was still ranting on, feeling sorry for himself. 'Accountability, my father always said, was what mattered. It's my own stupid fault.' Eventually, he stopped, noticing I had folded my dress up on to my thigh and that my glass was empty. 'Please let me get you another drink?' he said.

'Sure.'

Within an hour, my hand was on his thigh, and he was considerably more cheerful.

I remember telling him I was in Ireland on holiday to visit a cousin who lived in Donegal. I was staying one night in Dublin, I lied. I vaguely remember we left the hotel and went across the river to the Clarence Hotel. The same river I had been rescued from a lifetime ago. After that, it was hazy. Flashes of conversation. Kissing up against the wall in the corridor of the Clarence under the stairs, like drunken teenagers. I don't remember any mention of a wife, but then I never mentioned Jack either. I remember a taxi journey, but after that, it's all a blank.

64

I woke in this stranger's house. The second man in six weeks. On the bedside table (obviously his wife's side) there was an old photo of them kissing under a garlanded arch when his hair was dark as opposed to absent, and another more recent one of them with their hands on the shoulders of a young girl who was wearing the cloak and mortar board of a new graduate, taken in what I recognized to be the main quad of Trinity College. I thought about Lucy, also a Trinity graduate. I wondered what Lucy would think if she knew where I was, if she knew what I had done. What I had done now and what I had done then. This mother and daughter in the picture frame were redheads, though the daughter's was natural. The wife whose bed I was in was older than me. She squinted in the sunlight at the camera and her furrowed brow was Botox-free. Also on the table, an old-fashioned alarm clock and a transistor radio, both of which told me that the time was 6.14 a.m. There were five different types of medication, none of which I could identify except for a blister pack of anti-inflammatories.

My head pounded and I felt a surge of nausea rising. I took deep breaths to contain it. In for four and out for six. I raised my head from the pillow to further take in my surroundings. It hurt. I quietly took three pills out of their blister pack. I knew the recommended dose was two, but my brain felt inflamed this morning. I felt sick, emotionally and physically.

The corniced ceiling, the luxuriant drapes, the soft bedlinen and plush carpet in tones of cream, beige and gold, told me he was a man of means. Fitted mirrored wardrobes lined one end of the room, and against the interior wall, a walnut dressing table on spindly legs was strewn with cosmetics and jars of lotions and potions, the expensive brands. I could see my handbag on the cushioned seat beside it, an imposter, it's royal blue clashing with everything else in this room, apart from my matching shoes lying at opposing angles as if they didn't want to be a pair. My dress was crumpled into a ball in a corner. I could see the strap of my bra sticking out underneath it and flashed back to vigorous kissing in that corner as we had torn at each other's clothes. This stranger and me.

'You'd better go,' he said, startling me. He was awake. 'I'm sorry, I don't . . . this isn't . . .' he mumbled, his voice clouded by a hangover I shared. I sat up and turned to face him, grabbing the duvet to cover my breasts, noting now the hair on his chest, more plentiful than that on his head. Was he an addict too?

'Me neither,' I lied. 'I had too much to drink.' And that was true.

'I was upset,' he said, clearly desperate to make excuses for cheating on his wife. 'It's Rebecca, you see, she's been having immunotherapy in Germany, it's experimental. It's a stressful time.'

'I'm sorry, I'll go. Rebecca is your daughter?' I nodded towards the photo of the graduate with her mother as I scurried to the corner, and he turned away, giving me privacy while I scrambled to get my underwear on and shrug the dress over my head.

'She's my wife. I know. I'm a terrible person.'

'What's your name?' I wanted to know more about this terrible person. Was he worse than me?

He seemed surprised. 'Christopher –' He was about to give his surname but stopped himself. 'You're Ruby, right?'

'Right.'

'And you're here on holiday?'

Is that what I had told him last night?

'Um, no, I live here.'

A flash of panic crossed his face.

'But you said . . . you're American? Your accent . . .'

'I moved here when I was seventeen. I guess I never entirely lost the accent. Where are we? I mean, this house? I'm a bit fuzzy about getting back here last night.' I did not want to admit to a blackout.

'You said you were going back home to Boston.' He seemed outraged at the lie.

'I live in Ranelagh, okay?' I was impatient now. 'Where are we?' I said again. 'I don't want to bump into you any more than you want to bump into me.'

'Castleknock,' he said, 'the other side of the city. You don't remember the cab ride home?'

I ignored the question. 'Okay, we're unlikely to be in the same tennis club. We won't be seeing each other in a local restaurant or the supermarket. It's okay.'

'Fine. You'd better go. Please. The cleaning lady often comes early.'

I left before he could tell me a third time, grabbing my handbag, reassured to feel the shape of my phone and keys inside it, although the orange and the Polo mints were gone. I made my way down a mahogany staircase to a Georgian front door with a fanlight above it. I pulled the door behind me and glanced around. It was still early, there was nobody about. I walked towards a junction at the bottom of the street and hailed a cab idling at the traffic lights. Time to face the music. While I wracked my brain to come up with a plausible excuse, my thoughts were astray with Rebecca, Christopher's wife. Poor Rebecca.

65

I took my phone out of my bag. Clearly, I had turned it to silent at some stage last night. Seven messages and eight missed calls from Jack and Lucy, the last one at 4.37 a.m. from Jack. One from Jane too:

> Jack knows you're not with Sinéad and me. Have you relapsed? We're worried about you. Hope you're only having an affair ☺

The earlier messages from Jack displayed fondness.

> Hey Rubes, want me to pick you up? I can zip into town around midnight. Lucy is upset again

read the first. But the later they got, the more the tone turned to concern and then to anger.

There were messages from Lucy after midnight, saying

> Where are you Mum?

Her last one, at 2 a.m., was all in caps.
The final message from Jack:

> I called Jane and Sinéad. I know you lied. I called the Trocadero too. You've relapsed. If you were having an affair, you wouldn't be this stupid about it. Lucy cried herself to sleep again. We can't go on like this.

I *had* been stupid. My plan had been to drink until about midnight and then make an excuse to hop in the shower when I got home and sleep in the spare room. Nothing had changed since I was sixteen years old. I did not think things through. Never looked at the consequences. What did he mean by *We can't go on like this*? Would he insist on couples therapy? Surely not now, when Lucy was going through her fake crisis.

The taxi driver watched me like a hawk. I wished he'd keep his eyes on the road.

As we bumped over Charlemont Bridge, I asked the driver to pull over. I needed fresh air and I needed a straightener. From practice, I knew there was only one way to quell the nausea. I wondered where I would get booze at that hour on a Tuesday morning. I walked back towards the bridge and looked underneath it. Sure enough, some of the tented community were awake, one of them shuffling like a zombie around a gas stove. I clambered down the grassy embankment to be confronted by a woman clad in filthy jeans and a black polo-neck sweater. She looked about sixty, but her face was destroyed by broken veins and dark shadows under her eyes. Maybe she was the same age as me. A small terrier mongrel ran around her feet, barking at me.

'What do you want?' she rasped in a cross between an Eastern European accent and a Dublin one, and the voice of someone who had smoked forty a day for forty years.

'Could you spare a can?' I said. 'I have money.'

'I don't want your money.' She looked me up and down. 'The shoes,' she said.

'What? I can't give you my shoes. I don't have anything –'

As I spoke, she ducked her head back into the tent and re-emerged a moment later with a cheap pair of trainers. They were clean at least. She turned them over in her hands and nodded towards my stilettos. 'Size six? I'll take your shoes for a can.'

My head was pounding and I could smell the perspiration pooling in my armpits. I needed the can more than I needed the shoes.

'Fine,' I said, grabbing the can out of her hands. I could have bought five hundred cans for the price of the shoes, but needs must. She eyed me with . . . was that pity?

'I can give you a number,' she said.

'For a dealer? I'm not a junkie,' I snapped at her. My relapse had been alcohol. No coke or pills.

'Yes, you are,' she said, 'your drug happens to be legal. I have a number for a treatment centre. You should call them.'

I resorted to sarcasm. 'That treatment centre clearly worked wonders for you.'

'You think I'm an addict? I'm homeless, love, but my son is an addict. They helped him there.' Her voice softened. 'He's doing great now. Got a job in a coffee bar.'

I was taken aback. I had always assumed that all these tent dwellers were addicts, asylum seekers or both.

'I'm sorry,' I said, and then, grasping for conversation, 'Are you safe down here?'

'Yeah,' she said, 'most of the time, but we're not all clean. Depends on who's around. You could be knifed for a can sometimes.'

I sat on the canal bank and drank the lukewarm lager, feeling the alcohol lacing itself around my synapses, restoring order to my stomach. I was pissed off about the shoes. How was I going to explain that to Jack? And the Guinness stains on my dress. As I drained the can and rose to my feet, I began to feel normal again. Traffic on the bridge was now heavy. It would soon be time for Jack to go to work. Maybe he'd have left before I got home. I hoped so.

66

I opened the front door with shaking hands and placed my keys on the hall table. Jack walked out of the kitchen. He was dressed for rehearsals, but his face showed the strain of a sleepless night.

'Luckily, Lucy doesn't have to witness this because she has already gone to work. Before you lie to me again, let me save you the trouble,' he said. 'You didn't stay with Jane or Sinéad, you didn't go to the theatre, and you didn't book into the Merrion Hotel. I was worried sick. Where were you between leaving this house at seven p.m. last night and –' he checked his phone for the time – 'eight fifteen a.m.?'

I couldn't think of anything to say. I began to cry, but he did not move to comfort me.

'I gave you the benefit of the doubt last time. There is mud on your dress, and you reek of alcohol. Take a shower before you go to bed. And, please, don't sleep in our bed. You can stay in the spare room until you sort yourself out . . . with somewhere to live. I'm running late. I have to go.'

'Jack! You can't mean –'

'Yes, I can. Our daughter has just come through the worst crisis of her life and you are refusing to do the one thing that you could to reassure her. I don't know what's going on with you, but don't give me that bullshit about being triggered. When you didn't want a second child, I allowed that excuse, but Lucy is the only child we have, and she's in trouble. Why can't you help her?'

I reached out to touch him as he passed me in the hallway,

but he shrank from me, almost flattening himself to the wall, and that's when he noticed. 'Where are your shoes?'

'The heel broke off one of them. I had to borrow these from Linda.' When you've been lying as long as I have, it comes naturally.

He paused for a nanosecond; he wanted to believe me, but common sense kicked in. 'Didn't Linda move to Galway last year?'

'Yes, she did, but she was back staying at her mother's –'

'I don't believe you, Ruby. Don't make it worse. Call Nasrin.'

The door slammed behind him.

I had pushed him too far this time. Was my marriage over?

67

I rifled through the medicine cabinet looking for anti-nausea meds and the codeine tablets that Jack was prescribed for kidney stones. I must have taken them all the last time. There were loose bandages, a single ear plug, paracetamol (I took three), some cough medicine (I had a swig) and a pack of Xanax prescribed for Lucy, but my need was greater. One would only take the edge off the jitters I was feeling, so I took two. I ran a bath and stuffed the shoes I was wearing into the outside bin, the clothes into the washing machine. I lowered myself into the hot water and relaxed my head on to the bath cushion.

I woke. My head was submerged, and I gasped for air, inhaling water. I pushed myself up and out of the now-cold water, shivering and coughing, my teeth chattering. I put Jack's robe on and struggled to dry myself off. Bed was what I needed. I had to sleep it off. I turned off my phone, went into the spare room and got into bed. It seemed like minutes later when I was woken by the slam of the front door. My phone said it was 1.45 p.m. I heard the footsteps and knew it was Lucy, home early. I called out, 'Everything okay, love?'

She appeared at the bedroom door. 'What are you doing in here? Where were you last night? I left loads of messages for you. Dad tried to pretend you were staying with a friend, but I know you weren't. Dad's a terrible liar.'

I ignored the questions. I had one of my own. 'Why aren't you at work?'

'Some of them were talking about how much they missed Simon. I thought I was going to have a panic attack. I had to get out of there. Why are you in bed? And why not in your own bed?'

'And how are you feeling now? Do you want to take a Xanax?' I hoped she wasn't keeping count.

She ignored me and went downstairs again. It was a stand-off. If I wasn't going to answer her questions, she wasn't going to answer mine.

As she had grown up, our relationship had become more difficult, but this new Lucy was even more spiky and suspicious. So was I.

Lucy was always a sensitive girl. As a toddler, she was compliant and affectionate to Jack and me. Her mouth naturally turned up at the corners. She had a resting smiley face. She was smart too, quick to catch on to new ideas, and she could always outargue me using logic and facts. As exhausting as this could be, she was still a sweet girl. Despite some deviousness as a child, she was a natural empath, crying when any of her friends were hurt as if she felt their pain too. Her adolescence, though, was hard on me. She was angry that I didn't know who her birth father was. She judged me. And it got worse as she got older. Everything that Jack said was right and I was always wrong. She tried to drive a wedge between Jack and me. I'm not sure how aware of it he was, but it was blindingly obvious to me. It was clear that Jack loved her more than he loved me. It awakened all those old feelings. Erin, Isobel Lucas, and now, my own daughter.

Lucy had visited my mother regularly and often took her shopping. She loved school and participated in all the social activities except for drama club, probably to annoy me. She had been an excellent student, a good netball player. She did a stellar Leaving Certificate. She was fiercely ambitious. She had loved going into the office every day because she was a social creature.

I should have been delighted with such a high-achieving child, but the way she hung out of Jack and avoided me was irritating.

It was her fault that I was drinking again. How was I supposed to help her when I couldn't help myself? I pulled the duvet over my head and went back to sleep.

68

At 4.30 p.m., I was still in bed. I could hear the tinkling sounds of YouTube or whatever Lucy was watching in her room. I was hungry. I had to get up and prepare us some food. I showered again first, washing every molecule of that man out of my body, my hair. How could I have slept with a stranger, again?

My feelings were confused. They had led me to that lost night with the man in the Merrion Hotel and then to the previous night. I had tried to carry on as normal, to ignore Lucy's moods. But now I had fallen off the wagon spectacularly, twice, and reverted right back to my teenage behaviour. The shame was back, tenfold.

I dried my hair carefully and dressed in jogging pants and a clean sweatshirt. My head was still pounding. 'Are you hungry, Lulu?' I asked as I knocked and opened Lucy's bedroom door. She slammed the lid of her laptop down.

'How many times, Mum? You knock, wait for me to say enter, and then you come in, okay? And my name is Lucy.'

'Sorry, I forgot. I wanted to check that you're okay. Feeling better? You want to come down and help me fix dinner? Your dad will be home soon.'

'Right, are we going to play happy families again? Do you know how bored I am with this game?'

She was a smart girl. The atmosphere in the house had not been good. I had been depressed and withdrawn since her incident. My disappearance last night and the night she told us, added to Jack's anxiety about it, must have shaken her.

'You're drinking again, aren't you?'

We had always been open with Lucy about our addictions.

'It was a slip, that's all. I don't know what got into me. It won't happen again. I'm seeing Nasrin tomorrow.' Lucy knew her and liked her. Maybe I *would* try to see her tomorrow.

Lucy looked up at me, her eyes pooled with unspilled tears. 'It's because of me, isn't it? You drinking, you and Dad fighting? It's because of what happened.'

Yes, I wanted to say, *it's because of you*. I shook my head. 'I promise you that's not true. Now,' I said, quick to change the subject, 'would you like a proper dinner or something simple, like beans on toast? Whatever you like. Or we could order Chinese?'

'Are you going to tell me what's going on or not?'

'I had a minor slip, that's all, and it was nobody's fault except my own.'

'Sure.' She didn't believe me.

'Please come down when your dad gets home.' It was selfish of me, but I needed a buffer between Jack and me tonight. 'I love you,' I said. Did I?

'Whatever.'

I closed the door and crept away.

Downstairs, I drank a full litre of water, a cup of tea and a can of Coke. I texted Nasrin and asked if she was free to meet tomorrow for coffee. She was the only person who knew everything. Well, not *everything*.

Jack came home. As soon as I heard the car, I called Lucy to come down. I didn't want a showdown tonight. She hadn't appeared by the time he came in, slinging his jacket on to the hook inside the hall door. 'Look, Jack,' I said, 'you were right and I'm sorry. I had a slip, and it was bad. I ended up passed out at some party over the other side of the city. I blacked out. I don't remember much of it. I'll go to a meeting in the morning. You were right all along.'

He didn't say anything, but I knew by the set of his jaw that he was livid. Then he spoke, his voice trembling.

'The first time, when Lucy came home hysterical and you just vanished that night, I believed you because I wanted to, but that was a lie too. I see that now. I could have forgiven that, but yesterday, you planned it. You lied about going to the theatre, you even mentioned the Trocadero so that I wouldn't expect you home until late. Things got out of control, as you should have known they would. You threw away your sobriety rather than discussing your own experience with your daughter who badly needs your help.'

'Stop, please, I can't. You don't understand –'

'Well, help me, then. We can all go to therapy together as a family. If you don't, we are finished. I can't believe you won't help your daughter –'

'Help me with what?' We spun around and Lucy was standing in the doorway of our kitchen.

'Lucy, come and sit at the table.' Jack sat and held a chair out for her and then one for me.

'Please, Jack, don't do this.' I started to cry.

'Your mother has something to tell you,' he said.

69

'Mum, why are you crying? Are you guys divorcing?'

'Your mother has something to tell you,' Jack repeated.

'Jack, no.'

'You tell her, or I do.'

'What did you do, Mum?'

'Your mother is a rape victim too.'

I disassociated myself from my body. I saw sixteen-year-old me clamping my legs around Milo's hips. I saw the confusion and then the horror on his face when he realized what I was doing. The way he turned his face away when I tried to kiss him on the mouth.

'Mum, why didn't you ever tell me?'

Jack answered for me. 'Your mum didn't want you to ever see her as a victim and it's still traumatizing for her.'

'Is that why you disappeared that night?'

It was. I was crying harder now, crying at the lies I didn't want to repeat again.

'And is that why you didn't come home last night? Oh, Mum.'

She was alarmed and put her hand on my arm. It was the first time she had touched me in a long while. It was not comforting. I moved my arm away.

'I'm so sorry, Mum, when did this happen?'

'In Boston, when she was young. He was arrested, there was a trial, he spent thirteen years in prison. He denied it all the way. Stupid asshole,' said Jack.

'He wasn't stupid,' I said, 'he was going to be a doctor.'

Jack looked at me strangely. I shouldn't have defended Milo. Lucy, undeterred, put her arms around me. 'What happened?'

I stiffened. I had for so long wanted to feel her touch, but not for lies. 'I don't want to talk about it. Your father *knows* I didn't want to talk about it.'

She stood up and went to the window. Jack went to put the kettle on. She turned to face me slowly. 'Mum, is your rapist my real dad?'

I was shocked. I couldn't say anything for a moment. Jack looked at me and then to Lucy. 'No, honey, of course not. She was sixteen,' he said.

I had always been truthful with Lucy. I had told her that she had been the result of a one-night stand. When she was old enough, I told her, 'I honestly don't know who your father is. I feel shame for that.' Jack and I got together when Lucy was three, though he had been in her life from the day she was born. She knew that.

We had been unsure of what to tell her and when. We broached the subject when she was seven, by telling her that Jack wasn't her real daddy, but she wasn't terribly interested then. I think she was nine when she began to ask questions: 'Do I look like my real dad?' 'Is my real dad rich?' 'Is his house bigger than ours?' 'Has he got a dog?' 'Is he dead?' I was tempted to say that he was dead to stop the questions.

I got called into the school once and a teacher told me that Lucy had been saying her mother didn't know who her real father was. The shame washed over me like a blood-red tide. It angered me that I was going to have to lie to this nosy bitch. I chose not to. When I didn't respond to what felt like an accusation, the teacher got flustered and implied that I should make something up until Lucy was old enough to cope with this information. I bristled.

'Are you suggesting that I lie to my child? She's coping fine.'
'Well, no, it's that she might be teased.'
'So she hasn't been teased yet?'
'No, not yet, but children can be judgemental.'
'So can teachers,' I said, standing up from the desk and swinging my bag on to my shoulder.

We had allowed everyone outside immediate family to assume that Jack was Lucy's father, and I think most of the time Lucy forgot that he wasn't. He certainly did.

But now nineteen-year-old Lucy had further questions. 'If my father was the rapist, I'd want to know.'

Jack stepped in. 'He wasn't. She was twenty-three when you were born, you know that.' Jack was doing all the talking.

'Mum, why didn't you ever tell me? You've told me everything else, haven't you?'

'It's a private thing. I didn't even want to tell your father. How many people do you want to tell, about Simon?'

'Ruby, for Christ's sake,' said Jack. I was furious with him.

'I'm sorry you went through that, Mum.'

When she went back to her room, Jack looked at me triumphantly. 'There, that wasn't so bad, was it? You didn't have to go into detail and Lucy feels less alone.'

'I don't believe her,' I said.

70

'What?' said Jack, and I could tell he was shocked.

'I don't believe her. There were so many inconsistencies in what she told us. Kids these days, they experiment with all kinds of sex, even violent sex.'

'But I met him, I confronted him. And he quit his job. If that's not an admission of guilt –'

'Yes, he was an asshole, but you said he denied it. Maybe he quit his job to save his marriage. You threatened him. But that doesn't mean he raped her. And that email she sent him –'

'But the bruises, the bite marks.'

'Maybe that's the way she likes it.'

'What? Why are you saying this? Whatever happened to "hashtag I believe her"? Whatever happened to the sisterhood? What kind of mother are you?'

'Jack, her behaviour since it happened, it's not normal.'

'What do you mean?'

'She went back to work last week. It's been twenty-six years for me, and I can't even go back to Boston. She's not acting like a real rape victim.'

Even as I said the words, I knew how twisted they were. How twisted I was.

'I don't think there's a rule book for how rape victims are supposed to behave.'

'Did you see her eating last night? She has her appetite back already.'

'So what?'

'I didn't eat properly for months.'

'Why are you saying this? Why don't you believe her? She told me everything. There's a lot she doesn't want you to know. There is no way she made this up.'

They were keeping secrets from me.

'What do you mean? You've been talking behind my back?'

'Yes, because you can't even look at her. She trusts me.'

'Is there something going on between you and her? You're not her birth father, maybe –'

'Fuck you,' he snarled. 'Please get out of this house.'

'What?'

'Your insinuations are disgusting. Please leave. I don't want to be around you any more.'

'I think you're forgetting that Lucy is *my* daughter. And this house was paid for mostly by me.' I knew these were low blows. We had been through crises before, but these were red lines, and I had crossed all of them. There was a pause.

'I'm sorry, Jack, I shouldn't have said any of that.' I reached out to him, but he backed away.

'You don't believe for one second that I have any romantic interest in *my* daughter. You're trying to hurt me. Well, congratulations, it worked. As for you paying for most of this house, what a joke. Your rich daddy paid off the Inchicore house, and you might remember that I strongly objected to moving here. We're always behind with the mortgage payments. Right now, the bank owns most of this house. And when I tell Lucy that you don't believe her, who do you think she is going to want as a parent? And who will she want to come home to?'

'Where am I supposed to go?'

'You don't even care about her. I couldn't give a damn where you go. You've always been a liar, from the first moment I met you. Who was it that said, "When people show you who they are, believe them"? You treat me like an idiot. I have never known what's going on with you. Even when you're sober, you're acting like an alcoholic. It never made sense why you wouldn't go to Boston, even when that bastard was in prison. You didn't go for your sister's wedding or your dad's funeral. Your mother asked me to persuade you, but you shut me out. When we got together, I thought your recovery was going well, but there's something not right about you –'

'Jack, please –' He did not let me interrupt him.

'And I can't trust you to be faithful to me. I can't trust you to be sober, and you know what? That affects my recovery too. All this drama. I'm two phone calls away from getting a few grams and a bottle of Jameson and I've never been more tempted than now, but you know what's stopping me? Lucy. She needs me. And she needs you, a rape survivor, to be on her side, but you have chosen not to believe her. How can I possibly live with you?'

71

I couldn't believe that Jack was throwing me out. I might have insisted that he leave, but I knew that, right now, they were allies. Lucy would go with Jack. Why had she always trusted him more than me? Why couldn't I convince him that our daughter was lying, the way I had convinced him that I was telling the truth?

It was late now, but there was a sliver of blue light visible under the door of Lucy's room. She had probably taken her iPad to bed. In tears, I went to our room and threw some things into a bag. Instinct made me take my passport. Perhaps a weekend in London or Paris would give everyone time and space to calm down. I knew what I wanted to do, and I knew what I needed to do. I had never bought into the Higher Power beloved of AA, but now I prayed that I would have the strength to make the right decision.

I didn't say goodbye to Lucy. This was only temporary. I'd probably be back next week. Jack loved me, he wouldn't stay mad forever. When I came back down to the kitchen, he wasn't there. The sitting room was empty, but the door to the study was closed and I could see the light was on.

'Jack?'

'What?'

'I'm going now.'

There was a silence. No last-minute reprieve. No promise to get in touch. I closed the front door quietly, got into my car and reversed out on to the road. I followed street lights, blurred by the rain and my tears. I passed the lit-up gas stations, another tented encampment of homeless people, the endless apartment blocks, the locked-up churches and the pubs and bars, with their inviting signs for beers and liquor in full neon razzle-dazzle.

I drove on to the motorway and then off it at the first exit and returned to the city. I pulled over into a deserted car park and called Nasrin. 'I'm sorry it's late, may I come see you?'

She hesitated a moment. 'Are you in danger of relapsing?'

'No, it's not that . . . look, it's all right, I promise. I'll give you a call tomorrow, okay?'

'If you're sure?'

'Yes, I'm fine.' I tried to keep the wobble out of my voice and hung up quickly, but she must have heard it because she called back immediately. I didn't answer and then she texted.

> Ruby please come, the girls have some friends here for a sleepover, but I could lock them in their room with crisps and Grand Theft Auto and they wouldn't even notice.

I didn't reply. I drove to the Intercontinental Hotel and booked myself in for the night. The bellboy didn't pay any heed to my casualwear. The more expensive the hotel, the fewer eyelids were batted in my experience, having stayed in luxury hotels with Jack when he was a film star. As soon as I had checked in, I went straight to my room. I opened the minibar to find the small fridge empty. The receptionist had said something about a QR code to get the room service menu. My frustration grew. Why couldn't I have a damn paper menu? I called down to room service and ordered two bottles of expensive red.

I stared out of the window at the rain, impatiently tapping my fingers on the sill. It was dark outside. I could see my reflection in the glass. My face looked hard; I was grinding my teeth. Jesus

Christ, what was I doing? I used my phone to find the Twelve Steps. I knew them well, but Steps 8 and 9 stood out to me. I usually skipped over them.

> Step 8: Make a list of all persons we have harmed and become willing to make amends to them all.

I had made the list long ago. Some of them were dead, some I didn't even know. Milo, his mother (dead), his sister, my mother, my father (dead), Jack, Lucy, the therapists I had lied to over the years, all the alcoholics I had lied to in AA rooms, not to mention all the real rape victims I had betrayed.

> Step 9: Make direct amends to such people wherever possible, except when to do so would injure them or others.

I read the last part of Step 9 again: *except when to do so would injure them or others.*

To tell the truth would almost certainly injure my family, my friendships, my career such as it was, and jeopardize Jack's business, as well as his sobriety. I would go to prison. I had googled it over the years. The conviction rate in sexual abuse cases was less than 3 per cent. It came down to he said/she said in most cases. The burden of proof was on the victim. Women who went through the courts felt they had been put on trial. Eighty per cent of them regretted reporting their assaults. And then the stats on the other side: 60–80 per cent of female prisoners were survivors of sexual assault. Courts did not look favourably on women who made false claims. A UK study had found that 2.5 per cent of rape cases fell under the false accusation umbrella, but some of those were due to lack of evidence or because the victim withdrew from the case. I would not survive prison among justifiably angry women if they knew what I'd done.

My confession would hurt many people and, most of all, real rape victims. I had let the #MeToo and the #IBelieveHer movements pass me by. Jack couldn't understand why I didn't go on those marches. 'The trauma,' I'd said, and so he marched for me.

In AA, they said that if you could not make direct amends, you had to find a way to forgive yourself. This had proved impossible. There had been some days over the last twenty-six years when I hadn't thought about Milo, but they were few and far between, usually when I was busy with Academy productions or when I had an acting job. I didn't like being by myself, having too much time to think. I had a radio in every room in the house. I buried myself in many books to stop myself from thinking, mostly Victorian novels, where 'incidents' didn't happen. My phone buzzed again.

'Nasrin?'

'Jack told me you've split up.'

Why did he tell her that? Did he mean it permanently? Surely my marriage wasn't over?

'Where are you?' she said.

'I've booked into the Intercontinental for tonight. I guess I'll go to my mom's tomorrow.'

'Are you drinking?'

There was a knock on my bedroom door.

'Hold on,' I said as I went to the door and sent the boy and the alcohol away with a hefty tip. I felt momentary relief. I'd done the right thing.

'Hi? No, I'm not drinking, but I drank last month, and again, last night.'

I heard her muffled voice. 'Marcelo? Can you keep an eye on them? I have to go out . . . yes, she's in trouble.' And then her voice redirected to me. 'Stay where you are. I'll be there in twenty-five minutes.'

I thought about running away, going to a local bar, but I knew I needed Nasrin. I closed the curtains, disgusted by my own reflection in the darkened window, and paced the room. Nasrin's inner Google Maps was entirely accurate. Twenty-five minutes later, she knocked on my door.

'I knew there was something up. You haven't been in touch for weeks. What happened?'

I told her the whole sorry tale about Lucy. The evidence for and against her. Jack's confrontation with Simon, Lucy's infatuation with him, the initial lies about the circumstances, Simon's denial. Nasrin asked plenty of questions. I laid out all the reasons I didn't believe her. Nasrin was silent for a moment, her brows lowered, staring at me.

'You don't want it to be true that Lucy was raped, right?'

'Of course not.'

'You'd prefer to think of her as a deceitful liar who enjoys rough sex.'

'No, it's not –'

'Which is it, Ruby? You know that women don't lie about being raped. Why are you making a case for the patriarchy here?'

'It's not true.'

'Why are you sure?'

'Because if it is true, it's my fault.'

'You've lost me.'

'Some women lie, Nasrin, they do. It's rare but they do.'

'And you think Lucy is one of these rare liars? If it's true, how would that be your fault? Do you want it not to be true because you think being a rape victim is hereditary? How fucked up is your thinking, Ruby?'

'I can't explain it.' I began to sob, shoulders heaving. How could I make her understand?

'Jack is upset, you know?'

Poor Jack. I had broken his heart.

'What are you not telling me?' said Nasrin. My relapsing and not believing my own daughter when she'd told me she had been assaulted did not make sense to Nasrin. It barely made sense to me.

'I lied,' I said.

'What?' she said, exasperated. 'About what? You *have* been drinking today?'

'No, I lied about being raped.'

72

Nasrin got up from the chair she was sitting in and took two steps back. 'I don't understand. You weren't raped at all? Why did you say that you were?'

In AA, everyone had a story that explained their drinking, and while these stories were rarely shared in meetings, the close bonds we formed with other addicts made us confessional, and most particularly with our sponsors. Jack had his screwed-up family backstory; Nasrin had her own story about being adopted into a family who had used her as a servant. In order to fit in, I'd told her my rape story. It was a lot more dramatic than the Kenny story. The impact far more explosive. She sympathized. The 'fact' that it had broken up my family, uprooted me from my home. She understood why I drank. The truth was, I'd had an idyllic childhood. A comfortable home, a strong faith, loving parents, good friends, a great school. Until Kenny Carter. And a huge lie.

Now Nasrin was staring at me, waiting for a reply.

'I was jealous.'

'Wait, what, I don't understand? You lied about being raped. What does that have to do with jealousy?'

'The boy I accused. He was my sister's boyfriend, remember? She was always perfect. I came second to her all the time. Then he went to jail for thirteen years. His mom committed suicide. I destroyed his life.'

'You didn't just lie about it, you framed a boy? And you never set the record straight in all this time? You were a kid, right, when this happened, or did you make that up?'

'I was sixteen, he was nineteen.'

'Why would you do that to your sister? He didn't assault you in any way?'

The tears were streaming down my face.

'No,' I whispered.

'Were you drinking when this happened?'

'No, I'd never had alcohol in my life at the time.'

Nasrin gathered her bag and her jacket that she had left on the bed.

'That poor guy. You fucking bitch. It didn't have anything to do with your alcoholism. I believed you, but I forgot you're an actress, and you're convincing. You had us all fooled. Does Jack know? Is that why he kicked you out?'

'No.'

She went to the door, her face full of hurt and anger.

'You have a week to tell him, and the cops, and everyone else who needs to know that you are a lying piece of shit responsible for a massive miscarriage of justice. One week, or I tell everyone. Don't look at me like that. I owe you nothing.' She stopped as she opened the door. 'And by the way, don't judge your daughter by your own standards. She was raped. You call yourself a mother? You're a monster.' The door slammed.

I never got to tell Nasrin that my mother told me not to tell the truth. But even now, I knew that was a stupid excuse.

I could have told the truth at any time in those thirteen years Milo spent in prison. Or at any time in the twelve years since he'd been released.

I could have saved my sister from years of heartache.

Nasrin was right. I should be at home comforting my daughter. I didn't want to believe her, because if it was true, that was karma coming to bite me on the ass.

I called room service again. 'I'm sorry, I've changed my mind, could you send up a bottle of Absolut.'

73

The same room service guy delivered the Absolut with a bucket of ice. As soon as he left, I unscrewed the lid and sloshed it into the glass, adding a handful of ice cubes. As I lifted the glass to my lips, my phone flashed with an incoming call. Lucy.

'Hello.' My voice was hoarse from crying.

'Where are you?'

'I'm at Nasrin's house –'

'Dad told me you're separating.'

'Did he?'

'Yes. Why, Mum? Is it because of me?'

I let the silence grow. I felt mean, and angry.

'Mum, I didn't mean to drag up the past for you. If I'd known –'

'Really? What would you have done if you'd known? I don't believe you, Lucy.'

'What do you mean?'

'I think you made it up. I think Simon Perry rejected you and you made up the whole rape accusation.'

I knew this would wound her, but I wanted to hurt her. The badness within me was taking over.

My head jerked back as I heard her phone drop on to a hard surface. I guessed she was in the kitchen. I heard her wailing. I heard Jack in the distance, 'Lucy, what's wrong, what did she say?'

I didn't need to hear any more. I hung up. Almost immediately, my phone flashed again with an incoming call. Jack. I ignored it as it flashed three more times. Then it stopped. I took a swig of the vodka. And then another. I was an alcoholic. Why not give in to it? A voicemail alert came in from Jack.

> *I don't know who you are, Ruby. You didn't need to tell her you didn't believe her. Why would you deliberately hurt her like that? We've had some great years, but I don't understand why you are such a shit mother. You loved her when she was a baby, when she was a toddler, but something changed. Every time I tried to talk to you about your relationship with Lu, you deflected or changed the subject. She could feel it too, you know, and that made it worse. You've been pushing her to move out since the day she left school, in the middle of a housing crisis. I want her here. And tonight was the icing on the cake. I'm calling Pete in the morning about a divorce. Get your own lawyer.*

His voice was full of hatred and anger. My ice was melting in my drink as I took another large mouthful. I felt the welcome surge of warmth as it immediately hit all the dopamine triggers on the way down.

I had read all the books on addiction. I knew exactly why I was an addict. I had all the excuses too, ready to roll out. It was only a matter of time before everything came flooding out, a tsunami of truth that would wash me off the face of the earth and take all the people I cared about with me.

I went to the bathroom, emptied the glass into the toilet and did the same with the vodka bottle. I had one week left until Nasrin was going to blow the whistle. I needed to get my affairs in order. And to do that, I needed my head straight. I had to start over. I plugged my phone in and began looking at flights to Perth, Australia.

PART FIVE

74

Erin

By 2025, Nick was living independently in a studio downtown. He'd had one episode the previous year when he had decided the meds were slowing him down and stopped taking them. He'd come to our house and threatened to burn it down. Out of desperation, I allowed Vince to call Milo while I checked into a hotel. Inevitably, Milo had come to the rescue and, soon enough, Nick was back on the straight and narrow. I knew Vince liked and trusted Milo, and it felt like a betrayal.

My abduction hadn't really made the news. I was only missing for just under two hours, though it had seemed to me like days of sheer terror. Nobody connected it with Milo and I couldn't tell Nick the part that his mentor had played in my kidnapping. I didn't tell Mom, she would only get upset. And, really, what would have been the point in telling Ruby? She'd made it clear by her silence and absence that she wanted nothing to do with me.

Very occasionally, I'd come home and catch Milo in my kitchen with Nick and Vince. I would leave the house and not return until I was sure he was gone. I had to give Vince an ultimatum. It was either Milo or me. I knew Vince would choose me. We went back to sharing a bed because we both had physical needs, but the bond of trust between us had broken. Neither of us had cheated and yet our marriage was dead. We didn't have the courage to end it. We lived our lives separately.

I got on with things, work was busy, and Cooper Rivera had expanded further. Carla was taking time off with her first child after her third round of IVF treatment. She deserved it, but it meant that I didn't have much time to think about anything else. I had, however, worked on a short story collection of my own. I had dealt with enough literary agents in my time to know who to approach about my own work, and April Ngeow agreed to look at it after first querying why I wouldn't want to publish it myself. I was honest: 'I need the validation.' Two days after I'd submitted, she called me.

She represented a children's writer and a spy novelist I edited so I was pleased to note the same excitement in her voice when she talked about my work.

'Erin,' she said, 'this isn't like anything else I've ever read.'

'Uh-oh,' I said, dismayed because I knew how publishers wanted to label their books, and I didn't fit into any box, or I fit in too many of them. I had turned down submissions for this very reason. What section of the bookshop is this going to fit in? I had foreseen all these problems.

'First of all, I would like to represent you.' My heart lifted. April had her own agency and a significant hit rate with her authors. She knew the taste of every editor in New York and beyond.

'But,' she said, 'I think we're going to have to go the long way round with this.'

She explained that rather than putting it out to the big five publishers and their various imprints, she wanted to submit a story to the *New Yorker*.

'The *New Yorker*? I can't imagine a magazine that prestigious would be interested in my weird little stories.'

'Listen up, buttercup, if I ever hear you belittle your own work like that again, I'm going to come up there and stomp your ass, you hear me? These stories are works of art. We have to make sure the whole world knows it.'

A wave of relief washed over me. If you were an unknown writer who got published in the *New Yorker*, it was almost a guarantee that editors would be knocking on your door.

I waited three months before April told me the first story from my collection had been accepted. I wasn't sure who to call. Vince read books that I gave him to read, but I don't think he would choose to pick up a book if I didn't nudge him. Nick was more of a reader, but non-fiction mostly. I knew Carla would be thrilled for me, but she was enjoying time out with her long-awaited baby. I called Saima, my oldest, newly divorced friend. Saima was the only person who knew everything that Ruby and I had been through. She knew about Nick and his friendship with Milo, and Principal Bermingham and the abduction.

'Awesome,' she said when I told her the news. 'Where are we going to celebrate?' It was just the right thing to say, especially as we had yet to celebrate her divorce from Binto. She booked a table at Mooo. As we were on our second cocktail, she asked, 'Look, none of my business, but why are you not celebrating this with Vince?' I explained that we'd grown apart, that we didn't communicate much and how that had all started with him befriending Milo.

'Erin, don't get me wrong, but why do you think Milo knew about you being stalked by Bermingham? He was the one who called the cops and got you rescued.'

I paused before I answered. I could not countenance the thought of Saima betraying me too.

'He used to visit Milo in prison –'

'Yes, but only for the first year or two. Milo stopped him visiting because he was saying such awful things about Ruby and you. Milo thought he was unhinged.'

'How do you know this, Saima?'

'Vince told my brother-in-law.'

Saima's brother-in-law was good friends with Vince. I had

first met Vince at Saima's. It seems they had been talking about Milo and me behind my back.

'Yeah, what else did he tell him?'

'I'm not saying this to hurt you, Erin, but Vince knows Milo well now. Says he's a reformed character, that if he raped Ruby, he has learned his lesson. Says that Bermingham kept turning up at Milo's diner when he got out of prison, trash-talking you.'

There it was. '*If* he raped Ruby? Saima, you are supposed to be my best friend. How could you say that?' I had pulled my chair back from the table.

'Hey, don't shoot the messenger. I'm sorry, I'm just telling you what Vince told Tony, and Tony told my sister. Let's change the subject. I must tell you about Binto –'

I let it go. I couldn't lose Saima. I sat up close again. 'What's the asshole done now?'

She looked perturbed. 'Actually, we've been talking about getting back together.'

The night of celebration fizzled into awkwardness.

Later, when I told Vince my news, he was pleased and congratulated me. He didn't really understand what a big deal this was, but he was distracted, glued to a hockey game on TV.

My story was published in the *New Yorker* and I was thrilled. And then it went viral. It was shared on social media platforms all over the world. It was read by millions of people. There was a bidding war for my short-story collection and my agent sold it to the editor I liked best for a 'significant six-figure deal unprecedented for a short-story collection'.

Vince was thrilled for me. Carla was too but worried that I would now leave the company we had built together. I assured her that I would not, but I intended to work an academic year going forward, from October to May. She was relieved.

My publishers threw a huge launch party in New York. I got

the best make-up artist in the city to cover my scar. Vince tried to tell me that nobody would notice, but I noticed. Nevertheless, I had the most wonderful night. I invited everybody I knew from the publishing world apart from the head honchos at Watling and Harris who had treated me so badly for years. My mom came over from Dublin, and Kathy came too, with Aunt Rachel, Vince and Nick, Carmine and his wife, Saima and Ginnie, Cisco and even newly divorced Fabian, plus others from school, a lot of friends from Harvard and everyone from Cooper Rivera. It was like a flashback of everyone I'd ever known from every walk of life – everyone except Milo and Ruby.

75

In September 2025, I got a call from Dad's widow, Kathy. She said she was selling up in Boston. She and some of her girlfriends were moving to Florida. I was surprised. I'd always kept in touch with Kathy, but after Dad died, we had less in common. I'd assumed she would marry again, but when I asked her, she said, 'No, your dad left me enough money, so I don't have to. Marcia and Jade and I are opening our own little store there in Florida, in St Augustine.' Florida was a state that people retired to because of the weather and accessibility, but Kathy was only in her late fifties.

'Aren't you a little young for Florida, Kathy?'

She laughed. 'We're going to sell knitting pattens, yarn, needles and hooks, and craft kits. It's been a dream of mine since I was a little girl.'

Her girlish enthusiasm was infectious, and I knew she loved crafting. In fact, when Dad and Kathy got married, she had turned the spare room into a craft room. After he died, she would host knitting workshops in the house on weekends. She made a whole new group of close friends out of a hobby. You had to admire her.

'I'm clearing out the house, so please come over and take any furniture you want. I can't take the contents of a four-bedroom house to a one-bed apartment in St Augustine.'

I couldn't think of anything I wanted, but it was unlikely that I would see Kathy again, and she was a sweet person who had loved and cared for my dad. Also, although my life shattered in that house, I had some great memories of it. I arranged a time to go over.

I roamed the rooms of the house, thinking of the last time I'd been there to reassure myself that Ruby had not spied on us through a keyhole. I was still mad that Milo expected me to believe such bullshit. The room that had been Mom and Dad's was swathed in baby-pink and blue lace, lampshades, curtains and quilt. It was like a child's dream of a Cabbage Patch doll bedroom. How had Dad reacted to this? I think he must have let her have free rein over this room as long as she left the rest of the house alone. Kathy hadn't touched the other bedrooms. Which was a pity as my old room was an eyesore. The wallpaper was peeling and the busy floral pattern that had seemed cool nearly thirty years ago brought on an instant headache. No wonder Mom had said it made her dizzy. The room was used for storage now. There were three old baseball mitts, framed awards that Dad had won for humanitarian work, a broken keyboard on a stand that used to be downstairs, several old sewing machines, a box of shoes of all sorts on top of a bookcase. I reckoned most of this could go to Goodwill or to a garbage dump.

I went into Ruby's old room, still with its candy-pink wallpaper, and it was neat as a pin, most of Kathy's equipment packed and stacked and carefully labelled. I caught my reflection in the mirror on the wall. That mirror had been there forever. I remembered Mom saying that it was a wedding present from her cousin. I wondered if she would like to have it back, but then she hadn't taken it in the divorce. It looked like an antique, though. Maybe I could take it home and put it in our hallway. Kathy would be disappointed if I didn't take something.

The mirror sat on the floor. I pulled it towards me, examining the old mahogany frame for woodworm. As I turned, something on the wall caught my eye. A piece of what looked like a large Band-Aid curled up at the edges was stuck there. Had it been attached to the mirror? I pulled it away to reveal a deep hole about one inch in diameter. The mirror used to hang off a nail there, I recalled. I felt a creeping sensation at the back of my neck. I went back into my old room and removed the box of shoes from the top of a bookcase. It had not been there in my time. When I got real close, I could see a hole. I peered through it and into Ruby's room. I stood away from the wall and the hole just disappeared back into the pattern. My stomach churned.

I went back into Ruby's room, up to the hole on her side, and looked through. The view of my room was perfect. I could see exactly where my bed would have been and where the desk would have been. I could see where the trash can had been.

I ran downstairs and made an excuse to Kathy about being late for an appointment, telling her I would be back for the mirror. I went out, got into my car and drove to the nearest secluded spot. I pulled over. My hands were shaking, and I had a headache like I'd never had before.

76

I'd tried calling Ruby first, but she wouldn't answer. I called Mom instead. It was the middle of the night in Dublin, but I didn't care about that. As soon as I told her what I suspected, Mom started blubbing.

Mom had *known*. That was what hurt the most. She had found out the night before the sentencing. She was scared stiff. She had sacrificed her marriage to keep Ruby's secret. She preserved Ruby's lie and let Milo be sent to prison to protect Dad's investment clients, his congregation, Ruby's reputation, and to have an excuse to go home to Ireland.

Did she even think about me? My love for Milo was not a childhood romance.

Mom chose Ruby. There was no *Sophie's Choice* scenario. There was no moral dilemma. There was right and wrong. And Mom chose wrong.

It had nearly destroyed me. Years of loneliness and the fear of truly trusting anyone until I met Vince, a perfectly nice man who couldn't believe his luck when a woman sixteen years his junior agreed to marry him because she was dying of loneliness. Perfectly nice and perfectly dull. He knew at his core that I did not love him. Our marriage was over but neither of us had the courage to declare it.

And then there was Ruby's twenty-six years of lying. I called her again, some twenty times. She didn't pick up. I drove around for an hour. I could not discuss this with Vince. I needed to see Milo.

I walked into Billy's Diner and asked to speak to Milo. He came out from the kitchen and looked surprised to see me.

'Milo, I need you to take a drive with me.'

He looked confused. 'Why? And where? I'm working.'

'Please, Milo.' I started to cry. He put his hand out but stopped himself from touching me.

'Is it Nick? Is he in trouble?'

I couldn't stop crying, my body heaving in spasms of distress. I shook my head.

'Erin, you better sit down.' He pointed to a table at the back.

'You don't understand. I can't do it here.'

'Do what? Tell me.'

I ran towards the door, but Milo came after me. He called to someone, 'Hey, Marky, I gotta go. Close up for me, okay?'

I got in my car and Milo sat beside me. 'What's this about?'

I pulled away from the kerb and managed to control myself. I remembered what he'd told me about his theory, but I'd found it disgusting and unbelievable. Now I needed him to repeat it. After he told me, I cried again.

'What do you know, Erin, did she admit it?'

I took him to Kathy's house and introduced him as my friend, Michael. I told Kathy we had come to get the mirror. It was after ten o'clock. Kathy questioned if I was okay. I guess I looked like shit compared to a few hours earlier. I asked for aspirin and a glass of water. Milo accepted a coffee, and we made polite conversation for about two minutes before he and I climbed the back stairs. I showed him where the mirror was and the hole in the wall behind it. I demonstrated how the tape had covered it, and then we went into my room and I showed him the spot on the wall above the bookcase.

Milo went quiet. He sat down heavily on the floor and his

face was ashen. I tried to comfort him. 'Milo, I'm sorry, I should have believed you.'

I tried to put my arms around him, but he shook me off. 'I was right,' he said.

'Yes, you were, and I'm so sorry.'

His face lost its colour. 'It's been twenty-six years. My mother jumped into the Charles River because nobody would believe me. You and me, we had planned a life, kids, a whole future. All those years in a stinking cell. Why?'

There were tears streaming down my face. I wanted to hold him but he left the room, and I heard him go down the stairs and out the back door. I followed, expecting to find him standing by my car, but he was gone.

77

Ruby

At forty-two, I was young enough to start over somewhere else, and a town five hours from Perth, Australia, seemed like the ideal place. I checked the visa criteria; I applied for a holiday visa online. The website said it would take forty-eight hours to process, but on a lot of chat forums about holidays, it said that you could get it in a matter of hours. It entitled me to ninety days there. I was sure Uncle Dennis would be pleased to see me, particularly if I was sober. I had run the Academy often single-handedly and admin was admin wherever you went. Surely a mining company had databases and payroll like every other company. He would give me some kind of job and sponsor my work visa. Later, I could investigate citizenship. I could marry a local if necessary. I was leaving Lucy behind, but she would be better off without me. I was a terrible mother. She deserved better. Jack would be a better parent on his own. I loved Jack too. It had been clear to me from when she was about fourteen years old that he loved Lucy more than me. I had wanted to hurt her for taking Jack away from me. I was physically and emotionally exhausted. I changed into my nightwear and got into bed.

It was about 4 a.m. when my phone woke me again. It was Erin. She knew the time difference between Dublin and Boston. It was 11 p.m. there. Was it a pocket dial or had Jack called her? They had only met once, around the time of Grandma's funeral, though they had spoken on the phone a couple of times when we first got married. I let it go without answering. It flashed again over and over. Whatever it was could wait until morning. I was just drifting off again when my phone buzzed and flashed once more. This time it was Mom. It must be serious. I picked up.

'Erin knows. She called me, almost hysterical.'

I was confused and half asleep. 'Sorry, what about Erin? What does she know? It's the middle of the night, Mom.'

'About you and Milo, how you framed him. She's furious with me.' Mom started to cry. 'She said she's never going to speak to me again.'

I was wide awake now. 'You admitted it, you told her the truth?'

'She knew. Milo worked it out first. Kathy is selling your dad's house. Erin went to collect some furniture and discovered the hole in the wall.'

'Milo knows too?'

'He guessed that you must have seen them and used the tissue, and Erin found the hole behind the mirror. She hates me.' Mom gasped for breath, in between gales of tears.

'Oh my God, what is she going to do?'

'I don't know. They discovered it tonight. Ruby, what have you done to me?'

'Me? What have you done? You confirmed it. You could have denied it. There's no proof. This is your fault.' I went on the attack.

'Don't you understand how hard this was for me? It destroyed my marriage. I have lived with this awful guilt for twenty-five years. You think it hasn't taken its toll? I was protecting *you*. I prayed for that boy every night. I'm glad your father isn't around to hear this.'

'Mom, wait, stop, what is Erin going to do? Is Milo going to the cops? Who would believe him?'

'I don't know. She's been trying to reach you –'

I hung up.

78

Lucy

I heard Mom and Dad fighting in the kitchen that night. I had gone to bed early but, while they were fighting, I received a brief text from Miranda Hayes, the girl who left ComStat in a hurry.

Is this about Simon Perry?

I knew instantly that she was another victim of his. I replied.

He raped me.

Nothing happened for a moment and then the three dots told me she was writing a reply. And then they disappeared. Shit, maybe I had misjudged her response, but why had she asked specifically about him? Eventually, the dots started moving again.

Me too. #METOO

I needed to talk to her. It was after midnight but I texted back.

Can I call you? Is it too late?

She rang me immediately and told me her story. The grooming and the gaslighting were near identical. The fancy new restaurants. Playing her off against another pretty girl in the office. It was all the same. Waking up in his apartment with bruises, cuts and bite marks, and no memory of what had happened. She also thought he might have used a wine bottle. But Miranda hadn't told anyone, because she had thought nobody would believe her. She had developed a crush on him too, but he had been subtly seducing her, grooming her with daily praise of her work, 'accidentally' brushing up against her. Her parents were divorced, and she lived with her elderly father. She had been a wild child when she was younger. I told her that Simon had left the company after Dad confronted him.

Miranda had been struggling with depression. I encouraged her to come back to ComStat. We could go together to the HR Head and tell our stories, get Miranda's job back. We might even go to the police. We talked about potential other victims. Miranda thought there might have been others, before us. It was a game to Simon. We hung up, having agreed to meet for coffee the next day. I felt sorry for Miranda, who had nobody she could talk to. At least I had Dad. And then I heard Dad banging things around in the kitchen, his voice raised on the phone. I slipped on my dressing gown.

Dad was sitting on the sofa, his head in his hands.

'What's the matter, Dad? Are you okay?' I sat beside him and put my arms around him and felt his shoulders heave. He was crying. I was alarmed. I'd never seen him cry before. 'Where is Mum?'

'Your mum is . . . gone.'

'What?'

'I'm sorry, honey, but it's best if we divorce.'

'Divorce? What happened? What did she do?'

'I can't explain.'

'Dad, she'll be back. She told me it was a slip.'

'It's more than that. I can't explain. I asked her to go.'

Dad had always adored Mum, no matter what she did. If he'd asked her to leave, it must be serious. I put the kettle on to make some tea. I called Mum. Dad tried to stop me, but I clung on to the phone while she dripped poison into my ear.

'*I don't believe you.*'

My own mother didn't believe I'd been raped.

I remember a time when she loved me. There's video footage of her smothering me with kisses, lifting me up in the air when I was a toddler. I remember her telling me bedtime stories, and then, when I was old enough, I'd read stories to her. I remember baking with her and shopping expeditions to get me a new outfit. I don't recall exactly when I started to feel unloved by her. It was gradual. I asked Dad what I'd done wrong, knowing he would report back to her, and in front of him she would put on a show, calling me 'sweetheart' or 'Lulu', but it was all different when I was alone with her. I tried my best to please her. I studied hard. My final school exam results were among the highest in the country. Dad was ecstatic and so was Mum until he left the room and then she picked up the book she was reading again. I met her indifference with anger.

My degree course was notoriously hard to get into, but I waltzed in on the strength of my results. And yet nothing I did would please her. I was never good enough. When I got involved with Casey in college, I told them both, and Mum asked me if I was going to move to Canada to live with her. It's clear to me now, that's what she wanted. How disappointing it was for her when Casey broke up with me.

When I told her that I had got the internship at ComStat, which might result in a full-time job, she asked me if that meant I would be moving out. She really wanted me out of the house, and I would have gone if there was anywhere to go, but Dublin was in the middle of a worsening housing crisis. Dad told her not to be so ridiculous.

Fuck Mum. Dad and I were better off without her. I didn't tell him about Miranda. Dad was upset, it wasn't the right time, and I was shocked by Mum's words. Dad swept me into his arms.

'It's not your fault, it's not your fault. I believe you. Anybody would. There's something wrong with her.'

79

Erin

Ruby was not taking my calls. Milo didn't answer either. I texted him to let him know that Dad never knew and that I was sorry for everything. I had hurt him in so many ways, and his family, and all because of Ruby's devious behaviour. He didn't text back.

Maybe he had gone to the cops? He was owed an apology. He needed his conviction to be overturned and to be taken off the sex offenders register. He needed to be compensated for the thirteen years of his life, his future as a doctor, his future with me, the children we would have had. No amount of money would make up for this. My call to Mom had been in the middle of the night Irish time, but I could not wait until morning.

That night, I had to tell Vince what had happened. He was shocked. He knew that I was estranged from my sister, and he thought originally that was Milo's fault. But since he'd gotten to know Milo, he said he could not imagine him hurting anyone. He saw how tenderly he had treated Nick and asked for nothing in return. 'I knew you were angry with him, but you know I never thought he was capable of . . . my God, your sister is crazy.'

'I should have listened to you. Your instincts were better than mine even though I knew him better.'

'What's going to happen now?'

'I have to go to Ireland tomorrow. I need to confront her. Mom will have told her that we know.'

'Are you sure you want to get involved, Erin?'

I looked at Vince in disbelief. 'What are you talking about? I am involved.'

'It's between Milo and Ruby and your mom, though, right?'

'They betrayed me. I betrayed him. I loved him.'

'But that was years ago . . .' He stopped mid-sentence. There was a long silence. Neither of us wanted to say it. Eventually, he did.

'You still love him?'

I couldn't answer. I went back to the spare room and tried to sleep, but sleep was like a butterfly that night, occasionally settling but flitting from one thought to another, remembering the horrible words that I'd said to him. How cruel I had been on that one visit to Whiteshore. The way I had treated Margie. Mom had let me think I was crazy for trusting a man who had never done anything wrong. Years of therapy. Milo would not speak to me, but I sent him one more text before I turned out my light.

> I'm going to Ireland and I'm going to bring her back with me. You can decide what to do with her. I will not stand in your way.

I took the noon flight from Logan Airport next day. I was physically and emotionally exhausted and thankfully slept most of the way after two Jack Daniel's. I didn't tell any of them that I was coming. When a taxi delivered me to a large Victorian house in Ranelagh, it was after midnight Irish time.

Jack answered the door quickly. I recognized him instantly from his screen appearances. I had not woken him, he was still dressed, but his surprise was obvious. 'Erin . . .? Hi . . . I . . . I wasn't expecting you.' He opened the door wider, and I rolled in my small overnight case.

'Hi, Jack, I'm sorry to intrude –'

'Did Ruby invite you?' He looked exhausted.

'No. I'm sorry I didn't tell you I was coming, and I'm sorry it's late, but I need to talk to Ruby urgently.'

Very slowly, he took my jacket and hung it up as I was led down a corridor to a beautiful sitting room at the back of the house. There was a tear-stained girl sprawled on the couch. I realized quickly that this must be Lucy. Mom always had photos to show me when she visited. Pretty girl. 'I'm . . . I'm sorry, Lucy?'

'Yeah, are you Erin? I recognize you from Granny's photos.'

Jack recovered himself from the surprise. 'Ehm, Ruby isn't here.'

They both looked guilty.

'Well, when will she be back?'

Lucy spoke up. 'Never, I hope.'

'Lucy,' said Jack, a warning tone in his voice.

'Well, it's true.'

I had obviously walked into the aftermath of some domestic row between mother and daughter. Jack cleared his throat. 'Ummm, I'm sorry, Erin, sit down and I'll . . . Can I get you something?'

'Do you have any red wine, please?'

'Um, we don't keep alcohol in the house. Can I get you a Coke, tea or coffee?'

I could have kicked myself. 'I'm sorry. I completely forgot. Just a glass of water will be fine. I tried calling her, but she didn't answer.'

Jack looked at Lucy. 'She won't answer my calls either. I'm afraid we . . . are separating.'

'I'm not trying to call her. I'm never speaking to her again,' said Lucy. This was more than a mother–daughter argument.

'What? Why? Sorry, it's none of my business, it's just that I need to talk to her urgently. It's not the kind of thing we can do over the phone.'

Lucy said, 'We don't know where she is. She stayed at the Intercontinental last night, but she checked out this morning.'

'When did you last speak to her?'

'Late last night.'

'Did she fall off the wagon?'

Jack's face began to crumple. He went to sit with his daughter. Stepdaughter. He looked beyond exhausted. They both did. 'We don't know. Did you call your mother?'

'I spoke to her last night,' I said. There was another long silence. I realized something big had happened here too.

'Maybe Ruby is staying with her?' said Jack.

I thought that was unlikely. Ruby was the last person Mom would want to see, though she must have alerted Ruby that I knew.

'Look, I've obviously walked into something here, and I don't mean to cause upset. Do you guys have Uber? I'll get a cab and a hotel room.'

'No, please stay,' said Lucy. 'I want to know what's going on.'

'I think I have to speak to you in private, Jack.'

'Why? I'm an adult and she's *my* mother.'

'I know, but it's . . .' I appealed to Jack with my eyes.

'Lucy, please, leave us alone,' he said.

'But –' she started to object.

He took her hands in his. 'Please, Lucy. Whatever it is, I'll explain it to you later, okay?'

She left the room reluctantly. I didn't say anything until I heard her go up the stairs.

'It's about something that happened when we were kids,' I said to Jack.

'The rape?' he said.

I was taken aback. 'There was no rape,' I said quietly.

'Steady on, Erin. We believe rape victims in this house,' said Jack, immediately defensive.

'So did I, but Mom admitted it to me last night. Ruby made the whole thing up. My boyfriend spent thirteen years in prison. She lied and Mom covered it up.'

'What?' Jack's face was stricken. 'No, you can't be . . . Jesus Christ.' He stared at me. 'Your mother helped Ruby to frame your boyfriend for rape?' He was incredulous.

'Yes, but Ruby only told her the truth the night before the sentencing. Ruby had lied to the police and the prosecution, and in court to the whole jury and his defence attorney. She planted DNA evidence . . . inside her. Milo never had a chance. There are more details but I'm not . . . Mom thought it was too late to overturn the case then. It would have impacted badly on our family. But after that, we could never *be* a family. We imploded anyway.'

There was a long silence while Jack processed the information.

'You know, she never told me what actually happened, just that she'd been raped by your boyfriend.' He then looked startled. 'That's why she didn't believe Lulu.'

'What? I don't understand.' It was my turn to look confused.

'Lucy was raped some weeks ago, but Ruby didn't believe her.' Jack was stunned. He barely moved. 'How could she do that? Why would she do it?'

I couldn't even begin to imagine why Ruby would think that her daughter would lie as much as she had.

'I'm so sorry. She's so young.'

'Does the guy –?'

'Milo.'

'Milo. Does he know?'

'Yes, I had to tell him.'

'What's going to happen to her?'

'I told Milo it's up to him. I recorded the conversation with Mom, and he has that recording now. He'll be the one that decides.'

'I think she's on the run.'

80

Ruby

I flew Business Class to Perth, Australia. I put it on Jack's credit card. I figured it would be quite a while until I was going to be in such an environment again. Perhaps I'd never come home to Ireland. I refused the glass of champagne and all the other alcohol I was offered. I tried to look forward to a whole new life with new people. I was sure it would be hard to settle in at first. Work would be different, but I'd get used to it. This was going to be a long flight, and my best option at that moment was to read *The Big Book* – written in 1939 by Bill W, it was the handbook of Alcoholics Anonymous.

81

Milo

In 1999 and 2000, everybody wanted me to lie. Once the DNA evidence came to light, the public defender wanted me to say that sex between Ruby and me was consensual. I was sure they'd made a mistake with the DNA, or that somebody had planted it. I couldn't imagine how, but it was my lawyer's job to find out. I'm sure she never believed me. But, in court, she questioned how the DNA was handled. The sexual assault forensic examiner was called as a witness, who explained that the semen sample taken from Ruby was brought to a lab where it matched with my saliva sample. My attorney cross-examined her. She was adamant that there would have been no chance of cross-contamination or that my sample could have been compared to another of my samples by accident. 'We are not amateurs,' she said in a haughty tone, 'there are no accidents.' I remember thinking to myself that she was lying on behalf of the DA.

Margie had done some detective work in the library. She had found a photograph of the Reverend Doug Cooper and the Boston DA together at a golf event. There were other people in the photo too, and they weren't standing beside each other, but it was proof that they weren't strangers. My attorney refused to bring this up in court. And afterwards, when I tried to appeal, no attorney would touch the notion that the city's DA might be complicit in framing me.

I went up for parole every couple of years after the first eight and they'd ask me if I regretted raping Ruby Cooper, and I would say no, I did not rape that girl, and then I went back to the slammer.

I survived those years because I had some protection. Even though Whitey Bulger, the notorious organized crime boss, had skipped town, his crew ran the prison, and my uncle Shaun had done some (legit) work for him and his congressman brother back in the day. I had some protection from the gangs. But I have scars on the inside that run deeper than the one I got when a psychopathic cellmate decided to cut my heart out. Those three weeks in the sanatorium were like a holiday. No wonder so many inmates were cutting themselves, eating crushed glass and provoking fights they knew would lead to injury. Some risked death, and for a few, the risk didn't pay off. Most of what I saw in prison is stuff I don't want to remember, but I know some things for sure. The worst thing you can be in America is mentally ill, poor or addicted, and you throw African American or Hispanic in there and you're double-damned.

I swore that if I ever got out, I would do something to help those guys on the outside, the ones who looked like they might end up inside or the ones who were out and doing their best to stay out. I suffered from depression. The black dog would descend on me. All I wanted to do was lie in my cell and not communicate with anyone. I would take a risk too, start a fight, or steal something belonging to a cellmate, anything to get a week or two in solitary confinement.

Margie came to visit me once a month without fail. I don't know what I did to deserve a sister so loyal, especially after Mom died. I didn't really want to go on after that, but I knew that if I gave in, it would leave Margie with nobody, and she deserved better than that. Surprisingly, Principal Bermingham came to visit in the early years. He had always taken a special interest in me when I was at Altman, I expect because he was from Southie too, but when he visited he spoke so violently about Ruby and Erin and what he wanted to do to them, it unnerved me. He lost his job at Altman but wouldn't tell me why. I took him off my visitors' list. Ben Roche came at least twice a year right to the end. He insisted on collecting me when I was released.

Getting out of prison was as confusing as going in. Southie as I knew it had completely changed. The whole Seaport area was developed with bars and restaurants and high-rise luxury apartment blocks. I had proper clam chowder and Boston baked beans and Brigham's Ice Cream and, man, they tasted like home. Whatever swill that passed as chowder in prison tasted like dog piss or human piss, most likely. My first St Patrick's Day back in the old neighbourhood also helped to rebuild my sense of belonging.

Uncle Billy gave me my job back and a room above the diner that was also a storeroom. It was smaller than my cell had been and, while I was grateful to Billy, it was hard not to be depressed. I ignored any young girl that came in the door and went out of my way to stay out of their lane. Some of Billy's regulars knew me and where I'd been, but the ones who knew me well, they knew I was innocent and gave me extra clothes and shoes. One of the old guys said I could have a room in his house if I helped out a bit. Mickey Dolan was in his early eighties. He'd been in Vietnam as a young man. His hands didn't shake because he was old, they shook because of what he saw there. He often showed up with cuts on his face from shaving. The first morning I woke up in his house, I got a bowl of hot water, shaving soap and a towel and gave that man the best shave of his life. I continued to do that every few days until the end.

I saved up some money working in Billy's, and when he wanted to retire, I was the obvious choice to take over. Billy had daughters who had moved up in the world, working in various computer jobs that we didn't understand. Hell, I could watch music videos on my first cellphone and that was like a miracle to me.

    I could have moved out of Mickey's place long before he died, but it got to the stage where he couldn't do much for himself. I stayed to return the favour and looked after him as best I could until he passed. When he died, I had enough to rent a studio in Southie, brand new. Mom would have been proud, I know it. Margie was living with a nice fella called Fred Dominguez, and they lived way out of town up in Salem, but we got together whenever we could. We went to Red Sox games like the old days, and we laughed and talked about Mom, and how funny she was, and how she had been proven right about the Catholic Church.

I was scared to date anyone for quite a while. How could I trust them? But there was one woman who used to come into the diner regular enough and we'd get to talking. I didn't have the courage to ask her out. Bonnie was gorgeous, she was like a fun-size Rita Hayworth, flaming red hair and as cute as a button. Eventually, after a couple weeks of exchanging views on politics, TV shows and baseball versus football, she said, 'Are you going to ask me for my number or what?' and the next day I called her up and asked her out on a date. We hit it off straight away. She made me laugh. But the first time we went back to her place, I had to tell her about my false rape conviction. I didn't want her to find out from someone else, and I needed to tell her before we slept together. We did not sleep together that night. But we continued to see each other. I answered every question she had as honestly as I could. And I knew she'd been googling the case and found it. My 'victim' was unnamed in the court records. I could not explain the DNA to her any more than I could to anyone else.

When I'd got out of prison, I thought those bouts of depression would lift, but from time to time I had to lock myself away and speak to nobody. Mickey understood it, but he was the last person I wanted to hurt. I told him about these moods straight up. He said it must be post-traumatic stress disorder from being inside, but I knew I'd been suffering before I went to prison. It was part of who I am. I didn't want Bonnie or anyone else to see me like that. I spent a lot of money going to a psychiatrist that Ben suggested could help me. He prescribed antidepressants. I didn't see the point in taking them when I wasn't feeling depressed, but when I went back to him six months later after a week in bed, he insisted I had to take them every day. Gradually, the moods began to lift. I was relieved when I noted a whole year had gone by without a depressive episode. It was like a miracle.

The first time Bonnie and I slept together, I stopped so many times to check she was okay that she ended up yelling, 'Just give it to me already!' We continued to see each other, and when she got to know me well enough, she said, 'That kid lied,' and Bonnie and me, we became like glue.

And then I met Erin down at the shelter. I was surprised to see her. She was older and a little heavier and as beautiful as ever, but she looked like she wanted to run away. The old guy with her turned out to be her husband. My heart pounded. He said his son was missing. Even though I owed her nothing, Erin had been in my thoughts since the day I met her. I would often recall the day we spent on Salisbury Beach, swimming in the sea, and how her body looked in that swimsuit, the sound of her laughter when we went go-karting afterwards. The shared future we had planned was in ruins, but if I could find her stepson, maybe she would think more kindly towards me.

Still there was Bonnie, and she was such a sweet girl. I never wanted to hurt her. But I think I did. About a year into our relationship, we were lying in bed one Sunday morning, untangling ourselves from each other's bodies in her apartment. I was cleaning myself up. When I was done, I threw the Kleenex towards the trash can across the room. I missed and, when I got out of bed, I picked it up on my way into the shower; it was wet and sticky, and that's when it hit me. That's how I would clean myself in Erin's room all those years ago. Ruby must have got hold of one of those tissues. 'Damn,' I hollered at the top of my voice.

Bonnie came running. 'What's up? Did you hurt yourself?'

'I know. I know how she did it!' I explained it to Bonnie, and she was a little doubtful at first, but then she agreed. That's what had happened.

I had to tell Erin, but that didn't end well. I couldn't remember whether there was a keyhole in the bedroom door or not. I knew there was no lock because the risk of getting caught in Erin's bed by her parents was real. Everything we did was silent, and the risk made it even more of a turn-on. I could think of nothing else the day I went to see Erin.

Erin said there was no keyhole in that door and that I was disgusting for even thinking of such a thing. I knew I was right about Ruby using the tissue. She must have watched us, but I had no way of proving it. Had Ruby been able to hide under the bed? Was she in the wardrobe? I gave up trying to clear my name and Bonnie got tired of hearing about how I'd been denied justice. A few months later, she broke up with me.

I had kept the flyer that Erin's husband had given me with his son's photo on it. I sought him out, asked around. Finding Nick wasn't a total coincidence. I had been training as a counsellor, and I finally saw him at a shelter downtown years later. I owed Vince and Erin nothing, but this kid was just the kind of guy that I had promised myself I would help, and at heart, I would still have done anything for Erin. The mess he was in was not his fault. Very gradually, I earned his trust. I enlisted the help of my old friend Ben Roche and eventually got Nick the right meds and supports to be able to bring him home. After I got to know Vince through Nick, I knew that he didn't believe I could hurt anyone.

But then Leo Bermingham started showing up at the diner, wanting to talk to me about what we could do to punish Erin. He'd been around Bonnie when I was seeing her, and she had told him everything. She should have known to keep her mouth shut. He had been put away in a state psychiatric facility twice. He had harassed his ex-wife, and his own mother was terrified of him. I told him not to come around the diner any more. I even tried to get a restraining order against him, but the cops weren't too keen on helping a convicted rapist. At least he didn't know where I lived. When Leo kidnapped Erin and called me to tell me, I could scarcely believe what he was saying. He made everything worse. I was arrested again. I was accused of conspiring with Bermingham in waging a campaign of harassment against Erin. I was only held for a few hours, because Bermingham admitted he'd done it all for me and that I didn't know a thing about it. Erin was really shaken and badly injured. Her beautiful face was scarred, though still beautiful to me.

When Erin showed up in the diner and took me to the old family home to show me the evidence of what I had long suspected and that her mother had confirmed, I didn't feel the overwhelming sense of relief that I'd been hoping for. I needed to process the information away from Erin. I could not handle her upset on top of my own.

I called Margie first. Who else would understand? She screamed. She wanted to bomb Erin Cooper off the face of the earth and tear Ruby limb from limb. We cried hard about Mom. She drove down from Salem and asked when they were going to be arrested. She wanted to call the cops right there and then, but I said no. It had been twenty-six years, what difference would a few days make?

I had a hard time getting my head around it. Why would that kid hate me so much? Yes, I absolutely rejected her, but like I foolishly said at the time, nobody had to know. I wouldn't even have told Erin. In court, Ruby twisted those words to make me sound like a pervert. I was nothing but nice to her, even though she was always weird around me. It took me twenty-six years to realize it was nothing to do with me. She wanted to hurt her sister, because Erin was prettier, smarter and a whole lot kinder than Ruby was, though I didn't see much evidence of that kindness from Erin after the so-called rape. Except for the fact that Erin kept sending me those parcels for thirteen years. She had denied it but who else could it have been?

Since I had been released, Erin's heart grew a hard shell and the way she looked at me and spoke to me on the few occasions we met was horrible. I know she's sorry now and I know she's upset and devastated and confused. But that's on her. I always loved that girl. The depression is back, but it's different this time. The pills don't help. I should be happy. Why can't I be happy?

82

Lucy

Erin stayed with us for a couple of nights while she tried to find Mum, but Mum had gone into hiding. Her passport was gone and Dad said she was probably drinking. Neither of us wanted to go looking for her. We gave Erin the names and numbers of her friends. Nasrin confirmed to Dad that, the night he had thrown Mum out, she had confessed to framing Milo Kelly. Erin flew back to Boston on her own after four days of searching. She did not visit Granny.

When I eventually went to see Granny, she was in a state. She told me the details, about how naive she had been, how she never meant for the family to split up, she was just trying to save her family's reputation. It struck me, not for the first time, that Granny wasn't smart, but trying to defend her actions around a false rape accusation wasn't just stupid, it was immoral. She was devastated that Erin wouldn't speak to her. I could absolutely understand Erin's hurt, but I felt sorry for Granny. She had made a really bad decision back then and, in a lot of ways, it *was* her fault. But it was up to Mum to come forward and tell the truth. She was the one who had told the lies.

Dad's sponsor, Graham, came over a lot. Dad did not do his show that whole week. They had to use an understudy. He had never missed a day of rehearsal or performing before in his life. I hated Mum for what she'd done to him. Poor Dad.

I met up with Miranda a few times and had long phone and Zoom calls with the other girls. Ríonna and Basira had similar stories and, when we finally met up after three weeks of talking, we had the most empowering night of our lives. We had all suffered at the hands of Simon Perry. Ríonna was the hardest to persuade. She felt that she had brought the attack on herself, but the truth was he had groomed us all. We went as a group to the Rape Crisis Centre and then to the guards, where we each made a statement. From there, we went to the HR department of ComStat Holdings. There was strength in numbers. Miranda did not want to return to ComStat and Basira was about to leave for Iran, but Ríonna was very glad to come back to a job that she loved, and my position was made permanent.

I still have good days and bad days. We all do. I don't know what is going to happen now, but we are being kept informed by the Garda Liaison Officer assigned to our case. Simon has been taken in for questioning several times. A case is being prepared for the DPP. Despite some initial fears, all our families are standing by us. Except Mum. No surprise.

83

Ruby

After the flight touched down in Perth, I took a cab into the city and checked into a hotel.

I thought about Lucy. Nasrin was right. She had been raped, and I'd told her that I didn't believe her because I was thinking about myself. I couldn't handle the thought that this was karma.

I found a meeting close to the hotel. I shared with the group that I was in self-imposed exile because I'd done a terrible thing a long time ago. People were supportive and urged me to make apologies. I left as soon as the meeting was over. I took an open-top bus tour of the city, taking in as much as I could. I did not call Uncle Dennis. I thought about all the new lies I would have to tell him if I just turned up there. It had to stop.

I took another long flight. This time, I landed in Boston.

On a Thursday afternoon a couple of days later, I walked an hour and a half from the Harvard Square Hotel to the Boston Police Headquarters, a shiny, new, glass-fronted building. I took a number at reception and waited for my name to be called. When it was, I made my confession.

84

Erin

Ruby turned up in Boston. She handed herself in and confessed but was released on bail.

Kathy told me she had turned up on her doorstep. Ruby told her who she was and what she'd done. Kathy had known about the 'rape'. Dad had told her all about what Milo Kelly had allegedly done. Even though she said she was horrified by the true story, she had taken Ruby in and let her stay there. 'Your father would not have turned her away,' she said. I couldn't argue with that. She agreed to let Ruby stay for a while but warned her the house was shortly going on the market.

Kathy passed on an apology from Ruby to me and asked if I wanted to come and see my sister. I told her to tell Ruby that I would see her in jail. I was so angry. She hadn't called or texted me. Cowardly. Now that I knew she was facing the consequences, I had no wish to see her as a free woman. From what I could glean, she hadn't implicated our mother in her confession.

Milo got a lawyer, who I paid for. He had to be cleared of all charges. My family owed him everything, but it could never be enough.

I drove to Margie's house in Salem. That was a difficult

encounter, but eventually she listened to me. She realizes that we are all victims of Ruby's lies. I apologized for all my suspicions, but I convinced her that I have only Milo's best interests at heart now.

Vince and I divorced finally in late 2025. We parted as friends, and Nick, now that he knows everything that happened, wished me luck. He told me that Milo still loved me. I clung on to that hope.

Ruby had a public defender this time but she was just as convincing in court as she was before. She was only an immature teenager at the time who had led a sheltered life, and in the intervening years she had been raising a daughter. She used the fact of Lucy's rape to elicit sympathy from the judge. As a mother of a real rape victim, she had realized how important it was to come forward and tell the truth even though Michael Kelly had now been free for as long as he'd been imprisoned. It was infuriating. Her crocodile tears did not fool me.

Ruby was sentenced to only five years after a plea deal. I find that extraordinary. The mitigating factors were that she was so young at the time and that she confessed voluntarily. How is that fair? She only confessed because she was caught. I would have turned her in. I would have had her extradited from Ireland if I'd found her there. She will have to pay Milo a huge amount in compensation. I don't know what she can afford. I was going to pay whatever she couldn't but I was going to make sure he got every penny he could from Ruby. I didn't care if she ended up homeless after her pathetically short sentence.

Her husband, Jack, and Mom came over from Dublin for the sentencing hearing. Jack is doing okay, I think. He is selling the unnecessarily big house. He told me Ruby was the best actress he had ever seen, but he didn't mean it as a compliment. He can't get over the manipulation. He and Lucy are closer than ever, and I have told them they are welcome in my home any time. Mom is trying hard with me, but I'm not ready to forgive her yet. I have told her it's going to take time.

85

I had to examine my behaviour towards Milo. I had managed to convince myself I hated him for so long because I believed he had hurt Ruby. I'd spent so many years thinking badly of him. Now, I texted him constantly, each one an apology. I told him how I understood his anger; it was justified. He did not reply.

I had moved out of the home I'd shared with Vince and camped out in Saima's spare room for a few weeks. She understood, and she held back from saying she'd suspected all along, though she probably did, particularly in recent years.

I wrote a story just for Milo, about a parallel universe in which Ruby did not exist. Nobody existed except us. There wasn't much of a plot. Two teenagers fall in love and get married and have perfect children and then they grow old together, have beautiful grandchildren and die happily in each other's arms in their nineties. I wanted to show Milo that we could still have many good years together, health permitting. I printed it up and hand-delivered it to the diner, hoping to catch sight of Milo, but he wasn't there that day.

The next day Ben Roche called me and said that Milo was depressed, and I should leave him be for a while. It devastated me that Milo was depressed again. He should have been happy; he was exonerated. It didn't make the news but everyone either of us knew was told the truth. I made sure of it. That evening, I ignored Ben's advice and called to Milo's apartment. When he heard it was me on the intercom, there was a long pause before he buzzed me up to the fifth floor. The door of 509 was open and I stepped into a good-sized room. The air was stale and Milo emerged from what must have been his bedroom in a creased shirt and sweatpants. He looked like he hadn't slept in a week. In his shaking hand was the story I'd sent him. He held it up.

'How would we do it, Erin? I mean, where would we start? It's not that easy.'

'Milo, if I were you, I'd probably never forgive me, but I'm begging you, please? A day at a time? What if today we start with a trip out to Salisbury Beach? Go see the Festival of Trees, maybe ice skate like we used to?'

'I don't know if I'm ready. I'm more tired than I've ever been in my life. I just want to sleep and be left alone.'

'Okay, but I'm here for you. I'll go now.' I reached the door and was about to open it when he spoke.

'Why, Eri? Why did you ever believe I could do something like that? And you were so cold to me, even after we connected through Nick.'

I started to cry then, the floodgates opening. 'There aren't enough ways to tell you how sorry I am, Milo, but I want you in my life. I'll show you. It's all I can do.' I craved his arms around me. I wanted to put my head under his neck and to feel his heart beating next to mine, but he didn't make any move to comfort me.

The next day I turned up again with a small Christmas tree, and while I was not welcomed with open arms, I got a smile from Milo. The day after, I brought him a hot chocolate with marshmallows and sprinkles from the place down the street. The next day was Sunday and I had prepared a hamper of books that I thought he'd enjoy. I noticed a difference that day. The place was tidy, the windows were open and Milo was clean-shaven. He asked if we could take that trip to Salisbury Beach.

*

I do not deserve him. It is early days in our relationship. But today, March 12th, we discovered I'm pregnant. I'm forty-five years old. The doctor told me the baby is in good shape so far but that I will have to be careful. Milo almost carried me out of her office. I am lying on the couch in my new apartment in South Boston, propped up by pillows, while Milo is preparing dinner. I have a ring in a box under one of the pillows. I hope he says yes.

86

Maureen

I failed as a mother. I can make a lot of excuses, but both my daughters deserved better.

For years, I convinced myself that I was the one who had made the sacrifice and lost my marriage as a result. I adored Doug, not because of the life he gave me, although that was beyond my wildest dreams, but because he was a good and decent man. I wonder now why we bickered so much. It was always about silly, inconsequential things. And I had betrayed him.

I bumped into Kenny Carter coming out of a grocery store when a bag split and my groceries went everywhere. He was the person who helped me chase down the tomatoes and the pineapple. He was Brad Pitt beautiful, and I think he knew it. That day he invited me for coffee and, stupidly, I went. I was so bored by then. My kids were growing up. I was losing my purpose and here was this beautiful younger man who let me know he wanted me. I used Bible Camp as an excuse to see him. He was a paramedic, and I offered him some work teaching first aid to groups of kids and he agreed. Afterwards, we got lunch together, and then a few times we went back to his tiny apartment and had disappointing sex. Our affair was short-lived. When I realized Ruby was going to be in his group that day, I asked him to be especially nice to her. She was finding it difficult growing up in the shadow of her sister, who was beautiful and brilliant in every way.

Kenny and I slept together three times. I felt terribly guilty for cheating on Doug and shortly after that I called a halt to the affair. There was something sleazy about the way he talked about women, but it was the guilt that stopped me.

At the time, when Ruby told me what she'd done and then what Kenny had done, I panicked. I called Kenny up and screamed down the phone at him. He didn't give a shit. He knew all about the court case. He knew that Ruby was no virgin and he told me triumphantly as if he'd played some mean-boy trick on me. I felt such disgust with myself. He wasn't going to the cops with that, though, he knew how it would make him look. I could hear his smirk down the phone.

I did not use the situation to get back to Dublin as Erin has accused me of doing, but I had to get us out of Boston fast. I had seen her name graffitied on walls in South Boston, and Dublin was the only other place I knew. Although the media never released her name, too many people in Boston knew: her friends, her school, some of Doug's congregation, Milo's friends and family, and Kenny Carter.

I prayed for Milo every night. I found a charity that anonymously sends packages to prisoners: new underwear, socks, hygiene products, sweets, books, craft sets of aeroplane models – they have a menu. I sent him a parcel once a month for thirteen years.

It was naive to think that Doug would follow me to Dublin. Maybe he didn't love me as much as I loved him, but I think the church always came first with him. When I look back, I can't see how I ever thought he would be able to start a church or a business in Dublin where the rules were so different. Desperation made me hope there was a chance. I thought that love would keep us together.

I could not believe that he wanted a divorce. Divorce was

only legalized in Ireland in 1996. It was still shameful to me. I buried myself in activities with my old friends from schooldays, I helped in a charity shop three days a week and I volunteered in an after-school club for primary age kids, and then I got a part-time job in a school for boys. It never crossed my mind to have a new husband or to date anyone. I had some offers, but I never felt that spark I had with Doug. And after Kenny Carter, I didn't trust my own judgement around men.

When I heard that Milo's mother, Elaine Kelly, had taken her own life, I was utterly horrified and felt entirely responsible. Ruby was devastated by that. If only I had told the truth at the time.

I am ashamed to admit that I did not notice Ruby's drinking was getting out of hand until it was too late and she jumped into the Liffey, and my own poor mother told me I'd have to put her into some rehab facility. But we got through it. And then, when she got pregnant, I thought the sky would fall, but I was determined that my daughter would not be treated like the girls in my day, who were locked up in convents and forced to give their babies up for adoption.

When Lucy was born, it was such a great start for everyone. That's what I thought at the time. And when Jack married Ruby, and they formed a family, I felt she had finally settled down and the bad days were behind her.

And Erin. Poor, sweet Erin. She never did anything wrong and yet in our last call she told me I'd abandoned her back then. That was never my intention. I visited her as often as I could, and after Doug died, I kept in touch with his sister, Rachel, who was always involved in Erin's life. And Doug's new wife, Kathy, became a sort of friend too, in a way. I heard all about Vince long before I met him. Rachel approved, though she said Vince was maybe a little dull for Erin. He had adult sons who were closer in age to Erin than Vince was. The wedding was lovely, though, and the two boys were respectful.

Years later, when I saw the scar on Erin's perfect face, I was taken aback, but she said she had fallen into a rose bush in her garden. I was surprised that a thorn could do so much damage. The scar faded and, by the time of Erin's book launch, it was barely visible. I was shocked to hear the truth about the scar. Principal Bermingham had always been a bit odd, but when Rachel eventually told me what he had done to Erin, I was ashamed that Erin felt she couldn't tell me. I hadn't been aware of the distance between us.

I wish I had known how much Erin suffered. I feel the weight of guilt for not knowing. But I never preferred one daughter over the other. A mother goes to the child who needs her most. I thought that was Ruby. She had done a terrible thing and had to live with it. I honestly thought her life was harder.

I could not have been prouder when Erin published her stories, and when they took off the way they did, I was so pleased. She has always worked so hard.

Erin has asked me not to call her. I hope she won't cut me off forever. All I can do is try. I suppose Ruby is thinking the same thing about Lucy.

What a mess I have made of their lives. If I could turn back time I would tell Doug what Ruby had done. He wouldn't have cared about losing clients, he would only have cared about doing the right thing.

I am going to move back to Boston. I have bought a small apartment near where we used to live on Fisher Hill. I will rejoin the congregation and try to fit in. Both of my girls need me. I need them too.

87

Ruby

I am always nervous in here. It's only been a month, but the days seem endless. My cellmates are all in recovery or active addiction, although there are many ways to get what you need if you want to. Drugs find their way into prisons very easily. As prisons go, it could be a lot worse. This wing is relatively safe. None of us are here for violent crimes. The women in this prison are here because they are poor; they have unpaid debts and they were selling their bodies, drugs or stolen property to feed their addiction. I have told them that I am in here for insurance fraud, but I know they don't believe me. I act tough although I am scared to death. The people who terrify me the most are the male prison guards. They know why I'm in here. The way they looked at my body when I was strip-searched, the comments they made. I am sure they weren't supposed to be present, but who could I complain to?

Mom sent a parcel full of toothpaste, shampoo and hygiene products. It is easier to share these right away than it is to worry about being attacked for them. There is a kind of alcohol available in here. They call it Pruno and God knows what it's made of, but I have resisted so far. Drones fly over the yard, dropping off everything from taco sauce to heroin, but the guards and their dogs are usually quicker than the inmates to get to the drop-bags.

Jack has visited, but his life is in Dublin. I don't expect

to see him here again. He is shaken by my lies, but he is getting good support from the fellowship and his recovery has survived so far. I have accepted that our marriage is over. I hope he finds someone he deserves. I was never good enough. I told him what I'd done to Isobel Lucas and he said he would contact her. I have asked him to wait until I've had a chance to apologize to her. I don't know whether he will or not – he owes me nothing.

There are AA meetings here. I have not missed one, and this time, I get it.

> Make a list of all persons we have harmed and become willing to make amends to them all.
>
> Make direct amends to such people wherever possible, except when to do so would injure them or others.

The list is long. I started with Lucy. I wrote a letter to her admitting my jealousy and the reasons why I didn't believe her. Her rape was my real punishment, and I couldn't accept it. My sentence in the penitentiary is nothing compared to the damage I inflicted on her. I need her forgiveness and I'll never stop trying until I get it. I apologized for not being able to show my love for her in recent years. I applauded her strength in taking a case against Simon Perry but warned her that court would be gruelling. Her reply was full of resentment and sarcasm. But I'm not giving up on repairing that relationship. She used to love me. I need to learn to love her again and maybe it will be easier if I'm not competing with her for Jack.

I put everything into words that I couldn't think of to say to Jack when I saw him before the sentencing. I have lost him for good, but I must accept the things I cannot change. My heart is broken, if I have one.

I wrote to Isobel Lucas, care of her agent, WME in LA. I only met her once and yet I did so much damage to her career, and all for nothing as it turned out.

I wrote to Mom. And I'm allowed to call her. She is distraught over what has happened and blames herself. I told her it's not her fault. She keeps me updated on what's going on with everyone else. I kept her name out of my confession and out of the court case, and even though Milo knows about her involvement, he has chosen not to incriminate her either. I assured her that what she did was for good reasons, even though it was wrong, and I told her it had been up to me to set the record straight at any time, especially after Dad died. There was no good reason not to face the music after that, or indeed at any time before.

Jack and Lucy stay away from her, and she is talking about moving back to Boston, now that both of her daughters are here. Mom is desperate to make amends with Erin. And she spoke to Milo on the phone. Mom says that she and I are too alike. That we never think things through.

I sent a letter to Margie too. I didn't know anything about Principal Bermingham until I got here and, though I didn't call the cops on Margie or harass her, the attacks on Dad's church and Erin would never have happened if I hadn't lied in the first place. I got no response from Margie, though I didn't expect one. I didn't get any response from Nasrin, Sinéad or Jane either. A lot of people think the worst of me. I think the worst of myself. What was it Dad said that day? *'I love her, but she doesn't make it easy.'* I think of that a lot.

Milo came to visit me yesterday. He looks ten years older than his forty-six years. I hadn't written his letter yet. It was going to be the hardest. He came in full battle mode. I'd never seen this side of him before. Stony-faced and silent. His hands were fists full of tension. He glared at me, and didn't say anything while

I stumbled over my words. I begged him to forgive me, told him I was a jealous child who had felt trapped in a disgusting lie, and that I knew I'd destroyed his life as a result. I tried to articulate how truly sorry I was about his mom, and Margie, about his future as a doctor.

When I had run out of apologies, I could see that my tears had moved him. His folded arms stretched out and he rested his fists on his knees.

'What about Erin?' he said.

Erin was having Milo's baby, according to Mom, who heard it from Aunt Rachel. They were getting married. She was making a fortune from her book, which I haven't read. She'd bought a fabulous apartment in South Boston, almost on the site of the building where Milo had grown up. Erin was happy.

I summoned up all my acting ability. 'I can never forgive myself for what I've done to Erin.'

For the one and only time during his visit, he opened his hands and looked me in the eye.

'I'm sure she'd like to hear that from you,' Milo said. 'I'll try to get her to come visit.'

I hope he doesn't try too hard. She isn't on my visitors' list.

The truth is, I try not to think of Erin. All she ever did was make me jealous. Her life is perfect all over again.

Milo and I have a secret. Erin doesn't know he came to see me. I think she'd be mad with him if she knew. Maybe I'll drop it into the conversation next time I talk to Mom.

Acknowledgements

First debt of gratitude, as always, to my agent Marianne Gunn O'Connor. She is a warrior, a mentor and knows how to talk this writer down off a cliff with endless encouragement and wisdom.

The second goes to my editor Patricia Deevy who took a chance on me and has worked with me to improve each book and has taught me so much about the process that I somehow manage to forget every time.

In Penguin Sandycove, I must thank MD Michael McLoughlin and Publicity Director Cliona Lewis; in Sales, Carrie Anderson, David Devaney and Kate Gunn; in Editorial, Joyce Dignam; and in Comms, Finn Roche and Emily Black.

In Penguin General UK, I am hugely grateful to MD Preena Gadher, a tremendous support; in Comms, smiling Rosie Safaty, Anna Ridley, Emily Moran and Yazmeen Aktar; in Sales, Sam Fanaken, Ruth Johnstone, Autumn Evans, Jess Adams and Becca Barrett; Audio Editor Brónagh Grace; and Richard Bravery and Charlotte Daniels in the Art Department for coming up with yet another beautiful cover. Copy-editor Karen Whitlock has always been so gentle with her very many grammar and logic corrections. Thanks also to the editorial management and production team in London: Ellie Smith and Charlotte Faber, as well as ace proofreaders Shân Morley-Jones and Jill Cole.

Thank you to Marianne's sub-agents who take my books around the world: Vicki Satlow, Milena Kaplarevic, Monica Martin and

Txell Torrent, Jeanine Langenberg, Gray Tan, Megan Hussein and Anna Jarota, Sebastian Ritscher and Piotr Wawrzeńczyk.

Thank you Moira Mullaney Shipsey and Matthew Mullaney for Massachusetts and legal advice (all errors are mine, some things are a bit too speedy for the sake of the story), James Ziskin for Boston info.

Thank you to H for info on sperm and its motility.

Emotional and story support came from so many early readers who also answered my questions and smothered my doubts: Sinéad Crowley, Jane Casey, Nita Prose, Robyn Harding, James Ziskin, AJ Finn, John Marrs, Julie Feeney, Jen Brady and Freida McFadden.

Thank you to AA members for their generosity, and to the Rutland Centre for giving me a blueprint on which to base my fictional rehab centre, Longhurst.

Thank you to everybody in the Tyrone Guthrie Centre over the last three years for giving me the time and space and sustenance to write. Speaking of writing, this book was drafted, researched, written and edited by human intelligence.

Thanks a million Marian Keyes, Maria O'Connell, Rachel and Mary Kate O'Flanagan, Bríd Ó Gallchoir, Claudia Carroll, Lucy Nugent, Gráinne O'Kelly, Sinéad Moriarty, Monica McInerney and Kate Thompson for unwavering support.

To my mum, Siobhan, in her ninety-fourth year, the bravest woman I know, and to my siblings, I know I haven't been a great sister in recent times. I will do better. Thanks for bearing with me. I love you all.

To all the people I have forgotten, I'm so sorry. I'll name you next time.